Hope on
the Inside

ALSO BY MARIE BOSTWICK

THE COBBLED COURT QUILTS SERIES

Apart at the Seams (Cobbled Court Quilts #6)
Ties That Bind (Cobbled Court Quilts #5)
Threading the Needle (Cobbled Court Quilts #4)
A Thread So Thin (Cobbled Court Quilts #3)
A Thread of Truth (Cobbled Court Quilts #2)
A Single Thread (Cobbled Court Quilts #1)

TOO MUCH, TEXAS NOVELS

Between Heaven and Texas
From Here to Home

NOVELS

On Wings of the Morning
River's Edge
Fields of Gold
The Second Sister
The Promise Girls
Just in Time

NOVELLAS

"The Yellow Rose of Christmas" in *Secret Santa*
"The Presents of Angels" in *Snow Angels*
"A High-Kicking Christmas" in *Comfort and Joy*

Hope on the Inside

MARIE BOSTWICK

KENSINGTON BOOKS

www.kensingtonbooks.com

KENSINGTON BOOKS are published by

Kensington Publishing Corp.
119 West 40th Street
New York, NY 10018

All Kensington titles, imprints, and distributed lines are available at special quantity discounts for bulk purchases for sales promotion, premiums, fundraising, educational, or institutional use.

Special book excerpts or customized printings can also be created to fit specific needs. For details, write or phone the office of the Kensington Sales Manager: Kensington Publishing Corp., 119 West 40th Street, New York, NY 10018. Attn. Sales Department. Phone: 1-800-221-2647.

Kensington and the K logo Reg. U.S. Pat. & TM Off.

ISBN-13: 978-1-4967-0926-4 (ebook)
ISBN-10: 1-4967-0926-8 (ebook)
Kensington Electronic Edition: April 2019

ISBN-13: 978-1-4967-0925-7
ISBN-10: 1-4967-0925-X
First Kensington Trade Paperback Printing: April 2019

10 9 8 7 6 5 4 3 2 1

Printed in the United States of America

The book is dedicated to . . .

The Coffee Creek Quilters

*who truly do bring hope to the inside
and without whom this book likely
would not have been written.*

With Many Thanks to . . .

Brad, my loving, handsome, astonishingly supportive husband. I know you don't like for me to acknowledge you in print, but too bad. Deal with it. It's high time the world knows what I always have—that I couldn't have done any of this without you.

Martin Biro, my perceptive and deeply dedicated editor. You are always such a pleasure to work with. Your comments and insights helped pull this story together and lift it to a higher level.

Liza Dawson, the best literary agent on the face of the planet. Your faith, vision, and unflagging optimism help me keep going on the days I think I can't. Your passion for story inspires me to dig deep, be brave, and write true.

Betty and John Walsh, my sister and brother-in-law and first-round readers. Without you, I'd be in big trouble, as would the readers trying to decipher my book.

Amy Skinner, publicist and superhero, who has saved my bacon on more than one occasion. Thank you for sharing my twisted sense of humor. Working with you is just a joy.

Faithful Readers. Without you, I'd just be a lady with a laptop and a pipe dream. With you, I get to do the work I love.

Chapter 1

On most days, Hope Carpenter was early to rouse but slow to rise.

It was a habit she had developed while a young and happily harried mother of four, including one set of twins, with a to-do list that would have required a twin of her own to complete. Setting her alarm to go off before the rest of the family stirred, Hope woke before dawn and lingered in the cocoon of covers for fifteen minutes, relishing the luxury of stillness and unstructured time.

Even now, with her children grown and gone, she still cherished those few precious, predawn moments of peace and quiet. When her cell phone began to hum on a Friday in November that seemed like any other, Hope stirred and stretched in the dark before shutting off the alarm. Careful not to waken Rick, she plumped her pillow, smiling to herself when she caught the scent of lavender.

Hope was acutely sensitive to smells. If somebody walked into her home wearing perfume, she could name not only the brand but also the various flowers, herbs, or oils in the blend. It was kind of her party trick—that and being able to touch her nose with her tongue, which her kids always found far more impressive.

But beyond the novelty of this admittedly weird talent, scents were very evocative for Hope, as they are for so many people, summoning up vivid memories and emotions.

Whenever she smelled boxwood, she was instantly brought back to her grandmother's tidy garden where she played hide-and-seek with her little sister, Hazel. Breathing in boxwood, Hope could see herself, counting to ten, then opening her eyes and pretending she couldn't see Hazel crouching behind the hedges.

When Hope smelled motor oil, she was suddenly sitting on the concrete floor of the garage, handing tools to her dad as he worked on his 1969 Boss 429 Mustang, the car he spent most of his adult life restoring.

Orange peel took her back to her mother's kitchen. She could see herself standing on a stool next to the stove, peering into the bubbling pot as her mom stirred batches of the thick, fragrant marmalade she always gave as Christmas gifts.

Thirty-four years before, Hope had made her own wedding bouquet—white roses, dusty miller, and fragrant French lavender. Moments before the church doors opened and the entrance music began to play, she was hit by a sudden jolt of nerves. Was she ready to be a wife? Taking a deep breath, she smelled lavender and felt suddenly brave and sure. Ever since, Hope believed that lavender imparted courage. That was why she sprinkled a little lavender oil on her pillow each night; it helped her sleep peacefully and embrace the day to come.

Most scents summoned up happy memories for Hope, remembrances of good times and good feelings. But not always.

The hospice where her mother died had an herb garden near the entrance with a huge and redolent rosemary bush. An avid and skilled cook, Hope enjoyed the scent of most fresh herbs. But since her mother's death, just five months after Hope's twenty-first birthday, Hope associated the smell of rosemary with ominous news.

Though Hope was wide awake and Rick was beginning to stir on that early Friday morning, the sun still wasn't up when the phone rang.

Reed, born seventeen minutes after his twin brother, Rory, was calling from Philadelphia. He'd just been offered a full professorship in the English department and was so excited to share the news that he forgot about the three-hour time zone difference between Oregon and Pennsylvania.

Five minutes after Reed hung up, McKenzie phoned. She and Zach had just landed in Seattle, returning from their Hawaiian honeymoon. As usual, McKenzie had dialed Rick's cell phone, but Hope, who was getting dressed for work by then, eavesdropped on the conversation.

When Rick said, "Yes, kitten, she's right here. Hang on," Hope was surprised. Usually, Rick had to prompt their only daughter to talk with her. That day McKenzie was eager to talk to her, sounding truly happy, almost giddy.

McKenzie chattered away about how she and Zach had hiked through a rain forest and had a romantic candlelit dinner on the beach. It was a lovely talk, gossipy, cozy, and close, the sort of easy conversation Hope always wanted to have with her daughter but rarely did.

It wasn't because McKenzie disliked her; Hope understood that. She just liked Rick more, always had. But that day was different. McKenzie, who never sought her mother's advice about anything, asked Hope to e-mail her famous goulash recipe.

"Not the noodles," McKenzie clarified. "Just the sauce. I'll put it over macaroni."

"Sure. That'll work," Hope said, even though she thought that serving the sauce over thick, chewy, homemade noodles was what made the dish so good. But she held her tongue, not wanting to say anything to spoil this all-too-rare moment of mother-daughter bonding. It was so good to hear McKenzie sounding so happy. Zach seemed to have turned out to be the right man for her after all.

After McKenzie's two broken engagements, Hope could be forgiven for having dragged her feet when it came to making wedding arrangements. She'd begun to doubt that any man could ever measure up to Rick in McKenzie's eyes.

When Hope finally realized her daughter was serious, she kicked into high gear. She oversaw the menus, found a good price on the lobster that McKenzie insisted upon, hand-calligraphed place cards, tracked and organized hotel reservations, and stayed up past midnight every night for a month, stitching and stuffing 120 heart-shaped, monogrammed sachets, filled with homegrown lavender, as favors for each of the wedding guests.

McKenzie thought that part was ridiculous. She said that nobody would care if there were favors or not. Maybe they wouldn't. But Hope thought those little details mattered. Besides, she was having fun.

Hope arranged all the flowers too, including McKenzie's fall-themed bouquet of mums and carefully preserved leaves. She had wanted to sew the wedding dress as well, but McKenzie was dead set on wearing Vera Wang.

Hope's mother had been an excellent seamstress. She'd often talked about making wedding dresses for Hope and Hazel when they grew up. But by the time Hope was engaged, it was too late. Her mother was losing ground against the illnesses she'd battled for so long and no longer had the strength to sew.

Instead, Hope made the gown, getting her mother's advice at various stages of construction. When it was finished, Hope brought the dress to her mother's room and sat down on the bed while she and her mom stitched the hem of the huge, flouncy skirt (it was the eighties; every bride wanted to look like Princess Diana), working from opposite ends and meeting in the middle. As they sewed, Hope's mother imparted every piece of marital advice in her arsenal, barely pausing between subjects, as if she had rehearsed it all in her mind beforehand.

It was a long talk.

At the end of it, she took Hope's hands in her bony grasp and said, "Make up your mind to be happy, Hope. Whatever comes your way, find the happiness in it. That's the real trick of life."

Thirty-four years later, Hope still tried to follow that advice.

The conversation with McKenzie went so long that Hope was nearly late to work, sprinting from the faculty parking lot and through the door of the high school just three minutes before the first bell.

After a nearly three-decade hiatus to raise her children, this was only Hope's second year back in teaching. Things had changed a lot in that time. For one thing, Home Ec was now called FACS, Family and Consumer Science, and the curriculum was completely transformed.

It wasn't enough to teach kids how to sew an apron or make a meatloaf anymore. Lesson plans were far more complicated and had to be structured around skills that connected across the curriculum.

For example, the apron project Hope used to teach sewing might be designed on a computer to reinforce what students were learning in the tech program. Meatloaf making might be accompanied by a research project on nutritional value and ingredient sources to support what they were learning in health or environmental science classes.

These were changes for the better, in Hope's opinion, and made the coursework more relevant to modern life. But it didn't make Hope's life easy. During her first year back in the classroom, she often felt overwhelmed. Staying one step ahead of her students required her to burn a lot of midnight oil.

But now, three months into her second year, Hope felt like she had a handle on things. The glowing review she had received from her principal that day confirmed it.

She tried calling Rick to share the good news, but he didn't answer his office phone. However, since it was Friday, she got to tell Hazel all about it when the sisters met at Café Provence for happy hour.

"It's funny, isn't it?" Hope said, taking the last piece of cheese.

"What is?" Hazel said, burrowing through her purse in search of her wallet.

"How things work out. I only went back to teaching because Liam surprised us all and got into film school at UCLA. If we hadn't needed the extra money for his tuition, I might have quit after the first month. But now, I love it. I really do."

"Why do you sound so surprised? You're a natural-born teacher. I mean, you raised four amazing kids. Well, five, if you count me." Hazel grinned. "What's motherhood besides a two-decade-long teaching gig?"

"Oh, it's way longer than that," Hope said, reaching for her own wallet. "Doesn't matter how old your kids get, you never stop being a mom."

When the waitress approached with the check, Hope nipped it quickly from the folder, earning an exasperated look from her sister.

"Come on," Hazel said. "At least let's split it."

Hope gave the waitress a stern look. "Trust me. You don't want my sister's money. She's a well-known counterfeiter."

The waitress laughed and thanked Hope for the warning, then thanked her again when Hope said she could keep the change. Hope and Hazel got up from the table.

"You should have let me get that," Hazel said. "It was my turn."

"Uh-uh. You got it last week. Besides, I've been sitting here and chattering about me, me, me for the last hour. How are things with you? How's business?"

Hope held the door open, then followed Hazel outside onto the sidewalk. It was chilly, gray, and wet—typical for early November in Oregon. The blue-and-white-striped awning over the door dripped a steady curtain of droplets onto the sidewalk.

"You know that listing we had on the lake?" Hazel asked, looking down at her phone as she scanned through her text messages. "The huge one with the flagstone terraces and the boathouse? Well, we're set to close next week and—"

Hazel stopped short, frowning.

"Oh no. Jinxed it. Hang on, Sis. I need to call the office." Hazel punched a number into the phone, switching to her all-business voice when her assistant answered. "Linda? . . . Uh-huh. Don't worry about it. I was about to head back to the office anyway. Just tell me what happened."

Hope stood there for a moment, not sure if she should stay or go. When Hazel said, "We are not going to lose a two-million-dollar transaction because Stan failed to read the contract. Put him on," Hope realized she was going to be a while.

If Hope had to sum up her sister in three words, they would be "loyal," "honest" (sometimes to a fault), and "single-minded." And not just about business. Hazel did one thing at a time and wholeheartedly.

Only twenty-eight years after closing her first real estate deal on a charming but cavernous Victorian with a roof that leaked and plumbing that functioned only intermittently—a fixer-upper that Rick and Hope were *still* fixing up—Hazel was the owner of Hazelnut Realty, with fifty employees and three offices, soon to be four.

Hope loved that name—Hazelnut Realty. At first glance, it seemed like a nod to the region—99 percent of the U.S. hazelnut crop is grown in Oregon—but Hope knew it was her sister's idea of a joke. Hazel took her business seriously, but not herself, which was one of the many things Hope loved about her sister.

Hope glanced at her watch, then squeezed Hazel's shoulder in farewell. Hazel made an apologetic face, mouthed a goodbye, and went back to her call.

Hope stopped by the market to pick up ingredients for goulash, thinking it would be nice to surprise Rick. Between work and the wedding, they'd been eating a lot of pizza and takeout Thai lately. Not that Rick had complained. He'd been working so late every night that he hardly noticed what he ate. It had been that way for months, ever since his engineering firm had been bought by another, larger firm.

But when Hope got home, she was surprised to see Rick's car was already in the garage. It had been months since he'd left the office early. Rick kept telling her that his crushing work schedule was just temporary, that things would settle down once people quit feeling like they had to outdo one another in proving themselves to the new management.

Maybe his prediction had finally come true? If so, it really *had* been a good day, for both of them. Hope took the groceries out of the trunk and carried them to the house, humming a happy tune.

But that was before Hope opened the door, sniffed the air, and felt her stomach clench like a fist.

Rosemary.

Chapter 2

Rick Carpenter stood six-four and weighed 220 pounds. He had deep blue eyes, short gray hair that matched his full gray beard, and shoulders so muscular that it was hard to find shirts to fit him. He had played for the Old Boars, the senior division of the Portland Rugby Club, into his early fifties. Even now, at age fifty-eight, he looked like he could kick the butts of guys half his age.

Rugby is a little like football but much rougher. Players eschew helmets and pads and consider injuries a badge of honor. Rick inherited his love of the game from his dad, an Irish dockworker turned welder who emigrated at the age of twenty with a chip on his shoulder and ninety dollars in his pocket and died from complications of an industrial accident when Rick was just fourteen.

His deceased father loomed large in his life. Rick was the stubborn son of a stubborn man, a man whose boyhood had been cut short and who had pulled himself up by the bootstraps, as his dad had done before him.

But the influence of Rick's mother, Ruth, was also strongly in evidence. Ruth showed him he could be smart as well as tough. She instilled in him a reverence for education and a belief that hard work would not go unrewarded. And when Rick's hair-trigger temper started getting him into fights at school, Ruth taught him to bake.

It was just what he needed.

Whereas other men might handle anxiety by pounding a speed bag at the gym or heading to the nearest bar in search of a drink and a fistfight, Rick vented his pent-up emotions by pounding his frustrations into a mound of warm bread dough.

In addition to life lessons, Ruth passed all her baking secrets and recipes on to her only son. Rosemary olive loaf, however, was Rick's own creation, something he baked only sporadically.

When Rick got home that day, around noon, he'd gone directly into the kitchen, practically tearing off his jacket and tie before putting an apron on over his dress shirt. He went directly to work, furiously chopping olives and rosemary before mixing it into the sticky dough, kneading it a good fifteen minutes.

By then, he'd calmed down enough to be able to think. After washing his hands and pouring a neat scotch, he sat down and did exactly that for the two hours it took the bread to rise. By the time he'd punched down the dough, kneaded it a second time, he had formulated a plan and felt much better.

The only thing he had to do now was deal with Hope. She'd be upset at first, like he'd been, but Hope was nothing if not sensible. And optimistic. Once she got past the emotional part, she'd realize that nothing had changed.

He just had to break the news gently.

"Hey," Rick said, giving her a peck on the cheek before lifting the hot loaves from the baking pans to a cooling rack. "Got home early and thought I'd surprise you. Don't they smell great?"

He bent down and took a deep, appreciative sniff of the hot bread before lifting his head. In spite of his explanation, Hope still looked surprised.

No, he thought, not surprised—concerned. Her expression matched the one she wore whenever they watched one of those spy movies that he loved and she tolerated, as though she wanted to put her hands to her face and peek through her fingers. She was carrying a grocery bag in one arm and clutching the neck of a wine bottle in her hand.

"Looks like a good vintage," he said, nodding toward the bottle. "Doesn't even have a screw top."

"What's wrong?" Hope asked, ignoring his grin.

"Nothing."

Hope shook her head. "Something's happened. What is it? Something with the kids? Did McKenzie call?"

"Nobody called," he said, opening a drawer and searching for a corkscrew. "And nothing's wrong. Why would you think that?"

"You only make rosemary olive bread when something's gone wrong and you're trying to break it to me gently."

Hope looked toward the cooling rack and stabbed the air with an accusatory gesture, like a character in a courtroom drama who's been asked to identify the culprit.

"*That* is bread for making the best of a bad situation," she said.

"Hope, it's only bread. Nothing's wrong. Really." Rick twisted the metal coil into the cork, avoiding her eyes.

"There is—" He paused. "A situation. But it's not bad," he said quickly as he took two wineglasses from the cabinet. "In fact, it's good. I'm retiring."

"What?" Hope's jaw went slack. She stood there for a moment, staring incredulously. "Retiring? What are you talking about? You're only fifty-eight years old. You love being an engineer!"

Rick tipped the bottle and poured wine into the first glass, watching the purplish liquid climb toward the rim. He did love being an engineer. And he'd worked harder than anyone he knew in order to become one.

When they first married, Hope was still teaching, supporting them both so he could go to school full-time. Then the twins came. For seven years, Rick worked construction during the day, all day, studied and went to class nights and weekends.

When he finally finished, Hope, Hazel, Rory and Reed, two-year-old McKenzie, who already had him wrapped around her little finger, and his mother were all there to see him receive his diploma. Ruth said it was the proudest moment of her life.

Rick's proudest day came two weeks later, when he threw away his worn-out work boots, putting on a brand-new suit for his first day of work as an engineer. His second-proudest day was every one after that, every day he spent working.

He *did* love being an engineer.

He loved taking a project from plan to completion, solving problems before they occurred, working in a team, visiting the jobsite, seeing foundations poured, scaffolds rise, and buildings climb, floor after floor, until they really did scrape the sky. He loved putting his stamp on the city of his birth, seeing his imprint on Portland's skyline.

And now he was retiring? No wonder Hope didn't believe his story. The doubt in her voice made him angry, because it made him doubt himself.

"You mean . . ." She hesitated a moment. "You mean they fired you?"

"No," he said, and handed her some wine, his movement so abrupt that a little of the liquid splashed over the rim. "They did *not* fire me. They offered an early retirement package to me and a few of the other senior engineers."

He poured another glass for himself and took a long draught. "And I thought, after twenty-eight years, what the hell? So I decided to take it."

Hope's eyes flashed, sparking with that blue flame he knew so well and usually found attractive. But not tonight.

"*You* decided?" she snapped. "Without even discussing it with me? Haven't we talked about this?"

They had, more than once. The last time was when Hope came home from a sisters' weekend with Hazel and found a brand-new SUV parked in the driveway. The argument that ensued was heated. They kept the car, but later, when they were in bed, Rick swore it would never happen again.

"We had a deal! You said you wouldn't mak
sions without—"

"I didn't decide! They decided for me! All right
the fury and frustration in his face and voice silen
decided! Are you happy now?"

Hope stood silent. Rick knocked back his v
down without tasting it, trying to swallow back the catch in his
throat.

"These people are vultures," he said, when he felt he could
trust his voice. "They don't have any loyalty, don't care about
the years I spent building the company. They gave me two options, retire early with severance or wait to be fired." He put
down his glass. "What else was I supposed to do?"

The anger in Hope's eyes melted. She laid her hand over his.

"Babe, I'm so sorry. Are you okay?"

"I'm fine," he said, his throat still tight. "Glad to be out of
there. It's been miserable since the buyout."

"It has," Hope agreed. "You've practically been killing yourself."

"Yeah. Well. Not anymore."

He topped up his glass and tilted it in her direction. Hope
touched the rim of her glass to his, returning his smile. Somehow Rick felt renewed. And forgiven.

"What would you say to Christmas in Hawaii?" he asked.

"Hawaii?" Hope said, laughing a little. "This doesn't seem
like quite the time for a vacation, does it?"

"It's the perfect time. McKenzie and Zach are planning to
spend Christmas with his parents. Rory and Reed will both be
too wrapped up with work to make it out here this year, but we
can bring Liam along. He'd love it. Wouldn't you rather spend
Christmas under a palm tree than pining for your absent fledg-
lings? The timing is ideal. You'll have a break from school, and
for the first time in forever, my calendar is totally open."

Hope smiled. "A real vacation? No interruptions or e-mails?
No calls from the office? Very tempting. What about Hazel? We
can't desert her over the holiday."

Tell her to come along," Rick said. "The more the merrier. We'll bring Mom too. I'll look for a condo we can rent, someplace we can stretch out a little."

"Well . . . okay. Let's do it," Hope said, her face splitting into a grin, but only briefly. "Assuming you haven't found another job by then."

She sipped her wine.

"You're not really planning on retiring. Are you?"

"Of course not."

Rick took a serrated knife from the block and sliced into one of the loaves. The crumb was tender, but the crust was crisp, cracking under the pressure of his knife and releasing a rich, mouthwatering perfume of rosemary and olives into the air. He cut off two slices, smiling at a job well done.

"Don't worry," he said. "I have a plan. I'm going to spend the next few weeks working on the house, knocking off the stuff that's been on my honey-do list for the last couple of years. Thought I'd start replacing the roof on the sunporch."

"Really?" Hope said, her face lighting up.

The number of years she'd been asking him to get to that was closer to five than two.

"Really. Then we'll fly to Maui for an amazing Christmas before I come home and start sending out résumés."

"But," Hope said slowly, "are you sure you want to wait that long?"

Rick took a stick of butter from the refrigerator and started slathering it onto the hot bread.

"Nobody will be hiring until January. I might as well take a little time off while I can." He handed her a piece of the bread, still warm and dripping with butter. Hope took it, sniffed it, but didn't taste it.

"Honey. We're fine," he said, seeing the wheels turn behind her eyes.

The two of them had grown up poor and stayed poor for a long time. Pinching pennies was a hard habit to break, harder for Hope than Rick. He wished she'd worry about money a little less and trust him a little more.

"Really. The package they offered me is pretty decent. Not lavish but not bad. It won't take long for me to find another job; you'll see. After all, who was the brilliant man who led the team on the bridge repair? And the waterfront reclamation project? Who engineered half the buildings in downtown Portland?"

"Let me think . . ." Hope said, giving him a lopsided smile. "Was it you?"

"Damn straight it was."

Hope laughed and bit into the bread. Rick did the same and groaned with pleasure. It was delicious, the best he'd ever made. This seemed like a harbinger of good things to come.

"I'll find a new job by Valentine's Day—St. Patrick's at the latest," Rick declared. "Then we'll bank the severance. Or maybe pay off the second mortgage we had to take out for Liam's tuition."

Hope's eyes widened a bit. "Do you really think we could? That'd be wonderful, wouldn't it?"

He nodded, thinking how beautiful she was and what a good team they made. He was nothing when they met, a part-time student and full-time drywall contractor. He'd made a full-court press to win her, giving her the hard sell, explaining that someday he would become the kind of man she deserved.

With Hope by his side, it had happened. They had a beautiful home, beautiful family, beautiful life. Rick took care of the finances and Hope took care of the house, and him, and the kids, and pretty much everybody who crossed her path, mothering every kid in a six-block radius. Rick was proud of her and the life they'd built.

Sure, they had their moments. Hope could be feisty when she felt like it and stubborn as hell when she dug her feet in, but so could he. That was part of the attraction. It gave him the chance to win her over, again and again. Not a bad way to spend a marriage.

"You know something?" Rick said. "I think this is going to turn out to be a good thing. I was getting too complacent in my job, too settled. It'll be good to get out there and do something fresh, take a few risks, work with new people. And financially speaking, by the time everything shakes out, we're actually going to pick up yardage."

Rick laid his arm over Hope's shoulders, kissed the top of her head. "Everything's going to be fine," he said. "You'll see."

Chapter 3

A year and a half later, everything *was* fine.

They weren't homeless or hungry. They had their children and health, which, as Hope often reminded herself, was what mattered. In the big picture, everything was fine. But it was also different. *Everything* was different.

Hope was angry about it. But not for the reasons you might think.

At first, things were actually pretty terrific. Rick spent weeks before Christmas replacing the porch roof and refinishing the dining room floor. When they first bought the house, they tackled those kinds of projects together. But as his responsibilities at the office increased, Rick had less time for home repair.

That was all right. Hope understood.

When the kids were young, she always felt she and Rick were on the same team and working toward the same goal—building a strong, secure family. She didn't earn a paycheck, but she worked just as hard as Rick did and had even longer hours. And she took her job very seriously.

Realizing what a strong influence friends could be, Hope set out to make their house *the* house, the place every kid in the neighborhood wanted to be. She scheduled playdates, and field trips, and game nights. She was the den mother, room mother, troop leader, and bus chaperone. She threw sleepovers, and campouts, and parties.

When McKenzie and her little friends reached those self-conscious, self-absorbed preteen years, Hope started organizing pageants for neighborhood girls. They competed and won crowns for titles such as Miss Community Service and Little Miss Bookworm. Hope wanted them to understand that having good hair is meaningless if there's not a good mind underneath it.

Hope's parties were legendary. The neighborhood kids had such a great time that they didn't even realize they were learning things. She organized pirate parades, leprechaun hunts, Greek mythology costume parties, Christmas caroling, and a backyard production of *The Little Engine That Could*. Her favorite was the Bastille Day party she threw when the twins were eleven. With Hope's help, the boys baked chocolate croissants and built guillotines out of foil and Popsicle sticks. That party truly cemented Hope's reputation as the fun mom on the block. After that, every kid in the neighborhood wanted to hang out at the Carpenter home, which meant Hope always knew where her kids were and what they were doing.

Hope and Rick approached the job of child-rearing much the way their parents had, dividing the work along traditional gender-specific lines. Hope understood it wasn't the only good way to raise a family, but it worked for them.

Rory, the older twin, was a doctor. Reed was a professor. McKenzie worked as an IT professional for the State of Washington doing things with computers that Hope couldn't begin to understand. Liam, the baby, attended the prestigious UCLA film school. Hope was sure he would win an Oscar before his thirtieth birthday.

Whenever Hope looked at her children, she thought, *Yeah, we did good.*

On that first Monday after Rick's forced retirement, Hope came home from work and discovered that Rick had torn the shingles off the porch roof. He'd also made dinner—roast chicken, salad, and homemade Parmesan rolls. That was a lovely evening. Rick was so talkative, excited about the possibility of a new career challenge. It reminded Hope of the conversations they'd had in the old days, when they were both bursting with optimism and plans for the future.

For a while, everything went according to plan.

Their Hawaiian Christmas was truly the trip of a lifetime. When they got home, Rick turned the dining room, with its newly refinished wood floor, into his "Career Change Command Center" and started sending out résumés.

That's when the plan started to fall apart.

Hope didn't blame Rick. He sent out scores of résumés, went to dozens of networking luncheons with former colleagues, and applied for every job posting that even vaguely matched his skills. For seven months, Rick made looking for work his full-time job. Nobody could have tried harder.

Then Ruth died. She caught pneumonia and was gone in a week.

At first, it seemed like Rick was taking it pretty well, especially considering how close he'd been to his mother. Yes, Hope caught him crying more than once, but why shouldn't he? Hope cried too. Ruth had been a wonderful mother-in-law and grandmother. They all missed her and it had happened so quickly. Still, all things considered, Rick seemed okay.

Then something changed.

Rick spent less time in his Command Center and more time in the kitchen baking and eating loaf after loaf of bread. When he wasn't doing that, he sat in the ratty recliner he saved from Ruth's apartment and watched the Food Channel.

For a while, Hope let him be. He was entitled to his grief and they were okay financially. Between Rick's severance and her salary, they were getting by.

But what would they do when Rick's severance ran out? What if he couldn't find another job? If you were thirty years old and trained in tech, things were booming in Portland. "Stumptown," so named because, once upon a time, it was purported to have more stumps than trees, was a hotbed of the new economy, *the* place to be if you were young, hip, and skilled.

But it wasn't working out for everybody. There were more homeless people than before, more drug addicts, and more tent cities. There were also more apartment buildings. It seemed like every time Hope drove downtown, a new one was going up, but not quickly enough to keep up with demand. Home prices and rents were rising by the day.

It should have meant more work for engineers, and it did. But not for those with the depth of experience that Rick had and certainly not at the salary he'd been able to command formerly. All those young, fresh graduates who crowded into town could be hired much more cheaply.

Rick was willing to take a job with lower pay. As much as a paycheck, he needed something to *do,* a reason to get up in the morning. He applied for a ton of lower-salaried positions and even got interviews for a few of them. But in each case, the people doing the hiring took a pass on him, saying he was overqualified.

After one such interview, Rick sat on the edge of his and Hope's bed with his head in his hands and said, "Overqualified. What does that even mean?" Hope sat down next to him. She didn't know either.

Then, Hope's principal called. Due to budget cuts, they were cutting the FACS department, not just at her school, at all the schools, statewide.

That's when Hope started to get scared.

With only two years of classroom experience teaching in a very specialized subject area that was no longer part of the curriculum, it was clear she wasn't going to get hired to teach anytime soon. She looked for other work, any work, finally taking a job at a discount department store. The hours were terrible, but at least she was bringing a little money in. She thought Rick would be happy, even proud of her.

He wasn't.

In spite of their generally happy home life and adherence to traditional roles, Rick and Hope weren't exactly Ozzie and Harriet. They never had been.

Rick was stubborn and opinionated. So was Hope. Like a lot of couples, she and Rick argued sometimes. But they always resolved things quickly and were careful not to cross the line from arguing to fighting.

Until Ruth died.

Two days after Hope started working at the discount store, they fought.

It started because Rick made a batch of sourdough starter and left it sitting on the counter. Thinking it was a baking experiment gone wrong, Hope threw it out. But, of course, it wasn't really about the sourdough. Big fights are rarely sparked by the stuff people pretend to be fighting about.

Rick snatched a beer from the refrigerator and slammed the door. "Hey! If you're sick of me hanging around the house all day, then come out and say it, all right? Do me a favor and be honest for once."

"Rick," she said through clenched teeth, working hard to keep her voice even. "I have no idea what you're talking about. I came in from work. I was tired. I was cleaning up the kitchen and the dough smelled funny, so I threw it away. I didn't realize you wanted to keep it. It was a mistake, not a criticism."

"Right," he said, making a show of nodding his head. "*You* were working all day. *You* were tired. No criticism there. Uh-uh. Why don't you come out and say it, Hope? Just ask me the question you're dying to ask instead of throwing out all the jabs and bullshit hints!"

Hope spread her hands. "What? What question? Rick, I have no idea what you're talking about."

"Oh yes, you do. You're just too busy pretending to be understanding and supportive to come out and say it." He cracked open the beer can and made his voice a nasal whine. "Poor hardworking Hope, slaving over a hot cash register all day long while her deadbeat husband stays home and bakes cookies all day.

"Please," he said, tossing back a gulp of beer. "You know what the question is! You want to know what the hell I do here all day while you're out working so hard!"

"Well?" she shouted, flinging her hands out in frustration. "What *are* you doing? Because from where I'm sitting, it looks like nothing. It looks like you've given up!"

Rick spewed a string of curses and got right up into Hope's face, so close she could feel the heat of his breath on her skin, smell beer and bitterness on his breath.

"Do you have *any* idea how many résumés I've sent out? What do you expect me to do? Keep pounding my head into the wall? Sign up for a few more rounds of humiliation? 'Thank you, sir! May I have another?'

"Is that what you want?" he shouted. "Or maybe you want me to learn from your example, take some crap job ringing up bags of stale chips and bottles of generic shampoo. Would that make you happy?"

"Hey!" Hope cried, pushing up on her toes, forcing herself into his space as he had into hers. "At least I'm making an effort. And bringing in some money. We can't go on like this, Rick. Don't you get it? When the severance runs out, we're toast. We could lose the house. We could lose everything!"

Rick let out a snarling laugh that made Hope feel as small, and angry, and hurt as he did at that moment.

"Well, well. Look who just woke up and realized that it takes money to live. You're about thirty years late getting to the party, but hey, I guess I should be grateful you showed up at all, right?"

Angry tears sprouted in Hope's eyes. She swallowed hard and blinked to keep them from spilling over, making a deliberate effort to calm her voice and defuse the ugliness between them.

"Stop it, Rick. You know that's not what I was saying."

"When I need a lecture on financial reality, I'll let you know, okay? In case you hadn't noticed, while you were staying home and playing house, *I* was the one carrying the burden around here. *I've* been the provider for this family, not you!"

That was what Hope was angry about.

For over thirty-four years she'd thought of them as a team, different in their responsibilities and spheres of influence but equal in their contribution. This was the belief she'd based her entire life and marriage on.

If Rick saw himself as an island and Hope as a millstone around his neck, then what *was* their marriage? What was her life?

What had they been playing at all these years?

Chapter 4

Hazel was sitting on the sofa in her pajamas, holding a glass of red wine cupped in her hands, staring into the flames of the gas fireplace, thinking about the phone conversation she'd had with her niece, wondering what, if anything, she should do about it.

When the doorbell rang at ten o'clock, Hazel was surprised to see her sister standing on the stoop. But not that surprised.

"If you've come for a drink," she said, raising her almost empty wineglass, "you're almost too late."

"Rick and I had a fight."

Hope told her sister all about the fight, how it started (stupidly), where it headed (downhill quickly), and how it ended (badly).

"He punched a wall?" Hazel's eyes widened in disbelief. She knew her brother-in-law very well. After all, he'd partly raised her.

Two years after Hazel and Hope's mother died, their father fell while repairing the roof, hit his head, and died four days later. Hazel was only sixteen. Hope and Rick, already struggling to make ends meet and expecting twins, took her in without a moment of hesitation.

Hazel understood that Rick had a short fuse, but he wasn't a violent man. For all his size and tough-guy appearance, most of the time Rick was a big teddy bear. And now he was punching walls? Things must be even worse than McKenzie said.

"Did his fist go through?"

"No, but he cracked the plaster," Hope said, slipping her arms out of her coat. "I grabbed the car keys and I got out, went up to the West Hills, and drove too fast for a while, then ended up here. Do you mind?"

Of course she didn't mind. Hazel hung up her sister's coat, poured her a glass of wine, then made her sit down and tell her the whole story again, but more slowly.

When Hope was done, Hazel offered to lend them some money. Hope refused.

"No," she said firmly. "I appreciate the offer, but no. I would never borrow money, especially from my sister, unless I was one hundred percent confident that I could pay it back. Anyway, Rick would never agree to it. And I wouldn't want him to. It'd be like plunging a knife into what's left of his self-respect. Besides, this isn't just about the money. It goes a lot deeper. After tonight, I'm wondering if I really know Rick at all. Or if he knows me."

Hope put down her glass and buried her face in her hands.

"Oh, Hazel. The things we said to each other . . ."

Hazel scooted closer and rubbed her hand over Hope's back in slow circles.

"You didn't mean it. Neither did he. You and Rick love each other, always will. You're doing the best you can, I know. But, Hope, you're tired, and worn out—"

"And broke. Or about to be."

Hope lifted her head and looked at Hazel.

"What are we going to do? My job at the store covers groceries and gas, but that's about it. We've got to come up with a plan before the severance money runs out. But what?"

Hazel reached for her wineglass. Only minutes before, she'd been sitting there, trying to decide if or when to talk to her sister about the things she'd been discussing with McKenzie. The time, it seemed, was now.

"Well," Hazel said after taking a breath, "I've been doing some research. Do you know what your house is worth in today's market?"

Hope didn't. So Hazel told her.

"Really? That much?"

Hazel bobbed her head. "House prices in Portland are sky-rocketing. If you sell, you'll have enough to pay off the mortgages and then some."

"Enough to buy another house in our neighborhood?"

Hazel shook her head.

"Oh," Hope said, her face falling. "Well . . . what about—"

Hope started listing various neighborhoods. Hazel kept shaking her head, finally interrupting to explain that the price hikes that would allow them to pay off their mortgages had also priced them out of Portland.

But Hazel had a plan.

"Olympia?" Hope said, sounding confused. "No. There has to be another solution. I've lived in Portland my whole life. So has Rick. All our friends are here, everybody we know. *You're* here. I've never lived more than ten miles away from you. Except for my honeymoon and two vacations, I've never gone more than three days at a stretch without seeing you. What would I do if I couldn't talk to you?"

Feeling a catch in her throat, Hazel took a sip from her glass. It was a question she'd been asking herself ever since McKenzie called.

During the long, slow, agonizing years of their mother's decline, Hope had stepped into the gap, taking care of everybody. For as long as Hazel could remember, Hope had been more than her sister. Hope was her anchor.

It would be hard, so hard, to see Hope move. But when you love somebody you do what's best for them, even if it's hard for you. Hope had taught her that. And if she gave her sister time to think it over, Hazel knew that Hope would come to the same conclusion. Hope was still the one who took care of everybody else. She would do what she had to do, for Rick. Fight or no fight, she loved him.

Hazel put down her glass and forced a smile.

"You know, Sis, there's this amazing thing called technology. Maybe you've heard of it? We can talk, or text, e-mail, or video chat every day. It's not like we'd have to start raising carrier pigeons to keep in touch, you know."

"Funny."

"I'm just saying, it's not that big a deal. McKenzie and Zach love Olympia. And they'd love having you closer."

Hope frowned. "You already talked to McKenzie about this?"

"Olympia is a great town," Hazel said, ignoring Hope's question. "It's about halfway to Seattle; you'll be able to go to Seahawks games. And it's not like we'll never see each other again. I can drive up there in two or three hours, tops. And you can come visit me. It's the Washington state capital, so there's a lot going on. And it's so much more affordable than Portland. No income tax either."

Hazel reached for the bottle and poured more wine into her sister's glass.

"I was born here," Hope said, staring sightlessly at the wall. "So were all my children. Portland has changed, but my roots are here. So is my house.

"I painted every wall, put up every roll of wallpaper, stripped out old carpets, tore out that awful linoleum, laid new tile all by myself. I remodeled the kitchen too. Replaced the cabinet doors, painted them by hand, replaced the sink . . ."

She shifted her gaze, looking Hazel in the eye.

"How can I leave all that behind?"

"Hope . . ." Hazel said helplessly. "You said it yourself; you and Rick can't go on like you have been. You need a plan."

"You're right," Hope said softly, looking at her sister with wet and shiny eyes. "But can't I have a different one?"

"Hope. It's just a house. Rick is your—"

"I know." Hope took in a deep breath and let it out slowly. When she spoke again, her voice was steady. "You talked it over with McKenzie? You called her?"

"She called me," Hazel admitted. "I guess she's been talking to Rick. She's worried about him. And she'd love to have you closer. Both of you."

Hope nodded quickly but broke eye contact, lifting her glass to her lips. "Well. It might be good for Rick, having Kenz closer. She's always been his favorite."

"You're his favorite," Hazel countered.

"Mm," Hope murmured absently.

"You *are*," Hazel insisted.

Hope put down her glass and looked into her sister's eyes.

Chapter 5

Once the decision to sell the house and move to Olympia had been made, the plan to make it happen unfolded with astounding, almost disorienting, speed. Most disorienting of all was how quickly Rick embraced the idea.

He was asleep when she got home from Hazel's that night. But sometime during Hope's shift at the discount store, Hazel talked to McKenzie, who talked to Rick. Anyway, Hope assumed that's what happened. She had no way of knowing for sure because McKenzie hadn't bothered to phone her, only Rick.

When Hope got home from work she found him in the bedroom, pulling out shirts and sweaters and battered pairs of running shoes from his side of the closet and tossing them into an empty box.

"What are you doing?"

"Getting rid of things I don't need. No point in paying money to move stuff I don't want anymore, right?"

The next day, Hazel showed up with her assistant and started staging the house, a process that primarily involved taking down and packing away anything that might remind potential buyers that actual human beings lived there.

That was hard. To Hope, it felt like they were erasing all signs of her family's existence, from framed photos to her grandmother's blue glass collection. They even got rid of the black, blue, red, and green pen marks on the kitchen doorway where, year after year, Hope had marked the kids' heights on the first day of school.

Hazel tried to scrub the marks off with an eraser sponge, but it didn't work. As soon as she called out, "Hey, Rick. Can you help me out here?" he stopped packing the teapots Hope kept on a shelf over the window and trotted down to the basement for a paintbrush. If Hope hadn't stopped him, he'd have painted over it before Hope even managed to take a picture.

That was her low point.

Her mother had a rule when Hope was growing up: Everybody is entitled to feel sorry for themselves but not more than once a day and not for more than ten minutes.

Saying she was going to rake the planters, Hope went into the garden shed, set a timer on her watch, and bawled for ten minutes. When her watch beeped, she wiped her tears, went outside, and started raking.

Hazel did a great job with the staging. By the time she was finished, the house looked like something out of a magazine.

But it didn't look like Hope's house.

By the end of the open house, they had two solid offers. The one they accepted was six thousand over asking but stipulated that they close in thirty days.

Thirty days? They hadn't even started looking for a new house yet. Where were they supposed to go? Hope felt like somebody had punched her in the stomach. Rick seemed jubilant, at least to Hope's eyes.

But on their last night in the house, after the furniture had been removed and the floors swept and mopped, and the empty rooms echoed with the sound of their footsteps, Hope realized she'd been wrong.

He stood in the front entry, at the foot of the grand oak staircase, staring up toward the dim corridor and empty bedrooms.

"Remember how the kids used to slide down the bannister?" he asked, his gaze glued to the staircase, as if waiting for someone to descend. "No matter how many times I told them not to, they kept at it. Even after Rory broke his arm, they wouldn't stop. Stubborn kids, every one of them. Can't think where they got it."

"Me either," Hope said.

"Remember McKenzie's prom? She came down the stairs wearing that green dress, looking like a princess. All grown up. Just like that," he said, his voice low and wondering. "That boy she was going with . . . What was his name?"

"Justin Striker."

"Justin. Justin Striker," Rick murmured, as if trying to burn the name into his memory. "The look on his face when she came downstairs. . . . His jaw actually dropped. Do you remember?"

"No. But I remember how you made him sign a contract before they left, swearing he wouldn't speed, drink, or do anything to endanger or disrespect your daughter and would have her home by midnight." Hope laughed softly. "Poor Justin. You actually made him believe it was legally binding. McKenzie was mortified."

Rick smiled but only for a moment. He turned to face her.

"I'm sorry."

Hope almost said, "For what?" but stopped herself. She knew what he meant.

"You're not failing anybody, okay? Especially me. You never have."

Hope moved close and placed her hands on either side of his rugged face, feeling the stubble of a long day prick her palms as she looked into his weary eyes, seeing creases at the corners that hadn't been there a year before.

"This is going to be good," she said. "A fresh start for both of us."

"You think?" Rick asked.

"Absolutely."

Her tone was so confident that she nearly convinced herself.

Chapter 6

The condo was on the fifth floor.

It had three bedrooms, two bathrooms, a dedicated parking space, charcoal-colored wood floors, a gas fireplace, a so-called chef's kitchen with granite counters and stainless-steel appliances, a large balcony, and walls of windows with jaw-dropping views of Budd Bay and Mount Rainier.

"The building was constructed in the mid-seventies, but this unit was totally renovated just last year, completely turnkey," said the Realtor, Marcia, who was hosting the open house. "You wouldn't need to do a thing."

She was right about that. Everything that could possibly have been done to the space already had been done. It was absolutely pristine.

Maybe that's what bothers me about it, Hope thought. *But the view . . . Wow.*

She walked to the window and stood next to Rick, who was gazing over a canopy of emerald green trees toward the marina and a flotilla of boats bobbing on the sapphire surface of the bay. It was a peaceful scene and, with the white frosted peaks and jagged black crags of the mountain towering over it all, sharp and powerful against the cloudless sky tinged with violet, a breathtaking one.

No amount of money could buy this view.

Hope turned away from the window and walked slowly toward the kitchen with the shiny new appliances and countertops that had never known a spill. She was aware that Marcia and McKenzie were looking at her with expectant, tongue-bitten expressions, as if they desperately wanted to say something but had taken an oath not to speak until spoken to.

"Are there any other units for sale in this building?" Hope asked. "One that hasn't been updated?"

McKenzie laughed incredulously. "Mom. Why would you want a fixer-upper when you could have this?"

"I just thought we might save some money by doing the work ourselves. Besides, I like putting my own stamp on things. This reminds me of one of your aunt Hazel's staging jobs; it's beautiful but blank. Could belong to anybody."

McKenzie rolled her eyes. "So paint a wall or something. Hang some pictures. Why go to the work of remodeling if you don't have to? Did you see the price?" McKenzie thrust a glossy brochure with photos of the condo and the listing price into Hope's hands. "You can afford this, no problem."

"It *is* well priced," Marcia said. "The owners were transferred overseas and want a quick sale. But it's the only unit for sale in this building. They don't come on the market very often. I'll be amazed if it isn't sold by the end of the week."

McKenzie bobbed her head in agreement. "I've had my eye on this place for a long time. Lucky thing we were driving by and saw the open house sign. There's not another building like it in Olympia."

"You can't beat the views," Marcia added. "Or the location. Just minutes from downtown and the capitol, so it's a really easy commute."

"My dad is retired," McKenzie said.

McKenzie was speaking for Rick more and more. Hope didn't like it.

She appreciated McKenzie and Zach's kindness in letting them stay with them this last month. She knew it was an inconvenience, especially for Zach. He'd given up his man cave and moved his treadmill and weights into the garage so Hope and Rick would have room to spread out.

Hope was anxious to get out of the kids' place and into a home of their own as soon as possible, but she also didn't want to rush it. Buying a home was a big decision. Was *this* the right place for them?

"Oh. Well, there are lots of retired couples in this building. You'd fit right in," Marcia said with an efficient little smile that irritated Hope.

How could she know? Or even suppose she knew? Did a few gray hairs and the fact that Rick wasn't working sum up the total equation of their lives? Was employment status—or lack of it—to be their whole identity now?

"You'll have no trouble meeting people. Some of the men get together for coffee and donuts in the community room at seven every weekday," Marcia reported with a smile. "And the ladies play Bunco on Wednesdays."

"Bunco," Hope said blankly. "You mean the game with the dice?"

Hope had played it with Hazel and some of her friends from the office once. The game was based on luck rather than skill, which was a good thing, since wine flowed freely during the evening. Several tables played at once and you moved to different tables for each round. The winner earned the privilege of wearing a plastic top hat covered with gold glitter. It was a fun, silly game. Hope had enjoyed herself. But every week?

"It's a very friendly building," Marcia continued, either ignoring or failing to pick up on Hope's skeptical tone. "The unit is all on one level, so there are no stairs to climb. Also, the hallways are wide enough to accommodate a wheelchair and the master bathroom is handicapped accessible."

Hope's jaw went slack as she tried to think of an appropriate response. Marcia seemed to mistake her expression for confusion and clarified her comments.

"It's something a lot of retired people are looking for, somewhere they can age in place."

"Age in place?" Hope choked out a laugh. "Thanks, but wheelchair-width hallways aren't exactly at the top of my must-haves list."

"Not yet. But, you know . . ." McKenzie said, then shrugged.

When she thought about it later, Hope still didn't quite understand what had gotten into her. It was a crazy thing to do. But something had been bubbling inside her for days. And when McKenzie shrugged, as if to indicate that, in her opinion, the days of her parents' dotage were fast approaching, the bubbles fizzed, sputtered, and spilled over.

Without stopping to think, Hope bounced onto her toes, tossed her hands over her head and her body into the air, and executed a perfect cartwheel, sticking the landing right in front of Rick, who let out a laugh and looked at her bug-eyed.

"Whoa! What was that about?"

Hope didn't know.

"Mom! Are you crazy? That dining table is made of glass! What if you'd crashed into it?"

The horror on her daughter's face brought Hope back to herself. McKenzie was right. What if she'd missed? Before Hope could answer, she felt Rick's arm around her waist.

"But she didn't." Rick looked at her. "Good job, babe. Nice landing."

Marcia, who seemed to have a special gift for ignoring elephants in the room and the emotional angst of possible clients, clapped her hands together and said, "Well, it's a very special home. Whatever your stage of life. If you're interested, I wouldn't wait too long before making an offer. I'm not trying to push you, but I'd hate for you to miss out on the opportunity."

Rick nodded. "How much are the homeowners' association dues?"

The figure she named wasn't astronomical, but it wasn't insubstantial either. When Rick raised his eyebrows Marcia said, "But that includes everything—maintenance, landscaping, insurance, and garbage."

Homeowners' fees, along with reduced square footage and

the lack of gardening space, were among Hope's objections to buying a condo. Convenience came at a price. And it wasn't like they didn't have time to deal with household maintenance themselves. Since coming to Olympia, they had nothing but time on their hands.

Hope needed people in her life and meaningful things to do. So did Rick. She had no objection to an occasional morning of coffee, donuts, and idle conversation or to playing Bunco now and again, but she wasn't going to make a career of it. And she wasn't going to let Rick make a career of it either, not if she could help it. Nor was she going to let McKenzie turn him into an old man before his time.

Initially, Hope thought that spending time with McKenzie would be good for Rick, raise his spirits and restore his energy. But rather than help him shake off his depression, it seemed to Hope that McKenzie was encouraging him to lean into it.

It was getting to the point where McKenzie barely let Rick do anything, even get up from the table to pour his own coffee. Didn't she realize that she was making things worse? Rick needed to get away from McKenzie's coddling, and soon.

"How soon are the owners planning on moving?" Hope asked.

"Already gone. All this is rented," Marcia said, casting her eyes over the color-coordinated furniture and accessories. "The new buyers can move in as soon as the paperwork is finished. Have you been prequalified for a loan?"

Hope started to answer, but McKenzie beat her to it.

"Yes. They're working with David Simms over at EBA Mortgage," she said, turning to her father. "Well? What do you think, Daddy? It seems like a perfect—"

"Excuse me," Hope said, addressing Marcia and interrupting McKenzie's interruption, "but would you mind giving us a minute? I think Rick and I need to discuss this, alone."

Even Marcia couldn't miss the pointed nature of Hope's tone. After an awkward moment, she excused herself and went down the hallway to the master suite. McKenzie followed but not before shooting her mother the sort of look Hope hadn't seen on her face since McKenzie was a teenager.

"Well? What *do* you think?" Hope asked when they were alone.

"You'd rather have a house," Rick said matter-of-factly.

"True. But none of the houses we've seen fit in our budget. Except that one in Lacey. The yard was awfully pretty," Hope said wistfully. "I loved all those evergreen trees."

"Three of them dead," Rick said. "Ready to topple over any day. We'd have to pay an arborist to remove them. Plus, the roof needs to be replaced. And did you check out the mortar on the fireplace?"

Hope shook her head.

"The floor in the dining room was warped," Rick reported. "I wouldn't be surprised if the foundation has issues."

There was no denying it; the house with the beautiful yard was in rough shape. Still, there wasn't anything wrong with it that time and money couldn't fix. The problem was, they couldn't be careless with either.

They weren't old. Not yet. But they *were* older. They couldn't pull decades out of their pockets the way they once had, when time seemed an infinite line and Hope had faith in their ability to overcome every setback.

"Well," Hope said, wandering toward the window and looking out at boats and blue sky, "we wouldn't have to do a thing here, would we?"

"Nope. And I like that it's so close to McKenzie and Zach. That's a plus."

Was it? Hope wasn't so sure.

Rick walked to the window and shoved his hands into his pockets. "Helluva view," he said.

Hope couldn't argue with that.

"Do you want to put in an offer?"

"That depends. Do you think you could be happy here?"

"Could *you*?"

"I like that it's move-in ready and within our budget. I like that it's close to the kids. And I love this view."

That wasn't quite as definite a response as she'd hoped for, but it was the nearest thing to enthusiasm Hope had seen from him in months.

Rick pulled his fist from his pocket, unclenched it, and took hold of her hand. He hadn't done that in months either. The warmth of his skin and gentle pressure of his fingers felt like a promise, or a down payment on one.

Maybe he *could* be happy here. And if he could, then she could too.

Chapter 7

McKenzie choked so hard that she practically spit ginger ale into her pasta.

"Real estate?" She laughed, her eyes wide and surprised. "You?"

"Yes. Me," Hope said. "Is that so impossible to imagine? Hazel's done really well with it." Hope stabbed her salmon with her fork and dipped it into the accompanying sauce. It was too spicy, but she ate it anyway.

"Well, yeah. Sure. Hazel," McKenzie said, her tone making it clear that her aunt's obvious success in business didn't mean it ran in the family.

Hazel shot McKenzie a look. "If your mother decided she wanted to be a Realtor," Hazel said, fixing McKenzie with a laser beam gaze, "then she'd be a brilliant one. Best in the business."

McKenzie shrank in her chair. Hope took momentary pleasure from her sister's defense, then quickly regretted it. McKenzie was her daughter, her only daughter. Why were they always at loggerheads, always competing?

Wait. . . . Am I competing with my daughter? Is she competing with me?

If it was true it was awful. And more than Hope was ready to deal with just then. She pushed the questions from her mind and took another bite of salmon.

"*Is* that what you want?" Hazel asked, turning toward Hope. "To become a Realtor?"

"Well, I like houses," Hope said, realizing she had spoken without really thinking things through. "I like fixing them up."

"You're good at that," Hazel agreed, spinning a knot of noodles onto her fork. "Selling them is different, though. You'd have to sublimate your taste and opinion to those of your buyers and sellers. You'd have to bite your tongue. But, if you're really interested—"

"I'm not," Hope admitted. "I just want to do . . . something. Or change something. I just want things to be different."

Hazel tipped her head to one side and waited.

Their mother used to do the exact same thing, with the same expression on her face. She would sit there for as long as it took. There was no use trying to obfuscate or change the subject. Like their mother, Hazel was comfortable with silence. And waiting.

And I am completely not.

Hope held out for all of ten seconds.

"I thought things would be different here, better. With Rick, I mean. For a couple of weeks, it was. Or maybe we were so busy unpacking and arranging furniture that I didn't notice? I don't know," Hope sighed. "Now he's just as miserable in Olympia as he was in Portland, maybe more. Back home, at least he had his old rugby buddies, Cal and Joe and the rest of them. They'd call him up and goad him into going out to watch a match or have a couple of beers. Now he never leaves the house."

Hope stopped herself and sipped some water, thinking about how that sounded, wondering how she'd gotten to the point where she actually *wished* her husband would go out drinking with his beer buddies. It did sound awful. Because it was. And Hope had no idea how to help him.

"Apart from watching cooking shows and staring out the window at the beautiful view that I am actually starting to despise, all he does is bake bread. And eat bread. I bet he's gained another ten pounds since the move. I know I have," Hope said, reaching down to the waist of her jeans and grabbing a love handle.

"Oh, you have not," Hazel said. "You look just the same."

"At *least* ten pounds," Hope said, knowing for a fact that it was fourteen because she'd weighed herself that morning. "But I don't care about his weight so much as his attitude." Before, he was morose; now he was angry.

"Last week, I saw a listing for a discussion at the library on a book about the rivalry between Thomas Edison and Nikola Tesla and asked Rick if he wanted to go. He practically jumped down my throat for even suggesting it. Apparently, me coming up with ideas for fun things he could do translates into nagging and impugning his manhood. Don't ask me how," Hope said bitterly, "but it does."

The waitress came by, proffering a basket filled with the last thing Hope needed—more bread. She waved her off. Hazel took another brioche.

"Maybe you need to try another approach, find something Rick is more interested in," Hazel said after the waitress left. "I saw somewhere that they're looking for new contestants for *Cake Wars*. Maybe Rick should audition."

When Hope snorted a laugh Hazel looked very pleased with herself, as if she was happy to have brought a little levity to what was supposed to be a fun girls' day out but had quickly become a downer. Hope laughed again, deliberately this time. She hadn't seen Hazel in a month. She didn't want to spend what little time they had together moaning and complaining.

"Anything but *that*," Hope said. "Bread is bad enough. If Rick starts baking cakes I'll get so big we'll have to remodel the whole condo—make the doors bigger, widen the hallways."

"Hey"—Hazel shrugged—"if that's what it takes to reignite his interest in engineering—"

Hope snorted again, for real this time. Hazel started in too. Among the many things the sisters had in common was an unfortunate, uncontrollable snorting laugh that came over them when surprised by humor, a noise their father had once compared to a sea lion clearing its sinuses.

The sound drew a few curious looks from nearby tables, but not nearly as many as followed when McKenzie, whose presence Hope had almost forgotten, practically shouted, "What is *wrong* with you! Daddy lost his job and almost his whole identity, and you sit here making *jokes*? He's depressed! Don't you get it?"

McKenzie's outburst caught Hope by surprise. She felt her cheeks get hot but from anger, not embarrassment. She waited a moment, until the other diners finally looked away, then glared at her daughter.

"You think I don't know that? I've been married to your father for more than thirty-four years. I think I know him at *least* as well as you do. Possibly even a little better."

"If you do," McKenzie hissed, "why don't you try to help him instead of making fun of him? Why don't you try being there for him?"

"Oh, come on, McKenzie. Nobody is making fun of your dad," Hazel said, not quite rolling her eyes but almost. "It's just a little gallows humor, that's all. Your mom is under a lot of stress—"

Hope interrupted her sister.

"McKenzie, I've left a home and life I love to be there for him, to be *here*. But I can't help him if he's not willing to help himself."

"What about counseling?" Hazel asked, looking at her sister.

Hope shook her head. "Rick will never go to a therapist."

"How do you know that?" McKenzie said; the condescension in her voice made Hope's jaw clench.

"Because I asked him. About two hundred times." Hope put down her fork. "Really, McKenzie. Do you honestly think I haven't tried? I would do almost anything for your father. But what I will *not* do is sit in that condo day after day, twiddling my thumbs and watching him bake yet another stupid loaf of bread.

"I've got to find something to do," Hope said, sounding almost desperate as she turned toward Hazel. "I'd like to teach, but it's no better here than it was in Portland. No openings, not even for subs. But, one way or another, I need a job. Maybe not real estate but something."

"I think that will just make things worse," McKenzie interjected. "How do you think that would make Daddy feel? If you find a job when he can't? If you need something to do, why not volunteer work?"

"Because, in addition to a reason to get up in the morning, I also need money. We need money."

"But I thought things were fine now," McKenzie countered, her worried frown giving Hope the sense that she was finally listening. "With what's left of Daddy's severance, the money from the Portland house, and the lower price of the condo, I thought you guys had enough to get by."

"Just enough," Hope said. "If we're careful. I don't mind that. When we first got married we didn't have two nickels to rub together and couldn't have been happier. I don't mind forgoing the extras, but I do mind forgoing insurance, especially at our age."

"Insurance? But I thought you still got it through Dad's old company."

Hope shook her head. "They had to keep him on the company policy for a while but not forever. They'll boot us from the plan at the end of next month. After that, I don't know what we're going to do. I checked out private policies and they are way out of our budget. The cheapest one I could find, with really lousy coverage, was over a thousand a month.

"I need to find a job," she said. "Not just for me. For us."

Their conversation was less heated after that. McKenzie grew quiet. Hazel changed the subject, talking about people they knew back in Portland. Hope told Hazel about a diet she wanted to try, only to have Hazel say she'd done the same one the year before, then gained back all the weight she'd lost and five pounds besides. Hazel also told her that she'd started taking yoga and was seeing a man she'd met at the gym.

"Really?" Hope said, her ears all but perking up in response. "Is it serious?"

Hazel laughed. "Not at all."

Nobody wanted dessert. Hazel was feeling a little tired, so she asked if the waitress could get her a go-cup of coffee for the drive back to Portland. After the coffee arrived, they paid the check and got up from the table.

Hazel needed to visit the ladies' room before leaving, so McKenzie and Hope stood in the lobby of the restaurant, waiting to say goodbye to her. A bowl of peppermints sat on a nearby table. McKenzie plucked two from the bowl and handed one to her mother.

"I shouldn't have yelled like that," she said, looking down at her fingers as she fumbled with the candy wrapper.

"No, you shouldn't have," Hope agreed. "But it's okay. You were just trying to be protective of your dad. So am I. McKenzie, you need to remember, when it comes to your father, I've got a pretty good idea what works by now."

McKenzie nodded, still looking down at her hands.

"It's not easy, is it?"

"What? Dealing with your dad?" Hope asked.

McKenzie shook her head and crushed the candy wrapper into a ball.

"Being married."

"No. Not always," Hope said slowly, dipping her head, trying to look into her daughter's eyes. "Kenz? Is there something—"

Just then, Hazel exited the restroom. She had a big, dark stain on her blouse.

"The stupid top came off the stupid cup," she growled. "And the stupid towel dispenser is empty. And the blouse is brand new. And it's silk!"

"Don't move," Hope said.

Hope jogged past the deserted hostess station and into the dining room, searching for help. It was late and the restaurant was nearly empty, but Hope finally found their waitress, who got her a handful of wet paper towels. When she returned to the lobby with the towels, McKenzie was gone.

"She bounced out of here in a hurry," Hazel explained. "She got a text and realized she was late for a conference call."

"A conference call? At this time of night?"

Hazel shrugged to indicate that Hope's guess was as good as hers.

"She's working too hard," Hope said. "I know she's ambitious and that she and Zach want to be able to buy a house, but I don't know. . . . Couples should spend time together, especially newlyweds."

"Well, they're not newlyweds anymore," Hazel reasoned. "Everybody works crazy hours these days. It's just a fact of life. Anyway, she said to tell you she'd see everybody next weekend."

"Oh, good. I was going to ask her. Liam's coming home for a few days, so I'm cooking a big dinner on Sunday, corned beef. I don't suppose you can make it?" Hope asked.

"Wish I could," Hazel said, dabbing at the coffee stain. "I'm hosting an open house that day. But I'll try to get back up here before he leaves, promise."

Hope nodded, trying to mask her disappointment. She knew Hazel was sincere and would try to visit during Liam's vacation, but she also knew she shouldn't count on it. The summer selling season in full swing, Hazel was swamped.

"What if Liam and I came down and saw you instead?" Hope asked, her face brightening at the thought. "During the week when you're not so busy? We could come down on the train."

"I'd love that!" Hazel exclaimed, tossing the used paper towels into a nearby wastebasket. "You can have the guest room and Liam can sack out on the couch. This will be fun!"

Hope agreed. It would be great to go back home, even if it was only for a couple of days.

"So," Hazel said as they were leaving, "how are things with McKenzie? Did you two make up?"

"I think so," Hope said. "Though, when it comes to me and McKenzie, you never really know."

McKenzie didn't really have a conference call.

She just wanted to be gone before Hope returned. Making that comment about marriage being hard was a mistake. She knew how Hope was.

Having opened the door between them and let herself be even the tiniest bit vulnerable, she knew that Hope would try to pry the lid off things that McKenzie really didn't want to talk about, especially to her mother.

Not that her mom would just come right out and ask her about it. No. Instead she would hem and haw and hint, trying to act casual and disinterested when McKenzie knew she was feeling just the opposite. When it came to her children, Hope could never just leave things lie or let them go. She had to know everything, wanted to be everybody's savior and best friend. It drove McKenzie crazy.

But that was only part of the reason McKenzie left so suddenly. A moment before Hope went off in search of paper towels, McKenzie's phone pinged with a text message. As soon as she read it, she was seized by a sudden panic.

She had to get out of there.

After making excuses to Hazel and jumping into her car, McKenzie sped out of the restaurant parking lot and headed across town. Distracted and anxious, she accidentally drove through a stop sign, slamming on the brakes just in time to avoid being hit by an oncoming SUV.

The driver inside laid on his horn. It had been a close thing for both of them and the fault was entirely hers, but at that moment she honestly didn't care. She averted her eyes from the wild gestures and angry visage of the other driver and drove away, moderating her speed, but not by much.

The freight forwarding company Zach worked for had its offices in an industrial park, in one of those ubiquitous gray metal buildings you can find anywhere in the country. In fact, the offices looked so much like those surrounding them that McKenzie mistakenly pulled up into the wrong parking lot.

When she saw it was deserted, her pulse started galloping. It wasn't until she'd made a complete circle around the building, her sense of panic increasing with every heartbeat, that her headlights fell on the sign for Manor Mile Blinds and she realized she was at the wrong building.

She turned the car around, drove two blocks east, then took a right, and spotted the sign for Double Time Logistics. This lot looked empty as well, but not completely deserted. There were a few cars at the rear of the building. A white pickup and a red sedan were parked near the door. A medium-sized blue SUV with vanity plates that said "GUD2GO" was parked near the edge of the lot, under a street lamp.

Spotting Zach's SUV, McKenzie took in a deep, ragged breath and let it out slowly.

Why had she let herself get so worked up? Zach was at the office and working late, just like he'd said. There was nothing to worry about, no reason to be suspicious or let her imagination run wild.

In fact, if she wanted her marriage to last, there was every reason to do the opposite. She had to figure out how to push through her fears, to trust him again. Only the week before, Zach had caught her skulking behind a half-open door, eavesdropping on his phone conversation.

"How much longer are you going to keep acting like this?" he shouted. "Huh? How long? I ended it. I said I was sorry. I even spent two hours with that stupid marriage counselor you insisted we see! What more do you want from me?"

"I don't know," she said, tears turning to sobs when she saw the look on his face and realized that wasn't what he wanted to hear. "I just . . . I'm sorry, Zach. I'm really sorry."

"Yeah?" he snarled. "Well, instead of being sorry why don't you try being different. How about you give trusting me a try? You say you forgive me, but then I catch you doing crap like this, spying on me! Quit searching the pockets of my pants after I get home, okay?"

"I wasn't spying on you," McKenzie said, her voice a bit firmer. "Not then. I was just cleaning out the pockets before I did the laundry."

"I don't care *what* you were doing, I just want it to stop." He turned his head away in disgust, as though he couldn't bear looking at her. "I mean it, McKenzie. If you can't get over it, then get *out*."

Remembering the files she needed to work on over the weekend, McKenzie left the industrial park and headed downtown, still thinking about what Zach said.

She was trying to get over it. God knew she wanted to.

It was a one-off, he'd assured her, a lapse in judgment that would never have happened if he hadn't had so much to drink. He felt terrible about it, embarrassed and ashamed. If she would forgive him, it would never happen again, he promised.

She did forgive him. But it wasn't easy.

Nothing about being married was easy. Even getting herself to go through with the wedding had been tough. That weekend when they'd gone to Zach's parents' place at the beach, a month before the ceremony, she'd nearly called it off.

But he talked her out of it. She *wanted* him to talk her out of it. Who wants to be the girl who calls off three engagements in four years?

When they were in Hawaii she was glad she'd gone through with it, really glad. The honeymoon was perfect. Everything was perfect. For a couple of months.

How had her parents made it work all these years? She knew it wasn't always easy for them either, she'd witnessed the rise and fall of tensions over the years, but things always got back to normal. She didn't even know what normal was anymore, not when it came to Zach. But he was right; she had to get over it.

He'd said he was sorry, cut way back on the beer; he'd gone to counseling—well, a couple of times. But that wasn't his fault. The counselor wasn't a good fit. He didn't understand them and was making it into a bigger deal than it really was. It was just a mistake, like Zach said, one bad choice.

Zach had done his part to make things right. Now the ball was in her court. She had to forgive him and mean it this time. She *had* to.

No more eavesdropping. No more checking his pockets. No more suspicion or spying. If he said he was working late, then he was. End of story.

And why wouldn't he be working late? She did, all the time. Zach was trying to impress his boss and get the promotion they'd been dangling in front of him for the last six months. If it happened, she and Zach would buy a house and start trying for a baby. It was what they both wanted. Thirty-one wasn't so old, was it? No. There was still time. Definitely.

Arriving at her office, McKenzie turned off the ignition and started digging through her purse to locate the keycard she'd needed to get inside after hours. It had to be in there; where else would it be? But she couldn't find it, not even after she pulled out her wallet, brush, and birth control pills. She started pulling out more things, smaller things—lip balm, eyebrow pencil, tweezers, half a roll of peppermints—until the bag was empty.

It was no use. The key was missing.

She laid her head down on the steering wheel and sobbed.

Chapter 8

The next day, Hope phoned McKenzie at work. Several times.

McKenzie didn't answer until the fourth call and sounded very annoyed, especially after Hope said that no, nothing was wrong. She just wanted to confirm that she and Zach would be coming over to the condo the following weekend, for Liam's welcome home dinner.

"Of *course* we're coming. I told Hazel to tell you we were."

"Just wanted to make sure. I need to know how much corned beef to buy."

"Mom, it's over a week away. It's not like we won't see you guys three times between now and then."

"I know. I just wanted to remind you."

"Mom, I've got to go. I'm late for a meeting."

Hope didn't believe it. But then, McKenzie hadn't believed that she called just because she wanted to check on the corned beef count, so maybe they were even.

Hope didn't get it.

Kids liked her, always had. Most confided in her at the drop of a hat. The boys told her *everything*—including a few things she could happily have gone her entire life without knowing. Even so, Hope listened to it all and gave them solid, nonjudgmental advice. To everybody, not just her own children.

At school, she was the cool teacher. In the neighborhood, she was the cool mom. From grade school on, McKenzie's girlfriends would show up in Hope's kitchen with their worries in tow—parental, romantic, academic, existential—and Hope would listen, advise, and encourage. Many of them continued to stay in touch. They invited Hope to their weddings, sent pictures of their babies. So why, after so many years spent listening to the soul-baring secrets and dreams of other people's daughters, was it so impossible to have a conversation with her own?

It didn't make sense. Apart from McKenzie, everybody on the planet seemed eager to share their life story with Hope. Rick called her Mrs. Friendly, joked that she could go through a toll-booth and come out with a relationship. It was exaggeration but not by much. People were always telling Hope their stuff.

It happened again on Friday morning in Starbucks.

Hope went to fill out a job application. Barista wasn't quite the career path she'd planned on, but she heard they offered insurance, even to part-time employees.

The manager, a young woman named Beth, looked harried but was nice enough to sit down and give Hope an interview. Somehow they got around to the topic of Beth's teething baby, how hard it was for working mothers who were trying to do it all, and how guilty Beth felt about wanting some time to herself.

Hope assured her that a crying baby didn't mean Beth was a bad mother, that crying was just part of how babies communicate. Then Hope suggested frozen peaches as a means of soothing for sore infant gums and a neighborhood babysitting co-op as a means of soothing jangled mommy nerves while finding some female support, something every young mother needs.

"Thank you," Beth said, sniffling a little. "I think I really needed to hear that."

"You're a good mom," Hope assured her. "But even the best mom on earth needs a break now and then.

"My mother used to send us to church camp every summer," Hope said. "The first year I was terrified. When the bus drove up and all the kids started climbing on, I held onto her and cried, very piteously, 'Why are you sending me away? Don't you love me?'

"My mother was incredibly devoted, spoiled us really, but that day she just peeled my arms from around her waist and said, 'I love you and I'll miss you. But I can't miss you if you don't leave. Now get on the bus, Hope. I'll see you in a week.' "

Beth laughed. "And did you like camp?"

"Loved it. Made a lot of friends and won the award for Most Improved Kayaker, which is the award you get when you have no athletic ability at all." Hope chuckled. "But it was fun. I went back every year until high school."

"That's a great story."

Beth smiled and looked down at Hope's application.

"I wish I had an opening for you. I really do. You'd be a good addition. I'll keep your application on file. But we're completely staffed up right now. I'm sorry."

"That's all right," Hope said, trying to hide her disappointment. "I understand."

Beth scanned the application again, biting her lower lip as she read. "You were a FACS teacher? That's the same as Home Ec, right?"

"More or less. The curriculum has changed a lot."

"So why would you want to work here?"

Hope was used to people spilling their guts to her, murmuring, "I don't know why I'm telling you all this," and then going on and telling her a whole lot more. She got it. Happened all the time. But it wasn't a reciprocal arrangement. Other people talked. Hope listened. But there was something about Beth's eyes. She looked like she cared.

Hope told her everything, way more than she intended. Halfway through, Beth waved to one of the baristas and asked him to make two mochas. Hope started to get up from her chair, embarrassed to have shared so much and taken up so much of Beth's time. But Beth said not to worry, that she was happy for the chance to rest her feet, so Hope kept talking.

When she was finished Beth said, "That really sucks. You really got a raw deal," which wasn't much in terms of advice but helped more than Beth knew.

Hope just needed to hear somebody say it. Not because it changed anything, just to know she wasn't wrong to feel that way.

Hope blew her nose into a Starbucks napkin.

"Sorry."

"Don't be," Beth said. "You're entitled. I just wish there was—" She stopped abruptly and looked away just as suddenly, her sympathetic expression replaced by a blank, wide-eyed look. She reached for her phone. "Hang on a second."

"Why?"

"Just hang on. I need to call my cousin," Beth said, and punched some numbers on her phone. "Nancy? . . . Hey, it's Beth. Remember that job you were telling me about? For the craft teacher?"

Hope felt a flutter in her chest.

Somebody was looking to hire a craft teacher? That would be perfect!

Assuming the pay was decent. And the job came with benefits. Not too likely on either count, she reminded herself, trying to guard against disappointment.

"Yes," Beth said, continuing with her half of the conversation, bobbing her head in response to whatever it was her cousin was saying. "But they're still accepting applications? . . . Oh. That many, huh? Wow."

Hope felt her stomach sink. Obviously, she wasn't the only person who thought teaching crafts was a dream job.

"Well, I'm sitting across from a lady I think would be perfect," Beth said. "She used to teach Home Ec. . . . Exactly. That's what I thought too. . . . Okay, I'll tell her. Thanks, Nancy. Tell John I said hello. . . . Uh-huh. I'll see you at Mimi's on Sunday. Bye."

Beth ended the call and looked at Hope.

"The job is still open. They'll be taking applications for another week."

"But they've had a lot of response?"

"Over two hundred applications so far," Beth said, then clucked her tongue in response to Hope's fallen expression. "Come on. Don't get discouraged. Just because they've gotten a ton of applicants doesn't mean they've gotten the *right* one—yet. Something tells me you might be just what they're looking for."

Hope nodded, but more to be agreeable than from any real conviction. "Yes. But two hundred applications?"

"I know. I was surprised too. It doesn't pay any more than you'd make working here, but it has benefits, good ones. They've got to hire somebody. It might as well be you, right?

"Anyway, it won't hurt to try. All they can do is say no. But you're going to have to get creative, find some way to make your résumé stand out from the rest. I mean, assuming you even want the job," Beth said, reaching for her coffee cup.

"Are you kidding?" Hope said, surprised that she could possibly doubt her interest. "I'd take it for the insurance alone, but teaching crafting is completely up my alley. Of course I want it."

Beth slurped the last drops of her mocha.

"Well. Before you get too excited, let me tell you more about the job. You might change your mind after you find out who you'd be teaching. And where."

Chapter 9

"Cut!"

Liam chopped the air with his hand before lowering his camera. Hope made a sputtering sound.

"Again? What's wrong this time? The lighting? The angle?"

Liam laid his camera down on Hazel's kitchen counter next to a piece of navy blue fabric and thick white cotton thread, supplies for the *sashiko* embroidery project Hope was supposed to demonstrate. Assuming they ever got that far. After fourteen takes, Hope still hadn't gotten through her introduction, let alone started teaching the project.

"Lillabet was about to walk into the shot," Liam said, plucking Hazel's cat from off the counter and depositing her on the floor, "but that's not why I stopped. It's the emotion. There isn't any. You're not giving me anything, Mom. You're not making me believe you."

"Oh, Liam, please." All Hope had managed to do so far was say her name, alma mater, that she had taught for two years, and that she'd like to be considered for the craft teacher job in a women's prison. "What's not to believe?" she said, putting the pink index cards with her major talking points down on the counter. "Just keep the camera rolling and let me just get through this, all right?"

"Mom," Liam said, heaving a frustrated sigh, "the whole reason we're filming your application is to help you stand out from the crowd, right? You've got to show them what's special about you, the stuff that they can't know just from reading your résumé—your passion, your commitment, who you are *inside*."

Liam pressed his hand to his heart for emphasis and Hope rolled her eyes at her darling and oh-so-dramatic youngest child.

"I should never have bought you that camera for your tenth birthday. Huge mistake."

Liam took the shade off of a lamp he'd borrowed from Hazel's bedroom, then started fussing with a makeshift reflector he'd created from cardboard and an entire roll of Hazel's aluminum foil. When it was set, he walked back to the spot where he'd been filming, made his fingers into a frame, and stared through them.

"Still don't like it," he announced, dropping his arms to his sides.

"Honey, is it possible you're overthinking this? We're making a video, not an artistic statement."

"I make films, not videos. And films *always* make an artistic statement."

Liam inched the reflector closer to the lamp, paused to observe the effect, and then twisted his lips, clearly dissatisfied with the result.

"The lighting in here is the *worst*. It's like filming in a dungeon. Are you sure we can't do this tomorrow, when we're back at the condo? That would be ideal, all those windows, so much natural light."

"No," Hope said, giving her head a firm shake. "I don't want Dad to know about this."

"Well," Liam said slowly and lifting his brows, the way people do when pointing out the obvious, "if you get the job you'll have to tell him."

"Yes. But that's a big if. Hundreds of people have applied for this job. If, by some miracle, they actually pick me then I'll tell your dad about it. After all the drama over my last job, I don't see any point in stirring the pot unless I have to."

Liam stopped fooling with the reflector and gave Hope a considering but slightly worried look.

"Are you guys okay?"

"Of course we're okay. Your dad and I have been married for about a thousand years. Now and then, you have to expect some of those years to run through a rough patch. That's all this is, a rough patch."

"You're sure?" Liam asked. "Because I am too young and emotionally fragile to survive a broken home."

Hope laughed. "You don't need to worry. Your dad and I have had our moments, but if I have anything to say about it, we'll go to our graves married."

"Okay," Liam said slowly. "But what if you don't?"

"Don't what?"

"Have anything to say about it."

"Liam, that's not funny."

"I'm not trying to be funny," he protested, touching Hope's arm when she looked away. "I'm just saying, my friend Julie's parents were married forever too. Then her father lost his job, just like Dad. Next thing you know, they ran out of money, lost their house, started fighting—"

"*We're* not fighting," Hope said.

"Yeah. I know," Liam said. "You're barely speaking; that's even worse. That's just fighting without words. You two are so mad you can't even talk."

"Liam, I am not mad at your father. None of this is his fault."

"I didn't say you were mad at each other, just that you were mad. Mad at life. Mad at how you did everything right and everything still turned out wrong. Mad at the people who effed you over," he said, but somewhat more explicitly.

"Watch it. You're not too old to get your mouth washed out with soap."

"I'm just saying, if you two keep shutting yourselves off and each other out, it's not going to end well.

"Right now, Julie's mom is in rehab for addiction to painkillers, court ordered because she missed a turn and drove her car through the front of a 7-Eleven. Her dad is in Malibu, shacked up with Julie's best friend's mom."

He crossed his arms over his chest again, the way he always did when he thought he was right. "That's two families destroyed. So far. Julie's thinking about breaking up with her boyfriend, a really nice guy, because she's decided that men can't be trusted and marriage is a sham."

Hope sighed. That was her Liam, always able to find the most dramatic, most extreme, most unlikely illustration. He was going to make a wonderful director.

"Honey, I'm sorry for your friend and her family, but you don't need to worry about us. I don't even like to take aspirin, let alone prescription painkillers. And while we might have our moments, your father would never cheat on me, not in a million years. We're just not those people."

"Mom, if there's one thing that living in LA and studying film has taught me, it's that under the right circumstances and enough pressure, anybody can be 'those people.' "

Hope frowned. "What are you trying to say? That I shouldn't apply for this job? That I should sit in that sterile box with the great view, doing nothing and watching your father eat two loaves of bread every day?"

Liam groaned and lolled his head backward. "Of course not. If that's what I thought I wouldn't have volunteered to film your résumé, would I? I think this is a really neat opportunity for you. But you and Dad need to talk and quit keeping secrets from each other. You should tell him what you're up to, that's all."

"Why?" she asked, throwing her hands out in frustration. "Why open a whole can of worms over a job that I've got next to zero chance of getting?"

"Because you're married," he countered. "Because married people should share everything, the good, the bad, and all the stuff in between. Because that's what you sign up for on the day you say, 'I do.' And do you know how I know this?"

Hope took in a deep breath and let it out slowly, vanquished.

"Because that's what I told you," she answered. "Because

that's what I said when I gave the toast at McKenzie and Zach's wedding."

"Did you mean it? Or was it just something you said?"

"Okay, okay. I get it. You're right. After this, no more secrets."

"Good. But why wait?"

"Liam," Hope said, "I know you mean well, but I can't handle one more thing right now. I don't have the energy to argue with your dad about a job I didn't get."

"But if you *do* get it?"

"Then of course I'll tell him. I'll have to. But the chances of that happening—"

"Are excellent," he interrupted, picking up his camera and peering at Hope through the lens.

"Yeah? What makes you think so?"

He pushed the camera right up into Hope's face, trying to make her laugh. Smiling, she turned her head away. More than any of her other children, Liam knew how to get around her. She couldn't be mad at him even when she wanted to. At least, not for long.

"Because," Liam replied, "you are a very talented woman who gave birth to a very talented son who is going to use those talents to show those people at the prison how truly fabulous you are."

He lowered the camera and looked into her eyes. Hope could see he wasn't joking anymore.

"You ready for another take?"

"Okay."

Liam placed the camera back on the tripod, then got two of Hazel's dining room chairs and placed them near the camera.

"No notes," he said when Hope picked up the stack of pink index cards and started flipping through them. "We're going to try something different this time. Take a seat," he said, motioning toward one of the chairs. "Good. No, don't look at the camera. Look at me. We're just going to talk for a while."

"Talk? About what?"

"About you. What's the first thing you ever made? The first crafty thing?"

Liam lowered himself into the other chair. Hope laughed nervously.

"Liam, this is silly. Why don't we just skip all the part with me talking and you just film me demonstrating the *sashiko* instead. Nobody cares about me; they just want to know if I can teach."

"Humor me," he said, then leaned forward and propped his chin in his hand, the way he used to when he was little and Hope told him stories at bedtime. "Tell me about the first craft you ever made."

"The very first? It was an elephant."

Liam just sat there, waiting for her to go on. She felt ridiculous, wondering what he thought this was going to accomplish, and groaned to signal her reluctance. But he just sat there, looking at her, waiting.

"It was a stuffed elephant made with pink and gray velveteen and two of those plastic googly eyes, the kind you glue on."

"How old were you?"

"Seven."

"Sounds like a pretty complicated project for a seven-year-old. Did somebody help you?"

"Oh yes," Hope said. "My mother. It was her idea.

"We'd gone downtown to run some errands and I saw a plush stuffed elephant in the display window of a toy store. It was just like the one that MaryAnn Traynor had brought to school for show-and-tell. I was obsessed with it," Hope said, shaking her head at the memory of her own foolishness.

"I asked Mom to get it for me and she said no, that it was too expensive. It cost something like seven dollars, which was a lot of money back then. Even before I asked I knew we couldn't afford it. But when my mother said no, I started crying and wouldn't stop. I cried during the entire bus ride home.

"It was ridiculous," she said, still feeling that way after all these years. "I was acting like a brat. I'm sure Mom must have felt like giving me a good smack, but she didn't. She just sat there, holding Hazel on her lap while the whole bus stared at us.

"When we got to our stop, I started crying even harder. I was sure Mom was going to punish me when we got home. Instead, she took me into her studio."

Hope hadn't thought about that day for a long time. But even now, after so many years, her mother's studio was vivid in her mind, and the memory of it made her smile.

"Studio" was a pretty elevated word for her mother's little hideaway. The house was small, only two bedrooms. But Hope's mother needed space for her sewing and crafts, so Hope's father added a room by enclosing two sides of an old sleeping porch and insulating it—sort of. In winter, even with the space heater running, the room was like an icebox. Suddenly, even though none was present, Hope caught a whiff of coffee and saw herself standing at the door of the studio, saw her mother sitting at the sewing machine, wearing a pink parka with faux fur on the hood. She saw the old Folgers Coffee can in a corner, positioned to catch drips from the leaky roof.

It wasn't a pretty space, or a large one, or particularly well organized. And since Hope's mother was always in the middle of a project, normally it was a mess. Every flat surface, including the floor, would be littered with fabric, yarn, ribbons, thread, buttons, sequins, feathers, and glitter, stuff she picked up for next to nothing at garage sales and flea markets. Hope's father always said his wife must have been part crow, because she was always scavenging shiny objects to bring back to the nest.

Hope loved that room.

Even as a little girl, she understood that her mother's studio was her sanctuary, the room of one's own that every woman needs. To Hope it was a veritable Aladdin's cave of treasures and mysteries. Until the incident on the bus, she had never been allowed to enter.

That day, her mother took her by the hand and led her inside.

"She dug through a box," Hope said, smiling even through the thickness in her throat, "pulled out a piece of pink velveteen, handed it to me, and said, 'Hope, you need to make peace with the fact that life isn't fair. Nobody gets everything they want or think they want. But the sooner you learn to make the most of what you have, the happier you'll be.'

"Then she shoved a pile of stuff off the table, took out a piece of butcher paper, and sketched out an elephant pattern. I took over from there. Mom stood over me while I worked, showed me how to thread the sewing machine, and made sure I didn't cut myself with the scissors. But I did about ninety percent of that project on my own.

"I called my elephant Pamela, Pamela Pachyderm," Hope said, smiling, still foolishly pleased with the name. "I took her to school for show-and-tell and told everybody that I'd made her myself.

"I was shy as a child and never more than average academically, but I'll never forget that day. Everybody made such a fuss, my teacher especially. It was like they'd noticed me for the first time, as if they'd looked around and suddenly realized I'd been there all along. Strange as it sounds, in some ways it felt like the first time I'd noticed myself as well, realized that I had something to offer and the ability to steer my own ship. . . ."

Hope's voice trailed off as she thought about that moment and how the lessons of childhood leave their mark.

Make the most of what you have.

Her mother's motto became her own, the core belief on which Hope hung much of her life and sense of self.

No, life was not fair. But because of her mother's influence, Hope came to believe that she could balance the scales of an unjust world by making the most of what she had. It was a belief that grounded her, helped her keep going even when she felt like giving up. It was a belief she had always shared with Rick, part of the reason she'd been attracted to him in the first place.

And that, Hope suddenly realized, was why she was so frustrated with him. Either he'd abandoned one of the core principles that had bound them together or he'd never really believed it in the first place.

No wonder she felt like she was living with a stranger.

"So that was a really big moment for you, right? Kind of a turning point?"

The sound of Liam's voice interrupted Hope's train of thought. He was still sitting there with his chin in his hand, waiting for the end of the story.

"It was," she said, pushing Rick to the back of her mind, talking to her son and not the camera, wanting him to better understand who she was and where she came from so that, by extension, he could better understand himself.

"You know," she said, "people spend a lot of time trying to figure out their purpose in life. In the details, it's different for everybody. But at the broadest level, I believe we're created to be creators ourselves, to leave our mark by making the most of what we have.

"That's what always excited me about teaching. Whether it was you and your brothers and sister, or the kids in the neighborhood, or the kids in my classroom—the moment I loved most was when I'd see their faces light up when they realized that they made this thing, this wonderful whatever it was, all on their own.

"We're created to create, Liam. When we lose sight of that, we lose sight of ourselves. When I teach somebody to make something they feel proud of, something beautiful and useful that they've crafted with their own hands, I am really teaching them who they are, why they're here, and what they're capable of.

"That's why I'm *here*," she said, making a fist and pressing it to her chest. "Because I—"

Lillabet, who had been curled up in a ball on the floor, chose that moment to leap onto the kitchen counter, knocking over Liam's tripod and camera in the process.

Startled by the sudden flash of yellow fur, Hope cried out. Liam spun around, dove for the camera, and managed to catch it before it hit the ground.

"*You* are a very bad kitty," Hope scolded when it was all over, lifting the cat from the counter. "Do you know how much that camera cost?"

Lillabet, unimpressed, extended her tongue and licked her

lips. Hope put her back on the floor and turned to Liam, who was checking over his camera.

"Is it okay?"

"It's fine. No worries."

"Well, it was a good save. You know"—Hope laughed—"I really did forget it was there after a while. Should we set it up and go again?"

Liam shook his head. "No, we're good."

Hope gave him a doubtful look. "Are you sure? I didn't demonstrate the *sashiko* yet."

"You don't need to," Liam replied. "Trust me. I got what I needed."

Chapter 10

Hope slipped out of bed the moment she opened her eyes and tiptoed into the bathroom to dress. She was pretty sure Rick was only pretending to be asleep but she was quiet just the same and left the house without saying goodbye.

What would be the point? They'd already said everything they had to say.

At precisely eight, Hope was standing at the prison gate as instructed, holding a heavy and cumbersome cardboard box. A grizzled and gray-haired guard with a paunch hanging over his belt and a ring of keys dangling from it approached.

"Hope Carpenter?"

When Hope nodded he pressed a button to unlock the gate, holding it open as she walked through, a gentlemanly gesture at odds with the scowl on his face. Hope smiled anyway and said, "Thank you," hoping to win him over.

"Not that way," he growled when Hope started walking toward a two-story beige brick building with rectangular windows and green hedges, a squat and innocuous structure that reminded her of a neighborhood middle school. "We're going to medium. The superintendent wants to see you."

The medium-security building definitely looked like a prison. It was tall and formidable. The gray brick exterior was the color of spent fireplace cinders. The upper story had only one window, very large, made from a single plate of thick glass. The lower floors had no windows at all.

Hope and Rick always slept with the windows open. What must it be like to spend days and nights shut away from the world, separated from friends, family, and all that was familiar, prevented from inhaling a free, fresh breath of air?

Hope took a sudden gasping breath and then started to cough. The guard's scowl deepened.

"You okay?"

"Yes. Fine. I was just—"

"All right then, put your box down on that bench, then go over and talk to Cindy. She'll give you a locker and get you checked in."

"A locker?"

"For your purse. You can't bring it or anything else inside. Didn't you read the e-mail they sent you?"

"Sure, yes. The purse isn't a problem," Hope said, glancing down at the box. "What about the rest of my—"

"You can't bring anything inside. That's policy. You got a problem with that, take it up with the superintendent. I don't have time to stand here arguing with *civilians* about *policy,*" he said, pronouncing "civilians" like it was a dirty word and "policy" as if it were the opposite, a force not just to be reckoned with but revered.

"Right. Sorry. Thanks for your help."

The guard sniffed dismissively, then squared his shoulders and turned on his heel, like a private on parade, and marched out the door. Hope set her box down and approached the other guard, a woman in her mid-forties with dirty blond hair.

"Don't mind Wayne," she said. "He spent four years in the Marines and never got over it. Best four years of his life, so he says. Everything since has been a disappointment."

"If the Marines was so great then why didn't he reenlist?"

"Probably so he could spend his days letting the rest of us know just what a disappointment we are. By the way, I'm Cindy," she said as she searched through the deepest recesses of Hope's purse. "Wayne's not so bad. Once you get to know him."

"Umm," Hope murmured. "Bet I'll never have the time to find out."

Cindy barked out a laugh, a single delighted yelp, and went on with her search. Hope smiled. Cindy, at least, seemed nice.

"Cindy, what's it like to work here?"

"Not bad. The hours are regular and the pay is decent. Good benefits. I like the people I work with. Mostly," she said, grinning as she glanced toward the door Wayne had walked out of. "But it's all right. Could be worse."

"And you're never scared?"

Cindy's eyebrows popped up, as if the question surprised her.

"You mean of the inmates?" She shook her head. "Not really. Just follow procedure, you'll be fine. That's why we have all the rules, to keep everybody safe, staff as well as inmates.

"I'll tell you something," Cindy said as she continued riffling through Hope's bag. "No matter how tough they are or what they did, most of our inmates ended up here for the same reason. One day they woke up and made the knucklehead decision to do something really stupid with, for, or because of some worthless—"

The door opened, interrupting Cindy's monologue. A petite young woman, just over five feet tall, with cappuccino-colored skin and a fringe of black blunt-cut bangs above her dark eyes, came in carrying an armload of books. She set them down on the counter without a word. Cindy started flipping through the pages, one after the other.

"How you doing, Mandy?"

The younger woman shrugged. Cindy picked up another book, shaking her head as she riffled the pages. "You sure read a lot."

"I've got a lot of time for it."

"Not too much longer, though. Seven months?"

"And four days," Mandy replied.

"Not that you're counting, right?" Cindy smiled, closed the

last book, and shoved the pile across the counter. "Okay, you're good to go. See you next week."

Mandy picked up the books, pressing them against her chest like a mother cradling an infant, and cast a glance in Hope's direction before leaving the lobby. Wondering what Mandy had done to end up in this place, Hope watched her walk across the path toward the beige building. She was so tiny and looked so young.

"That's exactly what I'm talking about," Cindy said. "That girl, Mandy Lopez? She's doing five years on a drug charge because she was dealing for some worthless man. Talk to most any of these girls and that's how they ended up here." Cindy clucked her tongue. "After what I've seen here, I'm staying single. Forever."

Cindy handed Hope her purse and pointed to the bench. "Leave it over there next to your other stuff for now. We'll give you a locker later."

"But my box," Hope protested. "I need it."

"Everything you brought has to be inspected and approved before it comes inside. We'll get it to you later. Right now, I just need you to walk through the metal detector. Hands down at your sides. That's it," Cindy said, waving Hope through.

The machine started to bleep and buzz. Hope's heart leapt like a startled gazelle, but Cindy wasn't the least bit perturbed. She pressed a button to turn off the alarms, then told Hope to take off her earrings and shoes and try again. The result was the same.

What had she gotten herself into? Would it be like this every day? Would she set off alarms every time she came to work?

"Let me guess," Cindy said. "You wearing an underwire bra?" Hope nodded. "Didn't you read the e-mail they sent you? The one with the list of what you can and can't wear onto the prison grounds?"

Hope had read the e-mail. There were a lot of rules about clothing. You couldn't wear blue jeans because that was what the prisoners wore, or T-shirts with obvious words or graphics, no hats, no gang colors (not that she knew what those might be), no sunglasses, no metal jewelry, nothing tight fitting, suggestive, or immodest.

She had taken all these things into account when choosing her outfit: khaki trousers, bright pink blouse, brown jacket, and moccasins with rubber soles. What she had not taken into account was the impact of underwear on metal detectors.

"Sorry, I must have missed that part."

"No worries. Just pop into the ladies' and take it off. But hurry up, okay? Superintendent Hernandez isn't a guy you want to keep waiting."

Hope stood there for a moment. Was Cindy serious?

"But . . . why? Are brassieres lethal weapons now?"

Cindy's smile disappeared.

"This is no joke. The rules and procedures in this prison are here for one reason, to keep everybody safe, including you. If we get slack and metal gets smuggled inside, trouble comes with it. Ask Wayne, or me, or any of the guards; we'll tell you about how creative inmates can get when it comes to making weapons.

"Some of the people who work here think that these girls are born bad and always will be, that rehabilitation is pointless because people can't change. I'm not one of them. But I've worked here long enough to know that in the right circumstances and under enough pressure, people are capable of almost anything."

Hope's cheeks went pink.

She wasn't used to being caught in a mistake or corrected so pointedly. She felt well and truly chastised. Why did those words sound so familiar? And hit so close to home?

For the first time since setting out on this path, it occurred to Hope that she might be out of her depth. In the grand scheme of things, she had lived a very sheltered, very predictable, and very safe life.

Hope's top was too heavy to see through, but she felt uncomfortable just the same. She couldn't remember the last time she'd gone braless.

However, as she sat on the hard metal chair that seemed to have been deliberately placed at a distance from the desk of Superintendent David Hernandez, it occurred to Hope that being bereft of her bra wasn't the only reason Hope felt awkward and vulnerable.

"If you're going to work here," he said, looking over the top of his black-rimmed glasses in a way that made it clear this was still a very big if, "it's not enough to read the procedures; you have to follow them. To the letter. Understand?"

"Yes. Absolutely," Hope replied, nodding deeply before adding a final, "Sir."

This seemed to mollify him but not much.

He sniffed and pushed his glasses up on his nose again but never took his eyes off her, as if to let her know that, as she had failed her first test in judgment, he never would.

"This program wasn't my idea. I want you to know that, up front."

Hope nodded. Message received.

"It's a waste of resources," he went on. "Why are we taking money from a budget that's already too tight, trying to turn felons into artists, when we could be using that money to teach them something useful? A trade or vocation. Something that might actually help them earn a living so at least a few of them won't end up coming back here?"

He shook his head and glanced down at one of the many pieces of paper on his desk. This particular piece of paper, Hope realized as she cast her gaze across the chasm that separated her chair from his desk, was her résumé.

She waited a moment before speaking, wanting to make certain he'd finished looking it over before she said anything else. Superintendent Hernandez didn't seem like the sort of man who appreciated having his train of thought interrupted.

"Well, sir, I can understand that argument. It's certainly something I've run across before, when I was teaching. Especially in an era of limited budgets, emphasis is placed on teaching skills that will help students get into the job market. I understand there's only so much money to go around. But I believe there's another argument to be made.

"The reason to teach crafts isn't because we're looking to create artists or even teach a particular skill. I want to impart broader concepts—self-confidence, patience, problem solving, determination, and the ability to stick with a difficult and unfamiliar project, seeing it through to completion. Those are the kinds of life skills and attitudes that help people succeed in whatever work they end up doing."

Hope leaned in a bit, warming to her subject and encouraged that he still appeared to be listening. "You know, one of my students, Taylor, was applying to Cal Poly for engineering. It's a very tough program to get into, especially if you're from out of state. She wrote her admission essay on what she'd learned while designing and sewing a jacket in my class.

"It was basically an engineering project, she said, but even tougher because it was a completely new medium for her, so she felt out of her depth. She talked about the frustration she felt when making mistakes, how she'd have to stop and take another approach when her first idea didn't work, the sense of accomplishment she felt after successfully completing the project, and how much she learned about perseverance because of it."

"Did she get in?"

"Oh yes," Hope reported, grinning at the memory of it and the e-mail she'd received from Taylor at the end of her freshman year at Cal Poly, thanking Hope for being so patient with her. "You see," Hope continued, scooting the metal chair a bit closer to the desk, "if you can teach students the skills to—"

"Inmates, Mrs. Carpenter. . . ."

He paused, glowering at her.

"These aren't a bunch of giggly teenage girls. They're felons. They're drug addicts and dealers, burglars, money launderers, check kiters, identity thieves, car thieves, pornographers, prostitutes, and child abusers. The women in our custody have skills, plenty of them. But not the kind that a housewife from Portland can probably relate to."

He released his grip on Hope's résumé. The paper fluttered from his fingers to his desktop, like a dead leaf falling from a tree.

"How many years did you teach?"

Hope's jaw tightened with irritation. He already knew the answer because he'd just read it on her résumé. She kept her eyes glued to his, refusing to be cowed.

"Four total; two before I had my children and two more after they left home."

"Four whole years of professional teaching experience," he said. "None of it in a correctional setting. Until today, I bet you've never set foot inside a prison." He tapped her discarded résumé with his index finger. "Do you honestly believe that a résumé like this qualifies you for this job?"

"That's not for me to say, Mr. Hernandez. But since I received a letter saying I was hired with instructions to report for work today, I have to assume that someone thought so."

"Someone. But not me. I was out of the office for three months, came back to work this week, and discovered that, in my absence, the arts and crafts program had been approved and you'd been hired as the teacher."

Three months? He'd been away that long?

Hope could only think of one reason for a person to be excused from work for such an extended period of time—because they were on medical leave. That could explain the yellowish tinge to his otherwise swarthy complexion and the loose fit of his suit. With his close-cropped hair and perfectly pressed white shirt, David Hernandez didn't seem like the sort of man who would wear an ill-fitting suit to the office, not unless he had recently lost a lot of weight because he was ill.

"You must be glad to be back," Hope said, feeling a bit more compassionate toward him as she tried to imagine what might force such a relatively young man—Hope guessed he was in his mid-forties—to take such an extended leave of absence. "I hope you're feeling better now."

"I was," he said. "Until I came in on Monday and found out that, in my absence, the associate superintendent, Jodie Whittaker, who conducted your phone interview, and the chaplain, Nancy Hendricks, made a hiring decision based primarily on a video of you telling a sentimental story about your mother."

He let out a sarcastic huff, turned his head away, and mumbled something. Hope couldn't be certain, but she was pretty sure she heard the words "women," "incompetent," "soft," and an expletive linked together in a way that, assuming she was hearing him correctly, wiped away her momentary sympathy.

"Excuse me?"

"You can't run a prison on sentiment," he snapped, ignoring Hope's affronted expression. "Look, Mrs. Carpenter, I'm sure you're a nice person. And I'm sure you did a perfectly fine job teaching a bunch of privileged, college-bound teenagers in the suburbs—"

"My district was in the city," she said calmly, "and my students came from a variety of cultural, financial, and family backgrounds."

He shook his head while she was speaking, making it clear that he wasn't listening. "I don't care where you taught before, Mrs. Carpenter. You're not qualified to teach *here*. If I'd been here to make the decision at the time, you wouldn't be sitting here today. I'm sorry if that hurts your feelings, but I believe in being up front."

"I'm glad to hear it because I believe in being up front, too. And the fact is, Mr. Hernandez, I *am* sitting here today. I received a formal letter of employment from your office. If you are trying to rescind that offer on my first day and without legal justification . . ."

Hope crossed her legs, sat up straighter in her chair, and smiled sweetly.

"In any case, and in spite of your reservations, I'm glad to be here. I'm going to try my best to do the job well and earn the respect of the inmates and staff, including you."

The superintendent pushed his glasses back up the bridge of his nose.

"Well, we'll see, won't we?"

"Yes, we will," Hope said stoutly. "By the way, as long as

we're being up front? I just want you to know that it's not as easy to hurt my feelings as you might think."

There was a knock on the door. Hernandez left off frowning long enough to bark out, "Come in!" to whoever was standing on the other side.

Hope folded her hands in her lap, happy to have had the last word. For now.

Was this a good idea? Did she really want to work for a condescending boss who had made up his mind to dislike her even before he'd met her? Maybe she should tell Hernandez to stuff his job, then go home and make up with Rick.

Did she really want to spend her life dealing with two grumpy men with chips on their shoulders? One at home and the other at work?

No. But she'd come here to do a job and she was going to do it. Neither Rick, nor David Hernandez, nor anybody else was going to stop her from doing it. Or at least from trying.

Would she fail? Maybe. The complications of simply getting inside the building had already shown her she had a lot to learn. But she had to try.

"Come *in*," Hernandez barked impatiently, responding to a second knock.

The door opened halfway. A woman's head popped through.

Her short salt-and-pepper-colored hair was gelled into stiff spikes on her head. She wore a black shirt with a white clerical collar. The bright blue rims of her enormous eyeglasses matched her blue eyes, which lit up when she spotted Hope's face.

"Ah! There you are! *So* sorry I'm late," the woman said in a low but lilting British accent. "I wanted to be here to greet you, but I was counseling a new arrival who was pretty upset and— Anyway, doesn't matter."

She waved her hand dismissively before grabbing Hope's and pumping it enthusiastically.

"Delighted to meet you, Hope! As soon as Jodie and I saw that video, we knew you were the right woman for the job!"

Hope's face lit up with recognition and relief. At least somebody in this place was glad to see her.

"You're Nancy, right? Beth's cousin."

"Yes, and the chaplain here. I'm so happy that you and Beth ran into each other. And even happier that Beth didn't have an opening for you!"

Nancy let out a laugh, then clapped her hands together and looked at the superintendent and Hope in turn.

"So? How goes it here? You two getting on?"

Chapter 11

Rick was sitting at a Thai restaurant, drinking hot chai and checking his phone for text messages every ninety seconds, wondering where McKenzie could be.

It was a busy place, crowded with office workers who were in a hurry to grab a bite and get back to work. He envied them for their urgency, for having someplace they needed to be and things they needed to do, too many things. To think that he used to complain about that; he wouldn't now.

The waitress came over for the third time to ask if he was okay and see if he was ready to order. "That way, your food would be here when your daughter arrives. Not trying to push you," she said. "It's just that the kitchen gets pretty backed up at lunchtime."

Rick glanced at his phone again—still no text. McKenzie was often late, but not this late. Had she forgotten about their date? He decided to give her another ten minutes.

Rick glanced at the menu, then up at the waitress. "How about some spring rolls to start. We'll decide on entrées once she gets here."

He would have preferred to wait until he saw the whites of McKenzie's eyes before placing an order, but the waitress was obviously anxious to turn the table.

Spring rolls seemed like a good compromise. The appetizers arrived about a minute before McKenzie.

He saw her trotting down the sidewalk in her high-heeled boots, head down and hands shoved into the pockets of her raincoat. He knocked on the rain-spattered window to try to get her attention, but she didn't see him then, not even after she entered the restaurant and he waved. When the hostess pointed across the noisy dining room toward his table, she finally recognized him and her face lit up.

"Sorry I'm so late, Daddy," she said, bending down to give him a peck on the cheek before hanging her raincoat on the back of her chair. "My meeting ran long."

"It's all right. You're here now."

Rick pushed the spring rolls to her side of the table. McKenzie plucked one off the plate and dipped it into the sauce.

"I'm glad you went ahead and ordered. I've got another meeting at one fifteen."

"Oh. Well, I only asked for the appetizer so far. I wanted to wait for you."

Rick caught the eye of the waitress and ordered spicy mango chicken. McKenzie asked what would be fastest and ordered chicken pad thai based on her recommendation. After she'd left, McKenzie apologized again for being in such a rush. Rick lifted a hand to let her know there was no need.

"Don't worry about it, kitten. I get it. I used to be the busiest man on the planet, remember? You do what you have to do. How's work?"

He took a sip of tea and waited for her to finish chewing, smiling to see how she attacked the spring rolls. She must have been starving, Rick thought. Probably rushed out of the house without eating breakfast that morning.

That was McKenzie. Always in a hurry but always late.

Hope was three weeks before her due date when McKenzie decided to make her entrance. Hope's labor had gone so quickly that Rick had to pull the car over and deliver his baby daughter by the side of the road, two miles short of the hospital. It was the greatest, most terrifying, and most exhilarating ten minutes of his life.

After the baby was born, he pulled off the sweater he'd been wearing, wrapped her up in it, and laid her in her mother's arms. Hope, lying on the back seat of the minivan, her face beaded with sweat and glowing with happiness, looked down at her daughter, then up at her husband, and said, "My hero."

Though he didn't realize it until just that moment, these were the words he'd always wanted to hear from her. He'd spent every moment since trying to live up to them.

"It's good," McKenzie said, bobbing her head and partially covering her hand with her mouth until she had a chance to swallow the entire mouthful.

Rick arched his brows, giving her a doubtful look.

"No, really," she protested. "It is. It's just a lot of hours. I always feel like I'm playing catch-up. But it's good," she assured him.

"Good. And how's Zach?"

"Fine. Still waiting to hear about that promotion. I really hope he gets it. He's been working so hard. Between his schedule and mine, we barely see each other. Thank God for weekends," she said.

The waitress arrived, apparently just in time. McKenzie practically fell on her food, shoveling the noodles into her mouth. Rick laughed.

"You're really hungry. Must not have eaten today, eh?"

McKenzie shook her head. "Uh-uh. I got a McMuffin on my way to work. I think the stress of the job just makes me hungry."

"Oh."

For two minutes that felt like ten, father and daughter ate in silence. It never used to be like that, Rick thought as he chewed. Before the move, he and McKenzie would talk on the phone three times a week and never run out of conversation.

But no. That wasn't quite right. It wasn't the move that had done it. It was losing his job.

The reason he never used to run out of things to say was because he was always talking about work, the latest project, the latest build, the latest problem he had solved, swooping in and saving the day when others had failed. That had been his reputation in the firm, his identity—Rick Carpenter: troubleshooter; the guy who got it done no matter what.

If Rick couldn't talk about work, he didn't know what to talk about. Certainly not himself. He'd fallen out of the habit a long time ago. And even if he remembered how it was done, nobody wanted or needed to hear all that. There's nothing as boring as listening to somebody complain.

What was it his mother always used to tell him? "If you have the time to complain about something, then you have the time to do something about it."

Now here he was, with nothing but time, and he couldn't seem to do anything about anything. God, how disappointed she would have been in him. He was almost glad she wasn't around to see it.

That was the kind of thing he thought about these days. Nobody needed to hear it, especially McKenzie. Better just to shut up and eat.

McKenzie slurped up a bunch of noodles and said, "So. How're things with you and Mom? She started the new job today, right?"

"Uh-huh," he said, giving a slow and knowing nod. "But I'm pretty sure you knew that. Kenz, is that why you invited me to lunch? Because you're worried that I won't know what to do with myself for a whole eight hours while your mother's out of the house?"

McKenzie swallowed her noodles but didn't say anything, just arched her eyebrows and looked at him.

"Kitten, I'm fine. Really. I've got plenty to do."

"Good. Like what?"

"Well, like having lunch with you for one thing."

"What about two things? What are you doing after this?"

Rick took a bite of mango chicken, chewing slowly to give himself time to think of a response.

"Thought I'd go look for some new pants," he said. "All of my old ones are too tight. Which reminds me . . ." Rick reached under his chair, pulled out a paper sack, and handed it across the table. McKenzie opened the top of the bag and sniffed.

"Rosemary olive loaf? Are you that upset about Mom taking this job?"

Rick shook his head and let out a disbelieving chuckle.

"Wow. You're as bad as your mother. Listen, for your information, I don't bake olive bread because I'm sad, or depressed, or trying to make the best of a bad situation. I make it because I *like* it. And I made it this morning because, with Mom out of the house, it seemed like a good time. She hates the smell of it."

"But, Daddy—"

"Hey," he said, reaching across the table, "if you don't want it, I'll take it back, okay?"

McKenzie smiled and hugged the bag to her chest.

"I'll take it home to Zach. Maybe. Unless I break down and make it my midafternoon snack. Smells so good. I can't believe Mom doesn't like rosemary."

"Neither can I. But your mother has always been a hard woman to figure out."

McKenzie tipped her head to one side. "So. You two okay? I know you've been upset about her going to work."

"Not true," Rick said, pointing a correcting index finger toward McKenzie. "I'm not upset about her working. If she wants to work, fine. She can. She doesn't *need* to. Now that we're in the condo everything's fine. But if she wants to work . . ." He shrugged, feeling a little silly for having snapped, and took a bite of his food. "I just don't like her working in a *prison*, that's all. Why would I? I don't think it's safe."

"Where is safe these days?" McKenzie asked, surprising Rick. He couldn't recall her ever coming to Hope's defense before. "You didn't have a problem with her working in a public high school. If you think about it, prison might actually be safer. I'm sure they've got . . ."

McKenzie rested her fork on the side of her plate and cast her eyes around the room, searching for a word. ". . . you know, procedures and stuff. Besides, Mom's smart. She knows how to look out for herself."

Rick shook his head. "Your mother is entirely too trusting. And she gets *way* too involved. First it was the kids in the neighborhood, then her students at the high school. Gets herself so worked up over a bunch of strangers that she doesn't have time or energy left for her family."

He stabbed a chunk of mango with his fork and put it in his mouth, then looked up and saw McKenzie staring at him with an expression he couldn't quite read.

"What? You don't agree?"

"Well," she said slowly, her forehead creasing into a frown, "I did until now. But hearing you actually say it out loud makes me realize I was being kind of a jerk about it."

Rick didn't really know what to say to that, so he scooped some rice on his plate, prepared to endure another awkward silence. But McKenzie had more on her mind.

"Sorry, Daddy. I wasn't saying that you were a jerk, just that *I* was. Trying to juggle job, house, and husband is making me appreciate Mom more. Honestly, I don't know how she did it. I drop into bed exhausted every night, and I don't even have kids yet."

At the mention of kids, Rick shifted his eyes from his plate to McKenzie's face, hoping this might be the precursor to an announcement, but none was forthcoming. McKenzie was scraping her fork across her nearly clean plate, trying to corral enough noodles for one more bite.

"I know you're worried about her," McKenzie said. "The prison and all. I get that. But you can't blame her for wanting to do something important with her life, can you? Beyond raising her kids? I mean, you can understand that, right? People need a purpose."

Rick bobbed his head but didn't say anything or make eye contact. McKenzie wiped her mouth with her napkin.

"So, listen. Daddy. I heard about this job opening for an engineer with the planning department. It's a temporary contract and only part-time, but I was thinking that—"

Rick lifted his hand to stop her.

"Thanks, Kenz. But no. I'm done."

"But, Daddy—"

"No," he said firmly. "I'm not going through all that, not again. Especially not for a part-time temp job. I'm retired. I'm happy. I'm fine," he said, forcing a smile to emphasize the point. "End of story."

"Okay," McKenzie said, sounding a bit defeated. "I was just trying to help. I really think you should get out of the house more."

"I'm thinking of taking up golf."

"Really? That's great!" McKenzie glanced at her phone. "Oh, shoot. I've got to run."

She pushed back her chair and reached for her purse, but Rick waved her off.

"I've got this."

"Oh, I don't . . . You sure, Daddy?"

Rick reached for his wallet. "Don't worry about it. You need to get back to the office. If it makes you feel better, you can pay next time."

"Fair enough. Same time next week?" she asked, popping up from her chair. "Unless, of course, you're out on the links."

"More likely stuck in a sand trap," Rick said, getting to his feet and returning McKenzie's squeeze.

After she left, Rick paid the bill. When the waitress brought back his change, a man who'd been sitting nearby got up and walked over to his table.

"Hey, I wasn't eavesdropping or anything, but I couldn't help but overhear your conversation with your daughter. A friend of mine works at a pro shop. If you're in the market for a set of clubs, I can give you his name. I'm sure he'd give you a nice discount."

"Thanks. But I don't play."

The man frowned a little. "But you told your daughter you were thinking of taking up golf?"

"Yeah," Rick said, counting out a few dollars to leave for the waitress before putting the change back in his wallet. "I think about a lot of things. But that's not the same as doing them, is it?"

Chapter 12

"David *is* gruff," Nancy admitted to Hope a few minutes after the two of them left the superintendent's office for a tour of the facility. "And bitter. Harbors an *intense* distrust of women."

"No kidding," Hope said. "Why is that?"

"I've never been able to get the whole story out of him. At least not yet," Nancy said with a small smile. "But I think it has something to do with his mother. But then, when it comes to men it always does, doesn't it? Some way or other?

"Anyway, from what I can gather, his mother was involved in some sort of nefarious activity when he was young. She was arrested and convicted and David was shipped off to foster care.

"Hard to know for sure, but I'm guessing that this is his way of punishing her," Nancy said, sweeping out her hand, and they walked through the noisy dayroom, crowded with tables and women, including a petite girl with dark hair who Hope thought might be the same one she'd encountered at the guard station when she first arrived.

Yes, Hope realized as they got closer, it was definitely the same girl. She had the same stack of books with her and, in spite of the chaos and noise surrounding her, seemed completely absorbed in reading one of them. *What was her name? Mandy . . . Mandy Lopez? Yes, that's right. Mandy Lopez.*

Leaving the dayroom and cafeteria, Nancy and Hope moved into a long and far quieter corridor, lined with blue metal doors that Hope supposed must open on to cells.

"But if he hates women so much, why stay here?" Hope asked. "Why not transfer to a men's facility?"

"Because," Nancy said, "he doesn't *hate* women. He distrusts us. And not entirely without reason. His wife walked out on him not long after his diagnosis."

"That's terrible. She left him because he got sick?"

"Oh, I doubt it," Nancy said with a shake of her head. "But that's what *he* thinks."

"Still," Hope said, feeling a bit guilty as she thought back on the pleasure she'd taken in getting the last word in during her meeting with David Hernandez. "That's got to be hard. Is he going to be all right?"

"Chemotherapy is never a picnic, but testicular cancer is highly treatable if it's caught early enough. My husband's an oncologist," Nancy said, responding to the question in Hope's arched brows.

"David should be fine. Though I do wish he had taken a few more weeks to recuperate," Nancy said, clucking her tongue with a motherly concern that made Hope smile.

She liked it that Nancy, though far from blind to his flaws, liked the cranky superintendent. But Hope suspected Nancy felt that way about everybody.

"There was no need for him to rush back. Jodie had everything under control," Nancy said.

"Maybe he was worried that the two of you would do some more hiring." Hope chuckled. "Or maybe he was just in a hurry to get back to the important business of punishing women."

Nancy stopped walking and turned toward Hope. There was no mirth in her smile, only kindness and such a sincere acceptance that Hope felt both ashamed and forgiven for cracking such a careless joke.

"David's not a bad man. He's rigid," Nancy said. "And complicated, even more than most men. Working here does that to you, highlights all of life's complications and contradictions, especially those that exist within yourself. You'll see, now that you're on the inside. I can't quite explain it, but . . . this place seems to attract people who, whether they know it or not, need to deal with their complications.

"Well. Perhaps excepting me. When I read that visiting and comforting the prisoner is the same as visiting and comforting Christ, I stupidly took it at face value." Nancy let out a haw of laughter. "That's me, I'm afraid. Thick as a plank. Not subtle enough to be complicated."

"Sounds like the opposite of stupidity to me," Hope said. "It sounds like wisdom."

"Oh, it is," Nancy said earnestly as they began walking again, turning left into still another long and brightly lit corridor, passing a guard and two inmates along the way, who all smiled as the chaplain walked by. "But it's not like I thought it up. I just try to follow it."

"I bet it's not easy."

"Not always. Especially in the face of those contradictions. I've been sent here to display mercy to these women and yet, by my very presence, I am participating in their punishment. You see the problem?"

"I think so," Hope said, thinking that, for all her claims to the contrary, Nancy was the furthest thing from thick, or unsubtle. "So how did you resolve that?"

"By realizing that there are two kinds of punishment: that which seeks merely to punish and thereby exact revenge, and that which seeks to correct and thereby redeem.

"The first is cruel, usually to everyone involved. Revenge isn't nearly as satisfying as we imagine and rarely accomplishes anything apart from making the world smaller and meaner. The second kind of punishment may be the most merciful thing we can do for someone who has lost their way, force them to face the truth about themselves and give them opportunity and support to redeem their lives and correct their course."

"And do they?" Hope asked.

"Sometimes. Not as often as I'd wish. The tough part is what happens after they leave prison. For most, it's a lot harder than life on the inside. Society is unforgiving, revenge hungry. The outside world neither desires nor believes in redemption. At least, not for these girls, the ones most in need of it."

Hope screwed up her face and closed her eyes, trying to recall the words she'd memorized long ago and almost forgotten.

"But when He heard this, He said, 'It is not the healthy who are in need of a physician, but those who are sick. But go and learn what this means, I desire compassion and not sacrifice, for I did not come to call the righteous, but sinners.' "

"Well done, you!" Nancy exclaimed, clapping her hands. "I didn't realize you were devout."

"Oh. Not really," Hope said, feeling suddenly foolish. "When I was a kid, I was a Sunday school suck-up," she admitted, smiling sheepishly. "They handed out candy bars to the kid who knew the most verses."

Nancy laughed. "Poor, poor Sunday school teachers. Whatever it takes, right? At least it stuck with you. And it's a very apt verse.

"If He walked the earth today, I'm convinced that *this* is where He'd be, which means it's where *I'm* supposed to be. Against all odds, a few of these women *do* manage to successfully turn their lives around. Now that you're here, maybe you'll be able to tip the odds a bit further in our favor?"

Nancy paused her progress, then took a step back, narrowed her eyes, and looked Hope up and down, as if she were trying to guess her height.

"Yes," she said. "I think you just might. Your name alone has to mean something, don't you think? In the ancient world, you know, names usually carried a meaning. They were more than something to scribble on a paper cup so somebody knows which latte belongs to you. Names denoted character, sometimes destiny. Perhaps Hope will be the one to bring hope to the inside?"

Hope smiled. "I don't know about that. But I'd like to try. That's part of why I wanted to work here."

"Most of us feel that way at some level," Nancy said. "Even David.

"For all of his gruff manner, his bitterness toward all the women who disappointed and deserted him, and that huge chip on his shoulder, in his heart of hearts David doesn't truly want to punish anyone. Not for punishment's sake.

"He works hard, sometimes too hard, because he so wants *not* to be disappointed. David wants to redeem these women and, in so doing, find redemption himself. The problem is, he's stopped believing it's possible. I'm not sure David Hernandez believes in anything anymore, himself least of all.

"But who knows, Hope on the Inside? Maybe you're the one who can change all that. Perhaps you'll resurrect David's faith in the rest of us."

Hope laughed and they started walking again. "At the moment I'd settle for getting through my first day without having him fire me."

"No worries there," Nancy said. "You've got a verified letter of employment. That's why I pushed so hard to hire you before he returned. To fire you, David would have to build a case against you, which would take at least five or six months. Unless, of course, you do something really stupid to give him cause—insubordination, blatant policy violation, dating an inmate, that sort of thing."

Nancy gave Hope a concerned look, as if she'd just remembered something. "You're married, right?"

"Very. To Rick."

The chaplain let out a relieved breath.

"Good. No worries about fraternization then. You're not permitted to have social or personal contact with inmates, you know. That would be a major no-no, *massive* policy violation, cause for immediate termination."

Hope shook her head. "Everybody around here is always talking about policies. There sure seems to be a lot of them."

"Because there are," Nancy said. "You've got to keep on the

right side of them. Otherwise, David can and *will* fire you. But, apart from that, you've got at least six months to change David's mind about the crafts program—and you.

"Ah! Here we are!" Nancy exclaimed as they rounded a corner and approached a plain wooden door. "Your classroom."

Nancy opened the door and stood back, allowing Hope to enter first.

The space was narrow, about ten feet wide by sixteen feet deep, and had no window. Long, narrow tables and orange plastic chairs ran along both walls, leaving a center aisle just wide enough to walk down.

At the far end of the room, Hope found a gray metal cabinet with a lock, a whiteboard and colored markers, and a small table and chair that she supposed was meant for her. The cardboard box she'd had to leave on the bench outside the guard station was sitting on top of the table.

"It's a bit tight," Nancy said apologetically. "It was a mechanical room until recently. When they replaced and moved the furnace, this space became available. That's when I started talking to Jodie about trying to find money in the budget for a craft program. Of course we had to wait until David was on medical leave to get it approved."

"You know something," Hope said, looking over her shoulder at Nancy before folding back the cardboard flaps on the box, "for a woman of the cloth, you're kind of devious."

"Only in search of the greater good."

Hope peered into the box and frowned.

"Hey. Some of my stuff is missing." She reached in with both hands and started digging through the box. "A *lot* of my stuff is missing."

"Really?" Nancy came over and stood beside her. "Like what?"

"My scissors, my rotary cutter, my pins, knitting needles, the mason jars I use for mixing paint colors, the acetone I use for cleaning brushes, and my glue!" Hope slapped her hands against her sides. "Why would anybody steal glue?"

"It wasn't stolen. It was removed." Nancy gave her a curious look, as if she didn't quite believe Hope's failure to grasp the situation.

"Hope, none of those kinds of items are permitted inside a prison. You can't bring in anything sharp, or anything with a blade. Acetone is highly flammable and the glue—I'm guessing it was model glue?" Hope nodded. "We have a lot of addicts in here."

Hope let out a huff of frustration. "Okay, fine. I get it. But . . . mason jars?"

"To you and me, a jar is a jar. But if somebody steals it and breaks it, the jagged edges or shards can become a weapon."

"Fine. So I'll keep them in there when I'm not using them," Hope protested, gesturing toward the gray metal cabinet, keys dangling from the lock. "Nobody will steal them."

Nancy laid a hand on Hope's shoulder. "You don't know that. Let me be clear: I love these women. So will you when you get to know them—they're such wounded birds. But they're here for a reason. Theft is second nature to some of them; so is violence, preying on the weak. You can't turn your back on them, Hope. And you can't bring supplies into your classroom that might be a temptation to some or cause harm to others."

"Well, that's just great," Hope said, making no attempt to mask her frustration. "How am I supposed to teach a craft class with no craft supplies?"

Nancy smiled and patted her shoulder. "You'll figure something out, I'm sure. You've got a whole hour."

"An hour? Wait. Are you saying—"

"Your first class is coming in right after lunch," Nancy said cheerfully as she walked toward the door. "Jodie will bring them over from the dayroom herself; she wants to meet you. But one of the guards will come to collect them later.

"Don't worry. There's only eight in this first group. We didn't want to overwhelm you, not on your first day."

"Gee. Thanks," Hope said, then reached into her supply box and pulled out a sheaf of colored construction paper, wondering if she could tear the sheets into strips and have the women weave them into . . . anything.

"Good luck!" Nancy called out, then turned in the doorway. "Oh, and Hope? If you're looking for a church, you're always welcome at ours, you know. Anytime."

Hope leaned forward, sticking her head halfway into the box, and pretended she hadn't heard. "Fat chance," she mumbled.

Chapter 13

Rick got into the car, turned on the ignition, and sat there watching the windshield wipers swish back and forth, trying to figure out what he was going to do with himself for the rest of the day.

He probably should go buy some new pants. The ones he was wearing were so tight he could barely button the waistband. But the thought of having to go to the mall, find a parking space, have conversations with chipper salesclerks, and face the reality of his bulging waistline was just too much.

Next, he considered going to the hardware store, not because he needed anything, just to walk around and see what they had. Ultimately, that seemed like too much as well, so he pulled out of his parking space and headed back toward the condo.

Maybe he'd make a batch of those cheese biscuits he'd seen on YouTube the day before, possibly a pot of chili to go with them. Having dinner ready when Hope returned from her first day of work might help ease some of the tension between them. Was he being a jerk, like McKenzie said? He turned the windshield wipers up a notch and considered the question.

No.

Why should he be supportive of something so stupid, even dangerous? Seriously. A prison? What man would support his wife working in a place like that? And it wasn't like she *had* to work—not that the money was that great anyway—they were getting by fine.

"But the insurance," she'd said, during their most recent fight on the subject, throwing *that* up in his face. He told her he'd figure it out and he would. Besides, they were fine for the moment. It wasn't like they were the only people on earth who couldn't afford insurance. Why was she always making him out to be the bad guy?

On second thought, he didn't think he would make dinner.

Hope was going to do what she was going to do—she already had, in spite of him. Maybe *to* spite him. There was nothing he could do to change that. She obviously didn't give a damn what he thought.

Eventually he would have to make his peace with that and with her. But not today. Let her squirm for a while. She wanted to be independent? Ignore him and his advice? Fine. Two could play that game.

He was tired, tired of all of it. Maybe he'd just go home and take a nap.

The road he would normally have taken back to the condo was closed. It looked like there'd been some kind of accident. Three police cruisers were at the scene, one pulled sideways to block the street. The officer standing next to it, rain streaming from the brim of his hat, waved Rick's car onto a side street.

Rick didn't know Olympia very well yet, so it took a couple of minutes to get his bearings. But soon he found another, less traveled road that ran more or less parallel to the one he'd intended to take. About a mile along his route, he saw a sedan pulled over by the side of the road, tilted in a way that suggested a flat tire.

Rick slowed down, not because he was planning to stop but to avoid splashing water onto the driver, who was bending down to examine the tire. Just as Rick's car was pulling alongside the stranded sedan, the driver straightened up, turning briefly toward the road, allowing Rick to catch a glimpse of her face.

For a moment, he forgot to breathe.

Rick swiveled his head to the right as he drove by, trying to get a better look. He would have stopped in the middle of the road if there hadn't been another car behind him. Instead, he accelerated, found a safe place to pull over about a hundred and fifty feet on, then jumped out of his car and ran back toward the stranded sedan and its elderly driver, who was, once again, bending down to look at the tire. He increased his pace as he closed the distance. His shoes crunched over the gravel, alerting the driver to his presence.

When she stood up and looked toward him, Rick felt a wave of disappointment wash over him. He slowed his steps, feeling suddenly drained, even more tired than he'd been before.

"Well! That was pretty quick after all!" the old woman exclaimed. "Are you from Triple A?"

"No, ma'am. I just saw your car pulled over and thought . . ." Rick licked his lips and wiped the rain from his forehead. "Do you need some help?"

"I do," she said. "But I don't want to bother you with this. I just called Triple A. They said they'd have somebody out here to help me in about forty-five minutes. Don't worry about me. I can wait in the car until they get here."

She looked at the tire again.

"I was just trying to see if I could figure out how to take care of it myself. You know, my husband used to handle all this sort of—" She stopped mid-sentence and frowned. "Are you all right?"

"Yes, I—" Rick took in a breath and let it out. "You just reminded me of somebody, that's all."

"Oh yes. I get that a lot. It's this Irish face of mine," she said with a laugh. "I look like everybody's mother, or aunt, or long-lost cousin Colleen."

Rick wiped his face again.

"Ma'am, why don't you get inside your car out of the rain while I change this tire for you?"

She shook her head. "Thank you, but no. I couldn't ask you to do that. You'd get soaked to the skin. The tow truck will be along soon."

"Well, I'm already soaked," Rick observed, holding out his arms. "So are you. I might as well change this tire so you can be on your way. Won't take me ten minutes."

The woman twisted her lips a bit, considering this.

"All right. But only if you let me watch you so I can learn to do it myself. Age and sex are no excuse for helplessness. Even if they were, you can't always count on nice young men pulling over to help change your tire, can you?"

Rick smiled. She didn't just look like his mother; she sounded like her too. Not just in what she said but in the way she said it.

"Do you have a spare?" he asked.

"It's in the trunk. There's a compartment under the carpet."

She walked toward the rear of the car. Rick followed her.

"By the way," she said, looking over her shoulder as she walked, "my name is Kate, Kate McGahan."

The tire didn't take long to change, even with Kate "helping" by loosening and tightening some of the lug nuts while Rick looked on. However, once Kate got behind the wheel, the car refused to start.

"I'm guessing it's a transmission problem," said the tow truck driver, the same one who had been summoned for the flat but arrived shortly after the tire had been changed. "But we won't really know until the mechanic takes a look. Is there a particular garage you want to use?"

"Peterson's Auto," Kate said. "Ask for Joe."

The tow truck driver pulled out his phone. Kate circled the car, staring at the sedan with an accusation in her eyes, as if she suspected it of sandbagging.

"I *knew* it. I should have gone over there when I heard that grinding sound yesterday. I hope it's not too expensive to fix. Well, it could be worse, I suppose. At least it's stopped raining."

She turned to Rick. "Say, how much do new transmissions cost?"

"Maybe it's just the fluid," Rick said, though he was pretty sure it wasn't. "Can I give you a lift somewhere?"

"Oh no. Thanks. I'll just ride along in the truck. Hopefully they'll be able to look at the car right away. If not, I'm sure one of the boys from the garage will take me home."

The tow truck driver took the phone from his ear.

"Joe says they're swamped but, since it's you, to bring it over and he'll try to take a look at it first thing tomorrow."

Rick arched his eyebrows. "Sure I can't drop you off at your house?"

"Oh, I couldn't," Kate replied, looking a bit defeated. "You were so nice to stop and help, but I shouldn't take up any more of your time. I'm sure you've got lots to do."

"Not really," Rick said. "Not one single thing."

Chapter 14

Deedee, a skinny, wiry twenty-two-year-old with ebony skin and close-cropped hair, pinched the pink paper between her fingers and picked up the object, examining it from all sides.

"What is it?"

"A crane," Steph said, rolling her blue eyes, then taking a corn chip from a bag and putting it in her mouth. "I told you before, a paper crane."

"Yeah. I know what you said it was," Deedee replied. "But really, what *is* it? Looks like a piece of folded paper to me."

"It *is* a piece of folded paper, stupid. It's origami. Some kind of Chinese paper-folding thing."

"Japanese," Mandy said without looking up from her book. "Origami is a paper-folding technique that originated in Japan."

"How would you know?" Steph asked irritably. "You didn't even take the class."

Mandy lifted her gaze, giving Steph a pointed look, and tapped her book with her index finger.

"It doesn't look like a crane," Deedee said. "I don't know what it looks like, but not a crane."

Steph snatched the crane from Deedee's hands and told her to shut up, then crushed the paper into a ball and tossed it directly into Deedee's face.

"Hey!" Deedee said. "Why'd you do that? I wasn't trying to dis you. It wasn't that bad. Better than anything I've ever made, that's for sure."

Another woman, Nita, who had also attended Hope's hastily thrown together origami class, crossed the room and sat down at the table. She was about thirty, broad shouldered and heavyset, and wore her light hair in a single thick braid down her back.

"Was that a joke or what?" she said, reaching across the table to filch one of Steph's chips. "It was like something you did in kindergarten."

"I know," Steph huffed. "Mine looked like a sick chicken."

"I thought it looked more like a rabbit," Deedee commented. "It was cute, though."

"Who asked you?" Steph elbowed Deedee before turning her attention back to Nita. "How did yours turn out?"

"Didn't finish it," Nita said. "Didn't even try. I'm just taking the class to kill some time. Need to look busy around here or they sign you up for kitchen duty. Making kindergarten cranes is better than scrubbing pots. But not a lot better."

"That teacher," Steph said. "Where did they find her? Could she be any greener?"

"Uh-uh." Nita laughed. "Did you see the look on her face when we all trooped in? Deer in headlights. I bet you anything she's never been on the inside before today."

"Got that right," Steph said. "She won't last long around here."

"Maybe a month. Two, tops." Nita grinned. "Hey, you want to bet on it?"

"On what? That she'll quit?"

"Uh-huh. I will bet you four bags of Fritos that Deer-in-the-Headlights-Craft-Lady will quit within two months."

"With your help?" Deedee asked.

"Could be," Nita said. "What do you say? You in?"

"Too rich for my blood," Deedee said. Nita turned to look at Steph.

"Four bags is pretty steep," Steph replied. "How about one month?"

"Sure," Nita said. "Ain't no jump for a show dog. But getting her to go in a month is gonna cost you five bags. Deal?"

Nita stuck out her hand. Steph thought it over for a minute before taking it.

"Deal," she said finally.

"Baby," Nita hooted, "that is one bet you are going to be sooo sorry you made. Because I am going to win this thing, no problem. Only downside for me is that I've got to wait a whole month to collect. Tell you what, let's add a side bet."

"Like what?"

"One bag of Fritos says that, within a week, she breaks down crying in class."

"A week?" Deedee said, her eyes widening. "I'll take some of that action."

"Me too," said Steph.

Nita started laughing. Steph and Deedee joined in. The three women made a racket as they teased one another, each claiming the other was going to lose and chortling about how delicious victory would taste.

Mandy, who had been reading with both elbows propped up on the table to cover her ears, dropped her hands and glared at the trio.

"Do you mind? I'm trying to study here."

"So? If you don't like it, you can move," Nita said.

"So can you. I was here first."

Nita glared back at her for a moment, as if trying to decide if arguing was worth the effort. "Fine," she said finally. "Why're you such a grouch today?"

"Because I'm trying to study and there's so much noise in here I can hardly hear myself think!" Mandy slammed her book closed and then covered her eyes with her hands. After a moment, she lowered them.

"Sorry. Maybe I should take a break."

Deedee got up from the table, stood behind Mandy, and started rubbing her shoulders. When Mandy's groan of pleasure was followed by a yelp of pain, Deedee said, "Girlfriend, you are tense!"

Deedee leaned forward so she could see the cover of Mandy's book.

"Advanced algebra? No wonder you're stressed. What're you studying that for? You don't think you're ever actually going to need that, do you?"

"Probably not. But I need it to graduate. You can't get a decent job on the outside if you don't have at least a high school diploma, so I've got to earn mine before I get out of here. If I can't get a job, I can't take care of Talia."

"How is she? You got any new pictures?"

"As a matter of fact," Mandy said, smiling as she reached into the pocket of her prison-issue khakis and pulled out a photo, "my mom just brought this one; Talia's first-grade picture."

Mandy turned the photo around and the women cooed and awed in response.

"Is she a sweetie or what?" Deedee asked. "Those eyes? Just like her momma. She's gonna be a heartbreaker when she grows up."

"Look at that gap between her teeth. Can't believe she's already in first grade. And losing her baby teeth," Steph said, shaking her head. "Time sure flies."

"Everywhere but here," Nita said. "But that is one adorable kid. Your ex sure makes cute babies."

"Yeah. That's about all he knew how to do," Mandy said, still smiling as she slipped the picture back into her pocket. "Besides dealing drugs and beating the crap out of me on a regular basis. But Talia makes up for a lot. All I want to do with my life is get out of here, get my kid back, and be a good mom. That's it."

"How much longer till you get your diploma?" Deedee asked.

"Hopefully within seven months and four days. It's going to be a photo finish, *if* I finish," Mandy said wearily. "I'm still short two credits to graduate. I need another class, but—I just don't know if I can handle any more. I'm studying myself cross-eyed as it is."

"Two credits of what?" Nita asked.

"Anything," Mandy said. "I'm good with my required classes, just short on credits."

"Well," Steph said, "what about taking this craft class?"

Mandy frowned. "What craft class?"

"The one we've all been talking about!" she exclaimed, grinning and shaking her head. "Don't you hear anything when you've got your head stuck in a book?"

"Not really," Mandy said. "So, this craft class would count as a credit toward high school graduation?"

"I think so. The lady in charge—" Steph snorted out a laugh when Nita dropped her jaw and widened her eyes in a "deer-in-the-headlights" impression. "Knock it off, Nita!

"Anyway, this lady used to teach Home Ec at a high school in Portland, so she must be a real teacher. Talk to her. See if you can get an art credit or something. Can't hurt to ask. And it's got to be easier than algebra, right?"

"That's for sure," Mandy said, casting a loathing glance at her algebra textbook. "Okay, thanks. I'll check it out. You know, I think I saw her when she was coming through security this morning. Kind of short, wavy brown hair, pink top, looked nervous?"

"That's the one," Nita said with a grin.

Excited by the prospect of a class that would get her the credits she lacked for graduation without requiring a great deal of effort, Mandy left the common room and went searching for Hope, without success. The door to the mechanical room turned classroom was locked and no one answered her repeated knocks.

On her way back to the common room, Mandy passed the chaplain and asked if she knew anything about the new craft class and if it was being offered for credit.

"That's a brilliant idea," Nancy said. "Why didn't I think of that before? Hope is a licensed teacher, so I can't think why not.

I'm not sure what the curriculum requirements might be, but I'll discuss it with her when she comes in."

"She's already gone?" Mandy asked.

"Yes. She was only scheduled for two classes this afternoon and had a bit of a headache, so she left a few minutes early. No worries, she'll be back tomorrow."

Chapter 15

"So? How was your first day?" Cindy asked when Hope came back through the security check to retrieve her jacket and purse. "Everything go okay?"

"Not bad. Could have been worse."

Cindy looked into Hope's eyes for a moment, then laid a hand on Hope's shoulder. "Hey. Around here any day that *could* have been worse and wasn't is a win. See you tomorrow?"

Hope forced a smile but didn't speak, lifting her hand in farewell as she walked out the door. Wayne was manning the outer gate, looking no more cheerful than he had when Hope came in that morning. He grunted to acknowledge her presence. Hope nodded but didn't look at him as she walked through the gate and into the parking lot and climbed into her car.

When the prison fences disappeared in the rearview mirror, Hope turned onto a side road and pulled over near a clump of trees. Then she turned off the ignition, checked the time on the dashboard clock, laid both her arms on the steering wheel, and began to cry.

Ten minutes later, she wiped her eyes and nose and drove home.

* * *

The condo was empty when Hope got home.

She dumped her purse on the sofa, kicked off her shoes, poured herself a large glass of Syrah, and carried it out to the balcony.

Ten minutes of tears had released some of the pressure, but she welcomed the chance to think through this awful day before Rick got back, read the defeat on her face, and started to crow.

Hope flopped into a patio chair, took a long, steadying drink, and stared sightlessly at the view, barely cognizant of the perfect September weather or the sailboats with their brightly colored spinnakers, puffed and billowed to catch the late afternoon breeze.

She didn't need Rick to tell her that she was in over her head. She was supposed to be the teacher, but those women had definitely taken her to school. It wasn't that they'd been unruly; she almost wished they had. She'd have known how to handle that.

But these women . . . They were just so . . . so quiet.

It didn't help that she'd had to wing her first project with less than an hour's notice—origami cranes were pretty elementary for a group of grown women. But no matter the project, she was sure it would have been the same. From the moment the women filed through the door of the classroom until the moment they filed back out, Hope felt their eyes on her. They watched her every word, move, and gesture, as if sizing her up and finding her wanting.

She'd tried joking around with them, thinking it might loosen them up, but her attempts at humor fell flat. Like everything else. The only hours in her life that felt longer than her first hour teaching in prison were those she'd spent in childbirth and her second hour teaching in prison.

Going home early felt like defeat, but she didn't think she could keep it together through a third class; better to fall apart in the privacy of her car than melt down in front of the inmates. It almost felt like that's what they were waiting for, even hoping for, to see if she'd burst into tears, run from the room, and never return.

Would they get their wish? Should she go back tomorrow?

Even after pouring a second glass of wine, she honestly wasn't sure. It seemed like everybody and everything was against her—Rick, David Hernandez, the inmates, and the circumstances.

How was she supposed to teach crafts if she couldn't get her crafting tools and supplies past the guards? And how was she supposed to connect with women who were so hardened that they actually wanted to see her fail? And not just fail but fail spectacularly?

One of the ones from the first class—*What was her name? Nita? Yes, that was it*—Nita, looked at her in such a way that Hope gained a new understanding of the phrase "daggers in her eyes."

But it was the silence that really got to her. Maybe because she'd been getting so much of the same from Rick recently. She didn't like arguing with him, but at least when they argued they were communicating. Anything would have been better than the chasm of silence that separated them since she told him that she was taking the job and that was that.

It was a relief to come home and find him gone. She hoped his absence meant that he and McKenzie had enjoyed their lunch date. It seemed like weeks since he'd left the house.

Halfway through the second glass of wine, Hope went into the kitchen and started chopping vegetables and lamb to make a stew. By the time her glass was empty and the stew was simmering, she'd found her courage.

Tomorrow would be better. For one thing, she'd know what to expect. Even if it wasn't, she'd never quit anything in her life and didn't plan to start now. She wouldn't give the inmates *or* Rick the satisfaction.

Where was Rick anyway? McKenzie said they were meeting up for lunch at noon. It was almost five.

"He said he was going to buy some new pants," McKenzie reported when Hope phoned. "Maybe he's still shopping?"

Hope shook her head. "He hates shopping, only goes when he absolutely has to."

"Did you see his pants?" McKenzie asked. "They're starting to look like sausage casings. Trust me, he absolutely had to."

Hope conceded the point. "Still, it shouldn't take this long.

His idea of shopping is grabbing whatever's closest to the door and throwing some cash at the nearest clerk. Did he seem okay at lunch?"

"He was fine," McKenzie said. "A little grouchy but no worse than usual. You know what? I bet he stopped by a golf course. Or maybe a pro shop."

"A golf course? Why would he do that? He doesn't play golf. Rick always said that golf is a good walk, spoiled."

"Well, he must have changed his mind, because he told me he's thinking about taking up golf."

"Really?" Hope turned the flame down on the stew. "That doesn't sound like him. But if it gets him out of the house and away from the loaf pans, I'm all for it.

"Oh, hang on," Hope said when she heard a key turn in the lock. "I think he's coming in now. Do you want to talk to him?"

"That's okay," McKenzie said. "I've got at least two more hours of work before I can get out of here. Tell him I said hi."

Hope started to tell her not to stay too late, but McKenzie hung up before she could get the words out. Rick came into the kitchen sans shopping bags, still wearing his sausage-casing chinos.

"No luck at the mall?" Hope asked. When Rick looked at her blankly, she said, "McKenzie said she thought you were going to buy some new pants."

"Oh. Right. Changed my mind. I'm going to try to lose some of this weight instead."

"And golf is part of that?"

Rick gave her another blank look.

"McKenzie said you mentioned something about taking up golf? I wasn't sure where you were and she said you might have gone to check out a golf course. It's good exercise," she said, reaching into the cupboard for another wineglass. "You know, as long as you don't take a cart."

"Yeah. Well. I'm thinking about it. This smells good."

Rick plucked a wooden spoon from a crock of utensils near the stove and gave the stew a stir.

"So. How was your first day?"

"Good." Hope handed him a glass of wine. "Lots to learn, but you know . . ."

Under normal circumstances, Hope and Rick would have picked up on each other's white lies. Years of marriage will do that. Besides, they were terrible liars, both of them. This was at least partly because they'd had so little practice, especially with each other.

As it was, they sat down at the table, ate Hope's good stew with some of Rick's most recent batch of bread, and had a conversation, of sorts.

Mostly they talked about the weather. But it was more conversation than they'd had in many days and so they played nice, relieved that they were speaking at all, avoiding unnecessary inquiries, anxious to maintain their uneasy and unspoken truce, each unaware that they weren't the only one at the table who was being less than honest.

Chapter 16

David Hernandez folded his hands into a church and rested his chin on the steeple.

"Needles? You want to bring needles into your classroom."

"Yes," Hope said firmly, holding up a long metal needle that was bent at the top, creating a small handle. "Felting needles."

"Felting needles," David said, his tone flat. He shook his head. "You can't bring sharp, dangerous objects into the prison. Do you have some sort of memory problem? We've been over this more than once. So why are you bringing it up again?"

"Because I was hired to teach crafting classes and I can't do the job unless the students have access to crafting supplies," Hope said through clenched teeth. "I've explored the limits and then some of what can be done with paper, watercolors, and Magic Markers. These are grown women, David. But because of the restrictions placed on me, I'm left with no options but to teach them projects that would be dull to the average fourth grader. It's no wonder they're acting out. They're bored!"

"Look, if you can't manage your classroom—"

Hope raised a finger and pointed it straight at him. "Hold it right there! Yes, this is a challenging environment. And yes, after nearly a month on the job I am still finding my way. But I am an *excellent* teacher; no one can say otherwise. And I am *not* giving up—not on my students and not on myself. So, unless you're prepared to have this same conversation, week after week, I suggest you and I start acting like adults and reach some kind of compromise."

David propped his chin back onto the steeple of his fingertips, regarding his angry supplicant. For a moment, Hope saw something in David's eyes that could have been a grudging glint of admiration but might just as easily have indicated the steely determination of a boss who has made up his mind to send an insubordinate employee packing. Hope's money was on the latter, but she held her ground, staring at David with silent indignation, refusing to flinch. If he fired her, then he did. But she was done with playing games, done with trying to win him over, done with being nice. She'd said her piece, stood up for herself and her students. If there were consequences, so be it.

Finally, after a long and tense silence, David narrowed his eyes, took in a deep breath, and then let it out in a long, slow whoosh, then disbanded the church, lowering his hands to the armrests of his desk chair.

"A compromise. What exactly did you have in mind?"

Hope took a deep breath as well, taken aback by both the question and David's, if not conciliatory, at least noncombative tone. She exhaled carefully and through her nose, so as to avoid clueing him in to her surprise. David, she surmised, was a man who admired strength and certainty. She needed to give him the impression that she'd planned to win all along.

"Every week, I'll submit my projects to you or Jodie in advance. I'll tell you what I want the students to make and exactly the sort of equipment or tools they need to do so. I'll do my best to keep anything that could be potentially dangerous to a minimum. For example, for the felting project I have in mind, all they'll need are these needles.

"I'll count them before every class, distribute one to each student, collect them at the end of the period, and count them all again. No one will be allowed to exit the classroom until every single needle is returned and accounted for. Between classes, I'll keep them locked in the supply cabinet."

David leaned back in his desk chair, rocking it back and forth steadily but ever so slightly, fixing Hope with the same steely glare he'd displayed earlier. This time, Hope was sure that his expression denoted anything but admiration. He hated her; she was sure of it.

She was also sure that the next words out of his mouth would be, "You're fired," or some version of the same sentiment, and experienced that sinking feeling that comes the moment before failure. *Oh, well.* At least Rick would be pleased. Maybe, after David called Wayne into his office to frog-march her off the prison grounds in disgrace, she could go home and have something approaching a normal, unguarded conversation with her husband.

David pressed his lips together, then made a sucking sound with his teeth.

"Lesson plans to be submitted one week in advance. Only one potentially dangerous piece of equipment allowed per project—needles or scissors, not both. Understand?" Hope nodded before he went on. "Nothing with a point or blade longer than four inches. All equipment to be checked in and out as you described. Inmates will be patted down by a guard before exiting the classroom. Inmates will not be allowed to bring anything, with the exception of fully completed projects, in or out of the classroom.

"Those are my terms. Agreed?"

Hope swallowed before answering.

"Agreed."

"Good. Now, if you'll excuse me, I have work to do."

David picked up a pen and Hope rose from her chair, more than ready to leave. But before she could make her exit, David looked up from the form he'd just signed.

"By the way," he said. "If anything goes wrong, I'm holding you responsible. One incident, one injury, one missing tool, and you'll be out the door the same day. Are we clear on that?"

"Perfectly."

David nodded again. Hope didn't wait to be asked to leave. As soon as Hope stepped out into the hall, she leaned back against the wall to catch her breath. She knew she'd been nervous, but until she stepped out of David's office she didn't realize how nervous. Her heart was pounding and her hands were shaking.

Hope had never been afraid to lock horns with Rick, not when she knew she was in the right. But, apparently, it was one thing to pick a fight with her husband and entirely different to pick one with her boss. Which made sense. After all, no matter how heated the argument, Hope knew that Rick loved her. With David, it was just the opposite. He hated her. She was sure of it.

But it didn't matter. She'd gotten her way. She'd won.

After taking one more deep, steadying breath, Hope shoved her hands in her pants pockets and walked down the hall toward her classroom, feeling like a champion.

The feeling was short-lived.

Hope might have won over David Hernandez or at least figured out how to get around him, but the women were much harder nuts to crack.

In the nearly four weeks that had passed since Hope began working at the prison, she had yet to see a single one of her students so much as crack a smile. The hostility and aggression emanating from most of them was so thick it seemed to generate its own brand of heat, but it was a passive aggression.

There were one or two bright lights in her classes, women who seemed at least mildly interested and made an effort, but not many. Mandy Lopez was one of them. She'd joined the class in the second week, after Hope had agreed to come up with a curriculum that would make her program qualify for credit as a high school art elective. Mandy was as subdued as the rest of them, almost as if she was purposely trying to fly under the radar. But Hope never felt anything approaching hostility from Mandy. She kept to herself, worked quietly, and did good, sometimes excellent, work. Hope had yet to give Mandy less than an A on any project. She did a particularly good job with the macramé bracelets, a project that Hope thought might finally win them over but hadn't. Only Mandy seemed to enjoy it. For a moment, while she was weaving in the beads, Hope almost thought she saw Mandy smile. But she couldn't be sure.

If only the rest of the women were as cooperative as Mandy, Hope's job would have been, if not a joy, at least tolerable.

But they weren't.

Though the women only rarely made eye contact with her, Hope could feel hostile gazes boring into her whenever her back was turned. They did not laugh, but Hope sometimes caught them smirking or snickering to one another and had the feeling they'd done so only because they wanted to be caught. They wanted her to see their contempt, to know that she was disrespected and unwelcome. They did not ask questions, make comments, or speak unless spoken to, and sometimes not even then.

And though the projects she presented were, for the most part, almost embarrassingly elementary, the finished projects of most of her students were poorly executed, almost as if they were purposely trying to do bad work. It hadn't been as bad on the first day—most of them had at least tried to fold a pretty paper crane. Their degrees of success had varied widely, but at least they'd made an effort. But that was the first and only time.

Now most of the women were either just going through the motions or actively trying to sabotage their own projects and the class as a whole. Obviously, David Hernandez wasn't the only one who hated her.

Why? She couldn't figure it out.

That Friday, things changed. But not for the better.

Of all the projects she'd presented thus far, Hope actually thought this one was kind of fun. They were making little desk-top-sized trees out of old books. It was something that Hope remembered doing when she was little with her mother. And since nothing was required for each tree beyond an old paperback book, some paste, an empty wooden thread spool, and scraps of ribbon or buttons, it was an ideal project for her students. There was nothing sharp, dangerous, or toxic involved. And though the execution wasn't complicated, the finished products could be pretty, even elegant.

Picking a book from the pile of paperbacks she'd bought

from the thrift store, five dollars for the whole box, Hope demonstrated the double-folding technique required to create the correct angle on the tree. When she was done, she looked up from her work and said, "That's all there is to it. When you're finished folding, you just glue the tree on the spool, which is like the trunk of the tree. Then, if you want to, you can glue on buttons or ribbon for decorations. Any questions?"

To Hope's surprise, Nita, the inmate whose eyes seemed to carry an even greater grade of loathing than the others and who smirked more contemptuously and turned in the most careless and shoddy work of anyone in the room, raised her hand.

"Yeah," she said without waiting for Hope to recognize her. "I've got a question. Where did you get your teaching degree? A Cracker Jack box? Because these crafts you keep bringing in are kid stuff, complete crap."

For the first time since Hope started her job, the sound of laughter echoed through her classroom. It wasn't the sound of amusement but of derision. The women looked down at their laps or hands, snickered, and exchanged sidelong glances, laughing at Hope's expense. The only exceptions were Steph, who was sitting quietly at her table, looking subdued and somewhat guilty, and Mandy, who lifted her head, looking from Hope to Nita and back again, a small frown creasing her brow.

Hope, embarrassed as well as angry, felt her cheeks begin to flame but quickly recovered her composure.

"Well, Nita, you had quite a lot of trouble with all the other projects. If you're able to complete this one with a little more skill, maybe you'll be able to move on to something more complicated."

There was another round of snickering. This time, however, the laughter was not at Hope's expense. Nita's head swiveled as she gave her classmates a furious glare. They fell silent. Nita stood up, looking at Hope with loathing.

"What are you doing here, anyway? Slumming? Seeing how the poor folks live? The drug dealers and dope addicts and prostitutes and thieves? Collecting material for a book? Or were you just bored?"

"What I'm trying to do is teach," Hope said. "But it's difficult when I keep being interrupted. Sit down, Nita."

"So you think you're better than us," Nita said, keeping to her feet. "Is that it? You thought you'd come down here and rescue us?"

"Nita, sit down."

Nita stepped out from behind the table and took two steps forward. Hope was standing at the front of the room, a good ten feet away. Even so, she had to resist the urge to step back, putting more space between herself and the inmate. But doing so, she knew, would be a mistake. The other women were watching. Hope saw something expectant in their eyes, as if they were waiting to see what she was made of, if she would crumble or stand firm. Though her heart was fluttering again, she chose the latter.

"That's it, isn't it? You think you're going to rescue us. Rich lady thought she'd come down here and civilize the poor savages, teach 'em how to fold paper cranes, and sit with their hands in their laps, and behave themselves. Isn't that right?"

With all eyes on her, all ears perked to hear her answer, Hope took a step forward and lifted her chin.

"No, that is not right. I'm here because I'm a teacher, one who thinks that all people are born with a creative spark and that tapping into that, even in simple ways, can make life more meaningful, no matter who we are, or where we come from. I'm here because I believe that the sooner you learn to make the most of what you have, the happier you'll be. I'm here for one simple reason, to teach. To share with you as much or little of what I know as you care to learn."

"Oh, I see," Nita sneered, taking another step forward and clenching her hands into fists. "So you're here because you're a teacher? Well, I think you're a lousy one, the worst. I think you ought to—"

Steph, who apparently *did* have something to say and couldn't keep it to herself any longer, jumped to her feet and stood in the aisle, becoming a roadblock between Nita and Hope.

"Knock it off, Nita! Seriously, that's enough."

"Ef you!" Nita spit, literally pursing her lips and flinging phlegm on Steph's sneakers. "Mind your own effin' business."

"She's all right," Steph countered. "She's just trying to help. So leave her alone already. It's the last day, Nita. Face it, you lost."

Before Hope had time to wonder what Steph meant by that comment, Nita lunged forward, grabbed Steph's hair, and pulled her to the floor. The two women began to tussle, spitting curses, landing blows, and receiving them.

"Stop!" Hope yelled. The women yelled too, some urging them to stop, some cheering them on. Hope then turned around and slammed her hand onto a red button on the wall behind her desk.

Within seconds, she heard the sound of pounding feet. Wayne ran into the room, breathless and red and brandishing a billy club. Cindy was right behind him.

Chapter 17

On Saturday morning, Hope and Hazel left for their annual sisters' road trip. They called it their Thelma and Louise weekend.

They took turns choosing the location and itinerary. Hope's inevitably involved some kind of craft-based activity, often a quilt show or crafting retreat, but once she'd signed them up for a three-day tour of wineries in Oregon's Willamette Valley, capped by a gourmet dinner at one of the tasting rooms.

Hazel's choices were eclectic but more adventurous and usually involved an element of danger—everything from rock climbing near Mount Rainier to a weekend in Seattle culminating in the mosh pit at a concert by one of the city's more raucous grunge bands. When it was over, Hazel walked out with a black eye from a very enthusiastic fan who had thrown an accidental elbow and Hope had a ringing in her ears that lasted for almost two days.

It was a great time, but they agreed that they might be getting too old for the mosh pit.

This year, it was Hazel's turn. Much to Hope's surprise, she proposed a road trip to Idaho's Sun Valley region for the Trailing of the Sheep, an annual festival of all things sheep—everything from knitting, felting, and yarn-dyeing classes, to an elegant Farm to Table dinner, sheepdog trials, and the famous Sheep Parade and picnic in downtown Ketchum.

"This," said Hope when Hazel picked her up at six o'clock on a chilly Saturday morning in October, "is without a doubt the absolutely coolest Thelma and Louise weekend in the history of the universe. You rock, Hazel. Do you know that?"

"Actually, I do. Now get in the car. I want to get there in time for the 'Secret Life of Sheep Ranchers' lecture."

"Really?" Hope asked, not even attempting to mask her surprise.

Hazel, who never missed a manicure appointment and wore four-inch stilettos to the office every day, had never shown an interest in even the most casual sort of gardening, like growing tomatoes in pots, let alone sheep ranching.

"Yes," Hazel replied, impatiently beckoning her sister into the car. "And we've got nine and a half hours of driving ahead of us, so shake a leg."

Hope closed the door and buckled her seat belt. "I checked the maps app on my phone and it'll take ten and a half hours."

"Pfft," Hazel sputtered. "Amateurs."

Hazel slammed her foot on the gas pedal so hard that the tires left rubber tracks on the pavement. Hope clutched at the door handle and yelped in response, laughing and squealing at the same time.

Two hours later, Hope was still smiling as she poured Hazel some coffee from the thermos she'd brought along and handed her a homemade glorious morning muffin.

"Thanks again for doing this," Hope said, sighing contentedly. "I really needed to get away."

"You don't have to thank me. It's really not a—" Hazel, who had just bitten into her muffin, stopped in the middle of her sentence and groaned with happiness. "Wow. I mean—Wow. This is maybe the best muffin *ever*. Seriously, this is like *incredibly* good. And still warm! What did you do? Get up in the middle of the night to bake?"

"Not exactly," Hope said. "I was too excited to sleep."

"What? You mean you stayed up all night?"

"Really, Hazel, you have no idea how much I've been looking forward to this. These last four weeks have been really tough."

As Hope told her sister about the frustrations, roadblocks, and the fight, as well as the self-doubt she'd been dealing with since taking the job, the frown lines that pleated Hazel's forehead got deeper and deeper. Finally, she lifted her hand to interrupt Hope's litany.

"Hang on. You get into your car every day after work and *cry*? Every. Single. Day. Hope . . ." Hazel took her eyes off the road long enough to look at her sister pointedly, her eyes silently asking if Hope understood how pathetic that sounded.

"I know, I know," Hope sighed. "But I never cry in front of anybody—though I have the feeling that's exactly what they'd love to see happen, some of them anyway—and I never let myself cry for more than ten minutes a day."

"Ah, Mom," Hazel said, shaking her head. "She may be gone, but her spirit lives on. Still, maybe this isn't the job for you. What's the point of having insurance if the work is so stressful it makes you sick? And a fistfight—weren't you afraid?"

"No. The guards were there before things got too crazy, it was over in a minute, and the inmate who started it is banned from my classes. So I don't have to worry about her anymore. Really, it's not that bad," Hope said.

Hazel cast another questioning glance in her direction. Hope laughed.

"Okay. It is that bad. But I can't quit, Hazel. I *can't*. I won't give Rick, or the inmates, or David Hernandez the satisfaction."

"So that's why you're going to stay in a job that makes you cry every single day? Out of stubbornness?"

"Don't knock stubbornness," Hope said, hugging her arms tight to her chest as she took a sip from her coffee cup. "It's spurred me on to conquer all kinds of obstacles. And you, too."

"It *is* kind of the family inheritance," Hazel admitted, "the gift that keeps on giving. But I'm worried about you. Besides, there's a difference between leaning into your stubborn streak to raise a family or build a business and doing so to hold on to a job you hate with a bunch of people you don't care about, just for spite."

"It's not just for spite," Hope said, slumping farther down in the seat. "I do care. That's the problem."

"About the inmates? Why? They've been awful to you; you said so yourself."

"Not all of them. Some of them seem like they're on my side. Steph stood up for me and got a black eye for her trouble."

"Steph? What's she in for?"

"Drugs."

"Dealing or using?"

"Both. A lot of them have drug convictions. Some are in for theft as well, but usually they stole to fund their habit. There's some minor stuff too, check kiting, shoplifting. Nita's in for substance abuse and vehicular assault. Tonya ran an identity theft ring, a big one, so I hear."

Hazel's brows shot up. "And she's in the minimum-security prison?"

"Unless somebody's done something really terrible—murder, terrorism, that kind of thing—the security level is determined by the inmate's behavior on the inside, not the crime she committed. If they behave themselves, they can stay in minimum. If they mess up, they're shipped back over to medium."

"So I take it that the lady who started the fight, Nita, went back to medium?"

"Not this time. It runs on a point system. She's been pretty good for a pretty long time. If it happens again, she'll be sent back.

"She's the one who really seemed to want to see me fail. It doesn't make sense," Hope said, shaking her head. "Why would she? She hardly knows me."

"Well," Hazel said, stretching out her right hand and waggling her fingers to indicate she wanted another muffin, "not to point out the obvious, but if these were the kind of women who always did things that made sense or played according to the rules, they wouldn't be in prison, would they?"

"True. Anyway, they're not all out to get to me. Some of them are just neutral," she said as she peeled the paper liner off a muffin and handed it to Hazel. "They don't seem to care one way or another. Or maybe they do? I just can't tell. I *know* they're thinking something. But what?

"That's the thing that's keeping me there. I just wish I could . . ." She paused to take another drink of coffee and find the right words. "I wish I could get to the bottom of these women, figure out who they are."

"Careful what you wish for. You might be better off not knowing."

Hope shook her head. "I don't believe that. What was it Nancy called them? Wounded birds. But birds just the same—beautiful creatures, born to soar and sing. But something happened to them along the way. They got hurt, damaged. Now they've forgotten how to fly."

"And you're supposed to help them remember?"

"Yes. I know it sounds crazy, but yes. I took the job because I like teaching crafts and needed the benefits. But I'm staying in it because I really think this is where I'm *supposed* to be."

"Teaching the caged birds to fly?" Hazel asked, arching her brows.

"Something like that. A few of them, at least," Hope said softly, thinking about Mandy, the petite, dark-haired girl who never spoke unless spoken to yet seemed so determined and so different from the others.

Though they'd exchanged perhaps a dozen words, this wasn't the first time Hope found herself thinking of this strange and quiet girl. In those moments, Hope felt, with a certainty she could not explain, that Mandy was the reason she was there, the one she had to hang on for, no matter what.

"Of course," Hope said, sighing, "it'll be easier to help them if I can come up with some class projects that actually interest them."

Hazel laughed. "Explored the limits of origami cranes, have you?"

"The limits and then some," Hope said. "When we get to the

festival, I want to check out the wool-roving and felting demonstrations. Hopefully, I'll get ideas for some interesting projects."

"Well, *I'm* going for the ranchers," Hazel declared.

Hope shot her sister a doubtful look.

"Ranchers?"

"Yep," Hazel replied, jutting out her chin. "I am sick and tired
of dating men who are prettier than me. A grizzled, muscle-bound
man with a beard, that's what I need. Somebody tough, honest,
hardworking, and straight shooting. An outdoorsman, somebody
who isn't afraid to get his hands dirty, a man who puts his brain
in gear before his mouth and doesn't speak unless he has something important to say.

"A grown-up," Hazel clarified, plucking her coffee cup from
the console and tossing back the last swallow with a grim determination. "Who is single."

"Oh, I seeee," Hope said, drawing out the word. "That's why
we had to be on the road at the crack of dawn. So you could be
there in time for the 'Secret Life of Sheep Ranchers' lecture and
meet the Marlboro Man of your dreams."

"Hey," Hazel said with a small scowl. "It could happen."

Hope gave her sister a sympathetic look.

"Let me guess. The guy from the gym? Jim? He's married?"

Hazel set her lips into a line. "Jim from the gym. *Really* married. As in twelve years, two kids, and a house in the suburbs'
worth of married."

"Oh, Sis. I'm sorry. That hurts. But better you found out
now, right?"

"Better if I'd have found out three weeks ago, before inviting
him in after dinner and letting him stay for breakfast."

Hope winced but didn't need to say anything.

Hazel sighed. "I know. It's my own fault. I make rules for
myself, then I break them. Serves me right, getting my heart
broken."

"You're heartbroken? When I asked if you were serious
about this guy you laughed and said no."

"Fine," Hazel groused. "My pride is wounded, then. The big

jerk. It wasn't exactly heartbreaking, but it was embarrassing. I mean, you think a guy really likes you, then find out that he was only playing you and you fell for it. It's humiliating.

"But," Hazel said stoutly, "after I find myself a hardworking, straight-shooting, strong and silent sheep rancher from Idaho and tell him what that jerk did to me, not to mention his wife and kids, he'll hunt Jim down and pound that slimeball into the ground."

"Shear him like a sheep!" Hope added.

"Brand him!" Hazel exclaimed, pointing to her forehead. "Right there, with a big letter *A*. Then everybody will know what a cheating, two-timing scuzzball he is."

"Dang straight," Hope said, smacking her hand against the dashboard to signal her support. "Marlboro Man will teach him a lesson!"

"Yes, he will," Hazel crowed. "My hero!"

When their laughter died down, Hazel switched on the radio and started looking for a station, then sang along to Taylor Swift, crowing about her eventual triumph and the misery of men who are perpetually mean.

Hope joined in on the chorus. When the song was over, she broke the last muffin in half and offered a piece to her sister. "Oh, I couldn't," Hazel said, then took some anyway. "So, enough about me," she said, shoving a crumbling piece of muffin into her mouth. "Let's talk about you."

"We *were* talking about me," Hope replied. "Mean girls in prison and crying in the car, remember?"

"That's just work. I meant your real life. How's the family?"

"Good," Hope said. "Liam called a couple days ago, all excited about some big contest he entered. He made it into the second round. If he wins, he'll get a check for ten thousand dollars and they'll show his three-minute film before the main feature at movie theaters all over the country. He was pretty excited."

"Good for him. I would be too. And the twins?"

"They're good too. Well"—Hope chuckled—"I'm assuming Rory is good. He's so busy with his residency that I hardly ever hear from him. But Reed drove down to see him a couple of weekends ago. Sounds like he's doing all right. McKenzie and Zach are fine. Both busy with work. Zach's still waiting to hear about the promotion.

"I'll tell you the truth: A part of me almost hopes he doesn't get it. McKenzie is already working all the hours God gives her. I don't think it would be good for both of them to be working so hard. But, aside from that, everybody's fine."

"And Rick?" Hazel asked in a way that made Hope think he was the one she'd been interested in all along. "What's he up to?"

"Believe it or not"—Hope laughed—"he's taken up golf."

"I *don't* believe it," Hazel replied. "Football, rock climbing, jumping naked out of an airplane with a knife in his teeth—*that* I could believe. But . . . golf? I mean, what would his rugby buddies say? Rick's always been such a macho man."

"A macho man who bakes bread and absolutely adored his mother," Hope reminded her. "That's one of the things I've always loved about him. Rick can't be bound by stereotypes. Part caveman. Part Julia Child."

"Now there's a mental image," Hazel said, shuddering. "Golf, huh? Well, if it gets him out of the house—"

"That's what I keep saying. He's lost about ten pounds, has gotten a little bit of a tan, and seems a lot less miserable."

"What's his handicap?"

"No clue. But it ought to be pretty good," Hope said. "He spends enough time playing."

"How much time?" Hazel asked.

"You mean actual hours? I don't know. But he plays nearly every day, usually doesn't get home until after me. What?" Hope asked, feeling Hazel's eyes boring into her.

Hazel shifted her gaze back to the road.

"Nothing."

Hope rolled her eyes. "What? I know that look, Hazel. Spit it out. Say whatever it is you're trying so hard not to. You know you will in the end."

"No, no," Hazel protested. "It's nothing. It's stupid."

Hope let out a frustrated sigh.

"Okay, fine," Hazel said. "It's just that—doesn't it seem weird to you? A month ago getting Rick to leave the house practically required setting it on fire. Now he's a dedicated golf nut? Playing every day and not getting home until after you do?"

Hazel turned toward her sister, searching her face.

"Hope. Nobody hits golf balls in the dark."

"Not in the dark," Hope said. "In the afternoon. It's cheaper."

Hazel gave her a blank look, as if she didn't understand the comment.

"Playing golf in the afternoons is cheaper. It's like . . ." Hope hesitated. "It's like going to a restaurant for the Early Bird special, but in reverse. The early tee times are in high demand, so they offer a discount to people who are willing to play later."

Hazel's expression was unchanged.

"Hazel. Rick is *not* having an affair. Come on!" She laughed. "You *know* him. We both do. Rick is the most monogamous man on the planet."

Hazel twisted her lips, frowning thoughtfully for a moment, then nodded. "You're right," she said, finally. "I mean, it's Rick, right?"

"Exactly," Hope said with a smile, her sister's more convinced tone quelling her momentary flutter of anxiety.

Hope fiddled with the radio dial, searching for an upbeat station with a clearer signal, then reached into her purse, pulled out her phone, and dialed Rick's number. He'd been asleep when she left, so she hadn't said a proper goodbye.

"No answer?" Hazel asked.

Hope lowered the phone from her ear. "He's probably asleep. Or in the shower."

"Probably," Hazel agreed. "It's still pretty early."

Hope slipped her phone back into her purse, then turned the volume on the radio up a bit and hummed along. Spotting a gas station, Hazel pulled in and then hopped out of the car to fill the tank. "I'm going to zip into the bathroom and grab another cup of coffee. You need anything?"

"Nope. I'm good. I'll stay here and keep an eye on the tank."

Hope watched her sister cross the parking lot toward the service station, tottering along on a pair of her "casual" heels that were only three inches high. As soon as Hazel was inside, Hope pulled out her phone and dialed Rick again.

Still no answer.

Where *was* he?

Chapter 18

Kate came around the side yard, carrying a mug of hot coffee and a plate of freshly baked homemade oatmeal cookies to Rick, who was nailing treads onto the once dangerously wobbly stairs he was replacing.

"They look wonderful!" Kate exclaimed as she handed over the coffee.

Rick took a quick sip from the mug and then stepped back to admire his handiwork.

"They're not going anywhere, that's for sure," he said. "The support posts are anchored in concrete footings that go down two feet. And I used a premium composite decking with a life-time guarantee. Come back in fifty years and these steps will still be here, just as sturdy as ever."

"I'll have to trust you on that. At this point in life I'm on the twenty-year plan," Kate said. "Even that, I suspect, is being wildly optimistic."

Rick flapped a hand, waving off her prognostication. "What are you? About seventy?"

"Seventy-four."

"Well, you can't tell by looking at you. I'm betting you'll live to be one hundred, at least one hundred."

"Thank you. Honestly, I'm not sure I want to hang around

that long. But it's nice to know that, when I do go, it won't be in a porch step collapse. Really," she said as he bit into a cookie, "I can't thank you enough for all you've done—replacing these steps, fixing the railing in front, replacing the broken doorbell, the grout in the kitchen. Oh, and the toilet! How could I forget? Here I thought it was just a little leak and it turned out the whole thing had to be replaced."

"Well, we didn't *have* to replace it," Rick reminded her. "But with it being so old and the seal ruined on the O-ring, it wasn't any more trouble to replace it than repair it. I'm just glad we got to it before the floor started rotting. That really would have been a headache."

"We? You're the one who did all the work. All I did was pay for the materials. Rick, the day you pulled over to help me with that tire was one of the luckiest of my life." Kate's smile became wistful. "With Lyle so sick those last few years, I guess I didn't realize how much things had deteriorated around here. Anyway, I'm so lucky to have met you. I've come to think of you as my guardian angel."

Rick chuckled, his mouth still full of oatmeal cookie.

"Trust me. I'm no angel. Just ask my wife."

"Well, then she must be an angel, letting you spend so much time over here, helping a poor old widow woman," Kate said, making her voice crackle like a crone's and resting the back of her hand helplessly on her forehead for a moment before resuming her usual cheerful tone and demeanor. "But seriously, are you sure your wife doesn't mind you spending so much time over here?"

"Nah," he said, and popped the last bite of cookie in his mouth, then washed it down with another slurp of coffee. "Like I told you before, she's at work all day. Coming over here and working on your place keeps me out of trouble."

"Even so," Kate countered, "there are probably plenty of things you could be doing around your own house."

"Not really," he said. "It's so new there's nothing that needs doing. That's one of the things Hope didn't like about the place. She'd rather have bought a fixer-upper. Couldn't see why at the time. For twentysomething years, I never did anything but work at the office or work on the house—never had time to just sit. Taking on another fixer-upper was the *last* thing I wanted to do.

"But," he said grudgingly, "I'm starting to see Hope's point. Our new place is nice but . . . a little sterile."

"Maybe you could paint?" Kate suggested.

"Yeah. I've been thinking about that," he said, though his tone indicated he hadn't been thinking very hard about it. "Maybe someday. But I enjoy helping you out, Kate. I forgot how much I like fixing stuff and making stuff. Feels good to get to the end of the day and know I actually accomplished something real, something I can see and touch, that will last."

Rick smacked his big hand onto the stair railing, gripped it tight, and then tried to give it a shake, smiling when he couldn't.

"I'm glad. But are you sure you won't let me pay you?" Kate asked, her voice almost pained. "At least a little? You've done so much for me and all you've gotten in return is lunch and a few cookies."

"What are you talking about? Your cookies are amazing. And, thanks to the exercise I've been getting while knocking off your projects, I've been able to work them off plus a few extra pounds to boot. Not a minute too soon," he said, slipping his thumb into the waistband of his jeans. "My pants were getting so tight they were starting to cut off my circulation."

"Well. You do look to be in a bit better shape than when we first met," Kate admitted. "But that's hardly what I'd call a fair trade for all your hard work."

"Hey, don't discount the value of those cookies. Just like the ones my mom used to make. She was famous for them. Every holiday and family gathering, Mom would show up with this ugly avocado-colored plastic carrier she bought in the sixties, filled with cookies. She'd put it down in the middle of the table and they'd be gone in five minutes.

"She shared all her recipes with me. Except that one. Always joked she would but not until she was on her deathbed. And then. Well . . ." Rick set down his empty coffee mug and picked up the hammer. "There wasn't time. And anyway, I never thought to ask her. It didn't seem important at the time."

"You miss her," Kate said.

"Yeah," Rick said, his voice becoming hoarse. "I think I always will."

"As it should be. She was worth missing." Kate laid her hand—delicate, small, and freckled from the passage of seventy-four summers—over Rick's big, calloused paw. "I'll always miss my Lyle. And aren't we lucky, you and I, to have someone we loved so dearly and miss so much? There are lonely people all over who would give anything to be able to say that."

Rick swallowed hard and pressed his lips together tight before nodding and drawing the corners of his mouth upward into a ragged smile.

"You know something?" Kate said, her countenance brightening. "I just figured out how I can repay you. That cookie recipe? It's been my secret too, for fifty-five years.

"On the night before Lyle and I got married, my mother came into my bedroom, looking white as a sheet, told me everything she knew about sex, which turned out not to be much"—she laughed—"and then handed me a piece of her good pink stationery with the secret family cookie recipe written out on it."

Rick grinned. "The recipe was part of your premarital counseling?"

"Oh yes. And believe me, it turned out to be a lot more useful than the rest of my mother's advice. Lyle and I buried many a hatchet over a plate of those cookies.

"I always assumed I'd pass it on to my children. But, since we never had any," she said with a small bow of her head, "I'm going to pass it on to you."

Rick's lips went flat. He swallowed again before speaking. "Well . . . Thank you. I'd like that."

Kate smiled. "I'll go inside and copy it down for you."

"Considering the size of the bonus," Rick said, fishing some nails from a pocket of his tool belt, "I'd better make an extra-good job of these steps."

"Maybe you should leave them until next time," Kate replied. She lifted her eyes skyward, examining a band of ominous gray clouds. "Looks like it's going to start raining any second."

Rick placed a level on top of the next board, eyeing it carefully. "It's all right. I'm just about finished here. A little rain never hurt anybody, especially the son of an Irishman. You could be standing in a deluge and my dad would call it 'a fine, soft day.' "

Rick positioned a nail, then drove it flush with the top of the board in three precise but powerful blows before pulling another from his belt.

"When I was a kid, my mom shooed me out of the house to play every afternoon, rain or shine. And if I'd complain about it, she'd push me right out the door, saying, 'Go on, then. You won't melt. You're not made of sugar.' "

Kate threw back her white head and barked out a hearty laugh.

"Do you know something? My mother used to say the exact same thing. I guess we're neither of us too sweet then, are we?"

"Guess not."

Kate went inside the house to copy out the recipe. Rick took a sip of coffee and got back to work. When the clouds split and the rain began to fall, soft and fine, he lifted his head and grinned, then drove in another nail.

An hour and a half later, with a sore right arm and an index card of cookie ingredients and baking instructions written in Kate's fine, clear script in his back pocket, Rick got into his truck and headed home, feeling better than he had in a long time. But the feeling was short-lived.

As he pulled into the parking lot, Rick saw McKenzie's car backed into his spot. McKenzie was standing in front of the car, her backside resting on the hood and her arms crossed over her chest.

For a moment, Rick was confused by her presence, worried, thinking something bad had happened to her. Or to Hope. He parked in one of the visitors' spots, hopped out of his truck, and walked toward her, his stride lengthening with every step.

She knew the code for the elevator and had a key to their front door. Why was she waiting for him outside?

"Kenz? What's up? Everything okay?"

McKenzie uncrossed her arms and shook her head.

"I'm waiting for you. I've been waiting for you for three hours. Where've you been? Playing golf? That's what you told Mom you were going to do. Is that what you wear to play?" Her withering glance took in his blue jeans, ripped at the knee, and the red and black plaid of his worn flannel shirt. "Where are your clubs?"

Rick's expression hardened into indignation.

"What are you doing here, McKenzie? Did your mother put you up to this?"

"No," she spit, as though the very suggestion was offensive. "Mom called and asked if you were with me. She was worried about you. Said she'd called your cell about ten times, but you never picked up and never called back."

Rick pulled his cell phone out of his pocket and frowned. There was a long list of unanswered calls, five from Hope, three from McKenzie.

"Guess I had the ringer on silent," he muttered before shoving it back into his pocket.

"So? Where've you been?" McKenzie repeated, her chin jutting toward his. "I went upstairs when I got here, wanted to make sure you hadn't had a heart attack or something. Your clubs are sitting in the foyer. By the way, that set of clubs you bought off craigslist? They're ladies' clubs.

"Where've you been, Dad? Because I know you weren't at the golf course. Have you *ever* played a round? Have you ever even hit a ball?"

"What I do," he said, setting his jaw, his voice low and sharp, his eyes smoldering like two blue-hot coals, "and where I go is nobody's business but my own. You're way out of line here, Kenz."

"Dad. How could you?" McKenzie's voice cracked as she grabbed at his arm. "You and Mom have always been—"

"McKenzie, I don't know what you're thinking, but I don't have to explain myself to anybody. Not to your mother. And certainly not to you."

He pulled his arm from her grip and pushed past her, striding toward the lobby doors. "You're in my parking spot. Don't let it happen again."

Chapter 19

Talia was getting so big that supporting her weight made Mandy's leg go numb. But she wouldn't have removed the child from her lap for anything. Instead, Mandy shifted Talia to the other leg and squeezed her even tighter.

"This is amazing," Mandy said, scanning Talia's most recent report card. "I'm so proud of you, baby. So proud."

Mandy kissed the top of her head. Talia looped her arm around her mother's neck.

"I'm proud of you, Mami. You had a good report card too."

"Well, not as good as yours," Mandy said. "I barely squeaked by on my algebra midterm, but as long as I get my diploma, that's good enough for me."

"You will, Mami."

"Hope so," Mandy said, kissing her daughter's head once again, breathing in the smell of Talia's apple-scented shampoo. "And after I graduate, get out of here, and find a job, we'll be together all the time. How does that sound?"

"Good," said Talia, nestling her head on Mandy's shoulder. "How much longer?"

"Not long now. About six months."

Mandy's mother, Lola, who accompanied Talia to the prison

every two weeks and had been sitting in a folding chair on the far side of the room, glanced at her watch and coughed.

"We should get going."

Mandy looked at the clock that hung on the wall of the visitors' room. "We've still got five minutes."

"I know," Lola said, reaching down and picking her purse up off the floor, "but I need to get Talia to her soccer game. Come on, Talia."

Talia hopped off Mandy's lap.

"It's our turn to bring the snacks—orange slices and Rice Krispie bars. I'm playing goalie today!"

Every minute spent with Talia was precious to Mandy, a reminder of the happiness they would share if she worked hard and stayed on the right path. She wanted to protest their early departure but decided to hold her tongue. They'd had such a nice visit; why end it on a sour note and upset Talia by starting an argument?

Besides, it looked like her mother had problems of her own. She'd hardly made eye contact with Mandy since they arrived. Instead, she sat in her chair without speaking, fiddling with her charm bracelet, the way she always did when something was bothering her. Though Mandy didn't ask, she figured the something was probably her dad.

She hadn't been able to see it when they first got involved, but Marcus was so much like her own dad. Both were impatient, demanding, and controlling, saw the world as a zero-sum, "us versus them" proposition, and were 100 percent certain that they were right, always.

Enrique, Mandy's father, was less reckless than Marcus. He didn't use or sell drugs and didn't hit women. But he knew how to wound without ever striking a blow.

When she got out of prison, she intended to be a much better person—steady, dependable, mature, understanding, and kind. She might as well start practicing now by giving her mom a break. After all, if Lola hadn't been willing to make the bimonthly trek to prison with Talia in tow, Mandy would hardly ever have seen her daughter. Enrique had never come to see her, not once.

"So, which are you more excited about?" she asked Talia, kneeling down to zip the little girl's jacket. "Eating Rice Krispie treats or playing goalie?"

Talia tipped her head to one side and opened her mouth into a wide, gap-toothed smile as she considered the question.

"Uhh . . . Rice Krispie treats!"

"Thought so."

Mandy laughed and looked up at her mother, wanting her to see how completely adorable Talia was, but Lola was standing there with her own coat already buttoned, purse clutched in her hand, eyes cast down, and left foot tapping the floor, obviously in a hurry to get going.

Mandy gave Talia one more kiss, then got to her feet and hugged her mother and then kissed her on the cheek.

"Thanks for coming, Mami. I know it's a hassle, but I really appreciate it."

"Yes. Okay."

Lola felt stiff in her arms. Mandy took a step back to examine her face.

"Mom? You okay?"

Lola bobbed her head. "Yes, fine. It's just—We need to get going. The traffic will be terrible. Talia, say goodbye to Mami now or we're going to be late."

"Bye, Mami."

"Bye-bye, *chiquita*. Be a good girl, okay? Oh, wait. Hang on a second," Mandy said, reaching into the pocket of her khakis. "I almost forgot. I've got something for you."

Talia's face lit up. "What is it? A present?"

"Uh-huh. Hold out your arm."

Talia complied and Mandy tied the present, a small bracelet of blue beads woven together with white cording, onto her daughter's slender wrist.

"Do you like it?" she asked. "I made it for you in my arts and crafts class."

Talia stared down at the bracelet with shining eyes. "It's beautiful, Mami. Did you get an A?"

Mandy laughed. "Yeah, I did. Guess I'm better at art than algebra, huh?"

"Talia, we have to go."

Lola took the child's hand, opened the door, and nodded to the guard who was waiting to escort them off the grounds. Mandy stepped out into the corridor to watch them go.

It never got easier. In fact, the closer she came to her release, the harder it became. But she held it together for Talia's sake. For her own too, she supposed. Tears wouldn't do either of them any good, would they?

And, as the chaplain had reminded her only the week before, she was winning the battle against time. All she had to do was work hard, keep her head down, stay out of trouble, and wait. She was close now. So very close.

Soon Mandy would be the one walking down the corridor, through the gates, and into the free, fresh air. Talia would be standing outside, waiting for her, and they would never be separated, ever again.

Thinking of this, Mandy swallowed back tears and forced a smile. Just before turning the corner, Talia looked over her shoulder and raised her hand over her head.

"Bye, Mami. Thanks for my pretty bracelet. I love you."

"I love you too, baby."

Chapter 20

On Monday morning, Hope walked to the front of the class-room, dumped a bag of soft, lusciously colored balls of wool out on the center table, and told the women they could pick whatever colors they wanted.

She didn't need to say it twice.

Within seconds, they were gathered round the table, oohing and aahing over the wool, comparing and trading colors, gig-gling like girls as they squeezed the balls of roving tight into their fists only to see them spring back into shape the moment they opened their fingers. Just like that, everything changed. Hope didn't understand it, not yet, but she felt so happy she could have cried.

"What is it? Where did you find it?"

"It's wool roving," Hope replied. "My sister and I went to a sheep festival in Idaho over the weekend. One of the vendors was selling it and I just about bought out her entire stock. Isn't it gorgeous? Hand-dyed."

"Mrs. C.?" Deedee asked, raising her hand. "What's a sheep festival?"

"Well, it's . . . a festival. . . ." Hope paused, trying to think how to explain it. "Like a fair, a celebration of all things sheep and the ranching lifestyle. There was a big parade of sheep through the town—that was really fun. And sheepdog trials with prizes for the dogs who were fastest at rounding up a flock of sheep and herding them into a pen—"

"I saw that in a movie once," one of the women, Tonya, said, sounding pleased to have made the connection. "The one about the pig who thinks it's a sheepdog."

"That's right," Hope said. "I saw that too."

"What else did they have?" Tonya asked, leaning closer, as if she wanted to be sure she didn't miss anything.

"Well, there were demonstrations on dyeing and spinning yarn and a bunch of other crafting classes. There were lectures too."

"Lectures? You mean like going to school?"

"Not quite like that. My sister made us leave before it was light so we would get there in time for a lecture on the secret life of sheep ranchers. But she wasn't quite as interested in the lecture as in checking out the rancher who was giving it. She's decided her future husband should be a manly man—tall, dark, handsome, and knows how to sit a horse."

"Oh, honey. Me too." Tonya heaved a wistful sigh that was echoed by several others in the group. "So? Did she find one?"

"Not quite," Hope said. "The man who gave the lecture was about twice her age. But he was very nice. We sat next to him at the Farm to Table dinner."

"Farm to Table?" Tonya asked. "What's that mean?"

Tonya, a string bean of a woman with gray hair that she wore in a ponytail, had missed the rise of the locavore food movement. And so many other things. Not for the first time, Hope thought about what different worlds she and her students came from.

There were differences from woman to woman, but, on the whole, it seemed to Hope that their exposure to the world had been limited even before prison. On the one hand, they hadn't done, or seen, or heard of so many things that Hope thought of as commonplace. On the other hand, she was pretty sure that they had seen, and done, and been exposed to all kinds of things that she had no clue about. Things that, perhaps, no one should have to experience.

It made her feel strange, presumptuous, and overprivileged and spoiled, to be telling them about her weekend and a fancy Farm to Table dinner. In truth, it hadn't been that fancy. They'd eaten off paper plates at picnic tables, but the food had been undeniably delicious. But the women seemed deeply interested in her story, almost mesmerized. Eight pairs of eyes were glued to her, waiting for her to continue, as if she were a messenger from a distant land, their only point of contact with the outside world.

In a way, she supposed she was, and so she went on.

"Farm to table dining is very popular right now," Hope explained. "People have started to realize that fresh food, produced locally on small farms or ranches, is healthier for you. And tastes a lot better too. This dinner was a chance for sheep ranchers to educate people about how to use the food that can be made from their herds: meat, cheese—"

"Cheese?" Deedee asked, her voice incredulous. "From sheep?"

"Sure. Sheep make milk too. You never heard of sheep's milk cheese?"

Deedee made a face. "I like Velveeta."

"That's not real cheese," Steph said, giving Deedee an elbow. "Says so on the package. They make it out of oil and chemicals and yellow dye."

"So what? Tastes good." Deedee looked at Hope. "What does sheep cheese taste like?"

"It comes in a lot of different flavors and textures," Hope said. "But the kind I had was crumbly and tasted a little bit sharp. They put it in a salad made with arugula, mint, and pomegranate seeds, served with garlic mashed potatoes and tiny, tender lamb chops grilled over hickory smoke."

The women, who were practically salivating by this time, issued a collective groan of longing and pleasure that brought a smile to Hope's face.

Though she'd been working at the prison for only a month, she knew that food was a hot topic of conversation. Inmates spent hours talking about the dishes they missed most, reciting the recipes that they, their mothers, or their grandmothers used to make, and dreaming aloud about the first thing they would find to eat when they were on the outside. Since the cafeteria served no red meat apart from hamburger, and then only rarely, steaks and chops often topped the post-release wish list.

"What about dessert?" Mandy asked. "What did they have?"

"They brought everybody a plate with five different desserts, just a delicious little bite of each one."

There was another groan.

"What kind?" Deedee asked. "Pie? Pudding? Cobbler? I need specifics here."

Hope stepped back from the table. "Tell you what. Before I do, what if everybody picks out three colors of roving they like and I'll demonstrate how we're going to use it to make one of these little felted birds, okay?"

Hope held up a felted cardinal, vermillion red with a bright yellow beak and beady black eyes, that she'd made the night before. The women murmured again, this time with the kind of cooing and oohing that accompanies the sighting of a newborn baby or gamboling kittens. Hope grinned.

"It's so cute. You really think I can make that?" Steph asked, tipping her head to one side, her skepticism evident.

"I *know* you can. Now, come on, everybody. Pick out your colors and let's get to work."

What should have taken five minutes—simply choosing their materials—took nearly twenty. Many of the women had a hard time choosing colors for their bird's body and wings.

Hope had noticed that before. So many of them seemed so uncertain, incapable of making decisions, as if frightened of making a mistake. It would have been faster and easier just to make their choices for them, but Hope recognized that, in some instances, helping the women gain confidence in their own choices and opinions was more important than imparting any crafting skills. Assuring them that there were no wrong decisions, Hope waited patiently until every student had made her choice.

Once they did, Hope was finally ready to begin teaching.

The basic felting technique she demonstrated wasn't hugely

difficult to master, but it did take time to complete a project. Hope showed them how to immerse the balls of wool into bowls of water, squeeze out the liquid to make them smaller and more dense, and begin stabbing the wool with their felting needles, over and over and over again to work the wool into the correct shape.

"Hey, make sure you stab the wool and not each other," Hope cautioned. "These felting needles are small, but I had to get special permission to bring them in. If anything goes wrong here, you're all back to origami cranes. Got it?"

For the very first time since Hope had begun teaching in the prison, her students laughed at one of her jokes. She savored the sound, feeling like she'd won a prize.

Hope worked the room, stopping to check in with each of her students, offering gentle instruction, correction, or encouragement, as the situation warranted. After working her way back to the front of the classroom, satisfied that each woman had a handle on the procedure, Hope plucked a ball of robin's-egg blue roving from the balls left on the table, took a seat, and began working on a bird of her own.

For a few minutes, the room was quiet but comfortably so. This was the peaceful, contented, homey silence that occurs when women enjoy what they're doing and the presence of their sisters. But then, as inevitably happens in these situations, one woman cast an admiring glance at the work of her neighbor and followed up with a compliment that was soon returned. Then someone asked for an opinion and there was another question, both received answers, and soon the room was humming with companionable conversation and soft, pleasant laughter.

In that moment, apart from the uniformity of their clothing, no one entering that room would have been able to tell that group of women from any gathering of needlewomen anywhere in the world or known that the members of this peaceable, productive sorority lived inside the walls of a prison. For a short time, the prisoners, too, forgot where they were.

Deedee held up her completed bird, a bright yellow canary with one pink wing and the other purple, and asked if it wasn't the cutest thing ever. After receiving a round of affirmation from the room, she asked Hope if she could make another one. Hope looked up at the clock, surprised to see that there were only ten minutes left in the class.

"Not today. We're out of time." She put down her own bird, with its cotton candy pink body and blue wings, and clapped her hands together. "All right, everybody. We need to wrap up. If you didn't finish your bird, leave it on the table for next time. Let's start cleaning up and handing in your supplies.

"Mandy?" she said, looking toward the student whom, though quieter than all the rest, she felt most connected to. There was such a glint of determination in her eyes. "Would you mind collecting everybody's felting needles and giving them to me? There should be nine. Nobody can leave until we have an accurate count."

"Only eight. You've got the ninth needle," Deedee said, pointing at Hope's hand. "Nita isn't here, remember?"

"That's right. I almost forgot," Hope said, wondering if Nita's absence might account for the sudden about-face in the collective attitude of her students.

"She'd have dropped out anyway," Steph said. "She only hung on because of the bet."

Hope frowned. "What bet?"

Steph looked like she'd suddenly swallowed a frog. She clamped her lips closed, but Deedee, who had a habit of engaging her mouth before her brain, was happy to answer for her.

"Nita bet Steph five bags of Fritos that you'd quit before you finished your first month."

"She what?"

"Oh yeah," Deedee said. "But that was the second bet. The first was that you'd start to cry during class, but that only paid out if it happened during your first week. I lost out on that one, but it was only one bag of chips. Not so bad.

"Tell you the truth, I really didn't think you'd last, but I'm sure glad you did. You turned out to be way cooler than I thought," Deedee said, her tone marked with admiration as well as surprise.

"Well. Thanks. I guess." Hope turned to look at Steph, who

was staring down at the tabletop with flaming cheeks. "And what about you? Did you win or lose?"

"I won," she said sheepishly. "Honestly, it's not as bad as it sounds. . . ."

"No?" Hope arched her brows. "Because even if you were hoping I'd stick it out, betting on whether a person could be so mean and behave so badly that it would make another person cry or quit her job *sounds* pretty bad."

Steph lifted her eyes to meet Hope's gaze.

"Sorry."

"So am I. Don't do it again. To anybody."

Steph nodded, then got up from her seat and lined up with the others next to the door. Mandy handed the needles to Hope, saying they were all accounted for.

"Thank you," Hope said as a guard who would escort the women back to the dayroom knocked on the door. "Hey, can you stay behind for a minute? I'll let the guard know I'm walking you back. I want to talk to you about something."

"Okay," Mandy replied.

Hope spoke to the guard, then said she'd see everybody on Thursday before walking back to the front of the room with Mandy. The women, holding the tiny birds cupped in their hands as if they might suddenly start flapping their felted wings and fly away, chorused back their thanks and farewells.

As the last of them were heading through the door, Hope looked over her shoulder and called Steph's name. Steph stopped in her tracks, still looking shamefaced. Hope pointed at her.

"Hey! *You* owe me a bag of Fritos. Maybe two."

Steph's lips twitched into a smile. "I'll bring them to the next class."

"I look forward to it."

Hope smiled and waved goodbye before turning back toward Mandy, who was studying her with a somber expression.

"Am I in trouble?"

"You?" Hope let out a surprised little laugh. "You're the least of my problems. I just wanted to thank you for your help today."

Mandy gave her a doubtful look. "Yeah, well . . . All I did was pick up some needles. It's not like it was real hard."

"No, you're right," Hope admitted. "What I really meant to say was thank you for . . . well, for everything. I know we've never really talked, but up until today I've felt like you were the only one who was actually on my side in all this. Now I think I know why."

"I wasn't part of the bet, if that's what you're asking," Mandy said. "I didn't know anything about it. And if I had, I'd have stayed out of it. Around here, the smartest thing you can be is Switzerland. Keep your head down and don't take sides."

"I'll keep that in mind," Hope said. "But Mandy, tell me something—I'm just trying to figure this place out—why would they have done something like that? Who bets on the misery of somebody they don't even know?"

"Oh, man. You really don't have this place figured out yet, do you? Did you ever read *Alice in Wonderland*?"

"Sure, a few times. My mother read it to me and I read it to my kids."

"Okay. Well. I didn't read it until I got here. Actually, I hardly ever read anything until I got here," she admitted. "Anyway, you know how when Alice falls down the rabbit hole and ends up in Wonderland, everybody she meets is kind of crazy and emotional and does strange stuff for no real reason?

"Well, it's like that. Outside the world makes sense, at least some of the time. But those rules don't apply in here. People just do what they do. They don't think. They just try to get through the day, kill the time. You know what the worst part about prison is?"

Hope shook her head.

"That," Mandy replied, and pointed to the wall clock. "Time moves slower here than anyplace in the world. You do what you have to do to make it pass. It wasn't personal, them betting to see if you'd cry or quit. They were just trying to fight off the boredom.

"Well," Mandy conceded, "maybe except for Nita. She did it to be mean. But even then it wasn't personal. Nita doesn't have anything against you one way or the other; she's mean because she *is*. She doesn't know another way. She's one of those people you should just try to avoid. If you can't, then you've got to stand up to her. Nita's one of those ones who can smell fear. But, come to think of it, they're all like that."

Mandy smiled. Hope had never seen her do that before. Seeing it, she felt like she'd been handed another prize, an even bigger one.

"But you did good today," Mandy said. "It's going to be easier now."

"From your lips to God's ears," Hope said, then shifted her weight back and took a seat at the table, motioning for Mandy to do the same.

"You're not like the others, are you? Most of them are doing just what you said, killing time. But you seem to be making the most of it. I mean, look, I'm sure you'd rather be anyplace but here—"

"Got that right," Mandy said.

"Still, you're taking advantage of every opportunity that comes your way—working toward your high school diploma, reading every book you can get your hands on, so the librarian tells me. Chaplain Nancy said you're taking parenting classes too.

"So . . . what's the difference between you and the others? They have access to the same opportunities that you do, yet they're marking time and you're not. Why?"

"Well, first off," Mandy said, "I'm not the only one. Plenty of us are trying to make the best of our time here and prepare for something better on the outside. They don't get noticed as much as some of the others because they're like me, just trying to keep their heads down. It's safer that way. Smarter too.

"But if you're asking why a few choose that smarter path when so many don't"—she shrugged—"look, I can't answer for anybody except myself, but I know what keeps me going. It's Talia, my little girl.

"When I first got here, I was convinced that I'd permanently screwed up my life. I was so depressed that they had me on suicide watch. I couldn't imagine that anything good would ever happen to me, so what was the point? But then Nancy came to see me and kind of kicked me in the butt.

"She said I was overselling myself, and that a person had to be way more dedicated to leading a life of crime than I was to screw up their entire life at twenty-one."

"Did she honestly say that?" Hope asked, laughing when Mandy bobbed her head. "She's really something, isn't she?"

"Yeah." Mandy grinned. "Her accent cracks me up too. Anyway, she convinced me that it really wasn't too late to turn my life around and that I had a very good reason to try—Talia. My daughter is my hope, my reason for waking up every day. I want to build a good life for both of us."

"Looks like you're heading in the right direction."

Realizing that she needed to escort Mandy back before her next class started, Hope got to her feet. Mandy did the same and they started walking toward the door.

"Hope so. Just six months to go. Sometimes I can hardly believe it. Once I'm out of here, I'm never coming back."

"Good. Don't," Hope said. "Nothing personal, Mandy, but when those six months are up, I sincerely hope we never see each other again."

"Me too."

When Mandy laughed her whole face lit up. She seemed transformed, like an entirely different person from the somber woman Hope had seen on her very first day at the prison. Now, as they walked down the hallway together, companionably as two friends on a stroll, Hope couldn't help but wonder if this was the quality that had first drawn her to that quiet young woman, an inner capacity for happiness that she kept hidden behind a mask of caution.

"Hey," Mandy said as they neared the dayroom, "I wanted to thank you for something. Those macramé bracelets we made last week? I gave mine to Talia and she loved it."

"Oh, good! I'm so happy she did."

"She was really excited. But you know who was even more excited?" Hope shook her head. "Me. It was the first time since I got here that I'd been able to give her anything. My mom buys her stuff for Christmas and birthdays and *tells* her it's from me, but . . ."

Mandy pressed her lips together and her eyes started to fill. Knowing what she was trying to say but couldn't, Hope felt tears in her own eyes.

For a mother, for any parent, there is nothing quite so heart-felt and instinctual as the desire to give gifts to her children. Helping Mandy fulfill that long-denied desire was a gift to Hope as well.

Suddenly an idea popped into Hope's mind. The moment it did, she knew, in a way that she hadn't only a moment before, exactly why she was here, at this moment and among these women.

She also knew what she needed to do about it.

Chapter 21

"Quilts." Nancy's eyes widened a bit, as if she wasn't quite
certain she'd heard Hope correctly. "You want them to make
quilts?"

"Yes," Hope replied.

"Right," the chaplain said. "Why? I mean, couldn't you just
stick with the macramé bracelets? Or ceramics. Let them paint a
coffee mug or something. Perhaps crocheting? My niece crocheted a scarf for me for Christmas last year. It was very nice."

"I'm sure," Hope said. "When's the last time you wore it?"

"About . . ." Nancy screwed up her face, thinking. "About
three months ago. My niece had a party—"

"And I'm sure it was lovely, the party and the scarf. But a
quilt is something you sleep under every night.

"*Think* about that," Hope said urgently, leaning forward,
clutching the edge of Nancy's desk. "Think about a child—let's
say a little girl, maybe five or six years old. Her mother is locked
away behind a wall and can't come out, can't tuck her in at
night, can't comfort her when she wakes up in the dark crying
after a bad dream.

"Now think about what it would mean to that same child to
get into bed at night and fall asleep under a quilt her mother

made with her own hands. Maybe the fabrics are purple and pink, her favorite colors, and maybe the border has unicorns on it, her favorite animal. She knows that her mommy picked out all those fabrics just for her, stitched every seam and every inch of that quilt with her own hands.

"Think about what that means to an innocent, vulnerable child who's never been arrested, or charged, or convicted of anything but has been punished just the same, sentenced to months or even years of separation from her mother. But when she falls asleep under her quilt, it's like her mother is there with her, protecting and sheltering her, keeping her warm and safe, reminding her that she matters and that, someday, they'll be together again.

"Now think what it means to the mother who makes that quilt, a woman who wakes up every day feeling guilty, hopeless, and ashamed because of the mess she's made of her own life, a woman who feels worthless—"

"She'd feel like she had something meaningful to offer," Nancy said, finishing Hope's thought in a quiet, almost introspective voice. "It would be a chance to tap into the best part of herself, a part she might not even have known existed, and share her love, diligence, and creativity with others, maybe for the first time."

Hope shifted back in her seat and folded her hands in her lap, satisfied that she'd made her point. Nancy cast her eyes toward the ceiling, took in a deep breath, and let it out slowly.

"Oh, Hope. I don't know. I understand the value in this. But . . . quilting. Are you sure there isn't some other way to accomplish the same thing? A craft that doesn't involve sharp objects?"

"Nancy," Hope said in a flat voice, "unless you want me to have them sit around all day doing origami or scribbling in coloring books, any craft I teach them is going to involve a certain amount of risk. You *know* that.

"If you're intent on inflicting injury or mayhem, a crochet hook can be just as effective as a pair of sewing scissors. It could be jammed into an eye socket or even somebody's throat if you use enough force. And those macramé bracelets we made? Slip some of the cording into your pocket when nobody is looking and you can weave it into a garrote and strangle your cellmate in her sleep."

"Garroting?" Nancy looked at her, aghast. "My, my. You *have* picked up a lot since you started working here, haven't you? Very nice."

"My point is, the only one hundred percent certain way to ensure inmates don't hurt themselves or others is to throw every one of them into solitary confinement and not teach them *anything*. Everything we do beyond that involves a certain amount of risk. Quilting wouldn't be any different. And we could take precautions—check out tools and equipment, count them before anyone is allowed to leave, limit participation to inmates with records of good behavior.

"Yes, there would be risks. But think about the benefits," Hope urged. "I've heard you say it a hundred times, the root reason most of these women ended up here was because they felt worthless. This program could change that."

"Just by making a quilt?" Nancy asked.

"Well, actually . . ." Hope cleared her throat and scratched her nose. "I was thinking about three quilts each. And a nine-month program."

"Three! Are you planning on opening a factory?"

"Hang on," Hope said, lifting her hand. "Just hear me out.

"Making three quilts, each a little more difficult than the one before, will give them that opportunity to really master the skills involved. Learning to quilt well takes time, patience, and dedication. From what I've seen so far, most inmates have way too much of the first and almost none of the last. Very few of them know what it means to take on a difficult task and see it through to completion.

"Learning to quilt will challenge them and sometimes frustrate them. But when it gets tough, I'll be there to help them stick with it and work through the problem. They won't fail. I won't let them," Hope said resolutely.

"When they finish their quilt and think about all that went into it, the mistakes they recovered from and all they learned along the way, they'll feel proud of themselves, especially after they see how that hard work can bless the life of another person."

"So, all the quilts they make will be gifts for family or friends?" Nancy asked.

"No," Hope said. "The first two, which will employ more basic techniques and patterns and fabric choices, will be given away to charity. My hope is to help them start envisioning themselves as contributors, not just to people they know but to society as a whole."

Nancy nodded deeply. " 'Tis more blessed to give than to receive,' yes? So many charities could make good use of some quilts— shelters, nursing homes, programs for foster kids. And think what a thrill it would be if the women got thank-you notes from people or organizations that got their quilts," Nancy said brightly.

"Exactly." Hope smiled, pleased that Nancy was catching on to the vision. "The third quilt would be their masterpiece. They'd choose all their own colors and fabric and use any technique they want. They can either keep it or give it as a gift. Not all of the inmates have family, so I thought it would be a good idea to give them the option of making a quilt for themselves. Either way, I want to help them make something they truly feel proud of, an heirloom that will last a lifetime."

Nancy nodded again and spread her hands in acknowledgment. "Okay, I'm sold. But as I'm sure you're aware, there's only one vote that matters here and that's David's."

"But you'll support me, right?"

"Of course I will. But I'm a pushover. David will be a much tougher nut to crack."

"Yeah, I know," Hope murmured, lifting her hand toward her mouth, chewing on the edge of her thumbnail. "And it's not as if I'm on his list of favorite people. That's why . . . Well, I was kind of hoping you'd present the idea to him."

"Me?" Nancy laughed. "What makes you think I'd have any better luck than you would? On any given day David finds me only marginally less irritating than he finds you."

"I know," Hope sighed. "But when the margin is all you've got . . .

"Nancy, I *know* this program could make a difference. I've never been so sure of anything. But if I'm the one presenting the idea, David's going to shoot it down before I can even ask the question. If you bring the idea to him, we might at least have a chance."

"Hope, I don't mean to discourage you, but I'd have to be the greatest peddler on the planet to get David on board with letting you bring pins, and scissors, and rotary cutters into his prison. Unless you're friends with the kind of person who could sell ice to Eskimos, I don't think you've got a prayer.

"Although," Nancy said, "that's not nothing. So it's not a completely hopeless situation. If you want me to pray about it . . ."

As soon as Nancy said she wouldn't present the idea to David, Hope slumped in her chair, discouraged. She'd known it was a long shot, but when it came to getting David's approval, Nancy had been her Plan A. She didn't have a Plan B—not until Nancy started talking about ice and Eskimos.

Why hadn't she thought of that before?

Hope jumped up in the middle of Nancy's sentence, leaving the chaplain looking surprised and a bit befuddled.

"That's a great idea," Hope said as she headed for the door. "You pray. I'm going to call my sister."

Chapter 22

David Hernandez was a very busy man.

So busy, he informed Hope when she dropped by his office seeking an appointment to discuss what she vaguely referred to as a curriculum proposal, that he didn't have an open spot during office hours for at least a month.

"What about after work?" Hope asked. "How about a drink on Thursday? The Dockside Bistro is nice."

Much to her surprise, he agreed.

"One drink," he said, holding up a single digit to drive home the message. "I've got a conference call with a blue-ribbon commission on prison reform early on Friday and I need to finish reading the report."

"Just one drink," Hope promised. "We'll be well prepared and to the point."

"We. Let me guess," David said wearily. "You're bringing Nancy and Jodie along to gang up on me about something."

"Nope," Hope said. "Just me. And my sister, Hazel."

"Your sister?"

"She's visiting from Portland."

"And she's joining us for a drink after work so we can discuss this thing you refuse to tell me about in advance?" David pushed his glasses up the bridge of his nose, magnifying the suspicion in his eyes. "I'm not in the market for a girlfriend. And if I was I'd set myself up. I wouldn't need anybody else to do it for me."

"No! Lord, no!" Hope exclaimed, aghast that he'd even suggest such a thing.

Fun-loving, lighthearted Hazel and humorless, policy-pounding David Hernandez? Perish the thought!

David sat up straighter in his chair and clutched his pen tighter. " 'Lord, no'?" He arched his eyebrows. "Geez. I'm not that bad, am I?"

"No, no," Hope said, laughing nervously. "Not at all. I just meant, 'Lord, no,' I would never do such a thing. Set you up, I mean. Clearly, if you wanted a girlfriend you would have one by now. Probably several. Not at the same time or anything, I just—"

Hope was never so grateful to be interrupted as when David, who scarcely seemed to notice her babbling, said, "I barely have time to get a decent night's sleep, let alone date. Besides, it's only been a year since my divorce. Too soon to start dating, don't you think?"

Hope stood there for a minute. Was he asking her opinion? The expectant look on his face indicated he might be. It was the first time Hope had ever seen him looking less than 100 percent certain about anything. She liked him the better for it.

"Not too soon," she said. "Not if you feel ready. Or lonely."

David sniffed enigmatically and picked up the pen again.

"So. Thursday, you said? At the Dockside."

Hope nodded. "Right after work."

"Okay," he said gruffly, and started writing. "One drink."

"Great. See you Thursday," Hope chirped, and then backed out the door before he could change his mind.

To Hope's complete shock, one drink became two and was followed by an order of crispy Point Judith Calamari, Beef Tenderloin Skewers, and Hot Artichoke Dungeness Crab Dip, then coffee all around and a slice of Key Lime Pie with three forks.

An hour and forty minutes into what Hope had assumed

would be a half-hour meeting, David still hadn't embraced the idea of letting Hope teach quilting to the inmates. But neither had he given a definitive no.

After outlining the basic idea, Hope backed off and let Hazel take over. "You set the hook," Hazel said when they'd discussed strategy over the phone. "I'll reel him in." It had definitely been a good call. Hazel, a world-class debater if ever there was one, continued to match him objection for objection and argument for argument. Hazel hadn't worn David down entirely, but he was still listening, intently.

In Hope's mind, even this was a victory, and something of a miracle. Recalling how hard Nancy had prayed about this meeting, Hope felt sure there had to be a touch of the supernatural in play. Looking away, she closed her eyes and added a silent prayer of her own, but her thoughts were interrupted when Hazel brought her back into the conversation.

"Look, ask Hope if you don't believe me. Teaching the women to quilt isn't just about giving them warm fuzzies. There are actual educational benefits here, hard skills that they can put to use after they're released."

"Such as?" David asked, the set of his mouth making his skepticism evident.

"Well," Hope said, "basic math for one thing. Reading a pattern and constructing a quilt involves addition, subtraction, multiplication, and an understanding of fractions—as well as a lot of geometry. It also reinforces reading comprehension and the ability to decode and follow instructions. When I taught high school, my lesson plans were all designed to help support and reinforce the concepts and skills taught in the core educational classes. There's no reason we couldn't do the same thing with the quilting program."

"See?" Hazel said, hooking her thumb in Hope's direction. "What she said."

David's expression softened. For a moment, Hope almost thought he was going to smile. Then something even more surprising happened.

Hazel grinned and stuck out her tongue, making a "so there"

face, and David completely cracked up. Hope couldn't believe it! She'd never even seen him smile, let alone laugh. Until that moment, she didn't know he could.

"Okay, okay," David said, spreading his hands. "So they'll learn something. But we've got classes for that already and I don't have to bring blades and sharp objects into the building to teach them."

"But we already talked about that," Hazel protested. "Anything that could pose a potential danger could be kept in a locked cabinet in Hope's locked classroom. Tools and equipment could be checked in and out at the beginning and end of each session. No one would be allowed to leave until everything had been returned to the cabinet and accounted for right down to the pins. You could have the guards do a pat-down if you want. Heck, you could even bring in a metal detector."

David shook his head slowly, but he was still smiling. Hope couldn't believe it. What was going on? Was it the alcohol? No. Couldn't be. He'd only had two beers.

"Do you have any idea how much an extra metal detector would cost? Speaking of money, where am I supposed to find the funding for all of this? As I'm sure your sister can tell you," David said, giving Hope a wry but not completely unfriendly glance, "she's already overspent her budget for the quarter. I can't just write a blank—"

"I'll raise the money myself!" Hope interjected, so buoyed by David's unexpected good humor that she spoke before really thinking it through.

David's smile faded. The look of skepticism returned.

"How?"

"I'll contact local businesses, fabric and craft shops. Maybe even national companies. I'll write grant requests. A project like this could be a good match for all kinds of charities and foundations."

"You think so?"

"Yes. Absolutely."

Hope had never written a grant request in her life. Nor did she know of any foundations whose mission focused on prisons or prisoners. But they had to be out there, didn't they? And if they were, she'd find them. Somehow.

"See?" Hazel said again but this time with a tone of professional certainty, as if Hope's hasty response settled all doubts and overcame all objections. "And what about that blue-ribbon commission?"

"What about it?" David asked.

"You said the commission had tasked you with creating new programs particular to the needs of a female prison population that would help increase educational levels, support societal integration and family reunification, and decrease recidivism."

"You left out the best part," David said with a disgruntled half snort. "I get a whole year and not one extra dollar to accomplish this impossible feat. They want me to present the results before the next election.

"Governors' commissions," he mumbled before taking a slurp of coffee. "I'd love to tell them all exactly where they can stick their blue ribbons. It's not like they actually expect me to do any of this. It just gives them a chance to grandstand and say they're working toward prison reform without actually, you know—" He slurped some more coffee. "Doing any actual work.

"I went into the justice field because I honestly care about justice. But these guys? Forget about it. It's all about looking good and sounding good and holding on to their jobs. Do you know what they—"

Hazel interrupted, waving her hands in front of David's face to get his attention.

"Hey. Much as I'd love to sit here all night and listen to you gripe, don't you get it? Hope's program actually fits all of the criteria the commission handed you—education, societal integration, family reunification, and recidivism," Hazel recited, ticking the list off her fingers.

"Besides, what could be more specifically geared to a female prison population than quilting? Even back in the day, back when society was even *more* uptight, male dominated, and misogynistic than it is now—"

Hope's jaw dropped. She couldn't believe her sister was talking to Dour David Hernandez like this, teasing and bantering and poking fun at his weak spots. Even more unbelievable was the fact that he actually seemed to enjoy it.

This really *was* a miracle. Had to be. Hope couldn't wait to tell Nancy.

"Even then," Hazel continued, "they still let poor, powerless, oppressed women sew stuff. In fact, I think they insisted on it, didn't they? Kept them too busy to think about things like having opinions. Or, you know, getting the vote."

Hazel grinned and bolted the last dregs of her own coffee. David sniffed and twisted his lips in a grudging but somehow respectful smile, silently acknowledging both the validity of her point and her skill in expressing it.

"Okay, sure," David replied. "Potentially, Hope's program could have a positive impact in those areas. Potentially. But you don't actually know that because you don't have any proof."

"So get some proof," Hazel countered. "Make it a pilot program. Start with a small, select group of prisoners and see how it goes. No matter what happens, you'll be able to fulfill the mandate of the commission. Since Hope's going to raise the money and find the equipment, it won't cost anything."

"A pilot program? Huh."

David sniffed again and narrowed his eyes. Hope's pulse quickened.

He was thinking about it! He was seriously considering the idea!

She was so excited, simultaneously fearful and hopeful, impatient for his verdict even as she dreaded it. She clenched her fists to keep from grabbing him by the collar and demanding a decision and found her palms were slick with sweat. Finally, after a minute that felt like a hundred, David sniffed again and looked Hope squarely in the eye.

"Okay. We can try it. Twelve inmates, twice a week for two hours. For nine months—a pilot program. When it's over, we'll assess. Does that work for you?"

"Yes! Totally!"

Giddy with excitement, Hope lurched forward, ready to hug him, then remembered her sweaty palms and who she was talking to and grabbed her coffee mug instead. When she clinked her cup of lukewarm brew against Hazel's mug, David, too, lifted a cup and joined in the unspoken toast. There was no end to the wonders of this day.

"Twelve inmates means twelve sewing machines, right?" David asked. "Twelve sets of scissors, plus irons and ironing boards, rulers, rotary cutters, and cutting mats?"

Hope nodded and gave him a curious look. How did David Hernandez know about rotary cutters and cutting mats?

"My mom made quilts," he said, as if reading her mind. "Well, for a while. Before she got hooked and started stealing to support her habit."

He cleared his throat and lifted his coffee cup to his lips, even though Hope was pretty sure it was empty.

"Anyway, you're going to need a lot of expensive equipment. The sewing machines especially. You sure you're going to be able to get all that?"

"Absolutely," Hope said, her voice radiating confidence she felt not at all. "Won't be a problem."

Out on the street, after saying good night to David and watching his car drive off, Hope threw her arms around her sister's neck.

"You did it! You actually won him over. You made him smile. And laugh! I can't believe it. Hazel, I always knew you were an amazing saleswoman. But I didn't know you were a curmudgeon whisperer."

"Oh, stop," Hazel said, waving off her sister's praise. "He's not so bad. Is he married?"

"Was. His wife left him and—Wait a second! You're not actually attracted to him, are you?"

"Why wouldn't I be? He's kind of cute. Seems smart too."

"He is. But he's also . . ." Hope paused, searching for the right word, trying to figure out exactly what it was about David

Hernandez that rubbed her the wrong way. "He's just so inflexible. And humorless. I told you, until today I've never seen him laugh. Not even once."

"Well, maybe he hasn't had much reason to laugh. Maybe he's hurting. You know, Hope, not all wounded birds are women. Not all of them are trapped inside the walls of a prison either. . . ." Hazel paused, fixing her sister with her eyes. "How's Rick?"

"Oh, crap. Rick! I told him I'd be home in time to make dinner. Hope he didn't wait for me. He'll be starving."

Hope pulled her phone out of her pocket and dialed the house. When Rick didn't answer, she dialed his cell phone. There was no answer there either.

"He must still be on the golf course," Hope said as she shoved her phone back into her purse.

"Playing with glow-in-the-dark balls, no doubt." Hazel cocked an eyebrow. "What's going on with you guys?"

"Nothing. I mean, nothing more than you already know about."

"Hope . . . This is *me* you're talking to. If you can't be straight with your sister, who can you be straight with? You know I won't judge. So, tell me the truth: Are you thinking of leaving him?"

"Leaving Rick? How can you even ask such a thing?"

Hazel said nothing in response to her sister's aghast expression. Instead, she arched her brows and crossed her arms over her chest, her posture an echo of the question Hope had yet to answer.

Chapter 23

In the weeks since he'd first rescued her from the side of the road, Rick had tackled seven years' worth of deferred maintenance on Kate's cozy Craftsman bungalow. By now, he knew every inch of the house. He knew nearly as much about Kate herself and her late husband, Lyle, a civil engineer, and how, for more than forty years, they had lived, loved, and cared for each other.

And Kate, after weeks of coffee, cookies, and conversation with her volunteer handyman, had gotten to know Rick pretty well, too. Well enough that Rick felt comfortable opening up to her in a way he hadn't to anyone else for a long time. Well enough that, on this day, Kate felt she could ask him some personal questions, including one that came so completely out of the blue that Rick choked on his coffee before he was able to answer.

"Thinking of leaving Hope? No. Never. Why would you even ask?"

"Because," Kate said, "from where I'm sitting, it looks like you already have."

"What?" Rick spread his hands and laughed, a deflection and knee-jerk response to a comment that made him feel uncomfortable and somehow guilty, in spite of his innocence. It was the same way he felt the time he'd been pulled over by a police cruiser for a broken taillight. He knew he hadn't done anything wrong, but even so, the sight of those flashing lights in his rearview mirror made his stomach clutch and his mouth feel dry, wondering if he might have unknowingly incurred an infraction or crossed some line.

Kate took a cookie from the platter and placed it on her plate but didn't eat it. Obviously, she wasn't going to speak until Rick answered her question.

"I'm not fooling around, if that's what you're asking. Even if I had the inclination, when would I have time?" he asked in a teasing tone, hoping his smile would convince her to abandon the inquiry. "I come here in the morning, hammer nails all day, and go home every night."

"Engineers," Kate sighed. "Why do you all have to be so literal? Do you think it's cute or something? Because it's not."

"What?" Rick said again, feeling genuinely perplexed. "You asked me if I'm thinking of leaving my wife. I'm not. What's cute about that?"

Kate got up from the table and crossed the room to pick up the coffeepot.

"You want me to spell it out for you? Fine. I will. There are plenty of ways to leave your wife without actually walking out the door. You can, for example, leave her emotionally," she said, her tone a study in exaggerated clarity as she filled Rick's coffee cup and then her own.

"You can cut off conversation and congress. You can move your lips but say nothing, limiting your discussions to the weather and the passing of the salt. Or you can say everything without uttering a word. Reproach and simmering resentment are, in fact, best communicated through ponderous silence. That's what passive aggression is all about, right? Inflicting maximum damage without leaving a trail? Giving yourself cover and plausible deniability while shifting the blame?"

Kate slid the coffeepot back onto the warmer, then sat back down and shook her head at him.

"Don't pretend you don't understand what I'm talking about,

Rick. Just as you can obey the letter of the law but violate the spirit, so you can violate the spirit of a marriage. Two people can occupy the same home and bed for months, or years, or even an entire marriage, yet live lives that are entirely separate. And terribly, terribly lonely. You know this because that's what you and your wife have been doing for a long time, at least since you moved to Olympia. Maybe longer.

"Why else would you spend every single day fixing broken steps, replacing leaky toilets, and installing smoke alarms in the home of a poor old lady you picked up on the side of the road?" she asked. "Because you don't know what to do with yourself, that's why. You come here day after day because, though your new home is half the size of the old, it echoes with the punishing silence you're too stubborn to break, even though that silence is about to break you.

"And you come here," she said more gently, "because I remind you of someone you miss terribly. Because, for weeks now, you've been waiting for me to tell you what she would have told you: Quit being a stubborn ass. Get on with it."

Rick laughed again, more hoarsely this time, then rubbed the corner of his eye with the back of his hand and blinked.

"How did you know?" he asked.

How *did* she know? Because, until she spelled it out, he didn't realize that this was exactly what he'd been hoping for, advice and a good kick in the butt from a wise and trustworthy woman.

He remembered his father's wake, how he and his mother had stood a few feet away from the casket, shaking the calloused hands of his father's friends from the port, who'd come to pay their respects.

One after another, they clapped him on the shoulder, looked him in the eye, and said, "You take care of your mother now, son. It's what your dad would have wanted." And his mother said, "Oh yes. Rick's the man of the house now. I don't know what I'd do without him."

Young and foolish as he was—and, yes, arrogant—he'd actually believed that the entire safety and security of the family rested on his shoulders. It was a heavy load for a boy to bear but one he picked up gladly, out of love for his mother and respect for his father, the desire to be the kind of man his dad was—steady, dependable, and strong.

He was strong, first for his mother and then for his wife and children.

But until his mother was gone and his depression and demoralization became an unscalable wall between himself and Hope, he hadn't understood that strength is a circle. The reason he could be strong for his mother and wife was because he drew his strength from them, and vice versa.

When he first spotted Kate standing on the side of the road his heart had skipped a beat. From a distance, she looked exactly like his mom. For an illogical instant, he'd thought, hoped, that it was her. But when he got close, he realized the resemblance wasn't particularly strong, a product of white hair, a particular spring in the step, and wishful thinking on his part.

He'd taken her home because it seemed like the right thing to do. He'd come back to help fix her porch steps because it seemed like she needed help and because he liked the idea of being needed, of having something to offer. He kept coming back because, in the ways that counted, Kate *was* like his mother. And Hope.

Kate was strong and positive and wise. Feisty too. She wasn't the sort of woman to throw her pearls before a swine, offering the benefit of her insight, until she was sure the message would be received. But somehow he'd known that if he hung around long enough, she'd tell him what he needed to hear, that she'd kick in enough dirt to help him climb out of the hole he'd dug for himself.

Rick sniffed and took another gulp of coffee, trying to wash down the lump in his throat.

"At first, I didn't know," Kate said. "I just thought you were a nice man with too much time on his hands. But I figured it out after a while. My cookies are good, but they're not that good. And you're not *that* nice a guy."

Kate smiled and squeezed her fingers around the dome of Rick's clenched fist. The skin of her hands was thin, veined with blue and freckled with age, and her knuckles knotted with arthritis, yet her grip was surprisingly strong and strangely familiar. So were her words and the no-nonsense way she delivered them.

Quit being a stubborn ass. Get on with it.

That's what his mom would have said, all right, just like that. How he missed her. And Hope. He had only himself to blame for that. For so many things—

"There's no point in beating yourself up about it," Kate said, as if reading his mind. "It wasn't entirely your fault. And as to the part that was? Well, what's done is done. Nothing's so broken it can't be repaired."

Rick lifted his eyes. "You sure about that?"

"I'm sure," Kate said, squeezing his hand once more before releasing it, "not for a man who loves his wife as much as you do. Angry as you are with Hope, with life, with everything, there's a spark in your eye whenever you speak of her.

"Talk to her, Rick. Go home and make things right with your wife."

"How? What do I say?"

"Start with 'I was wrong and I'm sorry' and take it from there. It won't be as hard as you think. Most women are pushovers and entirely too nice. A bouquet of flowers and a bit of groveling and we forgive everything."

Rick smiled. Kate pushed back her chair and got to her feet.

"Now, if you'll excuse me. I hope you don't mind letting yourself out. My poor old kidneys can't handle as much coffee as they used to. You don't have to do that," she said when Rick started clearing the dishes. "Get on home to your family."

"I will," Rick said, gathering up the cups and plates, "right after I rinse up and pop these into the dishwasher. Won't take me a minute."

"Oh, all right. If you insist. But you'd better be gone by the time I get out of the—" Kate's chiding was interrupted by the sound of the doorbell. "Oh, bother. Who could that be?"

"I'll get it," Rick said, turning off the kitchen faucet.

"If it's the Girl Scouts," Kate called over her shoulder as she trotted down the hallway toward the bathroom, "tell them I already ordered four boxes."

"Will do."

The doorbell rang again, twice, in quick succession. Whoever was on the other side of the door was very insistent. Rick wiped his hands on his jeans as he walked through the living room, walls lined floor to ceiling with bookshelves and Kate's paintings, toward the foyer.

"Hang on a second," Rick called out irritably when the bell rang yet again.

He fumbled with the dead-bolt lock he'd installed only the week before, momentarily forgetting whether it had to be turned left or right. Finally, the bolt clicked over and Rick opened the door. When he saw who was standing on the other side of it, Rick's jaw went slack.

"Kenz? What are you doing here?"

McKenzie crossed her arms over her chest and glared at him. "You first," she said.

Chapter 24

McKenzie stepped over the threshold without invitation, pushing past Rick and walking into the middle of Kate's living room.

She turned in a circle, taking in the decidedly feminine surroundings, the sofa of rose-hued velvet, bookshelves filled with volumes by Jane Austen, Edith Wharton, and the Brontë sisters, a collection of bird figurines, and framed pictures of landscapes and bouquets of pink, blue, and green that Kate had painted with her own hands.

"Well?" McKenzie snapped. "Who is she? How did you meet her?"

"Kenz. It's not what you think—"

"Isn't it? I've been sitting outside this house for five solid hours, watching the door, waiting for you to come out. What could you possibly be doing in another woman's house for *five* hours? So who is she, Dad? Your golf pro?" She laughed bitterly. "You might be able to fool Mom with that line, but not me."

When Rick opened the door and saw his daughter standing on the stoop, his initial shock was followed by mild amusement. That was McKenzie all right, emotionally over the top, jumping immediately to the most dramatic and completely wrong conclusion.

But after she confessed to having waited half a day for him to come out and Rick considered this incident in the light of their last confrontation, when she'd accosted him in the parking lot, amusement gave way to irritation.

"Hang on. How did you know I was here? What have you been doing? Tailing me?"

"No! Of course not! I drove up to the condo just as you were driving away and—" McKenzie screwed her eyes shut and raised her hands, as if she couldn't bear to see him or hear him. "You know something? Never mind. It doesn't matter. I don't care who she is. And I already know what she is." Opening her eyes, she let her hands flop against her sides. "Dad. How could you? How?"

"Okay, Kenz. Stop right there. You're not only out of line; you're really confused."

"*I'm* confused? What about *you*? Seriously, how confused do you have to be to get involved with a woman who has such terrible taste in decorating?" she asked, sweeping her arms out. "This whole place looks like something straight out of 1974!"

"Actually, the last time I redecorated was 1982," Kate said as she entered the living room. "But your point is well taken. It's due for an update."

McKenzie's jaw dropped. Kate's eyes crinkled and her mouth bowed as she stuck out her hand.

"You must be McKenzie. Your father has told me so much about you."

If the flames on McKenzie's cheeks hadn't made her mortification abundantly clear, the multiple apologies she offered after Kate enlightened her to the depth of her mistake would have.

The fifth time McKenzie said she was sincerely and truly sorry, Kate nodded and said, "It's all right, McKenzie. I understand. You were just trying to protect your family. As I said before, apology accepted.

"But if you'll forgive me for sticking my nose into things that are probably none of my concern," she said, her eyes shifting from McKenzie's face, to Rick's, and then back to McKenzie, "I think your father is the one you should be apologizing to, not me."

"You're right," she said softly. "Daddy, I . . ."

Seeing tears in her eyes and fearing they would spill over, Rick lifted his hand to cut her off. For all that she was given to dramatic impulses, McKenzie only rarely gave in to tears. Having almost broken down himself earlier that day, he wasn't sure he could take much more.

"It's okay, Kenz. Don't worry about it. It's getting late. We should get out of Kate's hair. Come on. I'll walk you to your car."

After saying goodbye to Kate at the door, Rick and McKenzie descended the porch steps and walked toward the street.

"Where's your car?" Rick asked.

"On the other side of the street, down by the corner. I figured I could catch you in the act without being too obvious."

"If you didn't want to be obvious, you probably should have thought twice before buying a bright yellow Hyundai," Rick said, shaking his head and smiling. "You'd make a terrible spy, Kenz. The worst."

Stopping at the curb, McKenzie turned to look at him.

"Dad? I really am sorry."

"It's okay, sweetie. I get it. You were just trying to protect your mother. And the family. Something I should have been doing all along. But don't worry, okay? I will from now on."

McKenzie let out a long sigh and shook her head as she examined his face. Seeing the disappointment in her eyes, Rick felt a fresh twinge of guilt.

"I don't understand," she said. "Why didn't you just tell Mom what you were up to? Why couldn't you just be straight with her?"

"I don't know," he said, taking McKenzie's arm as they crossed the street. "Because I was acting like an idiot, I guess. Because life threw me a curveball and all I could think to do was duck. And because, even when you love somebody as much as I love your mother, marriage is tougher than it looks."

"Right. Tell me something I don't already know," McKenzie muttered, clicking her remote to unlock the doors on her hatchback.

When he saw McKenzie's car, Rick's brows lifted with fatherly disapproval. The hatchback was stuffed with suitcases, bags, and boxes piled so high there was no way that McKenzie could see out the rear. It wasn't safe, driving a car she couldn't see out of.

"What's all this?" he asked. "Did Zach finally decide to clean out the man cave? Why didn't you ask me to come over and give you a hand? I'd have brought the truck."

"I know," said McKenzie. "That's why I drove over to the condo today. I wanted to ask if you'd help me. It's not Zach's stuff, Daddy. It's mine. I'm moving out. Zach's been cheating on me."

"What? Oh, baby . . . Zach? Are you sure?"

Rick couldn't bring himself to believe it. There had to be some mistake. Zach seemed like a good guy—a little short on ambition perhaps, a little old to spend as much time playing video games as he did, a little too fond of beer, and maybe not his first choice of husband for his baby girl, but still. Besides, what kind of guy would be stupid enough to cheat on a woman like McKenzie? She was smart, beautiful, athletic, funny, hard-working—what more could he ask for? Nothing.

No. No way would Zach cheat on his daughter. It was a mis-understanding. McKenzie must have seen something that looked a little weird and jumped to conclusions, like she'd done with him and Kate.

But when McKenzie stared at him, her eyes filled with pain yet utterly dry, as if she had no more tears left, and she slowly nodded her head, Rick knew it was true.

"Oh, Kenz."

Rick opened his arms. McKenzie walked into his embrace, leaning heavily against his chest, as if she couldn't support the weight of her own body anymore.

"I tried, Daddy. I know I'm not always the easiest person to get along with. I know I can be stubborn, and spoiled, a princess, but I really did try, honestly. The first time I caught him—"

"The first time? You're saying he's cheated before?"

McKenzie moved her head up and down but didn't look up, burying her face into her father's flannel shirt as if she were em-barrassed to be seen by him. Rick reached down and stroked her hair, providing comfort as best he could even as fury toward Zach bubbled inside him.

"A few months ago," McKenzie said, "I accidentally over-heard a conversation between him and his boss, Mercedes. I didn't have to listen very long before I realized they weren't talk-ing about work. Suddenly it all made sense: the late nights and weekends, him calling to say they'd suddenly called a late staff meeting. Hearing the things he said to her, I knew they'd all been lies. I felt like such a chump.

"I confronted Zach, but he said I was crazy. Then I told him what I'd overheard. He finally admitted to what had been going on but said it didn't mean anything. He said he'd only done it after his boss had come on to him and he was trying to get a promotion."

"And you believed that?"

"He made it sound almost like a sacrifice on his part, some-thing he'd done so he could get the promotion and we could af-ford to buy a house and start a family. By the time he was done, he'd almost convinced me. Almost. The truth is, I wanted to be-lieve him.

"I made him jump through a few hoops," she said, "mostly just to save face. He behaved for a while. He sent me flowers, came home right on time, and even went to a couple of counsel-ing sessions.

"When the questions got uncomfortable he blamed the coun-selor, said he was making it a bigger deal than it was, trying to sucker us into paying for sessions we didn't need. He quit going and I let him get away with it. I let him get away with a lot of things."

McKenzie lifted her head at last and looked at Rick, her gaze filled with sorrow and self-reproach. "It was never going to work, Daddy. There was no chance. In my heart, I always knew that. I should have ended it when I caught him snogging with that woman in the bar."

"Wait. What woman? You mean his boss?"

McKenzie shook her head. "Somebody else. About a month before the wedding, we spent a weekend at his parents' beach house. It was raining. I was reading and Zach was bored, so he decided to walk to the bar up the street and watch the game. I said I'd meet him later. When I got there, he was sitting at the end of the bar, hammered and making out with somebody."

When McKenzie started sharing the story of her betrayal, Rick felt an emptiness in his center, a sensation of being hollow and devoid of substance. Upon his learning that Zach's faithlessness had been apparent even before the wedding, that void was filled by a sense of failure.

Not McKenzie's. His.

"Kenz, I . . . I don't understand. Why didn't you call off the wedding right then and there?"

"I did. I threw half a beer in Zach's face, told him it was over, and stormed out. He followed me, said that he was sorry, that he was drunk—blah, blah, blah." She flapped her hand, dismissing Zach's excuses as exactly that, excuses.

"He was drunk but not *that* drunk. Not so drunk that he didn't know what he was doing. But I bought into it and let him off the hook. Four weeks later, I was wearing white and saying, 'I do,' " McKenzie said. "What else could I do?"

"What else could you do?" Rick echoed, shocked that she had to ask. "You could have stuck to your guns, that's what. You could have told Zach where he could stick his excuses. *And* his engagement ring. Dammit, McKenzie!" Rick barked as his ire toward Zach spilled over onto his daughter. "You could have been the woman we raised you to be!"

"How?"

In former days, McKenzie would have pushed back against his anger, thrust out her chin and gone ten rounds with him, toe to toe, her eyes flaming with a stubborn determination that stirred her father with equal parts of admiration and irritation. Today, Rick saw no sign of that stubborn, irritating girl with the hair-trigger temper. Her tone was as flat and defeated as the look in her eyes.

"The church was booked," she said. "The out-of-town family had bought nonrefundable airline tickets. Mom had ordered two hundred pounds of lobster and sewn two zillion wedding favors for the guests.

"Seriously, Daddy. At that point, how was I supposed to call it off? Especially since I'd already broken two engagements—one of them after the invitations had already been sent out. Nobody wants to be that girl.

"And the truth is, as much as you and Mom were amazing parents, the best on the planet, I'm *not* the woman you raised me to be. I'm just a loser. A big, fat zero. The girl who can't get anything right, not one stupid thing."

Rick stepped forward and wrapped his arms around her once more.

"Don't say that, Kenz. It's just not true. Everybody makes mistakes, especially when they're young. Heck, even when they're old. You don't believe me? Just look at the mess I've made of my life, and your mother's, for the past two years. Everybody screws up royally sometimes, ignores their own best instincts. That's not being a loser; it's being human.

"Losers are people who, after realizing their mistakes, sit around and wallow in them. The thing to do now is own it and do what you have to do to make things right. As a very wise friend of mine said recently, 'Quit being a stubborn ass. Get on with it.' "

He lowered his head and kissed his daughter's hair. "You're not a loser, Kenz. You're my little girl. My princess."

"Thanks, Dad," McKenzie said. "But, if it's okay with you, I think I'd just rather be your daughter."

"Fair enough," Rick said. "Either way, I'm proud of you."

"Would it be okay if I moved back in with you and Mom for a while? Just until I get myself sorted out?"

"Sure. Of course you can. For as long you need to."

"Thanks, Daddy."

"Zach," Rick muttered, the bilious anger flooding his body as he pictured the face of his adulterous soon-to-be-former son-in-law. "That lying son of a . . .

"You know, I never did like him. That day when he came over to tell me he was going to propose, I gave my blessing but said if he ever hurt you, I'd track him down and kill him. Slowly.

And with pain. The way I'm feeling right now, Zach better not come within five hundred yards of me. Because I'd have no problem carrying through on that threat."

"I know, Daddy. Me too. But we can't."

"Why not?" Rick growled.

McKenzie lifted her face toward her father's.

"Because I'm pregnant."

Chapter 25

Two months later

Like most of the offices in the prison, Nancy's was cramped, windowless, and, apart from the framed seascape photograph hung up on the gray wall, cheerless. But it was private and quiet, which was why Hope and Nancy had fallen into the habit of meeting there on Monday afternoons to eat lunch and catch up.

This week, there was a lot to catch up on. Nancy had just returned from a two-week trip to England, where she had stood as godmother at the baptism of a newborn great-niece, then spent five days trekking through the Cotswolds with her husband, John. The final week was spent visiting Nancy's parents, Elizabeth and Henry, in Nancy's hometown of Aldeburgh, a coastal town in Suffolk.

Though Hope had noticed a definite increase in squabbling and tension among the inmates in Nancy's absence, she was glad the chaplain had been able to make the trip. It couldn't be easy, living in a foreign country, so far from her family.

Hope laid the contents of her brown bag out on Nancy's desk and smiled to herself. Two weeks of contact with her home country had thickened Nancy's English accent. Her *o*'s were somehow rounder, her other vowels more clipped, and her *r*'s nearly nonexistent as Nancy told Hope about her mother, eighty-nine-year-old Elizabeth, who according to Nancy was sharp as a tack, an excellent cook, and drove her own car to a local community center twice a week, where she taught poetry to disadvantaged youth.

"So," Hope said, unfolding a paper napkin onto her lap, "now I know where you get your philanthropic streak."

"Comes from both sides really. Father a vicar and all." Nancy unzipped her insulated lunch bag and started pulling out a series of plastic containers. "Every Sunday dinner of my childhood started with Dad slicing into the roast, then looking around the table and saying, 'Now, children, tell me what you've done for others this week?'

"And heaven help you if you didn't have something to report," Nancy said with mock horror before her face split into a grin. "Really, they were very good parents. And Aldeburgh was a wonderful place to grow up."

"I'm glad you got to go home for a while. It seems to have done you a lot of good."

"It did. I love my job, but every now and again it's good to spend some time on the outside," Nancy said with a meaningful roll of her eyes. "Plus my parents were overjoyed to see us. Dad took us to every museum, church, and ruin in Suffolk and Mum almost literally cooked the fatted calf in celebration of our return."

Nancy lifted the lid of a plastic container to reveal a whitish-yellowish-greenish mess with the aroma of butter, cabbage, and compost.

"What is that?" Hope asked, making a face.

"Leftover bubble and squeak," Nancy reported happily, thrusting a fork into the container. "Mum sent some home with me. We packed it in dry ice and carried it home on the plane. Want some?"

"Uh . . . No, thanks."

"You sure? It tastes better than it looks."

"I'll take your word for it."

"Your loss," Nancy said, taking a bite and murmuring with pleasure. "This is much better than the sad excuse for a lunch you've brought."

Hope looked down at her lunch, a container of hummus and a bag full of carrot and celery sticks, and sighed. Nancy had a point.

"I'm doing it for Rick. Do you know he's already lost twenty pounds? I've lost five," Hope said, munching on a carrot stick. "Which is actually pretty good for me."

"Still. So unfair," Nancy replied. "As if childbirth and menopause weren't bad enough, God plagues womankind with a stodgy metabolism as well. It's the same with John and me. He eats one less cookie and loses five pounds by the next morning. I eat nothing but grapefruit and boiled eggs for a month and drop twelve ounces.

"Are you sure it's worth it?" Nancy asked, making a pitying face as she nodded toward Hope's hummus. "Don't you miss all Rick's home baking? The bread? The rolls? Those lovely little chocolate biscuits with the toasted almonds on top?"

"Not as much as I missed the old Rick. It's worth living on crudités just to have him back."

"Well, good," Nancy said stoutly. "Right, then. Enough of my chatter. How are things with you? All well? The kids are fine?"

"Oh yes. Liam's film didn't win the top prize, but he got an honorable mention and was offered a summer internship at some studio he's all excited about. McKenzie is doing as well as can be expected. She found a new apartment, five minutes from our place, and plans to move in after the holidays.

"You know, I never thought I'd be able to say it, but I'm actually going to miss her. It's been a terrible time for her, of course. Between the divorce and raging hormones, she cries at the drop of a hat, but we've really been getting along well. Now that she's pregnant, she's far more forgiving of my faults."

"Motherhood will do that," Nancy said. "As soon as my Roger was born, I called my mother to apologize."

"For what?"

"For *everything*," Nancy replied.

Hope chuckled. "Well, I really will be sorry to see Kenz go. But it's probably time. She needs to settle into her new place and set up a nursery before the baby comes. The divorce papers have already been filed, so things are moving along."

"No hope for a reconciliation?"

"Zach moved in with the other woman."

"Oh, dear. So soon?" Nancy tsked. "Bad form. Poor McKenzie. But the baby's doing well?"

"The doctor says everything's fine, no problems at all. Kenz felt the baby move last week. So did I."

Though she was smiling, Hope felt her throat tighten with emotion as she recalled laying a hand on McKenzie's stomach to feel the miraculous fluttering beneath, a greeting from a tiny stranger she couldn't wait to meet.

"Oh. How wonderful," Nancy said, clutching her hand to her breast, her voice almost reverent. "Do you remember what it was like? The first time you felt them move?"

"Oh yes. I'll never forget. Took my breath away. Every single time." Smiling, Hope touched a finger to the corner of one eye, wiping away the wet.

"Speaking of potential new family members," she continued, "Rory and Reed are coming home for Christmas. And Reed is bringing a girlfriend."

"Really? Sounds quite serious," Nancy said, arching her eyebrows. "What do you know about her?"

"Not much," Hope said. "Her name is Pamela. She works in human resources. She rides a motorcycle and has a tattoo of a koi fish on her shoulder. Reed thought he should warn me."

"Oh, well," Nancy said, waving her hand dismissively. "That's not a problem, is it? Did you tell him that most every woman you know has a tattoo? Which reminds me, I ran into Mandy and Deedee this morning. They were bubbling with praise for you and excitement about the quilting program. Oh, and I understand that Rick's friend Kate got her volunteer clearance to come in and help you with the program?"

Hope, not wanting to talk with her mouth full, nodded and then swallowed.

"She's my friend too, now. If she hadn't smacked Rick upside his head when she did, who knows how long it would have taken for us to start talking again? I owe her."

Nancy laughed. "And so you repaid her by letting her volunteer at the prison?"

"I know, right? But with her husband gone and no family in the area, she was looking for meaningful ways to fill her time, so this is working out well for everybody. I don't know how I ever thought I could manage the quilting program on my own. Trying to teach twelve women with zero sewing experience and a variety of learning challenges to quilt all by myself?" Hope spread out her hands. "What was I thinking?

"Once they get the basics down, it should get easier. But, right now, these women need a lot of personal attention. Kate's sewing experience is minimal, but being a painter, she's very good with colors, and helping the women pick out their fabrics. But most of all, she's a steadying presence. She's so funny and cheerful, she has a way of helping the women laugh off their mistakes. Everybody just loves her."

"Deedee certainly does. She went on and on about both of you. So did Mandy, and you know she's not much of a talker. And Mandy told me she's nearly finished with her first quilt top?"

Hope bobbed her head in response to Nancy's questioning tone and scraped a celery stick around the edge of the hummus container.

"Her release is coming up, so I'm trying to push her through the program a little faster than the other girls. Fortunately, she picked things up so quickly that I'm going to let her skip the second charity quilt and move right on to her personal quilt. She really wants to make a quilt for Talia."

"What a good idea," Nancy said. "She seemed a bit anxious when I saw her. On second thought, 'anxious' isn't quite the word. More like 'impatient,' 'antsy.' Time always moves slowly on the inside, but never more slowly than in those last months and weeks before release. It would be good for her to have something to help pass the time and keep her mind occupied."

"Well, the block pattern she wants to use—Dove in the Window—should do the trick. It's kind of advanced for a beginner, but Mandy's up to it. If she works hard and stays focused, she should finish the quilt in time for her release."

"And Deedee?" Nancy asked with a knowing smile. "Is she catching on quickly as well?"

"Oh, Deedee." Hope laughed at the mention of her most affable and most bumbling student. "Don't ask me how, but yesterday she sewed her quilt block to her sleeve. Twice." Hope laughed again. "She's such fun but all thumbs. However, even Deedee is making progress. I'll make a quilter of her yet. Just see if I don't."

"Oh, I believe you," Nancy said earnestly. "Any woman who can make the rounds of local businesses and quilt clubs and, in two weeks' time, come away with twelve sewing machines and all the fabric and supplies she needs is someone to be reckoned with."

"It wasn't nearly as hard as I thought it would be," Hope replied. "Once I explained what I wanted the supplies for, I was flooded with donations. Those women couldn't raid their fabric stashes quick enough. But then, quilters are generous by nature. After pouring so much time, money, and energy into a quilt, nine times out of ten they turn around and give it to somebody else. And the only thing that quilters love more than quilting is bringing new quilters into the fold."

Hope crunched another carrot. "And they could definitely afford to part with some of their stuff. Most quilters I know own more fabric than they can use in a lifetime. That doesn't stop them from wanting more. Donating yardage to a good cause means they've got space to store more of whatever they decide they can't live without the next time they go to the quilt shop."

"So donating to the quilting program just means they can buy even more fabric they'll never use?" Nancy clucked her tongue. "Sounds like we might be encouraging hoarding."

"It's harmless," Hope said, waving a carrot stick. "And for some people, it's even therapeutic. When my mother was going through chemo and was too sick to sew, she'd pull out different combinations of fabric from her stash, lay them out on the table, and dream about what she would stitch when she felt better. It gave her a reason to keep going."

Nancy put down her fork. "I think your mother would be proud of the work you're doing here, the way you're helping to heal our wounded birds. Like your mother with her fabric, you're giving them a reason to dream, something to look forward to. It's not always easy, but thanks to you, some of them are beginning to believe that they have something worthwhile to give. I can see it in their faces."

Hope ducked her head. Though Nancy's words touched her, she'd never felt comfortable accepting praise, especially if she felt it was undeserved.

"Well, good. I hope so. Because I think they do have something to give, every one of them. Even the really, really tough ones. The ones who are so warped by pain, and fear, and anger that they can't recognize the good in themselves or anybody else."

Nancy pressed her lips into a sympathetic line and tipped her head to one side. "You're thinking about Nita. Don't feel bad. She's a hard case, that one. You did what you had to do."

"Did I?" Hope asked. "I suppose. Once the fight broke out, I didn't really have a choice but to call the guards to break it up, even though I knew it meant she'd be kicked out of the program. I just wish I'd been able to reach her."

"I understand. But Nita's an adult," Nancy said. "She has to live with the consequences of her actions. Besides, think of all the others—the ones you are helping. You're doing a fantastic job, Hope."

"Thanks, but they're the ones who are doing the heavy lifting. Yes, sure, I prepare the lessons, teach them the skills, and cheer them on, but they're the ones who have to do the hard work. And I don't mean learning how to thread a needle or run a sewing machine.

"For people who've never done it before, the tough part of making a quilt, or doing anything creative, is figuring out how to silence the negative voices in your head so you can do the

work. Everybody carries around those old tapes from childhood, the soundtracks of all those people who said we were un-
talented or unworthy or somehow just not good enough. Mine
was my high school guidance counselor; she said I wasn't cut
out for college."

"Mine was my first-form art teacher," Nancy said. "She gave
my papier-mâché elephant sculpture a failing mark. I was so
convinced of my utter lack of artistic talent that I never took another art class. It took twenty years before I was willing to take
a chance on another creative outlet," Nancy said, tilting her
head toward the wall and her photographs of the Sussex coast-
line.

Hope puffed with disgust and threw out her hands. "See?
That's exactly the kind of thing I'm talking about. Fortunately
for me, my mother intervened. She had a few choice words for
that counselor, I can tell you. Until she let loose on Mrs.
Blalock, I didn't realize she even *knew* those words."

Hope laughed, recalling how her shock was mirrored in the
face of the guidance counselor. "The fact that she was willing to
stand up for me like that meant the world to me. It gave me
courage and made me determined, not only to go to college, but
to graduate magna cum laude, if only to prove Mrs. Blalock
wrong."

"For good or for ill, revenge can be a powerful motivation,"
Nancy said.

"It was for me," Hope said. "But the point is, those negative
voices everybody carries around have an outsized impact on the
way we look at ourselves. I mean, you're a strong person, raised
by loving and supportive parents. If the criticism of a snippy art
teacher rang powerfully enough in your mind that it kept you
away from art for twenty years, then how much harder is it for
these women?

"I bet fewer than two in ten had anything even close to a stable
family life when they were young. Many of them were abused,
debased, and degraded in ways that most people can barely imagine. From the time they were children, most of them have heard
one message, over and over: 'You're nobody. You're worthless.' "

"If this is about Nita . . ." Nancy's forehead crinkled with concern. "Hope, that's not your fault. You can't save everybody, you know. She's made her own choices. Think of all the women in here, most with backgrounds every bit as bleak as Nita's, who're making *good* choices, the ones who have decided to own their mistakes, face their fears, and do the best they can to plot a real future for themselves. Think about Mandy and Steph."

"I know," Hope said, pushing the empty hummus container and zipper bag to one side of Nancy's desk so she could lean closer. "That's exactly what I'm saying. In spite of what all these women have been through, all those bad experiences and critical voices, they're pushing through the doubt and taking a chance on themselves. I've had tough students before, kids who had low self-esteem and zero self-confidence, but these women seem like they had the cards stacked against them from day one.

"Did you know that Mandy's father threw her out of the house when she was sixteen years old? Or that Deedee lived under a bridge for two years? Or that Steph was born addicted to crack?"

"I did," Nancy said softly.

"And yet, after all that, they're trying. In addition to all the usual demons of human existence, these women are fighting against abuse, neglect, and plain bad luck, plus the dumb decisions that landed them here, to learn something that's new and, for most of them, really difficult, just so they can make a quilt to give to somebody else."

"Yes," Nancy said evenly. "Because you were willing to step up and teach them how to do it. They've been here long enough to know how hard it was to get this program to happen, to talk David and the powers that be into letting felons have access to sharp objects, and to go around town begging for supplies and funding. They know how you've stuck your neck out for them. And because you've shown that you think they're worth taking a chance on, they're starting to believe it themselves."

Hope rolled her eyes and Nancy clucked her tongue.

"You just can't take a compliment, can you? Fine. If you

don't believe me, maybe you'll believe our esteemed superintendent."

"David?"

"Uh-huh. He dropped by this morning to welcome me back. He sat right in that chair you're sitting in now and spent a good five minutes singing the praises of the quilting program as a whole and you in particular."

"Okay, now you are just toying with me," Hope said, tossing her trash into the wastebasket. "No way did David Hernandez sit in this chair and say nice things about me. He hates me."

"Well, I'm not sure that's true, but if it ever was, it isn't now. He thinks you're doing an amazing job with the women and that, thanks to you, he's actually going to have something of substance to say when he writes his report for the governor's commission." Responding to Hope's silence and doubtful expression, Nancy pointed to her white clerical collar.

"Hope. I am a woman of the cloth. Would I lie to you?"

"Well . . ." Hope said slowly. "No. I guess not. Huh. Well, I'm glad he feels like that. And it brings up something I'd been thinking about."

"What's that?"

"Inviting David to Christmas dinner. When Hazel came up from Portland to help me try to convince David to green-light the quilting program, I noticed a definite spark between the two of them."

"Oh, really?" Nancy said, arching her voice as well as her eyebrows and propping her chin onto the tent of her folded hands. "Do tell."

"There's nothing to tell, yet. But Hazel's been feeling a little down. So I was thinking, you know"—Hope shrugged—"maybe get the two of them together in a room and see if the spark—"

"Becomes a flame? Brilliant idea. And since I can now assure you, with one hundred percent ecclesiastical authority, that David Hernandez does not hate you and, in fact, thinks quite highly of you, there's no reason not to."

"Maybe not. But . . ." Hope blinked a couple of times. "David Hernandez. And my sister."

Nancy threw back her head and barked out a laugh.

"Come on, Hope. He's not so bad. And since Hazel has a truly dismal track record with men, I'd rate the chances of this turning into an actual relationship somewhere between slim and none."

"True," Hope said, feeling her anxiety ease a bit. "It was just one meeting. If they spend any real time together, they'll probably realize they have absolutely nothing in common and are completely wrong for each other."

"That's the spirit," Nancy said, hopping up from her chair, then across the room to pluck a blue metal watering can off the top of a filing cabinet. "Besides, it's Christmas! Room in the stable for everyone, right?"

"All right, I'll invite David. Also, I'm sure you already have plans and loads of invitations, but if you and John did happen to be available, we'd love it if—"

"Join you for Christmas dinner? Thought you'd never ask." Nancy carried the watering can to a small and serviceable but oddly placed wall sink that stood near the door and began to fill it. "Roger can't come home this year, so it was going to be just me, John, and one of those sad, over-processed little turkey rolls. We'd be thrilled to come. Can I bring anything?"

"Yes. As long as it's not bubble and squeak," Hope said. "How about a salad?"

"Done," Nancy said, and began watering a brown and brittle fern that, to Hope's eyes, already looked like a goner.

"As long as we're issuing invitations," Nancy said, "why don't you come to services on Christmas morning? It's going to be a first-rate sermon. And very short. I know this because I'll be delivering it."

"Oh. You're sweet to ask. But, you know, I'll be pretty busy that day. You know, cooking and getting ready for the party. Besides, I haven't been to church since—Well, not for a long time. The stained glass would probably shatter the second I walked in." Hope laughed, hoping her lighthearted response would convince Nancy to drop the subject.

Instead, watering can still at work, Nancy tilted her head to one side, regarding Hope with a slightly confused expression. Hope bit her lip. That poor fern. If it wasn't dead before, it surely would be soon. Nancy was going to drown it.

"Stained glass? Oh no!" Nancy exclaimed, righting the watering can as liquid started seeping over the rim of the pot. "I didn't mean *church* services. I was talking about chapel."

"Chapel. You mean here? At the prison?"

"Yes. We do it every year, right in the cafeteria. It's a sunrise service, five o'clock, and only lasts forty minutes, so you'll be back home in plenty of time to tend to your Christmas preparations, probably before the rest of your family are awake.

"It's a beautiful service, Hope. It would mean so much to the women if you came. And to me. Deedee is singing a solo. Say you'll come."

. Feeling cornered, Hope bit her lip once again. After a moment's thought, she opened her mouth, prepared to say no.

But then, for some reason, she didn't.

"All right. I'll come."

Chapter 26

When she began serving her sentence, Mandy was just twenty-one years old and, in spite of all the things she'd seen and done since her dad had thrown her out of the house at sixteen, still a little green. The first few weeks on the inside had been rough, but as Hope had observed, Mandy was a fast learner.

She learned quickly that the way to survive on the inside was to make herself as inconsequential and unobtrusive as possible. For five years, Mandy kept her head down, minded her own business, and made no enemies. But she hadn't made any friends either, not until she started taking Hope's quilting class.

Mandy wasn't sure what had changed. Maybe it had something to do with the fact that she was so close to release. Or maybe it was because quilting was such a communal activity; she and the other students were always asking one another's opinions on color combinations, sharing tips on how to sew straighter stitches or rip crooked ones out more quickly, or proudly showing off their finished blocks or quilt tops. It might have been any of those things. Or it might have been something about Hope, the way she made them all feel capable, and trustworthy, and safe.

Whatever the reason, for the first time since she'd passed through the prison gates, Mandy felt like she had friends, people who had her back, people she actually cared about and who, much to her surprise, she would miss when she left.

And that's why, when Deedee told Mandy that she was going to sing a solo at the sunrise service on Christmas and asked if she would please, please, please come, Mandy said she would.

Cindy, who Mandy actually thought was okay, gave her a firm but silent poke in the shoulder at twenty minutes to five. She'd lain awake for hours the night before, her brain busy trying to answer questions with no clear solutions.

Groggy, her brain fuzzy with the remainders of interrupted sleep, she rolled over and glared at the guard. When Cindy leaned down and whispered, "Merry Christmas," Mandy remembered why she'd been woken while it was still so dark.

She lay in her bunk for a couple of minutes, blinking, and nearly fell back asleep. But when she heard quiet rustling from a handful of other inmates who were getting dressed in the dark, she got up and did the same. Yawning, Mandy shuffled through the dark dormitory, the valley of bunk beds still mostly filled with slumbering women, and down the hallway.

The cafeteria was dark too, which surprised her. The only light in the room came from a single-pillar candle, set on a tall, silver lamp stand. Except for one near the front of the room, covered with a snowy white cloth and topped by a simple silver cross, the tables had been pushed to one side to make room for the chairs. There were eight rows with twelve chairs in each one, separated by a center aisle.

Nearly every seat was filled, another surprise, and no one spoke a word. In a prison housing more than a thousand women, silence was a rare and precious commodity. Its presence, and the glow that the single candle cast upon the faces of the silent worshipers, filled Mandy with a sensation so far distant from her memory that it took her a moment to identify it—peace.

After a moment, Mandy heard a hissing noise. Deedee, sitting in the third row, waved her over.

"I saved you a seat." Deedee's announcement was whispered with a mixture of excitement and pride, as if she was pleased with herself for having thought so far ahead. "For Mrs. C. too."

"Thanks, Deedee," Hope said with a smile.

Deedee bobbed her head and bounced halfway out of her chair, making room for Mandy to pass. "You sit there, next to Mrs. C. I need to sit on the aisle so I can get up when it's time for me to sing."

Mandy moved past Deedee's knees and took her seat. Hope smiled as she sat down and then reached over, squeezed Mandy's hand, and whispered, "Merry Christmas."

Mandy nearly flinched. It had been a long time since anyone had touched her in quite that way—not a caress, not a touch that invited or required a response, just a simple acknowledgment of her presence and humanity, a sign of affection.

Mandy smiled at her teacher. "Merry Christmas."

The service was, as promised, brief.

Nancy, who normally wore just a plain black shirt and white clerical collar over black trousers, entered the room at the stroke of five, dressed in a splendid flowing robe and a clerical stole embroidered with an intricate pattern of red, green, and gold vines.

Two inmates walked in front of her, one carrying a thick Bible with a gold cover, the other a shallow gold plate. After placing their burdens on the table, the women took seats in the front row. Nancy greeted everyone, wishing them a "Happy Christmas," which made a few of the inmates chuckle, including Mandy and Deedee.

They liked the chaplain. They liked her enthusiasm, her funny accent, and the weird way she said things—"Happy Christmas" instead of "Merry Christmas," "biscuit" instead of "cookie."

What they really liked was the way she treated them, with kindness. Not because she was trying to convert them or anything—Mandy had never attended chapel services before—but because that's the way she treated everybody, as though they mattered. When Mandy first arrived, Nancy convinced her that her life really *wasn't* over, that if you can hang on, life goes on. And now, five years later, here she was.

Debby Harper stood up and read the Nativity story from the book of Luke. Mandy had heard it many times, every year while watching the Charlie Brown Christmas special. After a moment, she stopped listening and started wondering.

Mandy wondered if Talia was awake yet. She wondered if she'd opened the present that Mandy had "bought" for her, courtesy of a charity that supplied gifts to the kids of inmates, saying they were from the parents. She'd asked them to get Talia a Barbie doll. Had they really done it? Did Talia like it? She wondered what it would feel like, next year, when she was able to pick out Talia's present herself and pay for it with money she'd earned. She wondered how she was ever going to live through the months until her release. And if she would finish Talia's quilt before she left.

Though she wasn't anxious to spend one more day on the inside than she had to, she really wanted to leave with a completed quilt to give to Talia. She and Talia wouldn't have a home of their own right away. Until she could find a job and save money to rent an apartment, they'd have to stay with her parents. That was probably for the best. Talia had lived there for so long. She would need time to adjust to the change and to start seeing Mandy as a real mother, not just some lady she visited on odd Mondays. And Mandy would need time to adjust too. Life was different on the outside.

Still, Mandy couldn't wait until she and Talia became a real family, with a home of their own. It wouldn't happen right away. But being able to walk through the gate, hold her daughter for as long as she wanted, and give Talia a quilt she'd made with her own hands would be a down payment on their life to come, her personal promise that someday they would be a family, complete in themselves, and never to be parted again.

The reading was finished. Chaplain Nancy stood up and gave a very brief sermon on the subject of unpaid debts, a concept her audience understood only too well. Every woman in that room was there because she had incurred a debt and society demanded payment. That was the way of the world. But heaven wasn't like that. And so, according to the chaplain, God came down to show what heaven *was* like, what He was like, and to pay humanity's uncollectable debts, to serve the sentence of the guilty, invite them to dwell in his home as family, forever and ever. Amen.

It was a good sermon and Mandy could just about believe it. But she wasn't in heaven, was she? She was here on the inside, in prison, counting the days until her release even as she worried about what would happen after she was released. God was God, but people were people. They didn't forgive so easily. Or forget. Not even after you'd paid your debts.

Life was different on the outside.

Would she be able to find a job? Even with a high school diploma in her hand, would anybody hire a twenty-six-year-old with a felony on her record and no real experience? Would her job pay enough for her to support Talia? Would she be able to find an apartment they could afford, in an area that was safe, and a landlord who was willing to rent to a felon?

The sermon was over.

Deedee bounced out of her chair so abruptly that Mandy, lost in a vortex of her increasingly anxious thoughts, jerked involuntarily. Hope shifted her eyes toward Mandy, looking concerned. Mandy pretended she didn't notice, training her gaze to the front of the room where Deedee stood, hands folded primly in front of her. Deedee took a deep breath, opened her mouth, and then, without accompaniment, started to sing.

The sweet, clear, rich, and beautiful sound that came from Deedee's tiny body filled the room and took Mandy's breath away. She had no idea that Deedee could sing, and especially not like that. The song she had chosen didn't mention wise men, or stars, or herald angels, or anything about Christmas. But it was exactly right for the time and place.

When Deedee got to the second verse, Mandy's eyes began to flood.

"Let not your heart be troubled," His tender word I hear,
And resting on His goodness, I lose my doubts and fears;
Though by the path He leadeth, but one step I may see;
His eye is on the sparrow, and I know He watches me."

Mandy felt like Deedee was singing just to her, just *for* her, as if she somehow understood all the worries that had taken root inside her, the questions and doubts that kept her awake at night. But that wasn't possible.

Deedee was an amazing singer. However, she couldn't possibly have known that this song, these words, were exactly what Mandy needed to hear right now. But someone must have.

It was like what Hope said about the quilt Mandy wanted to make. She'd been attracted to one called Dove in the Window because of the name. That was what she felt like right now, a trapped bird, peering out the window to the world beyond, heart thrumming with fear and anticipation for that thrilling but terrifying moment when the window would open and she would fly free.

But that quilt . . . it had so many pieces and looked so complicated. It was beautiful and she knew Talia would love it. But Mandy thought it was beyond her.

Hope disagreed.

"Before you talk yourself out of it, take a deep breath and listen, okay? The reason it looks hard is because you're trying to take it all in at once. If you look closely, you'll see that it's based on one block, made in different sizes, and that the block is just squares, rectangles, and triangles, shapes you've already worked with. It's just a matter of breaking it down, block by block, and not getting ahead of yourself. You can do this, Mandy. I'll be there to help you at each step. Trust me. You won't be in this alone."

Trust me. You won't be in this alone.

That's what Hope had promised. And now, as Deedee sang, she was aware of a quiet presence, nothing she could see or hear, but the assurance it brought was palpable, as powerful and true as anything she'd ever experienced.

The path ahead was steep and winding. She couldn't see the end of it, but that was all right. She didn't have to because she wasn't alone. All she had to do was trust and take one step. Then the next. And the next. And the next.

It would be all right. She wasn't in this alone.

The flood spilled over. Hot, cleansing tears, tears of relief, coursed down Mandy's cheeks. She wasn't the only one. All around her women were crying, crying from joy and not grief.

When Deedee reached the final chorus, she lifted her arms and held out her hands. The moment she did, every woman in the room sprang to her feet, eagerly accepting the invitation, and joined in the song.

"I sing because I'm happy. I sing because I'm free.
For His eye is on the sparrow, and I know He watches me."

They stood side by side and shoulder to shoulder and sang with one voice.

They sang because they were happy. And free.

In that moment, they were.

Chapter 27

Hope never met a holiday she didn't love.

Holidays were a perfect excuse to try out new crafts, decorating themes, and recipes. With a little thought and a dash of creativity, they were also an excellent means of teaching her kids or students about anything from astronomy to zoology and every topic in between without them realizing they were learning. Well, most of the time.

The Bastille Day birthday party had been a big hit with the twins and their friends in the neighborhood. Her students at the high school had greeted her Pie Day party, celebrating both the pastry and the mathematical constant, with equal enthusiasm. However, her Groundhog Day party had been less successful. Even with the inclusion of the chocolate pudding cups sprinkled with cookie crumbs to represent dirt and topped with a teddy bear cookie to represent an emerging groundhog, the kids recognized it for what it was—a ham-handed attempt to teach the geography of Pennsylvania.

Well, you couldn't hit the ball out of the park every time. Some holidays had more material to work with than others. Hope loved them just the same, all of them.

But none more than Christmas.

That was why, even though she'd been diligent in winnowing

down their possessions before moving from Portland to Olympia, even getting rid of the spinning wheel that she'd always told herself she would learn to use but somehow never did, Hope absolutely refused to part with the Christmas decorations—all sixteen boxes of them.

Even after she dragooned Rick and McKenzie into service as reluctant helpers, it had taken two full weekends to finish decorating the condo for Christmas.

The display included six homemade, hand-ribboned wreaths, Hope's extensive collection of snowmen, a sixteen-piece ceramic representation of a Dickensian village at Christmas, complete with Scrooge and Tiny Tim figurines, a tabletop crèche she had inherited from her mother, dozens of candles, three snow globes, two music boxes, and no fewer than eight Christmas trees.

The largest fresh-cut trees, placed in the foyer and living room, were hung with ornaments of copper, gold, and chocolate brown and traditional red and green, respectively. The master bedroom tree was hung with a variety of glass balls that had been hand-painted by Hope's mother. The tree in the guest room, currently occupied by McKenzie, was decorated with the ornaments the kids had made as children. Two live trees on the balcony, planted in enormous terra-cotta pots, sported silver spray-painted pinecones and so many strings of white lights that Rick had to go to the hardware store and buy extra extension cords. The guest bathroom and kitchen counter were home to two artificial tabletop trees.

The kitchen tree was the most recent addition and Hope's current favorite, decorated with child-sized teacups, cake pans, muffin tins, and tiny rolling pins she'd found at a secondhand store and which she and McKenzie had turned into ornaments with the aid of red ribbon and a hot glue gun. The tree was adorable, and the opportunity for crafty bonding with McKenzie was a plus for Hope and a good distraction for her daughter. Kenz was working hard to keep up a brave front, and seemed genuinely pleased to see her brothers, but, obviously, this wasn't the happiest or easiest Christmas of her life. Hope was worried about her.

Though the dinner guests weren't due for an hour, Hope lit the candles, illuminated the trees, and started playing Liam's carefully curated selection of Christmas carols on the stereo before sitting down at the kitchen island to finish making the fresh evergreen and holly arrangements for the table.

Hope hummed along with a choral version of "The Holly and the Ivy" while she worked, stripping needles from the lower part of the cedar's branches and then thrusting them into a block of floral foam.

Everyone had still been asleep when she returned from the chapel service at the prison, the twins sharing the second guest room, Reed's girlfriend, Pamela, sharing with McKenzie, and Liam sacked out on the sofa, snoring softly. Hope had plenty of time to brew coffee, put the breakfast casserole in the oven, slice fruit for a salad, and warm up Rick's homemade coffeecake before the family began to stir.

As was their tradition, they opened presents in their pajamas while enjoying coffee and cake, then got dressed and sat down to breakfast. The gifts weren't as lavish as in former days; even with Hope working, they still had to keep an eye on the budget. But the boys seemed to appreciate the pajama pants she'd sewn for them and McKenzie really loved her three pairs of maternity pants.

"Awesome!" she exclaimed, holding the light gray pants up against her bulging waistline. "All my others are getting crazy tight!"

Rick, as was his tradition, gave everyone a book. But he'd surprised Hope with a sterling silver bangle bracelet with two blue glass beads and a silver heart charm. "Those are just to get you started," Rick said. "I figured I could give you more charms for birthdays and anniversaries. You like it?"

"I love it. It's perfect," she declared before slipping the bangle onto her wrist and then leaning forward to give him a kiss.

"And I love my new sweater," he said, looking down at the cable-patterned fisherman's sweater Hope had knitted for him. "Must have taken you forever to make."

"I actually started it three years ago," Hope admitted. "But then, you know me, I put it aside and got involved in something else. I found it again when I was unpacking."

"Good thing I lost enough weight so I can fit into it." He laughed, giving her a peck on the lips.

"And it's a good thing that Pamela gave me this beautiful new yarn," Hope said, nodding toward a bag filled with six skeins of beautifully soft turquoise-colored merino wool and then at Pamela, who was sitting on the sofa with Reed's arm around her waist. "I was almost out."

"Oh, I doubt that." Pamela laughed. "If you're anything like my mom, you've got some extra stashed away here somewhere. She always says that there's no such thing as too much yarn or too much chocolate."

"Your mom is a knitter?"

"A knitter, a sewer, a baker, a crafter. She does everything. Like you," Pamela said, then turned to Reed and gave him a smile.

Hope smiled as well. They looked good together, those two. But her smile faded a bit as she noticed the shadow that briefly crossed McKenzie's face. Poor Kenz. It couldn't be easy for her, seeing the way Reed and Pamela looked at each other, the evidence of love written so clearly on their faces. Even so, she was doing her best to make Pamela feel welcome and not to let her own disappointments mar her brother's happiness. Hope was proud of her.

"Hey, Mom," McKenzie said after the shadow passed, smiling so brightly that only Hope would have sensed what an effort this required. "Did you know that Pamela quilts? One of her pieces was accepted to a quilt show in California last year and won a ribbon."

"Uh-oh," Liam said, shaking his head. "That does it. Pamela, I hope you like this family of ours. Because if you and Reed don't get married, my mother is going to insist on adopting you."

Reed turned toward Pamela, grinned, and popped up his eyebrows.

"You guys seem okay," Pamela said, flushing crimson.

"That's just because you don't know us that well yet," Rory

said, getting to his feet. "You don't, for example, know that the Carpenter family plays a very vicious and highly competitive game of full-contact Monopoly every Christmas. Nor do you know that, every Christmas, my poor, pathetic twin loses. Badly."

"All right," Reed said, hopping to his feet and clapping his hands together. "That does it, loser. Game on!"

Hope started poking the holly branches into her table arrangement and chuckled as she thought about that Monopoly game. Predictably, Reed had lost and, happily, McKenzie had won. As McKenzie leapt up from the table to do a little victory dance, fanning fistfuls of fake currency in her opponents' faces, Hope could tell she'd forgotten about Zach and the uncertainty of the future. At least for a little while.

It was good that McKenzie was there, with them. Nothing made Hope as happy as having all her children under one roof, even if that roof wasn't the one they'd gathered under for so many years. In spite of the changes, it was turning out to be a surprisingly good Christmas. Most surprising of all had been the chapel service at the prison.

She'd only gone to be supportive of Nancy and Deedee. She never expected to find herself so moved by the experience. To start with, there was Deedee. Who knew she could sing like that? It just went to show you: If you dug below the surface, you discovered that people had all kinds of hidden talents.

Another surprise was the way that the women got to their feet and joined in. They were so . . . "Transformed" was the only word Hope could think of to describe it. Tears and smiles and raw emotion were fully in evidence, even on the faces of the toughest, most hard-bitten inmates. The beautiful, almost angelic sound of their voices raised together gave her gooseflesh. She'd felt like she'd witnessed a miracle. Maybe she had.

But, for Hope, the most moving part of the service came when Nancy, resplendent in her robe and embroidered stole, walked to the front of the room holding the gold saucer filled with Communion wafers and invited them all to partake.

"Come to the table," she said. "For all are welcome."

As Deedee started the group off singing "Angels We Have Heard on High," most of the women began filing forward to receive the bread. Hope hadn't planned on going forward. But when it came time for the row to go up, Hope looked over at Mandy. Her eyes were dry now but still rimmed in red. In them, Hope saw a mixture of longing and uncertainty.

Hope leaned closer. "Do you want to take Communion?"

"I . . . I've never done it before. Do you know how it works?"

"I do. But it's been a long, long time. I haven't been to church since my mother died." Hope felt her throat tighten. She swallowed hard and looked into Mandy's eyes. "Do you want me to go with you? We can do it together."

Mandy bit her lower lip, thinking for a moment.

"Do you think it would be okay?"

Hope could tell by the tremor in her voice and the look of yearning in her eyes that the question was more complicated than it appeared to be.

"Yes," she said, and took Mandy's hand. "It's like Nancy said. Everybody is welcome."

They'd gone forward together, taken the bread, and gone back to their seats. Such a simple thing. But it changed something inside Hope. Broke something. Built something.

It was too soon to say what it meant. But when Hope came home, even before she began making breakfast, she took the sixteenth box from the closet, a box that had remained unopened for many years.

Unwrapping the once-white tissue paper, now yellowed with time, she took out her mother's crèche and placed it on a table.

Rick, who had been taking a nap before the guests arrived, shuffled into the kitchen, yawning and stretching just as Hope was putting the completed centerpieces in the middle of the table.

"People should be showing up pretty soon, right? You need any help? Where is everybody?"

"No worries. I've got everything under control. McKenzie's napping too. She still gets tired easily. I sent the boys and Pamela off on a mission to find some heavy cream. I need it to cut the eggnog; Reed made it way too strong. They should be back any minute."

Rick reached into a nearby bowl of spiced nuts, took a handful, and popped a few into his mouth. "Everything looks great, honey. Even better than it did at the old house. I can't believe I'm saying this, but I'm glad we kept all the decorations."

"It does look nice, doesn't it?" Hope said, eyeing her surroundings with satisfaction. "Thanks for your help. I would never have managed without you and McKenzie."

"Well," he said, tossing the remaining nuts into his mouth. "Seeing as I didn't have a choice, you're welcome." Hope gave him a playful slap on the forearm. "I particularly like this last-minute addition," Rick said, tilting his head toward the crèche. "Looks really nice there."

Hope bobbed her head. "It was time."

Rick took a step closer, wrapped his arms around her.

"Hey, Mrs. Carpenter. Have I told you recently that I think you are the most amazing woman on the face of this earth and that I'd be lost without you?"

Hope narrowed her eyes and pursed her lips, pretending to think back.

"Nope. Not recently."

Rick lowered his head and kissed her long on the lips.

"Hope Carpenter," he said, his voice low, "I think you are the most amazing woman on the face of the earth. Everybody in this family would be totally lost without you. And me more than anyone."

"Oh, Rick."

Hope pushed herself up on her toes and kissed him back, her arms twining around his neck, feeling contented, and stirred, and satisfied all at the same time.

They stood there, kissing and clinging, for quite a while, only breaking apart when Hope heard a soft sound of footfall and looked up to see McKenzie standing on the other side of the room. Her eyes were red. It looked like she'd been crying.

Hope wanted to cross the room and crush her in her arms,

tell her she loved her and was proud of her and that everything was going to be okay. If she hadn't known how much McKenzie would have hated that, she would have. Hope broke away from Rick's embrace, feeling almost guilty.

"Sorry," McKenzie mumbled, looking down at her shoes. "I didn't mean to . . . I heard car doors slamming and looked out the window. I think people are starting to arrive."

"Right. I'll go open the champagne," Rick said. "You want me to take those little cracker things out of the refrigerator?"

"The salmon canapés," Hope corrected. "Yes, please. I wish the boys would get back with the cream. Well, we'll just stick with champagne and soft drinks until they get back."

Rick headed toward the kitchen. Hope went to McKenzie and put an arm over her shoulders.

"You okay, Kenz?"

"I'm fine. Allergies," she said, pointing to her eyes, even though they both knew there was no pollen in December. "You need help? I can slice up the cheese if you want me to."

"Are you sure you don't want to go and lie back down for a while? Dad and I can handle everything if you need some time alone."

"No, I'm good. What can I do to help?"

Hope couldn't help but admire the taut and definitive way McKenzie brushed off her concern, the stalwart determination to keep busy and not wallow in despair. Perhaps they were more alike than Hope had realized. When it was all too much and the tears finally came, did McKenzie set her watch for ten minutes too?

"Well," Hope said, searching her brain for tasks that still needed doing, wishing she'd been a little less efficient in her preparations, "yes. You can help me slice that cheese for starters. Oh, I know! As soon as your brothers get back with the cream, would you mind whipping some for the pies?"

"Right away?" McKenzie said doubtfully. "Shouldn't it sit in the refrigerator for a bit? If it's not cold enough, it won't hold up as well, will it?"

"Not quite as well," she admitted. "But I'd like to have it

made in advance so everything's ready when it's time to serve dessert."

How did McKenzie know about pre-chilling cream before whipping it? Growing up, she'd always made such a point of making it clear that she couldn't be less interested in her mother's tips on the finer points of domestic science. Could it be that she actually *had* been paying attention to the things Hope said over the years?

Hope moved her arm lower down McKenzie's back, shepherding her in the direction of the kitchen.

"Kenz? I just had the most fabulous idea. Come on. I'll tell you about it."

Chapter 28

McKenzie wasn't stupid. When Hope pulled her aside to share her great idea, McKenzie understood exactly what her mother was up to and why. Hope worried too much. And it wasn't like Christmas had been a total disaster.

For one thing, McKenzie had gotten some nice presents. In addition to the maternity clothes her mom had made for her, she'd gotten a couple of interesting-looking novels from her dad. Normally, he gave her nonfiction titles, but maybe he knew that a literary escape was just what she needed right now.

Her soon-to-be-ex in-laws, Ted and Wanda, had sent several presents: a gift certificate for a prenatal massage, a copy of *What to Expect When You're Expecting*, and two sets of newborn-sized footie pajamas. The message there was clear; divorce or no divorce, they were excited about being grandparents and wanted to be involved in the baby's life. Which was fair enough. McKenzie wanted that too. Even if she hadn't liked Ted and Wanda as much as she did, she still would have wanted them to be involved. Just because Zach sucked at monogamy was no reason to deny her child access to a set of doting grandparents. That was a no-brainer. When it came to Zach, though, it was trickier. At the moment, she felt like she could go the rest of her life without ever seeing him again. If it was just her, she wouldn't have had to. But they were going to be parents and so, like it or not, they would be connected for the rest of their lives. For the sake of the baby, they had to find a way to navigate that relationship.

That was why McKenzie decided to buy Zach a Christmas present, a twenty-five-dollar Starbucks gift card, the most generic present she could imagine, a gift that said: *I don't care about you enough to put much thought into this, but let's just try to get along.* The day after she tucked it into a Christmas card and put it in the mail, McKenzie received an iTunes gift card from Zach in exactly the same amount.

So, at least everybody was on the same page. Christmas could have been a lot worse. McKenzie had to keep reminding herself of that, but it was true.

Even though it felt kind of weird to celebrate the holiday in her parents' sleek, modern condominium instead of the big, drafty, always-being-renovated house she'd grown up in, enough of the familiar traditions were in place so that it still felt like a proper Carpenter Christmas.

Her mother's roast turkey and secret recipe for stuffing were unchanged and just as delicious as ever. It must be. She'd had three helpings. But, then again, she had three helpings of a lot of things these days. Was it the baby who made her so hungry? Or was she using food to silence the confusion and ache of loneliness she felt in the wake of Zach's betrayal? Whatever the reason, she'd already gained twelve pounds.

But it had been nice, especially with everything else about her life so upended, to smell those Christmas smells she'd grown up with, to line up Hope's collection of snowmen, shortest to tallest, the way she always had when she was little, to enjoy her father's homemade coffeecake, still warm from the oven, while they opened the presents, to play Monopoly afterward, just like they always had, and then to actually win the game.

That was a first. Rory, the most competitive of them and an

adherent to what he called full-contact Monopoly, which meant buying up as much property as he could, as quickly as he could, usually won. But this year he'd hung back, passing up an opportunity to purchase a third railroad. Did he feel sorry for her? Had he let her win? Maybe.

But it was good to see him, good to see all of them. With her brothers spread far and wide, pursuing lives and careers that were far more glamorous than hers—doctor, professor, filmmaker—it was getting harder and harder to bring everybody together at the same time. She liked them more now that they were grown up.

Reed and Rory—being the oldest and smartest and boys, not to mention having that twin thing going on, where they could practically read each other's thoughts and often finished each other's sentences—had always made her feel like an outsider when she was a kid. And Liam . . . Well, Liam had been the baby, spoiled, indulged, her mother's favorite. Hope always said she didn't have a favorite, but come on. Who did she think she was kidding?

Looking down at her bulging belly, which seemed to get bigger by the day, McKenzie wondered if she would have a favorite child. If she did, it would probably be this one. She couldn't imagine ever getting married again. Not that this necessarily precluded her from ever having another child, but a second go-round as a single mother was definitely not part of her plan. Not that it ever had been. And maybe life was easier for only children?

But having grown-up siblings wasn't so bad. Liam was still Liam, the best at telling stories and getting noticed, which was probably what made him a good filmmaker. He had recently taken to wearing bow ties, an affectation she found irritating, but he was calmer now, less flamboyant, and a much better listener.

They'd had a long, quiet conversation about the symbolism in *Pan's Labyrinth,* one of her favorite movies, that was really interesting. Also, Liam was really excited about being an uncle.

He'd even bought the baby a *Star Wars* onesie for Christmas, which was kind of sweet.

Considering the circumstances, it really wasn't a bad Christmas, or wouldn't have been, if every second person she met hadn't been quite so in love.

She *was* happy for Reed. How could she not be? Pamela was awesome. If she and Pamela had met at the office, they'd definitely have become friends. Reed was head over heels for her and it was clear that the feeling was mutual. An engagement couldn't be far off. She was surprised that it hadn't happened during Christmas. Also grateful. An announcement and toasts to the bride and groom would have been more than she could have handled just then.

Then there was Aunt Hazel and her mother's boss from the prison, David Hernandez. They weren't as giddy as Reed and Pamela, but there was definitely something there. Hazel and David moved off into a corner to talk as soon as dinner was over and David raised his arm and leaned against the wall while they chatted. It was an unconscious gesture but a clear signal that he was trying to keep Hazel to himself, effectively fencing her off from everybody else, especially any men who might compete for her attentions.

Men were so obvious and so primal. Zach had been just the same when they were dating. And McKenzie wasn't the only one who noticed David's instinctive attempts to corral Hazel. McKenzie saw the way her mother, who had been standing at the kitchen island, chatting with Kate and Nancy, kept shifting her eyes toward the corner. When Hazel laughed at something David said and then reached up and picked imaginary lint off his shirt—more primal behavior—McKenzie saw the way her mother quickly extricated herself from the conversation and made a beeline for Hazel and David, plying them with offers of a second piece of pie.

It was weird, the way her mother was trying to get between those two. David didn't seem like a bad guy. McKenzie thought his haircut was kind of unfortunate—way too short—and he'd seemed a little tense when she'd first met him, overly formal. But he'd definitely loosened up around Hazel, so maybe they were good for each other. Why should her mother have any objections to him? It didn't make sense.

Then again, when it came to not making sense about the love lives of other people, McKenzie couldn't exactly go around throwing stones. Of all the displays of affection that got under her skin during the holidays, none bothered her quite as much as that of her mother and father.

Which was stupid. Really, really stupid. And selfish.

What was wrong with her? What kind of daughter wasn't happy that her parents, whose relationship she had so recently feared might be on the rocks, and which in order to save it she had skulked around after her father like some kind of 1970s, made-for-TV-movie private investigator, were, once again, so clearly in love?

She should be happy for them! And she was.

Except when she wasn't. Like at Christmas.

She hated herself for feeling that way, so much so that she'd actually said something to Liam. It was just an offhand comment, a joke really, about the stomach-clenching experience that ensued when you walked into a room and found your parents making out under the mistletoe.

But Liam, who was way more insightful than she recalled, wasn't fooled.

"It's a perfectly understandable reaction," he said, picking a toothpick out of his drink and sliding the first of three olives into his mouth.

He'd recently taken to drinking very dry vodka martinis with extra olives, which was also irritating. She got that he was searching for a persona, trying to stand out among a group of hungry and perhaps equally promising young filmmakers. But couldn't he just try being himself? Did he have to be Truman Capote?

"You and Dad have always been close," Liam said. "You're clearly his favorite."

"What are you talking about?" she scoffed. "I am not."

Liam tossed back a mouthful of martini.

"Oh, please. Yes, you are. You're his little princess. Always were."

"Okay, fine. So what if I am? You were always Mom's favorite."

He shook his head and swallowed. "Not really. Just her last chance to get it right. She really is crazy about all of us. Have you seen her today? You could light up Burbank with that smile, she's so happy. All her chicks back in the nest, it doesn't get better for her. Anyway, you're missing the point. What I'm trying to say is that, whether you knew it or not, you and Mom were always in competition for Dad's attention."

"That's not true."

Liam lifted his brows and gave her a look, as if he wasn't even going to waste his breath arguing over such an utterly inaccurate denial.

"Even so," Liam continued evenly, "in the wake of your lousy husband's infidelity, your sympathies swung toward Mom. Which makes perfect sense. I mean, you're both women and wives. In a few more months, you'll also be a mother. Of course you took her side. How could you not?" He picked up his toothpick and pointed it in her direction. "You guys play for the same team. And it only makes sense that you'd project the angst about your own crumbling marriage onto the situation you saw shaping up between Mom and Dad."

McKenzie opened her mouth, wanting to argue against his logic. When she couldn't, she snagged the second olive from his toothpick and ate it. Liam frowned momentarily in the wake of her theft and then went on.

"Then it turned out that Dad was not, in fact, cheating on Mom. The climax of the marital crisis that had been brewing between them since Dad lost his job didn't destroy their relationship. If anything, it made their love stronger," he said, looking across the room toward their parents, who were talking to John and Nancy. Rick had his hand on Hope's back and kept moving it up and down, as if he couldn't stop himself from touching her.

"Which was great for Mom and Dad but not so terrific for you. Not only did you lose your husband; you lost first position in Dad's affections. The princess usurped by the queen."

"I wasn't ever first," she said softly, knowing it was true. "I just wanted to be."

McKenzie took the last olive, dipped the end of it into Liam's glass, then put it into her mouth. Liam moved the martini glass toward her, signaling that she could have a sip if she wanted, but McKenzie shook her head.

"Am I really that terrible?" she asked.

"Kenz," Liam said, "we're all that terrible."

Were they? The fact that it might be true shouldn't make her feel better; she knew that. But she couldn't help it. She was so tired of feeling like the only one.

"I love you, Liam."

"Love you too, Kenz."

"But," she said with a sigh, shaking her head as she stared at the scrap of red and green silk around his neck, "I really, really, *really* hate that tie."

So, there it was. Everybody saw through her. Including her mother.

Even though McKenzie had tried as hard as she could to be brave and not let her troubles spoil Christmas for the rest of the family, she knew that her mother knew that she was sad, and depressed, and fat, and ugly, and abandoned, and jealous of everyone who wasn't as alone as she was and probably always would be.

Liam was incredibly insightful, especially for someone his age. But even he had failed to notice that behind the smile that could have lit up Burbank, their mother was worried about her daughter's happiness, racking her brain for something she could do or say to cheer her up.

That was the real impetus behind Hope's sudden urge to throw a baby shower in January, months before the baby would arrive. No matter how grown-up your kids were, no matter how illogical the timing, the compulsive maternal desire to kiss the boo-boos, wipe the tears, and erase the pain never faded. McKenzie knew this because, if it had been her daughter, she'd have felt the same way.

Maybe she and her mom *were* on the same side.

Chapter 29

When Hope tossed out the idea of a baby shower, McKenzie initially said no.

For one thing, it was too soon. Most expectant mothers didn't have showers until the final month or two of the pregnancy. Also, with several pressing projects at work and the upcoming move into a new apartment, not to mention ongoing, stressful, and quite expensive consultations with her divorce lawyer, she was just too busy. But more than anything else, she just wasn't in the mood for a party.

Of course she wanted to have a baby. She'd wanted it so much that she'd gone through with the wedding against her better instincts and foolishly turned a blind eye to Zach's long hours and late nights at the office, because he said it was all about him getting promoted and making enough money so they could buy a house and start a family.

Now she was getting her wish. But not the way she'd thought she would.

The idea of raising a child alone was still overwhelming to her. It was Zach's baby too, but given the way he'd displayed his trustworthiness, or lack thereof, McKenzie wasn't going to count on him. Thank heaven her folks were in the picture. In spite of the circumstances, they were totally excited about the baby.

McKenzie was sure she would be too. Soon. But not yet. For all these reasons, she gave her mother's baby shower proposal a big thumbs-down. Maybe later, but not now, she told her mother. Not when she was so far from her due date. And so depressed. McKenzie didn't mention this last part, but she didn't have to. Hope already knew.

Which probably explained why she just wouldn't let it go. Hope wheedled and whined, lobbed arguments and counterarguments, played the guilt card and devil's advocate. Finally, McKenzie caved. But only after issuing her caveat.

"All right, already! Fine! You can throw a baby shower. But you have to promise to keep it simple, okay? Cake, a few presents, a few people. Nothing crazy. Seriously, Mom. I just don't have the energy for more."

"Absolutely," she said, nodding her assent. "Just a nice little party to celebrate you and the baby. Nothing over the top." She held her hand out flat, as if taking an oath. "Promise," she said.

She totally lied.

Going behind McKenzie's back, she had called Zinnia, McKenzie's best friend from work, and gotten her to expand the number of office invitees from six to twelve. Hazel, Kate, and Nancy came, as well as Wanda, Zach's mother, who drove down from Bellingham and brought a huge basket full of baby gifts, everything from towels and toys to bottles and bibs. It was a little awkward, having Wanda there, but she seemed so happy to have been invited and McKenzie was glad she came. In addition, Hope invited every other female resident of the condo, so there were about twenty-four women in attendance. McKenzie's dad was there as well, to serve beverages and help out in the kitchen.

The decorations were beautiful and, yes, totally over the top. Why had McKenzie even gone through the motions of asking her to tone it down? And why had Hope pretended she could? It was like dangling a freshly caught fish in front of a cat and then asking her not to eat it, a futile request.

Even so, McKenzie couldn't help but smile when she opened the door and saw dozens upon dozens of yellow balloons bobbing near the ceiling, each wrapped with a square of gauzy, transparent tulle with a pattern of tiny silver stars and tied with yellow ribbons.

Since McKenzie had only just found out she was having a girl, Hope had kept the color scheme a gender-neutral yellow and white. The effect was fun and feminine without being fussy, and, when the sunlight streaming through the windows glinted against the starry tulle, kind of magical. The table decorations were just as fabulous. Each of the four tables was covered with a snowy white cloth overlaid with a topper of cheery yellow gingham and matching gingham napkins. Hope had sewn the toppers and napkins herself and made the fishbowl centerpieces. Each fishbowl, filled halfway with brilliant blue water, had a bright yellow rubber ducky bobbing inside.

"What could be simpler than a bowl of water with a plastic duck floating in it?" Hope said with an innocent smile when McKenzie accused her of violating their agreement regarding simplicity.

When it came to the food, Hope actually had kept it simple. At least according to Hope's standards.

Upon arriving, guests were offered appetizers, pretty much a repeat of those she'd served at Christmas, and cups of fizzy punch with lemon sherbet. The actual meal consisted of a "simple" salad bar.

After choosing between lettuce, spinach, kale, arugula, or some combination of the four, guests could top their greens with carrots, peppers, onions, radishes, and heirloom tomatoes, pickled beets, corn, and okra, artichokes and avocados, two colors of cabbage, and four varieties of cheese, as well as grilled chicken, shrimp, or steak, sunflower seeds or croutons. There was salad dressing too, five different kinds, and Rick's homemade sesame breadsticks.

It was the most extensive and impressive salad bar any of the guests had ever seen. Everybody oohed as they went through the line, choosing their favorites. But most impressive was the way Hope displayed the food. Each item on the buffet came in its own appropriately sized glass jar. Each jar was wrapped with a wide yellow ribbon, overlaid with a thinner white and yellow polka-dot ribbon, and had a small wooden chalkboard on the front, announcing the contents of the jar in yellow chalk and Hope's elegant script.

It all looked so pretty and fresh and, in its way, simple.

Then there was the dessert. Which was anything but.

McKenzie couldn't get on Hope's case about *that*. The dessert was all Rick's doing.

"Well, Kenz? What do you say? Do you like it?" Rick asked, crossing his arms as she admired the cake, all four tiers of it, iced with alternating layers of yellow and white, the edge of each decorated with a row of cheery marzipan duckies.

"Oh, Daddy. It's just . . . I don't even know what to say. It's stunning."

"Whew!" Rick replied, grinning and wiping imaginary beads of sweat from his brow. "That's a relief. If you knew how many episodes of *Cake Wars* I've watched since you moved into your new apartment, trying to get this right."

"Too many," Hope injected. "Then there were all the trial runs. He baked three prototypes before this one. Just when I was finally able to fit into my jeans. I don't think I'll eat another slice of cake for as long as I live."

Rick raised his brows. "No? Not even if it was lemon poppy seed cake? With raspberry filling?"

"Well . . . Maybe," Hope said. "Just a little piece. I mean, we're only having salad for lunch, right?"

"That's my girl," he said, pulling his wife close and kissing her full on the lips.

McKenzie stood there, watching them kiss, waiting to feel the usual twinge of jealousy and accompanying dose of self-pity. It didn't come. Instead, she felt happy for her parents and for herself.

Nobody's life is perfect, but it suddenly occurred to McKenzie that hers was way better than most and that she was very lucky.

"I love it. The cake, the food, the decorations. Just everything. Thanks so much. This is amazing. You *shouldn't* have done it," McKenzie said, her tone just slightly scolding. "But I can't say that I'm sorry you did." She looked down toward her swelling waistline, feeling that skittering bubbling sensation in her middle that signaled the baby's movement and, she felt, her approval. "I can't say that *we're* sorry you did. It's going to be a great party, guys. The best ever."

It was. Everyone had a wonderful time, McKenzie most of all.

But it wasn't about the decorations, the gifts, the food, or even her father's spectacular cake. It was about how all of it made her feel: loved, special, cherished, and anything but alone.

The mountain of gifts—blankets, bottles, and bibs and tiny, impossibly adorable sets of footie pajamas and sweaters and hats, a diaper bag from Kate, as well as a really sweet watercolor of a baby lamb resting in a field of flowers that she'd painted herself, a blue sling carrier from Nancy, a car seat from her aunt, the huge basket of gifts from Wanda, and the world's most beautiful vintage white wicker baby carriage from her parents, refurbished into perfect working order by Rick and fitted out with a yellow gingham carriage pad and tiny quilt sewn by her mother—sparked her imagination, got her to think about how a sweet baby, *her* baby, would look wearing those clothes, using those gifts, sleeping peacefully and soundly as McKenzie wheeled her down a tree-lined street or the quiet paths of a pretty park.

For the first time since seeing that blue line on the drugstore pregnancy test, just two days after coming to grips with the truth of Zach's infidelity, McKenzie felt fully awake, alive, and optimistic about her future, overjoyed at the prospect of impending motherhood, and bristling with impatience to meet her baby.

Hope's plan worked. For the first time in a long time, McKenzie was happy and very, very excited.

When the party was over and McKenzie was leaving for her new apartment, she kissed Hope and Rick in turn, saying, "How did I ever get lucky enough to score you two as my parents? It sure wasn't anything I did."

"Oh, stop," Hope said, giving McKenzie another squeeze. "You're a good person and a wonderful daughter."

"The best," Rick said.

"Well, we all know *that's* not true. But thanks for saying it anyway. And thanks for . . . Well, for everything. Not just the party." McKenzie rubbed her palm over her belly. "Until today, I was feeling scared, like it was all on my shoulders, worried I'd make a mess of everything. But now I feel like maybe I've got this."

"You do," Hope affirmed. "You're going to be a terrific mom. And if you ever need help, we're just up the street."

"Yeah," McKenzie said, relief apparent in her sigh. "How lucky was I to find a perfect apartment less than five minutes from here? And how lucky will this baby be to have her own personal daycare just up the street, right? It's going to make everything *so* much easier. Well, good night, guys. Thanks again."

"You're welcome," Rick replied. "Hey, I'll bring the rest of the presents over to your place tomorrow morning. Ten o'clock, okay?"

"Sounds good," McKenzie said. "That'll give me time to sleep off the sugar high from all that cake I ate."

Rick laughed. McKenzie joined in, then gave them each one more hug for good measure and headed down the hall toward the elevator, so blissfully happy that she didn't even notice the strange and somewhat stunned expression on her mother's face, as if she'd just been caught totally off guard.

Chapter 30

"That. Is. Beautiful," Debby Harper said, enunciating each word as she leaned over Mandy's shoulder.

After much sewing and ripping and resewing, Mandy had completed eight of her Dove in the Window blocks. But until that morning, she hadn't been feeling that great about the quilt.

Hope kept telling her to quit worrying, assured her that the finished quilt would be just as pretty as the one she'd seen in the pattern book and even prettier because Mandy had picked prettier fabric.

Mandy was less convinced.

The blocks were okay. She'd sewn them exactly according to the instructions. They were all the correct size and almost perfectly square. But Mandy just couldn't see how it was all going to come together. Each block was fine on its own, but when she tried to picture them joined in one big quilt it just seemed like there was so much going on. Maybe too much?

The fabrics *were* beautiful—a rich range of purple, blue, and gray. But maybe it had been a mistake to use so many different fabrics? Maybe she should have used fewer fabrics. Or fewer colors?

There were only about two months remaining until Mandy's release. Time was running short. She didn't want to spend what was left of it sewing block after block after block, only to put them together and realize that Talia's quilt was a big mishmash of colors and patterns. Mandy wanted this quilt to be perfect, something Talia would be proud to have on her bed so that someday, when they had their own place and Talia invited friends over, she would point to it and say, "Isn't it cool? My mom made it."

Hope said it saved time to finish all the blocks before putting them together, but finally, probably sick of listening to Mandy's worrying, she gave Mandy permission to stitch her finished blocks together. Mandy was so glad.

Her quilt was weeks away from being finished, but as soon as she joined those eight blocks Mandy could see the pattern emerge. She could see other patterns too, smaller, more subtle, and sometimes surprising secondary patterns that suddenly seemed to appear out of nowhere, pulling her vision in different directions and new discoveries, drawing her eyes into a maze of pattern, shape, and color.

And the colors! Oh, the colors were perfect! Her teacher had been right all along; she'd had no cause for worry. In spite of the range and variety—chambray, lilac, opal, berry, teal, deep gray, periwinkle—every color she'd chosen enriched and balanced the others, adding depth and harmony to the design. Her concerns about the patterns were likewise unfounded.

When Hope had brought in a huge bag of donated fabrics, saying she could pick anything she wanted for her quilt, Mandy had been immediately drawn to this particular collection, partly because it included that one incredible purple fabric, as deep and rich as the skin of the eggplants that had grown in her mother's vegetable garden when she was little. Purple was Talia's favorite color, lavender her second favorite. But when she took a closer look, it was the patterns printed on the fabrics that really caught her eye.

There was a vaguely industrial feel to them. One of them was actually printed with little gears and wheels. Another had a design of scallops edged with rows of pie-shaped spikes that reminded her of fencing. And another soft gray piece of material had a pattern that looked like a jumbled tangle of barbed wire.

But other fabrics in the collection were decidedly softer, sporting flowers, vines, polka dots, and clouds.

The imagery of those designs spoke to Mandy. They seemed like a perfect reflection of the tension she felt at this moment, still surrounded by fences and wire but teetering on the threshold of life beyond these walls, a land of open skies and flowering fields.

But this quilt wasn't for her. It was for Talia. Maybe she ought to choose fabrics that were younger and more girly. There was another purple fabric in the bag, printed with pictures of Disney princesses. Maybe Talia would prefer something like that?

"Not for long," Hope advised her. "She'll outgrow it in a year or two. The other collection will appeal to her for a lifetime. The colors are just beautiful, but the patterns are subtle. That's one of the things I love about using batik fabrics; those tone-on-tone prints influence overall impact of the quilt without overpowering the design. And I think it's good that the fabrics are speaking to where you are right now.

"Yes, it's going to be Talia's quilt, but it will also be yours. Even when given as a gift, a quilt should convey something meaningful about the maker. The piece of yourself that you put into a quilt is what makes it special. Years from now, this quilt will help remind you, and Talia, about how far you've come. It also might give you a way to talk to her about the journey."

Mandy was glad she'd listened to Hope's advice. As soon as she'd finished stitching her first few blocks together and could envision the finished quilt, Mandy knew she'd made the right choice. It was going to be beautiful. Talia would love it. Mandy already did.

Deedee had caught a bug and wasn't in class that day. Eager to show her handiwork to her sick friend, Mandy asked if she could take her partially finished quilt down to the infirmary so Deedee could see it. Normally, their quilting supplies were kept in the locked cabinet between classes, but since Mandy was just talking about fabric, nothing sharp or potentially dangerous, Hope said she could.

Mandy had gone from class directly to the cafeteria, intending to visit Deedee in the infirmary right after lunch. But then Bonnie Glazier caught sight of the folded-up fabric and asked to see the quilt. Mandy obliged, spreading the partially completed quilt out on the cafeteria table. Within moments, they were surrounded by other inmates, all of them oohing and aahing over Mandy's creation in progress.

"Can I touch it?" Debby Harper asked. When Mandy nodded, she leaned in and brushed her fingers across the blocks. "It's so soft. And I love the colors."

"It's for my little girl," Mandy replied. "Purple is her favorite."

"Mine too," Bonnie said. "Geez. This must have taken you forever."

"Not forever. But yeah, I had to put some time into it. This first block—" Recalling her frustration, Mandy let out a puff of disgust. "I ripped it out twice before I got it right, spent the whole class making just that one block. Really, I felt like tossing the whole thing at that point. But it got a lot easier after the first one. Once you understand how the block goes together, it's not that hard."

"For you maybe." Bonnie shook her head. "I could never make something like that."

"That's what I thought at first too," Mandy said. "But you just have to take it one step at a time. If you break it down like that instead of worrying about the whole thing, it's not so overwhelming. You could do it."

"Oh, please," Bonnie said, rolling her eyes. "I'm the least crafty person on the planet. I can't even sew on a button."

"What difference does that make?" Mandy countered. "When we started, about half the people in the program would have said the same thing. Now they're all making quilts. Deedee didn't even know how to thread a needle when she started."

"Oh, well . . . Deedee." Bonnie spread her hands, as if to indicate that Deedee's ineptitude shouldn't have surprised anybody.

"Hey. Don't start dissing Deedee," Mandy cautioned. "She's my friend."

"I wasn't dissing anybody. I'm just saying, stuff like this comes easier to some people. But I'm not one of them."

"Have you ever tried?" Mandy asked. Bonnie shook her head. "Then how do you know? I mean, look at Deedee. Who knew she could sing like that? Nobody. Not until she opened her mouth. People have all kinds of hidden talents."

"Yeah? Well, mine must be *really* hidden."

Bonnie's comment brought a murmur of laughter from the growing knot of women who had surrounded the table to check out Mandy's quilt and listen in on the conversation. Bonnie looked up, seemingly startled by the noise and the size of the crowd. Grinning, she delivered her next line in a louder and more expressive tone, playing to the gallery.

"I mean they are deep, *deep* down. Down where ain't nobody gonna find them."

The audience laughed again, even more appreciatively, quite a few of the women nodding their agreement. But Debby Harper, who had been listening carefully to the exchange, even as her eyes remained glued to Mandy's quilt, didn't so much as crack a smile. Instead, she looked at Mandy and said, "You really think I could learn to make something like this?"

"Definitely. If you're willing to put in the effort, you can learn to do just about anything. Of course," she said, thinking about her struggles with advanced algebra, "having a good teacher helps. Hope is fantastic. You should put your name down on the waiting list for the quilting class."

"Really? Do you think I could get in?"

"Sure. I mean, there's no extra space right now, but the pilot program is going so well that I bet they'll expand it. Shouldn't be a problem, as long as your behavior record is clean."

"You mean, shouldn't be a problem as long as you're willing to suck up to Hopeless Carpenter."

Mandy looked up, twisting to the right, searching the edge of the crowd. Nita elbowed her way through the cluster of women until she was standing next to Mandy, Debby, and Bonnie.

"It's a stupid program," she said, turning her back to the others and addressing Debby. "All of those craft classes are stupid.

Even if you didn't have to kiss Hopeless's ass to get in, become one of her little pets, it's boring. Total waste of time. That's why I dropped out of the crafting class."

"You didn't drop out," Mandy said. "You were kicked out."

Nita turned to face her.

"First off, you're full of it. I dropped out because the class was boring. Second, I wasn't talking to you." Nita uttered an expletive and followed it up by placing her hand on Mandy's shoulder and giving her a shove, not enough to knock her off balance but enough to make her challenge clear.

With this many women living in close quarters, many of whom had ended up there precisely because of their poor self-control and all of them with too much time on their hands, fights sometimes broke out among the inmates, but not that often. The quickest way to lose your privileges, or even get sent to medium security, was to get caught fighting.

Still, losing your privileges was one thing. Losing the respect of the other inmates was something else again. In the minds of many, failure to respond to a challenge made you a soft target, someone to be looked down on, someone to pick on when people were bored or feeling bad about themselves.

With such a short time left in her sentence, the risk was far greater for Mandy than for Nita. In addition to privileges, Mandy could also lose some of her "good time," days that had been subtracted from her sentence for good behavior, delaying her reunion for weeks or even months.

Nita made a sucking sound with her teeth, then crossed her arms over her chest, staring at Mandy. The rest of the inmates stood, silent and immobile as mannequins, waiting to see what would happen. There was, after all, no punishment for witnessing a fight, not if it just happened to break out in front of you. Besides, they were overdue for a good one.

Mandy unclenched her fist and got up from her chair. Nita took a step toward her, purposely invading her space, but Mandy stepped aside, pulling her quilt off the table before pushing her way through the crowd.

"Hey! Did you hear me?" Nita taunted, raising her voice. "I *said* I wasn't talking to you."

"Yeah, I heard you. Fine with me. I wasn't talking to you either."

On a normal day, one of the guards would already have stepped in and said, or done, or threatened something to help diffuse the situation. But the same flu bug that had sent Deedee to the infirmary had also made its rounds among the guards. The prison was short staffed, which meant the remaining healthy guards were walking the hallways and common areas rather than staying put in one spot.

Mandy kept her eyes in front of her and her progress steady but purposely unhurried. She couldn't afford to look like she was running away. Otherwise, every Nita clone in the unit would start coming after her. She had to appear tough and strong, not like she was backing down from a fight but like she couldn't be bothered to fight because Nita was simply beneath her notice.

It seemed to be working. Somebody in the crowd chuckled in response to Mandy's comment—she thought it might be Debby. Then a couple more people joined in. The laughter was light, but it was directed toward Nita, not her. Mandy found herself smiling. She shoved her hands in her pockets, slowed her pace even more, ambling instead of walking, and started to whistle.

That was a mistake.

With Mandy less than twenty feet from the door, Nita pushed through the knot of bodies, following in Mandy's wake, lengthening her step with every stride to close the distance between them and shouting.

"Did you hear me? Hey! You better turn around and listen because I'm talking to you. Did you hear me? I'm talking to you!"

Mandy continued on her path, eyes still to the front, but took her hands from her pockets and clenched them into fists, readying herself for the blow that seemed all but inevitable.

Nita's shouting was growing louder and more insistent. Mandy could tell she was getting close, was practically on her heels. Mandy stopped, ready to turn around and make a stand, but before she could do so, Nita lunged forward, shoving Mandy so forcefully that she stumbled and very nearly fell.

"Hey!"

The shout was louder than Nita's and more reverberating, the shout of a man, an angry one. Regaining her balance, Mandy looked across the cafeteria and saw Superintendent Hernandez coming through the door opposite, eyes blazing, arms pumping like pistons as he strode across the room. The crowd of women parted before him, then hung back to watch, their faces bright with anticipation. They'd been cheated out of their fight, but being able to see the superintendent rip into the failed combatants was almost as good.

"What's going on here?" He came to an abrupt stop in front of them, looked from one face to another. "Nita? What did you push her for?"

Having been forced into close proximity for several years, Mandy knew that Nita was a practiced and very accomplished liar. Still, it was sort of impressive to see her in action. Mandy could tell a lie if she had to and thought she was pretty convincing. But Nita? Nita was in a class by herself.

She didn't flinch in the face of Hernandez's ire, didn't bite her lip, or shift her eyes, or blink, or do one single thing to tip her hand. Nita would have been an excellent poker player. Instead, she looked at Hernandez with an expression of very slight confusion, nothing too overblown, obvious, or innocent. She paused for a moment, as if it took her a second to figure out what was bothering him.

"I didn't. Everybody was hanging out, talking, and then Mandy got up to go, but she forgot her quilt. So I grabbed it and ran after her. I didn't shove her. I just tapped her on the shoulder, trying to get her attention."

"If you just tapped her, why did she trip?"

"Dunno." Nita shrugged, as if it were really none of her concern and he'd be better off asking Mandy. He did.

"Mandy?"

She lifted her brows, attempting to appear somewhat but not

overly surprised to hear him speak her name, mimicking Nita's manner. This was one of those moments, the moment when you had to lie.

"Why did you trip?"

"Like she said, I didn't hear her coming. I was thinking about my algebra test next week. She tapped me on the shoulder and it startled me, so I tripped."

Hernandez stared at Mandy long and hard, waiting for her to crack. She didn't. Finally, he relaxed his stance, gave his head a slight shake, and said, "Okay."

Nita turned around and walked back toward the tables. He watched her the whole way, as if he wanted to make sure she felt his gaze so she would know he had his eye on her and always would. When Nita took her seat, he turned toward Mandy.

"You on your way somewhere?" he asked.

"Well, I was just—"

"Walk with me."

They were halfway to the end of the corridor before he broke the silence. Mandy figured he was trying to do the same thing he'd done with Nita, use the power of his presence to send the message: Nothing got by him.

"Nice work," he said at last, glancing toward Mandy's partially finished quilt.

"Thanks."

"What's it doing out of Mrs. Carpenter's classroom?"

"Deedee's sick and I wanted to show it to her, so I asked Mrs. C. if I could bring it down to the infirmary and she said I could."

"She did?"

The tenor of his question and the abrupt way he'd asked it made Mandy wish she could take it back. She should have lied, told him she'd slipped it out of the classroom when Mrs. C. wasn't looking. If somebody was going to get in trouble, Mandy would rather it was her.

"I shouldn't have brought it to the cafeteria," she said, trying to deflect the blame back onto herself. "That was stupid."

"Yes. It was."

Hernandez halted his steps and turned toward her. His eyes were still angry, but there was something else in them too. Mandy felt like she'd disappointed him and it embarrassed her.

"Mandy, I remember when you first got here. I remember how scared you were. I wasn't sure you were going to make it. I wasn't sure you wanted to."

He was right. She hadn't wanted to make it. What she'd wanted was to die. Well, maybe not die exactly. What she really wanted was just to disappear, quit being, quit hurting, quit making mistakes that made other people suffer—her mother, Talia.

The chaplain convinced her it was possible. Not that she could erase her mistakes; what was done was done. But she could quit making new ones, make something of herself and her life, and make a future for Talia.

"You've done an amazing job of turning yourself around," Hernandez continued. "You kicked your habit, got an education, and maintained a relationship with your little girl. You also kept your head down, didn't attract attention to yourself, didn't make enemies. That's half the battle around here, Mandy. And you know that.

"What were you thinking, bringing this in there?" he asked, grabbing the quilt, fisting the fabric, and then shaking it in her face. "It doesn't take much to make people jealous around here. You know that. So why would you start showing off about things you get to do that others don't? Especially in front of somebody like Nita? She's the type who doesn't care how far she falls or how hard, as long as she brings somebody else down with her."

Hernandez shoved the quilt back in Mandy's direction, shaking his head. Some of the perfectly pressed quilt blocks showed wrinkles and creases where he'd crushed the fabric in his fist. She quickly rolled up the quilt and tucked it under her arm.

"You're right," she said, hanging her head as she realized exactly how right. "Sorry. It was a stupid thing to do. I wasn't thinking."

"Well, *start* thinking. You're so close to release, Mandy. Don't do anything to jeopardize that. From here on out, your only job is to steer clear of trouble. Understand?"

She looked up at him. "Mr. Hernandez? Don't be mad at Mrs. C. This was my fault, not hers. She didn't know—"

"Maybe not, but she *should* know. In here, not knowing can be dangerous. But don't worry about Mrs. Carpenter. She's my problem. You just worry about you, okay? Worry about walking through that gate and back to your family."

"Yes, sir. Got it."

Chapter 31

"Do you know he didn't even offer me a chair? The man called me to the carpet and then literally left me standing there on the carpet!"

Hope lifted her wineglass and tossed back another swallow, then shifted her phone to the other ear.

"He just sat there behind his desk, chewing me out like some kind of wayward sophomore he'd caught skipping out of third period. The nerve. It's January; has he already forgotten that we had him over for Christmas dinner? The man was our guest—"

"He's also your boss," Hazel said. "One doesn't preclude the other. If you thought it did then maybe you shouldn't have invited him."

"I was trying to be *nice*," Hope countered.

"Good. Then keep being nice and admit you were wrong. You knew you weren't supposed to let students remove anything from the classroom. You said so yourself when we presented the program to him; you promised to keep everything under lock and key between classes."

"Well, sure," Hope said before taking another sip from her glass. "Scissors and pins and rotary cutters—anything that could be potentially dangerous. This was just a little bit of patchwork. Not exactly hazardous."

"But it sounds like it could have been," Hazel said, "if David hadn't shown up when he did. Look, whether you like it or not, everybody has a boss. And whether you like *him* or not, David is yours. He might be younger than you, but he knows more about running a prison than you do. So stop being defensive, learn from your mistake, and move on."

"Hey, just because he's your boyfriend doesn't mean you have to take his side all the time. I'm your sister. I was here first."

"Okay, first, David isn't my boyfriend."

"No?" Hope asked, refilling her glass. "Why not? Sure looked like he was at the Christmas party."

"Well, for beginners, David has a job in Olympia and I own a business in Portland. I've done the long-distance thing before, too many times. It never works."

"Sure it does. If you want it badly enough, you make it work."

"Would you make up your mind?" Hazel said. "One minute you can't stand him; the next minute you're saying I should upend my entire life for him."

"Good point," Hope said. "I revert to my earlier position; I can't stand him. He's too rigid and all wrong for you. Unless . . ." Hope paused to take another drink. "Unless he has hidden qualities that I don't appreciate and you're crazy about him and he makes you really happy. If *that's* the case, then make it work."

Hazel laughed. "Wow. You're just a hot mess tonight, aren't you? How much wine have you had?"

Hope glanced at the half-empty bottle on the counter. "Too much. It's been a rough week."

"So? Tell me what happened. Because I know this is about more than David chewing you out."

Hope told her what had happened at the end of the baby shower, after Hazel and the rest of the guests had departed, explaining how McKenzie had dropped the bombshell about her expectation that Hope would be providing full-time childcare after the baby was born.

"What?" Hazel gasped. "Why would she think that? She just expects you to quit your job to become a full-time babysitter?"

"Apparently."

Hazel's laugh was incredulous. "Well, that's interesting. What did she say when you told her it wasn't happening?"

Hope was silent.

"Oh, Hope. Come on. You're not really thinking about doing it. Are you?"

"I don't know. Maybe. I mean, it's my grandchild. I haven't even met this baby and already I'm in love. Of course I want to help take care of the baby; I'm looking forward to it. What grandmother wouldn't? When Mom was dying, at the end, do you know what she said to me?"

"No. What?"

"Of all the things she regretted leaving behind, the biggest was the chance to meet her grandchildren. Mom never had that chance. But I do!" she said urgently. "I can be part of my granddaughter's life!"

"Yes, of course. But you shouldn't have to quit a job you love to do it. This is McKenzie's baby, not yours. She needs to raise it, just like you raised your children."

"For the first time in our lives, McKenzie and I are really connecting the way I always hoped we would. I don't want to lose that. Besides, McKenzie needs me. I have Rick, but McKenzie's all alone."

"And your students at the prison? They don't need you?"

Once again, Hope was silent. She rubbed her hand over her forehead, then pinched the bridge of her nose where a headache was coming on. She was so tired. She'd felt like that ever since Christmas. Maybe she should have given herself a little time to recover from the holidays before organizing the baby shower. Was she getting old? If she couldn't even manage to throw a party without feeling exhausted, how could she possibly find the energy to take care of a baby?

"What does Rick say about it?"

"Just that it was good the timing worked out so I'd be able to get the first group of quilters through the pilot program before the baby came."

"So he just assumes you're going to walk away from all your students and the program you created, and not only created but practically went begging door-to-door to get funded?"

"Hazel," Hope said, speaking in a purposely calm and modulated voice, hoping her sister would follow suit.

"No! Uh-uh. After all you've been through, the way you've supported him? This just *really* ticks me off. Hey, I've got an idea. Why doesn't Rick stay home and take care of the baby? Now that he's retired from both engineering *and* golf, he's got time on his hands."

"Don't," Hope said. "Seriously, Hazel. Don't go blaming Rick. None of this is his fault. If I asked, he would take care of the baby. I know he would. But I don't want him to. I didn't say anything yet because he asked me not to tell anybody, not until he's sure."

"Sure of what?"

"Well, don't tell him I told you, but you know he started volunteering at that housing charity, Many Hands, right? Once he fixed absolutely everything that could possibly be fixed at Kate's house, he needed something to fill his time. Anyway, somebody on the staff saw that he really knew what he was doing, then found out he's an engineer. Now it looks like they might offer him a job as the project coordinator. It would only be half-time, at least to start with, and the pay would obviously be a lot less than he used to make. But he's really excited about it."

"Well, that's great," Hazel said, her tone softening slightly. "I hope it works out."

"So do I. He's so much better than he was, but even so, he needs this."

"Okay, but what about your needs? Doesn't that count for anything? I mean, you've already walked away from your career to raise your kids. Why does—"

"No, I didn't," Hope said, interrupting her sister and then shushing her when Hazel began to argue. "Hazel, I didn't walk away from my career to raise a family because raising a family *was* my career. It was the career I wanted more than any other. And I was really, really good at it."

"Yes, you were," Hazel said. "But you did the job, Hope. Mission accomplished. Now you've got a second career that you're also really, really good at. Something you love.

"Unless, of course, I'm wrong about that. Unless the women—Mandy, and Deedee, and Steph, and all the others you're always talking about—don't mean as much as I thought they did."

"Don't be stupid," Hope snapped, and slurped at her wine. "And don't try to play mind games with me, Hazel. I love my job, and my students. I don't want to walk away from them. They need me."

"So doesn't it make you mad that McKenzie just assumes that you'll quit?"

"Yes!"

"Then why don't you *tell* her that? Tell McKenzie that you don't want to be her babysitter?"

"Because I do!" Hope shouted. "Don't you get it, Hazel? I *want* to take care of my grandchild. I can't wait to hold that little bundle in my arms. And I want to take care of McKenzie too. I want to be there for her, to support her as she undertakes the most difficult and important job of her life, the way I wish our mother could have been there for me. I want to take care of Rick. And my boys. And my students. And you. I want to take care of everybody!"

"But, Hope . . . you can't. Nobody can."

"I know!" Hope shouted again, this time putting the phone in front of her mouth, making absolutely sure she was heard. "That's why I'm so mad!"

Hope pinched the bridge of her nose again. Her headache was getting worse. Much worse.

"So?" Hazel asked after a moment's pause. "What are you going to do?"

Hope sighed. "I don't know. McKenzie and I are getting together on Saturday. She wants me to help her pick out a crib. Hopefully, I'll figure it out before then. Or be kidnapped by aliens. Or drafted. Does the military accept nearsighted women in their fifties?"

"Wow," Hazel said after a long pause. "You really are a mess."

"Tell me something I don't know," Hope said, and emptied her glass.

After visiting several furniture and department stores and finding that prices for new cribs far outstretched McKenzie's budget, Hope suggested they check out consignment shops. At the second one, they found an inexpensive crib and changing table that were nearly identical to models that McKenzie had liked at the department store.

The only problem was, both pieces had a dark cherry stain. McKenzie had her heart set on doing up the nursery with white furnishings and light gray walls, with coral and yellow fabrics for the quilt and curtains. Once Hope assured her that they could paint over the stain, McKenzie bought the crib, asking the shop owner to hold the furniture until Monday, when Rick would come with his truck to pick it up.

After four hours of shopping, McKenzie was hungry, so they walked over to a storefront café not far from the consignment store. Peering through the window, Hope saw ten tables, all empty, and hesitated before going inside. In her experience, empty tables were often the sign of a bad chef. But there weren't any restaurants nearby, and as McKenzie said, "Burgers are burgers. Besides, I'm starving," so Hope let it go and they went inside. Later, she wished she'd listened to her instincts.

The atmosphere was casual, more diner than restaurant, with only one waitress on duty who took orders at the counter, then delivered food to the table. Hope ordered a BLT, sweet potato fries, and an iced tea. McKenzie ordered a double cheeseburger, large fries, strawberry milk shake, side salad with extra Thousand Island dressing, and took a menu to the table so she could decide on dessert later.

After they had placed their orders and sat down, Hope grinned at McKenzie. "You should have just ordered the whole left side of the menu. It would have saved time."

"Oh, I thought about it. Believe me."

McKenzie pulled a sleeve of crackers out of her purse, tore open the package, and shoved a saltine into her mouth. Hope gave her a curious look.

"You're still getting morning sickness? Maybe you should mention that to the doctor. It's usually over by the second trimester."

"Not sick," she mumbled, her mouth full. "Starving. These are my emergency crackers. I never leave home without them. Were you this hungry when you were pregnant? Last week, I went to buy groceries and ended up eating half of a rotisserie chicken, an apple, and a package of cookies before I even got home. And it was ten o'clock in the morning."

"Maybe not quite that hungry," Hope said, sipping iced tea through a straw. "But once, when I was pregnant with the twins, I decided to make your dad a cake for his birthday. You know, as a surprise. By the time he got home from work, there was one slice left."

McKenzie grinned and stuffed another cracker in her mouth. "Good. I'm glad I'm not the only one."

"I gained forty-five pounds when I was pregnant with you."

McKenzie's eyes went wide. She chewed quickly and then swallowed, ridding her mouth of the crackers. "Forty-five pounds! Seriously?"

"Seriously. Remember, you were a pretty big baby. Seven pounds and four ounces, even though you were early."

"Well, I always did like making an entrance," McKenzie said, flipping a hank of hair over her shoulder and pretending to preen. "But forty-five pounds . . . How long did it take you to lose it?"

"Who says I did?" Hope said, then flapped her hand and laughed when she saw the stricken look on her daughter's face. "Honey, it was a joke. Actually, I'm down another five pounds. Since your father cut back on his baking, they keep melting away. If this keeps up, I'm going to have to take in some of my pants."

"Fine," McKenzie groused. "Rub it in, why don't you?"

"Honey. Stop. You're growing an entire human. Of course you're gaining a little weight. But don't worry; once the baby is born, you'll lose it in no time. Running after kids is amazing exercise. And you're planning on nursing, aren't you?"

"For as long as I can," McKenzie said. "Between maternity leave and my saved-up vacation days, I'll be able to stay home for two months after the baby is born. But once I go back to work, I don't know."

"The longer you can nurse, the better it'll be for the baby. And for you, best weight loss plan ever. Plus, you'll save a fortune on formula. Nursing is just a matter of planning ahead, even when you're working. What if Dad and I get you a pump for your birthday? A really good one?"

"Sure," McKenzie replied. "I mean, I did have my eye on this really gorgeous red handbag I saw at Nordstrom. But what girl would want a new purse when she could have a really sweet breast pump?" McKenzie broke out laughing and Hope joined in.

How nice this is, she thought to herself. *Cozy and close and absolutely right.*

Each of Hope's children was her favorite child. Collectively and individually, she loved them with every ounce of her breath and being. She didn't know another way, not when it came to her children.

And yet from the moment of McKenzie's birth, the love she had felt for her daughter, though equal to that which she felt for her sons, was somehow different.

Perhaps it had something to do with the circumstances of McKenzie's very dramatic entrance into the world.

Years later, Hope could still remember the terror that gripped her when she realized that they weren't going to make it to the hospital and Rick pulled the car over to the side of the road. She recalled the searing, unanesthetized pain that racked her body as she strained to bring forth her child and the heart-exploding ardor she felt for her strong, calm, heroic husband. Until that moment, she hadn't imagined she could love him more than she already did, and yet she had. And she remembered, too, the relief, exhaustion, and giddy joy she'd felt when, after she channeled every last drop of energy into that final, agonizing push, Rick looked up at her and cried out, "It's a girl!"

She had worried, during her pregnancy, that she would not be able to love this new baby as she had her twins. But the moment when Rick then wrapped the child, slick, wet, and squalling, in his sweater and laid her on Hope's chest was the moment she learned that love was a well with no bottom. She could draw again and again and again, and it would never run dry.

And the new baby was a girl. A girl!

She had dreamed of having a daughter, a child with whom she could relive and renew the intimacy and shared bond of womanhood she'd felt with her own mother, sharing food and laughter and inside jokes, stories and wisdom, passing the torch of all she had known and learned in life to the next generation.

And now, finally, after all these years, her dream had come true. And soon, a granddaughter.

No, the well never runs dry.

The waitress arrived, carrying a tray loaded with their lunch. Hope scooted her single plate as close to her side of the table as possible to make room for McKenzie's several. As soon as the waitress disappeared in the back, Hope shoveled half of her sweet potato fries onto McKenzie's plate.

"You sure?" McKenzie asked, her eyes lighting up at the sight of her mother's offering.

"You go ahead."

McKenzie was so focused on sating her hunger that several minutes ticked by before another word passed between them. When McKenzie's burger was gone and she slowed down somewhat, Hope took a sip of iced tea and cleared her throat.

"So, Kenz. Speaking of maternity leave and you going back to work, we should probably talk about childcare."

McKenzie lifted her hand, bringing the conversation to a halt until she could finish chewing. "I know," she said at last. "I was wanting to talk to you about that. After I got home from the baby shower, I realized that I made it sound like I was signing you up for free babysitting for the rest of your life. But I want you to know, I'm planning to pay you."

"Kenz," Hope said, shaking her head. "You don't need to do that."

"Yes, I do. It's only fair. And if you're worried that I won't be able to afford it, don't," she said, spearing a chunk of green pepper with her fork. "I just found out that I'm getting a promotion to department head and a pretty nice raise to go with it."

"Oh, McKenzie! That's wonderful. All your hard work is paying off. Good for you, sweetie. I'm proud of you."

McKenzie shrugged, but her smile signaled her satisfaction. "My supervisor said it had been in the works for a while, but I think they sped up the timeline because of the baby. A lot of people go on maternity leave and never come back.

"I never understood that before," she said, reaching down to rub the dome of her stomach, "but I do now. Crazy, isn't it? I haven't even laid eyes on this baby, but I already know how tough it will be to go back to work. Good thing I've got somebody who actually knows what she's doing to take care of her," McKenzie said, looking up with a grateful smile. "Really, Mom. Makes me feel so much better about everything."

The surge of love that Hope felt in her heart at that moment was accompanied by a smaller but palpable feeling of disappointment, the sensation of standing behind a door that was closing. But what else could she do?

"I'm glad, Kenz. Happy I can help."

McKenzie's grin and nodding response said that she was happy too.

"I mean, can you imagine what would happen if I had to raise this poor baby unsupervised?" she said, looking down at her stomach with affection and then laughing. "I'd probably drop her on her head or go into the store to buy milk and forget she was asleep in the car seat or something."

"No, you wouldn't," Hope protested.

McKenzie started eating again. "Well, maybe not *that*. But we both know I'd find some way to screw things up. Anyway," she said, washing down her fry with a slurp of strawberry milk shake, "I'm just glad this baby will have a *real* mother to look out for her, somebody who knows what she's doing."

A bell jingled as the door to the café opened. A man wearing a bomber jacket, Oakland A's baseball cap, and green tennis shoes with a weird faux alligator pattern walked up to the counter and grabbed a menu from a rack near the register. Hope glanced at him briefly, then leaned closer to McKenzie and lowered her voice so they wouldn't be overheard.

"McKenzie," she said, fixing her eyes on her daughter, "you know how thrilled I am to be a grandmother. And you know I'm going to support you in every way possible. But this baby can only have one mother, and that's you."

"No, no. I get that," McKenzie replied, speaking casually but failing to meet Hope's gaze. "But compared to you . . .

"I mean, you were an amazing mother, the best in the whole neighborhood, maybe in the whole world. Everybody thought so. My friends always used to say that I didn't know how lucky I was, having you for my mom." McKenzie touched her fingertips to her stomach, very lightly and cautiously, as if she were testing the heat of a candle flame. "Until now, I'm not sure I did.

"Let's face it," she said, finally looking up, cracking her lips into a stiff smile. "I couldn't even manage to keep a marriage together for more than two years. Just imagine the havoc I could cause in twenty years of parenting. Everybody knows how selfish I am. Zach was always telling me that and he was right."

Hope felt her jaw tighten. She wanted to remind McKenzie that Zach, having explored new depths of selfishness, was hardly one to speak. But remembering her personal promise not to get into the habit of speaking ill of her grandchild's father, she held her tongue.

She tried formulating a more diplomatic response but was distracted by the movements of the man in the bomber jacket. He'd been shifting his feet and sniffing ever since he came through the door. He was probably in a hurry and impatient for service, but for some reason Hope kept looking toward him. Something about him bothered her.

Now he smacked the bell on the counter. The waitress came out from the back. The man tugged his baseball cap lower on his head, shielding his eyes, and leaned across the counter.

"McKenzie—"

"You know it's true," she said, talking over her mother. "I'm selfish. But mothers can't be. That's why it'll be better if you can handle more of the mother thing. I'll be more like the dad. I'll pay the bills, start a college fund, that kind of thing. And then be around on weekends for the fun stuff—taking her to the park, or soccer games, or out for ice cream."

Hope wasn't listening. Her eyes were glued to the scene playing out at the register. At first, the waitress hadn't seemed to understand what the man was saying to her. When he leaned even closer, he said it again and grabbed her sleeve.

"McKenzie—" Hope said more urgently, reaching for her daughter's hand.

"Mom, I know. Okay? I know what you're going to say. But you don't—"

The waitress's eyes had gone wide and color drained from her face. She shook her head. When the man reached into his jacket pocket, the hair stood up on the back of Hope's neck.

The waitress let out a short, sharp cry. Hope saw fear in her eyes, a glint of steel from the man's pocket.

"McKenzie!" she shouted. "Kenz, get down!"

Hope kicked her chair backward and sprang across the table, pulling McKenzie to the floor amid a clatter of dishware and silver. She shoved McKenzie as hard as she could, pushing her under the table, then spread out her arms, making her body a shield between her daughter and unborn grandchild, and the man with the gun.

Chapter 32

It happened so fast that almost before McKenzie realized what was happening it was over. One minute she was eating French fries and minding her own business, and the next minute her mother was screaming and pulling her down and McKenzie was on the floor, covered in spilled strawberry milk shake, trying to figure out what was going on.

The gun was real and loaded, but Hope's shouts and the cacophony of clattering dishware had distracted the gunman. He turned momentarily toward the sound, and the waitress, thinking quickly or perhaps not at all, snatched a vase full of half-dead flowers from the counter, dashed the stale and stinking water into his face, and then smashed the vase over his head. Later, the police officers said that she'd been very lucky and should have just handed over the money.

They'd all been lucky. The man dropped the gun, grabbed his bleeding head, and fled on foot through the door. Alerted by the commotion, the café's chef-owner ran in from the kitchen at almost the same moment, wielding a cleaver.

The police were called and arrived almost immediately, as well as an ambulance. McKenzie insisted that she was fine—the baby started moving around as soon as McKenzie got up from the floor—but Hope was even more insistent. To appease her,

McKenzie agreed to go to the hospital for a checkup and an ultrasound. The baby was fine. Apart from a cut on her forearm,
caused by contact with a broken plate, Hope was unharmed as
well.

The police searched the area but were unable to locate the
gunman. Later that afternoon, however, one of the officers who
had been on the scene came into the emergency room on other
business and noticed a man sitting in the waiting room, waiting
to be treated for a gash on his head. He was wearing a bomber
jacket, greenish tennis shoes with a strange alligator pattern on
the uppers, and held a bloody Oakland Athletics baseball cap in
his lap. The waitress was able to identify him in a lineup. After
his fingerprints were matched to those found on the gun, he was
charged with attempted robbery.

So it all turned out well. No one was hurt and the bad guy
was caught.

To McKenzie, it still seemed kind of surreal. It was just so
crazy. By the time she went over to her parents' place to share an
extra-large pizza that evening, she was making jokes about it.

"Hey, Dad? From here on out," she said, "I advise you to
tread lightly around your wife. Seriously, I think she's been taking Tae Kwon Do lessons in secret. One false move and boom!
You could find yourself on the floor."

"I'll keep that in mind. Another good thing to remember," he
said, "should you suddenly decide to embark on a life of crime:
Never wear alligator shoes to a robbery."

"Or really anywhere," McKenzie mumbled through a mouthful of cheese and pepperoni. "Those were some butt-ugly shoes."

"And always, *always* root for the Mariners," Rick said.
"Right, honey?"

"Right."

The wooden tone of Hope's response caught McKenzie's attention. She was suddenly aware that she and Rick were the
ones doing all the talking. Judging from the frown on her father's face, she guessed he'd picked up on the same thing. Rick
reached out and laid his hand on Hope's shoulder.

"Hey. You feeling okay?"

"I'm fine," Hope replied, pushing her chair back from the table. "Just tired. I think I'll turn in early."

"Good idea," Rick said, squeezing her shoulder. "You had a crazy day."

Hope nodded. "I'm sure I'll feel better in the morning."

McKenzie hadn't really let herself think about what could have happened, partly because she didn't want to. But it must be different for Hope. She was the one who'd sensed danger, reacted to the reality, and saved the day. For her, it must have been all *too* real. No wonder she was so quiet; she must be exhausted.

"Actually," McKenzie said, getting to her feet, "I should get going. I'm supposed to meet Zach for coffee in the morning."

Rick's brows came together into a single, disapproving line. "What's that about? He's not trying to get you to take him back, is he?"

McKenzie choked out a laugh. "Definitely not. He probably just wants to discuss some of the financial stuff. One thing we're agreed on: The more we can work out between the two of us, the less ends up going to the lawyers."

McKenzie walked over to her mother, wrapped her arms around her, and squeezed her tight.

"Hey, I was just kidding before. I thought what you did today was amazing. You're my hero," McKenzie said, realizing it was true.

"No," Hope replied. "Just your mother."

"Same thing, right?"

Hope returned McKenzie's smile.

"Sometimes. Depends on the day."

Zach's eyes flew open and his jaw dropped. "A gun! Like an actual loaded gun? Are you okay?"

"I'm sitting here talking to you, aren't I?"

"And the baby's okay?" he asked, looking down toward her stomach. "You went and got checked out?"

"Yes. I had an ultrasound at the hospital. Everything's fine." Though Zach nodded deeply, his eyes still looked a little glazed, making McKenzie wonder if he'd really heard her. "Zach? It's okay. Really."

"Yeah. But you must have been scared."

"Not really. There wasn't time. I almost didn't know what was going on until it was over."

"Man. Thank God your mom was there. I don't know what I'd do if anything had happened."

McKenzie felt her jaw tighten. How very like Zach, making it all about him.

"Well, it didn't. Now, what did you want to talk about?" she asked, and took a drink of her coffee.

Zach rolled his eyes. "Kenz. Come on. Are you planning to stay pissed at me forever?"

Almost gasping at the audacity of his question, McKenzie practically spit coffee onto the table.

"Are you serious? First off, Zach, this is still pretty new. Our divorce isn't even final, so I don't think I'm exactly out of line here. Second, since you cheated on me, more than once—Yeah, I think I will be pissed at you forever. In fact, that seems like an excellent plan!"

"Well, if it makes you feel better," Zach said, shifting his shoulders in a maddeningly nonchalant manner, "then go right ahead. But seriously, Kenz. It can't have come as that much of a surprise. I mean, you knew who I was from the first, didn't you?"

Ignoring his question, McKenzie took another drink of coffee. "How's Mercedes?"

"Ah." Zach sniffed. "That didn't quite work out the way I hoped it would. Probably for the best. She was very jealous, stifling."

"Uh-huh. So you haven't changed."

Zach shook his head. "If anybody could have changed me, it would have been you. Honestly, I was sort of hoping you would. But I am who I am, Kenz. We both know that."

McKenzie pressed her lips together and glanced down at the table, saying nothing because there was nothing to say. Zach was right. He was who he was. She'd known that going in. Had he hoped she would be able to change him? Maybe. And why not? She'd hoped the same thing.

"So, listen," Zach said. "I get that you're still mad. Maybe you always will be. And I know I deserve it, but, with the baby coming, I was hoping that we could call a truce."

"A truce." Zach bobbed his head. "What would that look like?"

"Well, for one thing, besides child support, I want to pay for half the childcare expenses. And I want to start a college fund for her too, direct deposit so it would come right out of my paycheck."

"Zach. If this is about custody—"

He held up his hands and shook his head, vigorously. "I swear to you it's not. Yes, I want to be involved in her life, but I'm not cut out to be a full-time father. Or even a part-time one. I kind of envision myself as more of the fun uncle type, the one who takes her to Mariners games, or the water park, buys extravagant birthday presents. That's the part I'd be good at."

McKenzie cast her eyes down, feeling her cheeks grow hot.

"There's something else. I'd like to be there when she's born," he said, nodding toward McKenzie's ballooning waistline. "In fact, I'd like to come to the birthing classes with you, be your delivery coach."

McKenzie blinked. She hadn't seen this coming.

"I don't know, Zach. That feels like it would be pretty awkward."

"Only if we make it awkward," he said, his voice urgent, almost pleading. "Kenz, like it or not, you and I are going to be parents, so we're kind of stuck with each other. You can spend the rest of your life hating me if you want to. I could do the same. But for the baby's sake, for ours, too, what if we tried to be friends?"

"Friends?" McKenzie scoffed. "Why? We never were before."

"I know. But maybe we should have been. Because I liked you, Kenz, right from the first. You were funny, and smart, and cute, and a total pain in the butt." He laughed. "But then, you know, me being me, I had to try and get you into the sack and then it became this whole other thing." Zach turned out his hands in a helpless gesture.

"I still like you, Kenz. If you were willing to give it a go, maybe we could be friends. We couldn't be any worse friends than we were lovers. So, what do you say? Can we give it a try?"

Zach stood outside the coffee shop watching as McKenzie climbed into her car. When she pulled away from the curb, he raised his hand. McKenzie didn't wave back, but she nodded before driving away.

In the end, she'd said he could participate in the birth if he wanted to, but only if he showed up for all of the birthing classes that she'd signed up for. It was a test, one she was quite certain he'd fail. Reliability had never been Zach's forte.

As for his other request, that they become in divorce what they'd never been during their marriage, friends, she hadn't given him an answer one way or another. Time would tell, she supposed. On the one hand, it was hard to imagine a time when she wouldn't look at him and feel the way she felt now—hurt, humiliated, and betrayed. On the other hand, she was open to the possibility, as much for her own sake as for the baby's.

Being this hurt and this angry was exhausting. She'd really like to spend her energy doing something else, if that was possible. She'd have to think about it.

The thing that was most on McKenzie's mind was Zach's description of the kind of relationship he envisioned for himself and their daughter, casting himself more in the role of playmate than father.

When he'd talked about that, McKenzie had felt her cheeks flush red. His words, or at least the attitude behind them, sounded embarrassingly familiar. Thinking about Zach and what he said, then thinking about her mother and father, made her realize that Zach had no clue.

Maybe she didn't either, not until today.

Being a parent, a good parent, wasn't a part-time proposition, something you picked up or put down according to what was convenient for you. You couldn't pick and choose the parts you liked. It wasn't about being popular or making your kid like you. It *was* about doing your best, however imperfect your effort. It was about sacrifice and putting your child first, always, no matter the consequences. It was, as her parents had demonstrated so clearly, about love—all-in, 100 percent, never-take-a-day-off love.

Zach was right; he was who he was. And he would probably never change. He didn't want to.

But McKenzie did. Very much.

Chapter 33

In spite of her assurances to Rick, Hope didn't feel better the next morning.

Though she'd fallen asleep quickly, her slumber was restless. She dreamed she was back in the café. Everything happened just like before up to the point where Hope shouted to McKenzie, pulled her down to the floor, and shielded her child with her own body.

But in the dream, instead of getting beaned over the head with a vase and running out the door, the gunman turned around and pointed the gun right at them. Hope woke up sweating and gasping.

Rick was sound asleep next to her, snoring softly, so she lay in bed and took slow, deep breaths until her heart resumed a more normal rhythm. She forced herself to go back to sleep only to wake up twice more in the same condition. In the morning, she was so exhausted and anxious that she called in sick.

The pattern of nightmares and interrupted sleep continued. She called in sick for five days in a row. Days weren't much better than her nights. Rick was being kind and patient, but she found herself snapping at him over the littlest things. Kate came over to visit and brought over a pan of lasagna, which was awfully sweet and much appreciated. Hope just couldn't summon the energy to cook or do much of anything.

She felt anxious too, nervous and unsettled, but couldn't figure out what was making her feel that way. The incident in the café was on her mind, of course. It was a frightening experience. But she didn't think that was the root cause of all this, not that she was able to think very clearly about anything. She tried to stitch the binding on the quilt she was making for the new baby, thinking that doing handwork would help settle and soothe her anxiety. Then her hands started to tremble and she had to put it aside. She didn't tell Rick about it; he was worried enough about her already.

On Friday afternoon, when she was trying, unsuccessfully, to take a nap, Hope heard the soft scuffing of feet on carpeting. She opened her eyes and saw Rick standing just outside the bedroom door.

"Sorry," he said when she opened her eyes. "I was just checking on you. Didn't mean to wake you up."

"It's okay. I wasn't really asleep."

Hope yawned and scooted herself into a sitting position, pillows wedged behind her back. Rick came into the room and perched himself on the edge of the bed, crooking his left leg onto the mattress but leaving the right leg straight, his foot anchored on the floor. Seeing this, Hope smiled.

"Do you remember how, when you would come over to the house to see me and we'd go into my bedroom to talk, Mom would always yell, 'One foot on the floor at all times, you two!' "

"That's right. I'd forgotten about that." Rick grinned. "Your mom didn't trust me as far as she could throw me."

"And she was right not to." Hope smiled. "You were one big bundle of testosterone."

"When it comes to you, I still am." He took her hand and lifted it briefly to his lips. "Nancy called a few minutes ago. She said to tell you hello and that everybody misses you, your students especially. She wanted to know if you're coming back to work on Monday."

Hope pulled her hand from Rick's grasp, pushed her hair back from her face, then put her hand in her lap.

"Oh. Well, it was nice of her to call."

"So are you?" Rick asked. "Going back on Monday?"

Feeling her heart flutter, Hope took a quick breath and looked away. She'd been asking herself the same question for a couple of days now. She gave Rick the same answer she'd given herself.

"I don't know. I want to. But I don't know if I can. I feel so strange, anxious and exhausted. I don't know what's wrong with me."

"Maybe you should talk to somebody," Rick said gently. "I mean, after what you went through, it makes sense that you'd be nervous about going back to the prison. Until now, I'm not sure it really sank in that your students were real criminals, that some of them might have been involved in things every bit as terrible as what you experienced in the café."

"No," Hope said. "That's not it. I always understood what I was getting into and who I was dealing with. I didn't kid myself about the reasons my students ended up where they were. But now . . ." Hope shook her head. "I'm just not sure I'm up to it. If I'm going to quit in a few months to help McKenzie with the baby anyway, would it be better to do it now?"

Rick frowned and shook his head. "I don't think so."

Hope frowned, surprised by his response. "Why not? You were never happy about me taking this job. We barely spoke to each other for weeks after I went ahead and did it anyway, remember? So what's changed?"

"A lot of things," he said. "First off, I'm not quite as much of a self-centered jerk as I was back then." Hope tried to interrupt him, to say he was being too hard on himself, but Rick waved off her justification. "I was, Hope. I acted like a total jerk. McKenzie told me so when we went out to lunch one day and she was right. I'm not saying that I should have been excited about you working with felons; I'm just saying I should have handled things better. I'm trying to make up for it now.

"Besides, I know you. If you quit now, back out on the commitment you made to those women, you will hate yourself for it later."

"But if I'm going to end up quitting anyway—"

"To take care of the baby? I'm not sure that's a good idea.

"Wait," he said, holding a hand out flat. "Let me clarify. I'm not sure *you* think it's a good idea. We haven't talked about it much since I picked you and Kenz up from the hospital, but I've got the feeling you're not convinced. If you really want to quit working at the prison and take care of the baby instead, fine with me. And if you don't, that's fine too."

"Honestly, I don't know what I want right now. I just can't seem to focus."

"Hope. Are you sure you don't want to talk to somebody?"

She knew what he was saying and why; the symptoms she was displaying, sleeplessness, anxiety, irritability, could all be signs of post-traumatic stress. And of course it all made sense. Though the outcome had been all they could have hoped for under the circumstances, no one was hurt and the perpetrator was captured, the incident *had* been traumatic.

In the moment, she hadn't really thought about what she was doing. She merely acted on her instincts and did what came naturally, protecting her progeny. It wasn't until later, when she was sitting in a curtained-off cubicle of the emergency room, watching a technician spread lubricant over the mound of McKenzie's stomach prior to performing the ultrasound, that she started to think about what *could* have happened. A moment later, she experienced a trembling in her hands.

That was the first time. It had happened a few times since then. Sometimes it came on while she was thinking about the café, but sometimes it just seemed to come out of nowhere, once while she was thinking about what to get Hazel for her birthday.

Just because she wasn't consciously thinking about the robbery didn't mean that it wasn't bubbling around somewhere in her subconscious; the fact that she kept dreaming about it proved the point. And she *was* anxious—anxious about going back to work, or not going back, anxious about taking care of the new baby, or not, anxious about Hazel's birthday present, and the state of national affairs, and where Rory might be sent for his residency, and whether she should make a hair appointment for the end of that month or the beginning of the next.

She was anxious about everything, the monumental as well as the piddling, with no sense of proportion about any of it and, seemingly, no ability to stop herself from being anxious. The pep talks she tried to give herself did no good. Her thoughts were one big jumbled mess of worries. Was the trauma of what had happened in the café at the center of it? She didn't think so, but on the other hand, what else could it be?

"I need a few days to think things through, the weekend. I'll make up my mind to go back to work or not, by Monday. And if I can't . . ." She lifted her eyes, met Rick's worried gaze. "If I still can't, then I'll talk to someone. Okay?"

"Okay," he said quietly, and kissed her hand again. "Whatever you decide is fine with me. I just want you to be happy. That's all I've ever wanted."

Hope tipped her head to one side, then lifted her hand and rested it on the side of his face, felt the prickle of his beard on her palm.

"My hero."

Chapter 34

Mandy's hands were shaking as she inserted the prepaid phone card into the telephone kiosk, then punched in the number with trembling fingers. While waiting for the call to be accepted, she took slow and deliberately deep breaths, trying to hold it together. But the minute the call connected she lost her resolve as well as her composure and started to cry.

"Hello? . . . Mandy?"

She opened her mouth to answer, but all that came out was a strangled sob.

"Mandy, are you all right? You shouldn't be calling me. I'm not supposed to have any personal contact with inmates."

"I know. I'm sorry," she said at last, swallowing back her tears as best she could. "It's just . . . I don't know what to do. My dad just left and he—Hope, what am I going to do?"

"Mandy, what's wrong? Try to calm down and tell me what happened. Your dad came to see you? And he had bad news? Is something wrong with your mom?"

"No, no," Mandy said. "It's about Talia. He came to tell me that they are going to court to try and get permanent custody. He said I'm an unfit mother, a thief and an addict and that Talia won't be safe with me. They're going to take my baby away! Please come back. Please! I don't know what to do!"

Hearing the words from her own mouth brought it all back again. Even with her eyes screwed shut, she could see his face, the disgust and loathing in his eyes. He hated her.

All the work she'd done over the last five years, the agony she'd gone through to get clean and stay clean, the hours of effort she'd poured into getting her diploma and turning her life around—none of it mattered. Not to her father. Maybe not to anybody. In his eyes, she was what she had always been, a failure and a disappointment, barely fit to live, let alone raise a child.

If I get my way, you'll never get to see Talia again.

That's what he'd said. Mandy had no doubt that he meant it, just as she had no doubt that—unless someone helped her—he would get his way. He always had before.

"Please, Hope. I need help. There's no one here I can talk to."

"Mandy? Mandy, quit crying and listen to me, okay? You've got to try to calm down. Is Nancy there today? Have you tried to see her?"

At the mention of the chaplain's name, Mandy felt anger bubble up like bile inside her throat.

"No. I don't want to talk to her," she snapped, spitting the words. "She lied to me. She said that if I got it together and turned my life around, I'd get Talia back. And I was so stupid that I actually believed her!

"For all these years, everything I did or didn't do was about that, about being able to get out of here and be with Talia, about getting a chance to make up for all the ways I failed her. Talia was the only thing that kept me going. If I can't be with my daughter, then it was all for nothing, worthless. Just like my life.

"Nancy lied to me. I shouldn't have listened to her. I never will again."

Hope's voice came through the line again, lower and more stern than before. "Mandy, you've got to listen to me. Your life is *not* worthless; do you hear me? You're not thinking of ending it, are you?"

"You can't end what's already over," Mandy said bitterly.

"But Talia's been through so much already and all of it is my fault. I won't do that to her as well."

"Good," Hope said, relief evident in her voice. "Now you listen to me: You can't give up. You've been strong for a long time, for Talia's sake. You've got to keep on being strong. Just because your father says something doesn't mean it's going to happen."

"You don't know what he's like," Mandy said, letting out a small, derisive laugh. "He always gets what he wants. Always."

"Not this time," Hope said, her voice so stalwart that Mandy wanted to believe her. "You're not an unfit mother, Mandy. Maybe you were before but not anymore. You *have* turned your life around. Don't give up before you've even started, Mandy. You can't let your father tell you who you are. You've changed and you know it. You've got to fight him."

"I don't know how," Mandy said, tears threatening to choke her again. "I never did."

"Well, you've got to now," Hope said. "You've *got* to. For Talia's sake."

Mandy bobbed her head. She knew Hope was right; she had to find a way to fight back. She didn't know what the way might be, only that she couldn't do it alone.

"Where have you been all week? People are saying you're sick."

"I've been sick," Hope said. "Something bad happened to me and my daughter."

"What?"

"It doesn't matter," Hope said. "You just worry about you right now."

Something about the tone of Hope's voice worried Mandy.

"But you're coming back, aren't you?"

The answering silence from the other end of the line transformed worry into panic. There was no one she could trust. No one who believed in her like Hope did. If Hope deserted her . . .

"You've got to come back. You've just got to! My father—I can't fight him by myself; I just can't. Please! Please say you're coming back."

* * *

Rick walked into the kitchen just as Hope ended the call.

"Babe? Are you okay? You look like . . . Well, I don't know exactly what you look like but not good. Do you need to sit down?"

Hope took in a deep breath, let it out with a whoosh, and then nodded her head. "No, it's okay. I'm fine.

"On second thought," she said, frowning and then smacking her phone down onto the countertop, "I am *not* fine. I am ticked off. Really ticked off!"

"What's happened?"

"That was Mandy. Her dad came to visit her today—first time he's ever done so, as far as I know—to tell her that he's going to go to court to try to have her parental rights terminated. He said she was unfit to be a mother.

"How can he say that about his own daughter?" Hope said, throwing out her hands. "And how can her mother stand by and let this happen? She's brought Talia to visit the prison every two weeks for five years. She knows how hard Mandy has worked so she could be a mother to Talia. She *knows* that!"

Rick was standing by, watching her pacing back and forth across the kitchen, her anger growing with every step, but he didn't look like he was actually hearing what she was saying.

"Mandy called?" Hope nodded and Rick shook his head. "I thought you weren't supposed to have any personal contact with inmates."

"I'm not," she admitted. "But she wouldn't have called unless something was really wrong. What was I supposed to do? Tell the operator I wouldn't talk to her?"

Rick didn't speak, but the look on his face said that yes, that was exactly what she was supposed to do. Hope's ire deflated and was replaced by a twinge of guilt. What if she'd gotten Mandy into trouble?

"I couldn't just blow her off, Rick. I couldn't. Not when she needs help."

"I know," he said, a small smile tugging at the corners of his mouth. "You've never been able to say no to anybody who needs help. So? What are you going to do?"

"Go back to work," Hope said. "At least until the baby is born. I don't know if I can help Mandy or not. But at least I can be there and support her. She needs to know that somebody really cares. They all need to know that."

"Well, you're the one I care about," Rick said, putting his arms around her. "You're sure this is what you want?"

"I'm sure."

Rick nodded his head slowly.

"Okay. Good. Then that's what I want too."

Chapter 35

"Hey! Mrs. C.!" Deedee exclaimed when she came through the door of Hope's classroom on Monday morning. "I'm so happy you're back!"

"And I'm so happy to be back," Hope replied as the rest of the women filed into the room. Mandy brought up the rear. She looked simply awful. The bags under her eyes stood witness to what must have been a sleepless night. Even so, when she caught sight of Hope a small smile bowed her lips.

"I was afraid you weren't going to come back," Mandy said.

"Don't be silly," Hope said, grinning broadly in a deliberate attempt to lighten the mood. "You didn't think you'd get rid of me that easily, did you? Anyway, it had nothing to do with the robbery. I just wasn't feeling good. Even teachers get sick sometimes."

"But you're better now?" Mandy asked.

"Oh yes," Hope said, with more certainty than she felt. "One hundred percent."

"See? I told you," Steph said, giving Mandy an elbow and then turning toward Hope. "You wouldn't let some bad guy with a pop pistol keep you away from us for long, would you, Mrs. C.? I told everybody; if you scared that easy you wouldn't have ever started hanging out with us in the first place, would you?"

"I don't know about that," Tonya said, "I think we're a pretty scary bunch. You especially, Steph. If I could get away from you, I totally would."

"Hey!" Steph exclaimed, propping her fist onto her hip. "What a crummy thing to say. Who just gave you her extra pancake at breakfast, huh?"

"I was just kidding. Sheesh." Tonya rolled her eyes. "Can't you take a joke? Besides, the only really scary one around here is Nita. Ever since that thing in the cafeteria, she's been a real witch. I mean, even more than usual. And she's really got it in for you, Mandy. You better watch your back, girl."

"She doesn't have to. We got Mandy's back," Deedee said stoutly, putting an arm around Mandy's waist. "Nobody better mess with her when we're around, am I right?"

The women murmured to affirm their response. Mandy sniffled and ducked her head.

"Uh-oh. Don't go starting that again. Mrs. C.? Will you talk to her or something?" Deedee asked, jerking her head toward Mandy. "She's a mess, was crying all night long. You won't let them take her baby away, will you? I know you won't. So, tell her to quit blubbering. Everything's going to be okay."

Was it going to be okay? Hope's brief conversation with Nancy before heading down to her classroom left her wondering. From what Nancy told her, Mandy's father was already lawyering up, ready to fight and fight hard. Mandy, with no money and no connections, would have to represent herself.

Kate's arrival saved Hope from having to respond.

"Sorry I'm late," Kate said, sounding flustered and a bit out of breath. "I had to go through the metal detector three times. Seems that my new shoes had metal in the heels. Fortunately, Cindy found these beauties in the Lost and Found."

Kate glanced down at her feet, which were encased in a pair of much too big, squashy white bedroom slippers that had heels that flapped when she walked. The women all laughed.

"Okay," Hope said, clapping her hands together to get the

group's attention. "Enough gossip. Let's get to work. Mandy? You and Kate can start checking out everybody's machines and equipment."

Following Hope's instructions, the women began moving around the room, falling into their familiar routine, lining up in front of the cabinet to wait their turn to receive their supplies. Hope walked up to the front desk but stopped a few paces short, suddenly feeling out of breath. She laid her hand on her chest; her heart was galloping. Kate came up behind her.

"Hope? Can I get the keys?"

Hope took a quick but deep breath and exhaled through her nose, trying to calm her racing heart. When she reached into her pocket for the cabinet keys, her hands were shaking.

"I'm fine," Hope said quickly, dismissing the concern in Kate's eyes. "I should have eaten more at breakfast. Don't worry. I've got a granola bar in my desk."

"You sure you're all right?" Kate said, doubtfully.

"I'm just hungry, that's all. Seems like I'm always ravenous these days. Maybe I'm spending too much time hanging around McKenzie, sympathy hunger pangs or something."

Hope laughed, trying to sound more convinced than she felt. Apparently, it worked. Kate smiled, then took the keys and went to unlock the cabinet. Hope dug the granola bar out of her desk drawer and consumed it greedily. It seemed to help a little; her heart was still racing, but her hands stopped shaking. She really hadn't eaten much at breakfast; maybe it was just a blood sugar thing. She'd probably feel much better soon.

Hope tossed the wrapper into the wastebasket and looked around the room. Deedee and Carla were already plugging in their sewing machines and setting up their workstations. The others were standing in line, waiting to check out their equipment and fabric. As each woman approached the table in front of the storage cabinet, Mandy found the cardboard box with the woman's name, checked the contents, even counting out the number of straight pins inside—they were allowed twenty apiece—and then reported the numbers to Kate, who checked off the information next to the inmate's name on her list.

Hope was glad she'd put Mandy in charge of the checkout process. Especially today, it was good that she had a job to do, something to distract her from her worries. It was good, too, that she was here with her friends. Like Deedee said, the girls had her back.

Whatever the course—crafts or quilting—Hope had noticed that students in her classes seemed calmer and kinder to one another than those in the general population. Participation in communal creativity seemed to have built bonds of camaraderie and a stronger degree of tolerance among the women.

Her quilting students were developing such truly close friendships. Perhaps their shared status as mothers had something to do with it. Almost every woman in the group had signed up with the hope of being able to make a quilt for her own child. That probably helped explain their extraordinary focus too. They only had two hours to sew, twice a week, and didn't like to waste a moment of it.

Mandy was the furthest along, but a couple of the others, Carla and Linda, had already completed their charity quilts. Mandy had chosen to donate her quilt to a battered women's shelter, Tonya to a nursing home, and Linda, who was also a little older and had some previous sewing experience, to a camp for children with cancer. When Hope came into work that morning, she found a letter in her inbox, written on lavender stationery with a border of peonies.

The woman who had received Tonya's quilt, age ninety-three and with no children and, Hope supposed, few, if any, visitors, had written a note of such heartfelt thanks for the quilt that it brought Hope to tears. She planned to give it to Tonya later, knowing she would feel just as moved.

Nearly all the women had their equipment now and at least half of them were already sewing. For the moment, at least, they all seemed to be doing fine. Knowing how quickly that could change, Hope pulled an enormous bag, filled with the red, white, and blue fabrics, out from under her desk. Those were the colors Tonya had requested for her personal quilt, which she intended to give to her son, who was halfway through his Army basic training. Helping Tonya choose her fabric was the first thing on Hope's list that morning. She knew she had to get to it before—

"Mrs. C.?"

Hope looked across the room toward Deedee, who was pointing to her own wrist. Somehow, yet again, Deedee had managed to sew her yellow and blue pinwheel block to her sleeve.

Hope sighed. *Oh, well. At least her points are looking better.*

"Hang on, Deedee. I'll get a seam ripper."

Somehow Mandy had believed that simply having Hope back in the building, being back in Hope's classroom, would make her feel better. Weird how much this had come to mean to her.

Here she was among people who liked her. Here she didn't have to be careful or keep her head down. She was at the head of the class, the best student in the room. Everybody here knew that and was okay with that; they respected her for it.

Here she felt safe. And capable. That was Hope's doing.

Hope never talked down to her, never made Mandy or any of the women feel like she was better than they were or that she was doing them some kind of favor and they should be grateful that she was willing to spend her time with so unsavory a crew. If anything, Hope behaved as if they were doing *her* the favor. Every time one of them did try to express their appreciation to her, Hope waved off the compliment, saying something like, "Are you kidding? I love my job! I'm the luckiest teacher in the world. And I have the best, most talented students."

Were they so talented? Was she?

Mandy came to the end of the seam, backstitched to secure the thread before cutting it, then raised the presser foot and took the block out from under the needle and inspected her work. The seams met perfectly.

Smoothing her hand over the fabric, Mandy thought back about how nervous she'd felt when Hope had first shown her the quilt pattern. It had seemed impossibly complicated. There were so many angles, so many points and pieces. She didn't think she was up to it; after all, she'd only ever made one quilt. But Hope was right; when Mandy focused and took it one step at a time, it wasn't beyond her.

Hope made her feel capable, and smart, and trustworthy. In another place, another life, being put in charge of distributing and keeping track of needles, pins, scissors, or rotary cutters wouldn't be a big deal. In here, it was. There were people who would give plenty to get their hands on some of those items. On the inside, even a few straight pins could be valuable currency. That's why making sure that every single item, down to the last pin, went back under lock and key at the end of class was a big responsibility. And Hope had entrusted it to her.

Since entering Hope's orbit, crossing the threshold into this small, safe, and supportive company, Mandy had started to feel like nothing was beyond her.

Then her dad showed up.

Mandy's jaw tightened as she pinned the next block, thinking how stupid she'd been.

In the nearly five years of her incarceration, Mandy's dad had never come to visit her, not even once. She'd actually been excited when a guard came to tell her that her father was in the visitors' room. So close to her release, she thought he'd come to bury the hatchet between them, or maybe even apologize.

Instead, he'd come to destroy the only dream she had left, to take away her hope of obtaining the one thing that had kept her going all these years, the chance at a new life with her little girl. And while he was at it, he made a point of reminding her that she was stupid, unreliable, irresponsible, dishonest, untrustworthy, and unfit.

"You might have fooled a few of the do-gooder types around here into thinking you've changed, including that bleeding-heart chaplain, but not me. You're just as worthless as you've ever been. I won't have you ruining Talia's life the way you ruined everything else. Look at you," he snarled, looking her up and down. "Just as worthless as ever. You've had your chance. I won't give you another, not with Talia."

Mandy ducked her head and swiped her hand across her eyes.

In this room, this box inside a box, the inside of the inside, people saw her as intelligent, capable, worthy, and changed. Inside this room, that's how she saw herself.

But if people on the outside couldn't see that she was different from before, if they'd never even give her a chance to prove it, then what was the point? If there was no hope of redeeming her past mistakes, what was the point of trying? Or living?

Twin tears dripped onto the block Mandy held in her hands, leaving two dark splotches in the fabric, turning them from lavender to grape. Mandy felt a hand on her shoulder and looked up.

"You okay?"

Hope looked so pale, not like herself at all. She'd seemed fine at the beginning of class, but now Mandy could see her teacher was tired and weak. Mandy felt a twinge of guilt. Hope was only here because Mandy had begged her to come. Why had she done that? It wasn't as if it would change anything. Her father would get his way: he always did. And she'd known Hope was sick. Although not this sick.

She looked awful. Mandy wiped her eyes and frowned at her teacher.

"You should go home."

"No, no. I'm fine." Hope bent down to inspect Mandy's quilt block. "Let's see what you—"

Hope stopped in mid-sentence and opened her mouth wide, as if she was gasping for air. Her hand, still resting on Mandy's shoulder, started shaking. A moment later, her whole body started to shake. Hope clutched her hand to her chest.

Mandy let out a cry and sprang from her chair. Hope collapsed into her arms. Mandy looked across the room toward Kate, who was helping Linda.

"Kate! Kate, help!"

In an instant, the room was filled with exclamations of alarm and fear and a tight circle of bodies pressed in on Mandy and Hope, who was conscious but still gasping and seemed unable to speak, her eyes wide and frightened. Mandy heard Kate's voice.

"Stand back! Let me through," she demanded, and then, "Oh, my Lord."

For a moment, the old woman looked almost as weak and white as the teacher, but she quickly came to herself.

"Linda! Pick up the phone and dial eight. Tell whoever picks up that it's an emergency and we need an ambulance, right away. The rest of you, stand back and give her some air. Mandy, help me put her on the floor so we can cover her up with one of the quilts. We need to keep her warm until the ambulance gets here."

She helped Kate lower Hope the rest of the way onto the floor and then covered her with a quilt, but as soon as the older woman took command Mandy felt numb, almost frozen. She couldn't respond on her own or think for herself. Her whole being was consumed with the belief that Hope was dying and that it was her fault because everything she ever did was wrong and everything she ever touched got ruined.

Cindy and another guard were on the scene in less than five minutes and the EMTs were on the scene shortly after that. To Mandy, it seemed like time stood still.

The EMTs strapped Hope to the gurney. Kate turned toward Mandy.

"I called Rick. He's on his way to the hospital. I'll ride along in the ambulance and meet him there. I need you to take charge here and check in all the machines and equipment," she said. "Can you do that?"

Mandy blinked. "Yes. Okay."

"Make sure everything is accounted for and give Cindy the key when you're done. I'll call as soon as I know anything."

Mandy bobbed her head.

Kate frowned. "Are you going to be all right? I can ask one of the others to handle the check-in if you're not feeling up to it."

"No. You go on to the hospital. I'll handle things here. Really," Mandy said, responding to the deepening doubt she read in Kate's eyes. "I'm fine."

And if she was or if she wasn't, did it matter anymore? Did anything?

Chapter 36

Hope wasn't quite asleep when she heard a tentative tap on the bedroom door. Opening her eyes, she saw Rick standing at the threshold, looking apologetic.

"David Hernandez is here. I can tell him to come back another time if you're too tired."

"No, that's all right," Hope said, sitting up. "I'll put on a robe and be out in a couple of minutes."

"He brought flowers," Rick said.

"You're kidding," she said. Rick shook his head no. "Well. In that case, I'll be out in thirty seconds."

David was already sitting on the sofa, drinking coffee and eating a slice of Rick's homemade pumpkin bread, when Hope came out of the bedroom. The bouquet David had brought, pink carnations and white daisies, was sitting on the coffee table.

"Thank you," Hope said, nodding toward the flowers. "You're very kind, but honestly, I'm embarrassed over all the fuss."

"Sounds like you gave everybody quite a scare. They thought you were having a heart attack."

"So did I," admitted Hope.

"Do they know what caused it?"

Hope shook her head. "They kept me a couple of days and ran a bunch of tests. We don't have the results yet, but I'm feeling much better."

"Good," David said, bobbing his head. "That's good to hear."

David fell silent, his head still bobbing, avoiding eye contact. Funny, Hope thought to herself, he always seemed so in control, one of those people who never had trouble speaking his mind. Not today. The silence between them was awkward enough that Hope was just about to tell him to spit it out when Rick came in from the kitchen, carrying a coffee mug.

"I thought you might want some tea," he said. "It's herbal."

"The doctor wants me to lay off caffeine until we figure out what's going on," she explained to David before thanking Rick.

"Right," Rick said after putting the tea down in front of his wife. "Well, looks like you two have things to talk about. Honey, I'm going to go down to the jobsite, just want to see how the foundation is looking. Will you be okay on your own? I won't be gone more than an hour, hour and a half at most."

"Honey," Hope said with a small roll of her eyes. "You can stay for as long as you want. I'm fine."

Rick bent down and gave her a peck on the lips. "See you in an hour," he said, and headed out the door.

"He worries too much," Hope said after Rick had left. "I'm feeling so much better. As soon as the doctor gives me the green light, I'll be back at work."

David finally made eye contact. The look on his face, the way he said her name, as if it was an apology, made Hope's stomach sink. "Hope, I . . ."

Hope licked her lips. "Ah. So this isn't a social call."

"I wish it was," he said, sounding utterly sincere. "All incoming and outgoing calls from inmates are recorded, so I know about the phone call between you and Mandy on Sunday. I'm sorry, Hope. I have to let you go."

"David. David, come on. We talked for about three minutes."

"Four," he said. "And twenty-seven seconds."

"Okay, four. Fine. It wasn't like we were planning a breakout or jewel heist. She was overwrought, desperate, and sobbing. What was I supposed to do? Hang up on her?"

"What you were supposed to do was not accept the call to begin with. And you know that, Hope. I've told you before, every policy we put into place—"

"Is there for a good reason," she said, finishing his sentence for him. "I know. And you're right. It was a mistake. I was wrong and I'm sorry. It won't happen again; I promise. Give me another chance."

"I can't."

Hope felt her pulse beginning to rise. This time, however, it wasn't the wild galloping that she had no control over but the anxious uptick that comes from realizing that something you truly care about is about to be taken from you and that you're the one who caused it.

"David. Please. Please listen to me. I know I deserve whatever happens to me, but the inmates are the ones who'll suffer, especially the women in the quilting program. They've been making such incredible progress. Not just on their sewing but in things that matter a whole lot more. They're calmer and more confident. They're able to focus and make their own choices. And they're more responsible."

David held up his hand. "Hope, you don't need to convince me. The inmates in the quilting program have made huge strides. I've noticed it and so have the other staff members. Even Wayne has noticed. Just last week he told me that the inmates in the quilting program are the best in the facility."

"See?" she said, throwing out her hands. "I know you're a stickler for the rules, but if even cranky old Wayne sees a difference . . .

"Come on, David. Give me another chance." David moved his head slowly from side to side. "At least let me come back for a couple of months. That'll give you time to find a replacement and me time to help the women warm up to the idea of a new teacher."

David looked at her. His gaze was clear and his voice was firm.

"Hope, I'm shutting down the program, permanently."

"What? David, you can't! Why? Why would you do that?"

David picked up his coffee mug, cupping it in his two hands, and sighed heavily.

"I don't have a choice. Nita and Mandy got into an altercation in the bathroom and a fight broke out. There was a razor blade involved. Nita got cut on her hand, nothing very deep, thank God. Fortunately, Cindy heard some noise and broke things up pretty quickly. But it could have been a lot worse.

"Nita admits that she was the one who started it. There's been some tension between them for a while now; I got between the two of them in the cafeteria a couple of weeks ago. According to Nita, she was giving Mandy a hard time, made a comment about Mandy's father suing to remove her parental rights, saying it was a lucky thing for Mandy's little girl that he was—"

David paused when Hope's gasp interrupted his story, and then went on.

"You know what Nita's like. She has a talent for knowing how to hit so it hurts. Anyway, according to Nita, Mandy lunged for her. They tussled around for a minute and then Nita says that Mandy pulled the razor on her. Mandy denies it, says that Nita was the one who pulled the blade, but . . .

"It was a round blade, Hope. Same kind as the ones you use in your sewing program."

"And you think Mandy stole it?" Hope's jaw went slack. "Never. She wouldn't do that, David. Mandy is the most responsible, hardworking student in my class. No matter what was going on between her and Nita, Mandy would never do something like that, especially not when she's so close to her release."

"A week ago, I might have agreed with you. I sent Nita back to medium for a month. I just cut back on Mandy's privileges and took back some of her good time, so she'll be staying with us a little longer. That's the best I could do. But"—he took in a breath and shook his head—"this thing with her father has hit Mandy hard. I listened to the phone call she made to you, Hope. She's not the same person. You said it yourself; she's distraught and desperate.

"She's also the only one who had access to the cabinet where you keep those rotary blades," he said. "When they were taking you to the hospital, Kate left her in charge. Cindy was supposed to keep an eye on the check-in process and do a pat-down when the women left the room, just like always. But things were pretty confused that day and those blades are thin and small, small enough to conceal. Obviously, she missed something."

"No," Hope stated definitively. "I don't believe it. No matter how confused things were, there is no way that Mandy would take advantage of the situation just so she could settle a score with Nita."

"I'm not saying she took the blade because she wanted to hurt Nita." David rubbed his hands around his coffee mug, as if he were trying to warm them. "I think she had someone else in mind."

Recalling Mandy's phone call, the desperation in her voice, Hope felt her stomach clench.

"No," she said slowly. "No. She wouldn't do that. She's got so much to live for, Talia. Talia means everything to her."

"And now her father is trying to take Talia away." David tilted his head to one side, letting his words sink in for a moment. "Mandy has a history of depression. We had her on suicide watch when she first got here."

"That was years ago," Hope protested.

David put the cup on the table and got to his feet. "I'm sorry, Hope. You're fired. You're a good teacher and the quilting program was a good idea. I wanted it to work as much as you did. But my first instincts were right; it's too risky. The experiment is over, Hope. I'm shutting down the program."

Chapter 37

Three days after Hope was released from the hospital, McKenzie came to visit, bearing an African violet in a terra-cotta pot and a plate of homemade cookies. Hope, glad for the distraction, invited McKenzie to sit down in the kitchen while she made a pot of tea.

"Wow. So he came over here specifically to fire you?" McKenzie moved her hand in front of her lips, as if she'd just realized that her mouth was full of cookie. "That's got to hurt."

"It does," Hope admitted, pouring chamomile tea into McKenzie's mug and then her own. "But I'm more sorry for the women than myself. It's just so unfair."

"Yeah, but . . ." McKenzie said slowly, as if she hated to disagree with her mother but couldn't quite bring herself not to. "You can't really blame him, can you? I mean, if students are smuggling razors out of class . . ."

"*If,*" Hope replied, unable to keep the bitterness from her voice. "I'm not convinced that's what happened. Quilting class was the highlight of the week for these women. They wouldn't do anything to jeopardize the program, Mandy especially."

"Well," McKenzie said slowly, still proceeding with caution, "then where do you think the blade came from?"

"Not from any of my girls. I'm sure of it."

Hope sighed and rubbed her forehead. She'd felt a dull ache

behind her eyes all morning. Whether her headache was caused by the stress of losing her job or anxiety over the uncomfortable conversation she needed to have with McKenzie was impossible to say. Probably some of each.

"Anyway," Hope sighed. "It's done now."

McKenzie sighed as well, signaling her sympathy.

"I'm really sorry, Mom. I know the quilting program meant a lot to you. I'm sure it meant a lot to the inmates too." She laid a hand on the shelf of her pregnant stomach. "But, on the upside, maybe it's good you have some time to recover?"

Just then the baby kicked, so hard that McKenzie's hand bounced. McKenzie laughed and then looked up at her mother.

"Did you see that? I swear she's doing kickboxing in there. She was doing the same thing all during our last birthing class at the hospital. I was lying down and Zach was pretending to time the contractions. All of a sudden the baby did a complete somersault! My stomach was rippling like a waterbed that somebody was bouncing on. You should have seen Zach's face. He looked like he thought an alien was going to come popping out of me any second." She laughed.

"You'd better rest while you can, Mom. Because once your granddaughter makes her appearance, I think it'll take every ounce of energy you've got just to keep up with her."

The throbbing behind Hope's eyes spread to her temples. She swallowed her tea and took a breath.

"McKenzie. Honey, there's something we need to—"

"Well, I'm off!"

Rick bounded into the kitchen, wearing jeans, a red and white flannel shirt, a brand-new pair of work boots, and a grin. He grabbed three cookies from the paper plate that was sitting on the kitchen table between Hope and McKenzie.

"Big day. Need to keep up my strength." He winked and took a bite of cookie. "Kenz, did you make these? They're fantastic!"

"What can I say, Dad? I learned from the best."

"Chip off the old block."

Rick bent down to kiss McKenzie's head before looking up at Hope.

"It's only a half day today. Ben's just going to show me the ropes. I should be back by one. You'll be all right until then?"

"Yes," Hope said wearily. "I'll be fine."

The news that Rick had gotten the job as a part-time construction coordinator for Many Hands Housing could not have come at a better time. His concern over her health was touching but tiring. He asked how she was about every five minutes.

His first real day on the job wouldn't be until the following week. And though he was already a different man than he'd been during those dark days of depression, it seemed to Hope that he'd suddenly found another gear. He was like a kid again, bursting with energy and enthusiasm, chomping at the bit to get back to work. The salary was less than a quarter of what Rick had earned in the past, not surprising for a three-day-a-week job at a nonprofit organization, but Hope knew Rick would give the job his all and then some. She was proud of him.

"Did you take your pills?" he asked.

Hope picked up the prescription bottle from the table and gave it a little shake.

"Don't forget the ones at lunch. I'll keep my phone on. Call if you need me."

"I'll be *fine*."

Rick grabbed his keys off the kitchen counter. "You going to stick around for a while?" Rick asked McKenzie, who bobbed her head. "Keep an eye on your mother. Don't let her overdo it."

"Would you please get out of here and go bring home some bacon?" Hope tilted her head backward. Rick bent down to give her a goodbye kiss and then headed out the door, whistling a tune.

"Somebody's happy," McKenzie said, grinning and shaking her head.

"So happy. You have no idea. If he'd won the lottery, he couldn't be happier. I'm so proud of him."

"Me too," McKenzie said. "I think this will be better for him, don't you? Daddy was always so driven, such a workaholic. When he lost his job, I really wasn't sure he'd be able to bounce back. But now he's like . . ." McKenzie paused and took a sip of tea. "I was going to say he's like his old self, but that's not quite right. I feel like he's better than his old self, you know? More balanced. I think I might like him even better now, don't you?"

"Well, I don't know that I'd say I like him *better*. But I think he likes himself better and that's good for everybody. He's thrilled to be going back to work, especially for this organization, where he's building something more meaningful than corporate profits. You get to a certain point in life and you start to think seriously about your legacy, how you've spent your time, and what you'll leave behind." Hope lifted the cup to her lips, smiling. "I don't know if the people over at Many Hands realize what a brilliant hire they just made or not. If they don't they will, probably before the end of his first week.

"It's funny," Hope said. "I still miss Portland but not the way I used to. Back then, we thought we had it all—house, career, lifestyle, security—but somewhere along the way, we'd lost track of each other. Rick will work hard at this job, he doesn't know another way, but I think he's got his priorities set straight now. I think we both do."

"So? You're never too old to grow up?"

Hope laughed. "Yeah. I guess."

"Well. That's a relief." McKenzie looked down at her belly. "You hear that, kid? Don't be discouraged. There's still a chance that, someday, your mother won't be a *total* train wreck."

"Don't say things like that," Hope chided. "McKenzie. You are *not* a train wreck."

"I'm kidding!" McKenzie countered, lifting her hands. "It was just a joke. And I think you're right. Even grown-ups can still grow up. Or at least change. I think we've changed in the last few months, haven't we? I mean . . . you and me?" McKenzie waved a finger between herself and her mother, indicating their connection rather than their individual personalities.

"Yeah," Hope said, her voice a little hoarse. "I think so too."

"I don't know why it took so long, but . . . I think it's better this way."

"So do I."

McKenzie bobbed her head a couple of times and then cleared her throat. "Right. Well, anyway. What were you saying before Dad bounced in here?"

"Saying?"

Hope felt her pulse quicken. She couldn't do it. Not now, anyway. Not after McKenzie had just told her how much better their relationship was now. For the first time in thirty years, they had the kind of close, cozy connection Hope had always longed for.

From the moment Hope first laid eyes on McKenzie, naked, red as a beet, and squalling her head off, as though she'd taken that first glimpse at the world and already found it wanting, Hope had loved her daughter. Nothing McKenzie said or did or didn't do or didn't say could change that. But, in these last weeks, for the first time, Hope could honestly say that she *liked* her daughter and that if she and McKenzie had shared not one drop of common blood Hope would still have enjoyed spending time with her. Yes, things had changed between them. Much for the better. But how quickly would things change for the worse if Hope told McKenzie that she wasn't going to be a full-time babysitter for her grandchild?

And yet she had to say it. Becoming her granddaughter's principal caregiver would be a mistake for all of them: McKenzie, Hope, and the baby.

McKenzie needed to gain confidence in her own mothering instincts and abilities. Yes, she would be a different kind of mother than Hope, but that was fine. Actually, it was better. McKenzie needed to see that! And the baby needed to look to McKenzie as the most important person in her world. Hope planned to be a doting and very involved grandparent; so did Rick. Already they were talking about the things they wanted to do with the baby, the places they wanted to show her and things they wanted to teach her. But the child could have only one mother—McKenzie.

And as for Hope? She had spent a lifetime rearing her family. She wouldn't trade a single day of that experience for all the money in the world. But now was the time for her to do other things. She didn't know what those things were, not yet. Her firing had come so out of the blue, like a punch to the gut. But working at the prison had proven to Hope that she had something meaningful to offer to the world, as well as a duty to offer it.

Hope had thought it through from every possible angle and she knew what she was doing was best for everyone. Rick agreed with her. Would McKenzie?

She had to have the conversation eventually. But things were going so well between them. She didn't want to lose that, not yet. She would wait for another day and another moment, a better one.

When would that be?

She had no clue. She hoped that when the moment came the right words would come as well and that, miraculously, McKenzie would be able to hear them. But now was not that moment. Today, she just wanted to enjoy her daughter.

"I didn't say anything. Or if I did, I don't remember."

"Sure you do," McKenzie said casually, taking a cookie from the plate and dunking it into her tea. "We were talking about how the evil David Hernandez fired you and canceled the quilting program, and I was saying that maybe it wasn't all bad, you getting a chance to rest and recover before the baby was born, and then you said you had something to tell me."

McKenzie glanced up from her tea, soggy cookie still in hand, looked into Hope's pained face, and turned suddenly pale.

"What's wrong?" McKenzie dropped her hand. A glob of wet, gooey cookie fell onto the table. "You're sick, aren't you? You said it was just something with your thyroid, but it's something else, isn't it. What? Your heart?"

"No, no," Hope said urgently, grabbing her daughter's hand. "It's nothing like that, Kenz. Really. The doctors did all kinds of tests and it's exactly what I told you—my thyroid. Nothing else."

"You're sure?" McKenzie asked. "Because you looked really

funny just then. Like you were trying to figure out how to share bad news."

"It wasn't that. I was just thinking about—about getting fired. That's all."

It was true, at least partially.

"Okay," McKenzie said slowly, her expression relieved but still tinged with suspicion. "And you're sure. It's nothing with your heart?"

"Nothing with my heart," Hope replied, lifting the cup to her lips and taking a sip before going on. "All those things I was experiencing—anxiety, rapid heart rate, tremors in the hands, weight loss even though the appetite increases—are symptoms of hyperthyroidism. The medication to normalize my heart rate is already working; I'm feeling a lot better.

"It'll take at least six weeks for the anti-thyroid medication to kick in, but once it does, the other symptoms should disappear. I was kind of hoping I could lose the tremors and rapid heart rate but keep the weight loss thing. But the doctors said it was all or nothing, so . . ."

Unable to resist temptation any longer, Hope plucked an oatmeal cookie from the plate and then took a bite, an expression of rapture crossing her face.

"Oh my gosh, Kenz. These are heaven."

"Thanks. It's Kate's recipe. It's weird, but all of a sudden I'm overcome with the urge to bake, and clean, and organize everything in sight. Yesterday I stayed up until midnight, putting my spice rack into alphabetical order."

"I've always done that," Hope said. "Makes it so easy to find things when you're cooking."

"Yeah, I know," McKenzie replied, taking another cookie for herself. "But that's you. I'm the girl who wanted kayak paddles and Bose speakers in her bridal registry instead of flatware, remember? The only reason I even have a spice rack is because you gave me one when I graduated from college."

"You've gotten new spices since then, right?" Hope asked. "Because if you haven't you should. They only stay fresh for about a year. After that, they're not as flavorful."

"Yes," McKenzie groaned, rolling her eyes and letting her head flop to one side, as if she were too weary to hold it up. "I know. You only told me that about fifty thousand times when I was growing up. That's kind of my point.

"As soon as I got pregnant, and this was even before I knew I *was* pregnant, I woke up on a Saturday morning and made a special trip to the grocery store to buy all new spices. It cost me close to two hundred dollars! Now I'm staying up half the night and alphabetizing them." McKenzie shook her head and rubbed her hand over her belly, which was now approximately the same size and shape as a July watermelon. "I don't get it. I used to be the least domesticated person on the planet. Now I'm turning into Martha Stewart. Or you."

"It's called nesting," Hope said. "Happens to most expectant mothers. It has something to do with hormones. But don't worry; it doesn't mean you're turning into me."

McKenzie groaned again, rolled her eyes again, let her head flop again, this time to the opposite side, and even tsked for good measure, displaying the full range of nonverbal cues that daughters employ to signal their disgust with their mothers.

"Stop, okay? Just stop."

"Stop what?" Hope asked, her confusion genuine.

"Doing that thing you do."

Still confused, Hope looked at her askance. McKenzie pointed toward her own lips, making a circling motion with her index finger.

"That thing you do with your mouth when your feelings are hurt. Stop it."

"What thing? I don't do a thing."

"Oh yes. You do." McKenzie broke her cookie into two pieces, took one for herself, and placed the other onto Hope's plate. "Would you try not to take everything so personally? All I meant was it's weird, the way these urges have come over me; I wasn't saying that I don't want to turn into you. If anything, lately I'm wishing I was more like you. A lot more."

Hope started to protest, but McKenzie lifted a hand to cut her off before she could say anything.

"There's something I've been wanting to ask you. But you have to promise not to get all, you know, the way you get."

"The way I get about *what*?" Hope said, throwing her hands out, feeling more confused than annoyed.

"The way you get when you are too happy about something small. The way you *get*," McKenzie said, opening her eyes wider, as if this and repetition would make her meaning clear. "Excited. Too excited."

"Fine," Hope said. "I have absolutely no idea what you're talking about, but I promise I won't—Wait." Hope's face lit up as she considered the possible list of things that would be exciting. "Oh, Kenz! Are you having twins?"

McKenzie laughed. "No. I am *not* having twins. I know you love the idea of two-for-the-price-of-one grandkids, but one baby at a time is plenty for me, thank you. I wanted to tell you something else. Well," she said, "to ask you really: Would you teach me how to crochet? I want to make something for the baby, but something easy. A hat or something?"

Hope clenched her fist and pressed it against her mouth.

"Oh no," McKenzie moaned, her neck hinging backward. "You're not going to cry, are you? I shouldn't have said anything. I should have just looked for a YouTube video or something."

Laughing, Hope wiped away her tears. "It's okay. I'm just happy, that's all. Do you have any idea how long I've been waiting for you to ask me something like that?"

"About thirty years?" McKenzie guessed.

"Twenty-eight. I figured I had to give you a couple of years to learn how to talk first. But yes," Hope said after taking in a deep breath and blowing it out, moving past her happy tears. "I would love to teach you how to crochet. But are you sure you wouldn't rather try quilting? I know I've already made you a baby quilt, but you really can't have too many. And I'd be a far better quilting teacher than crochet teacher. I mean, I *can* crochet, but it's never been my strong suit. I can show you the basics, but that's about all."

"I know. That's the reason I asked." McKenzie leaned forward, looking somewhat sheepish. "Okay, I know it sounds stupid. But one of the reasons I never wanted to get into sewing, or quilting, or furniture refinishing, or cooking, or any of the twelve gazillion things you're so incredibly good at is exactly that: You're just *so* good. At everything. How can I ever hope to compete with you? Or even keep up?"

Hope opened her mouth to argue, ready to say that they weren't in competition and never had been. But then shut it again, thinking back to that day when McKenzie had mocked her ill-considered plans for a career in real estate, the pleasure she'd felt when Hazel came to her defense and how it had turned to self-reproach when Hope realized it stemmed from a desire to score points against her own daughter. Hope ducked her head, trying to catch hold of McKenzie's downcast eyes.

"But we're not like that anymore, are we? I think we're both playing for the same team these days, don't you?"

McKenzie lifted her gaze, nodding to signal her agreement. "Yeah. We're good now. But I think I'd still rather stick with the crocheting. Not because I'm worried that you'll show me up. It's hard to explain, but I kind of want to figure it out for myself. . . ." McKenzie paused briefly and bit her lower lip. "Mom, if I tell you something, can you promise not to take it personally?"

Hope frowned. She wasn't quite sure where this was going.

"Well. I don't know if I can promise, but I'll try."

McKenzie paused a moment more before continuing. "You were an amazing mother. The best. I've always known that. So did everybody else.

"When I was a teenager and most of my girlfriends were barely speaking to their moms, they'd come up to me and tell me that you were so great, and cool, and such a terrific listener, and how lucky I was to have you for my mom. And I knew they were right because you were. Basically, you were perfect."

"McKenzie, I wasn't. Nobody—"

McKenzie let out a little growl of frustration. "Okay, okay. You weren't perfect; you interrupted a lot. Oh, and you and Dad would stand in the kitchen and kiss in front of me, which, frankly, still skeeves me out." She closed her eyes for a moment and waved her hand in front of her face as if trying to shoo away the image. "But you were *close* to perfect and that was incredibly annoying.

"I mean, for one thing, everybody acted like I wasn't entitled to have any problems because I had this amazing mom, so how bad could my life possibly be? But more than that was the feeling that no matter what I did, I could never, ever do it as well as you.

"I know that you and everybody else think I broke off my first two engagements because I didn't think Shawn or Andrew measured up to Daddy. But that's not why I called the weddings off. I was afraid that *I* wouldn't measure up, to you. I wanted to get married. I wanted to have a family. But I also knew that I could never be the kind of wife or mother you were and so . . ." She shrugged. "I chickened out. But then Zach proposed and I thought, 'I'm almost twenty-eight years old. If I'm not ready now, when will I be?' The answer, obviously, was never."

"Kenz, this divorce was not your fault. You can't be in a marriage with three people. At least not outside of certain counties in Utah."

"Funny," McKenzie deadpanned. "But whoever is at fault, it's over. But this . . ." McKenzie looked down and stroked her stomach. "This will never be over. It's for life. Ready or not, in another ten weeks I'm all in. And probably over my head. But one way or another, I'm going to be a mother. I know I won't be the kind of mother you were—and are. I can't be. But I've been thinking about that a lot lately. And I think that I can be, that I *have* to be, my own kind of mother. Right or wrong, I'm going to have to find my own way to screw up my kid."

"As every parent does," Hope said. "Including me."

"Nah. You did good. I mean, sure, Liam's a total pain. But otherwise . . ."

McKenzie cracked an impish grin and Hope smiled.

"Anyway, the reason I came over—apart from keeping myself from eating the whole batch of cookies—was to ask you to teach me to crochet. But there's something else too."

McKenzie pressed her lips together and winced, almost as if she were anticipating a blow.

"Would it hurt you terribly if I found somebody else to be my babysitter?

"I know you were excited about it and I know you'd be amazing. But Mom, even though they fired you, I think this work you were doing at the prison was really important. I wasn't sure you'd be able to handle it at first, but I was wrong. I underestimated you. You will be an amazing influence on the baby, but I think you should spread that influence as far as you can. It's like you said: You get to a certain age and you start thinking about your legacy. I think you need to chart your own path, apart from just our family. And as a mom, I need to chart mine."

Hope swallowed hard. For a moment, she was unable to speak. But had she been able to, she'd have told her daughter that she was already charting her own path and that, as her mother, she had never been prouder.

She hadn't just raised a daughter; she had raised a woman. And should Hope's next breath be her last, she knew her legacy was already secure. And profound.

Chapter 38

"Hang on. Let me get the door. You're dropping stuff everywhere."

Hazel took Hope's key ring, unlocked the condo door, and then held it open for her sister. Hope carried her burden into the kitchen and set the overflowing box down onto the counter.

"You want some tea?" Hope called out over her shoulder.

Hazel, who had been following in her sister's wake, picking up the objects Hope had dropped along the journey from the front door—an issue of *Life* magazine, several valentines from the seventies, some neon-colored swizzle sticks, and a ball of red-and-white-striped twine—put everything down on the counter next to the box.

"What I want is a glass of wine," Hazel said, opening the refrigerator and examining the contents. "And a snack. What's Rick been baking lately?"

"Not much." Hope took two wineglasses out of the cabinet. "He's been pretty busy with the new job. Also, we're both trying to cut down on the carbs. Rick's even started running again; he's looking very trim these days. He said he'd pick up some steaks for the grill on his way home from work. In the meantime . . ."

She opened the pantry, pulled out a yellow package, and held it out so her sister could see. "How about some cheese and gluten-free crackers?"

"Cheese, yes. Gluten-free crackers, no. I'd just as soon eat cardboard. In fact, I'm pretty sure it'd be the same thing. How about this pear?" Hazel asked, turning away from the refrigerator. "You got plans for it?"

"That's fine," Hope said as she uncorked a bottle of Pinot Grigio. "Slice it up and we'll have it with the cheese."

After the glasses were filled, the pear and a chunk of smoked Gouda sliced and plated, Hope and Hazel clinked their wineglasses together.

"Thanks for coming up," Hope said. "It's been a really fun day."

"No problem. What are sisters for if not to help cheer you up when you hit a rough patch? Although how this is supposed to help cheer you up I have no idea." Hazel plucked a very worn, circa-1950s copy of a Hardy Boys mystery from the box on the counter.

"I told you," Hope said. "I'm making junk journals—little notebooks or scrapbooks made with recycled or vintage paper. You can use magazines, books, old photos, postcards, scrap paper, or just about anything for the journals. Then you can embellish them however you want. I was thinking I'd dig into my button box to decorate some of these. And maybe sew some rickrack on the edges. It'd be a good way to use up some of the stuff in my stash."

"Yeah. And you only had to buy an entire box of stuff that nobody else wants so you can use up that handful of buttons and yard of rickrack. Junk journals." Hazel shook her head. "Well, at least the name makes sense. You know that this book is missing half the pages, right?"

"That's why I was able to get it so cheap. But the cover is perfect. I'll use it and a few of the interior pages to make a journal for Rory—he was always crazy about the Hardy Boys. Those old movie posters and the popcorn boxes are for Liam's journal.

And this," Hope said, picking up the copy of *Life* magazine, "I'm going to use it in McKenzie's journal. It was printed the same week she was born."

"Very nice. And these?" Hazel took a mason jar filled with neon-hued swizzle sticks out of the box. "Are we planning on opening a tiki bar?"

"No," Hope said, frowning in response to Hazel's sarcastic tone. "I just liked them, okay? I'll figure out something to do with them. I know! I'll use them as plant markers for my herbs!"

Hazel took a sip of her wine and shook her head. "Wow. You are so bored you hardly know what to do with yourself, aren't you? Sis, you have *got* to find another job."

"Believe me, I'm looking," Hope said. "I mean, even with Rick working part-time, I *can* keep busy. I've been working on my sewing backlog and doing some of the deep cleaning I'd put off. I reorganized the spice drawer on Thursday. And these junk journals really are going to be adorable. I'm going to give everybody one for Christmas." Hope frowned. "Though I guess I shouldn't have told you that."

"I swear I'll act surprised," Hazel said, holding her hand out flat.

"The thing is," Hope continued, "being busy isn't enough anymore. And I don't think a job would be either, not a job kind of job." Hope sighed and took a deep draught from her wineglass. "Working at the prison may have wrecked me for regular life, which is pretty funny considering how miserable those women made my life for that first month. But after that, I don't know. . . . They changed me. Every day I spent with them felt like an important one, a day when I was really making a difference."

"I know," Hazel said, nodding sympathetically. "But that doesn't mean you can't make a difference someplace else. Maybe you should start applying at some nonprofits."

Hope picked up a pear slice and layered a piece of cheese on top.

"I already have. There's an opening at a food bank, another at the Boys and Girls Club. I sent my résumé yesterday."

"Do you think you'll get an interview?"

Hope bit into her pear and cheese stack. "Maybe. Having the prison job on my résumé should help. Assuming David doesn't slam me if they call for a recommendation."

"He won't," Hazel said quietly.

Hope frowned and swallowed her cheese. "How do you know? Are you two seeing each other?"

Hazel shook her head. "We text sometimes. If we lived closer, I think that I *would* see him. Maybe. Even if you do hate his guts."

"I don't hate David's guts," Hope said. "How could you even think that? Am I happy he fired me? No. I still think he made the wrong decision, but I never thought he was being malicious. The two of us are oil and water, personality wise. But whatever he does, he does because he thinks it's the best thing for the inmates."

"Well, good," Hazel said. "He doesn't hate your guts either, you know. The things you said about him? He said basically the same thing about you. And he felt terrible about having to end the quilting program. It took a while for him to get on board, but in the end, he saw how the women were responding. He said it was a terrific program and that you were a terrific teacher. He'll give you a good recommendation, Hope. I'm sure of it."

Hope sipped her wine.

Given the number and depth of insights that Hazel seemed to have into David's thoughts, it was hard to believe they were only texting, "sometimes." Hazel had cycled through more than her share of heartthrobs and heartbreakers over the years, but Hope had never heard her sister speak of a man in quite that way, with a sort of wistful longing in her voice.

"If you did want to start seeing David, I'd be okay with it. You know that, right?"

Hazel pressed her lips together momentarily. "But you don't like him."

"That's not true." Hope clucked her tongue with exasperation. "I was just saying nice things about him."

"What you said was that you didn't hate his guts."

"And I don't." Hazel's brows arched to a skeptical angle. "Okay, sure. Would I pick him for myself? No. David's too by-the-book for my taste, too much of a rule follower. But he's different around you. I've seen it. For one thing, he actually seems to display signs that he has a sense of humor when he's with you. Not a great sense of humor, mind you, but at least it's something. When I talk to him, it's like trying to have a conversation with Rain Man. He's so literal. But with you . . ."

"Anyway," Hope said, giving her hand a dismissive flap, "all I'm trying to say is: If you really like him and want to see him, don't let me stand in the way."

"Even though he fired you?"

"Yes. Even though he fired me. David's okay. I'm not saying I'm going to make him a junk journal or anything—"

"Sure. Let's not go crazy." Hazel grinned. "Thanks. I really do appreciate that. I do like David. But the distance thing, our jobs, our personalities . . . I don't think it would work."

Hope didn't think it would work either. But stranger things had happened. Look at her and Rick. Plenty of people had doubts about the two of them.

Hope remembered that night, sitting on the edge of her mother's bed as the two of them hemmed her wedding gown, meeting in the middle. Though her mother never came right out and said so, it was obvious she had doubts about the match. At one point, she had gone so far as to remind Hope that marriage was forever and that a woman—"a woman," she said casually, as if she were talking about any member of the sex and not Hope specifically—would do better to call things off, even at the last minute, than to go through with the ceremony if she wasn't 100 percent sure.

"I'm sure," Hope replied.

It was the only time Hope could recall being truly angry with her mother.

Because she wasn't sure, not 100 percent. She had been only a few minutes before, but then the mother Hope idolized, the oracle she had thought infallible, had spoken and the seeds were planted.

Her great-aunt Marilyn's tactics had been less subtle. She sent Hope and Rick a glass fruit bowl as a wedding present and left a receipt inside along with a note saying that the bowl could be returned within ninety days. According to Aunt Marilyn, this was about thirty days longer than she expected the marriage to last.

It was an ugly bowl, an amber color with bubbles in the glass and tan swirls like burnt crème brûlée near the bottom. Hope hated that bowl, but she had kept it on the kitchen counter ever since, right next to the stand mixer, as a symbolic "so there" to her cranky old aunt. Rick thought it was funny. Every year for as long as she lived, Rick insisted on writing a personal note in Aunt Marilyn's Christmas card, thanking her yet again for the fruit bowl.

Hope thought it was funny too, now.

She had forgiven her mother many years before, not long after the twins were born. That was when she realized that her mother was not a saint after all, just a woman, as human and fallible as Hope was herself and just as prone to snap judgments. And wrong ones.

"Maybe it won't work," Hope said to her sister. "But you never really know until you try. That's how you figure out what matters to you, and how much you're willing to sacrifice for it."

Hope picked up the bottle and refilled Hazel's glass. "Not that anybody's opinion matters in this except yours, but I do like David. And now that I think about it, under certain circumstances I actually *could* see myself making a junk journal for him."

"Yeah?" Hazel asked.

"Yeah," Hope said.

"Well, then. I shall take that under advisement."

As the sisters lifted their glasses to their lips, noises started to come from the front foyer, the jingling of keys and opening of doors and clomping of heavy feet.

"Rick?" Hope called out. "If you've been at the jobsite take off your boots, okay? I washed the floors this morning. Rick?"

"Already did," he said, entering the kitchen in his stocking feet and setting down his bag of groceries before giving Hope a peck on the lips. "Hey, Hazel. What's all this?" he said, nodding toward the overflowing box.

"Treasures," Hazel said.

"Oh, good," he said, and took the last piece of cheese. "Because we were almost out."

"Funny." Hope peeked into the grocery bag. "Did you get the steaks?"

"Yup. Three T-bones. And some stuff for salad. And some local strawberries too, first of the season. Oh, and there's a package in there too. I picked up the mail on the way in. Looks like it came from the prison."

"The prison?"

Hope reached into the bag and fished out a padded manila envelope, addressed to her. She ripped open the top, reached inside, and felt the soft kiss of cotton brush her fingertips. At the first glimpse of purple, gray, and periwinkle, Hope knew what it was and why it had come to her.

"Oh no," she murmured.

"What is it?" Rick asked.

"Mandy's quilt top."

"Her quilt top? Why would she send it to you?"

Hope didn't answer; she barely heard him. She pulled the fabric from the envelope, unfolded the quilt, and spread it out on the counter. As she did, another smaller envelope fell out.

"Wow. This is beautiful," Hazel said, running her hand across the patches of plum, lilac, heather, and teal and then leaning down to examine the tight and even seams, the perfectly met points. "I thought you said she was a beginner."

"She is," Hope said, unfolding the letter she had taken out of the smaller envelope. "A very talented beginner. And a very motivated one. Until now."

As she read the letter, the scrawled and anguished words, splotched and smeared with the tears of the writer, Hope's heart clutched with shared anguish. She pressed her hand against her lips and shook her head. Rick moved close, put his arm over her shoulder, and read along with her. Halfway down the page, the muscles in his neck twitched as he clenched his jaw.

"That's just not right," he murmured. "It's her word against that other lady. How can they know for sure who's telling the truth?"

"What's it say?" Hazel asked. "Why did she send you the quilt? I thought she was making it for her kid."

"She was," Hope said, eyes still scanning the letter. "But now, since that fight with Nita, they're delaying her release. Not by a lot, but still . . ." Hope sighed heavily. "David and his stupid policies. Didn't he realize what would happen next?"

"What's David got to do with it?" Hazel asked, looking uncomfortable.

"It's a policy that when inmates are involved in fights they can have some of their time off for good behavior rescinded," Hope said. "Two weeks would be the minimum in this sort of case, which tells me that David was trying his best to be lenient. But the problem is, now Mandy's dad is using this as ammunition in his court battle to deny Mandy's parental rights. He's trying to paint her as violent, unstable, and unreformed."

"That's terrible," Hazel said. "But can't her lawyer just fight back? That's what they do in court, right?"

"Mandy doesn't have a lawyer. She's got to fight this all on her own and from inside a prison. And, honestly, I'm not sure she's got any fight left in her. That's why she sent the quilt, because she says she'll probably never get to see Talia again and so she's sending it to me so I can finish it for McKenzie's baby."

Rick, who was still holding the letter, read the final lines aloud.

" 'In a month I'll walk through the gate. They say I'll be free, but it's not true. No matter what I do in the future or how hard I try, I know I can't be free of the past. People never let you forget, not ever.

" 'Anyway, I hope your granddaughter will like the quilt. It's nice to think that some little girl can use it, even if she's not mine.' "

Rick stopped reading.

"She sounds terrible. All that stuff about her father? How can her father claim she hasn't changed if he never even went to visit her? I don't care what my kid did," Rick said, shaking his head. "No way would I let them rot in jail for five years without ever going to see them. How does this jerk think he's a fit parent anyway?"

"That's what I say," Hope replied, her sorrow swallowed up by the anger and indignation she shared with her husband. "Mandy may have given in, but I won't. She's paid the price for her crimes and worked hard to turn her life around. She deserves a chance to be with her daughter."

"But how can you help?" Hazel asked. "You're just her teacher."

"Not anymore," Hope corrected. "Which could turn out to be a good thing. As an employee of the prison, I couldn't have any personal contact with Mandy. But now, as her friend . . ." Hope walked across the room and started rummaging through her purse. "Hazel, next time you text David, tell him I said, 'Thank you for firing me.' "

Hope took her phone out of her bag and started dialing.

"Who are you calling?" Hazel asked.

"Kate. She's lived here her whole life, worked at the capitol, knows everybody. If there's a lawyer in town who'd be willing to take Mandy's case, Kate will know how to find them."

Rick grinned. "Hey, Hazel. Why don't you and I cook up these steaks and toss some salad while Hope gets busy avenging injustice?"

"I'm on it," Hazel said, putting down her wineglass and pulling a head of lettuce from the grocery bag. "You know, I almost feel sorry for Mandy's dad. He doesn't know it yet, but making my sister mad? That was a big mistake."

Chapter 39

Kate did know an attorney, Diane Waverly. She wasn't very encouraging.

"It's always a crapshoot in these situations. So much comes down to the judge. It's good that you're willing to testify to Mandy's character," Diane said, looking at Hope and Kate in turn, "but I don't know how much of a difference it will make. I'll be honest with you: The fact that Mandy was involved in a fight involving weapons so soon before a judge will be ruling on her case is not good."

"But Mandy didn't start the fight," Hope protested. "Nita did. There is no way she would have stolen a blade from the supply cabinet, not in a million years. I'm sure of it."

"I know you're sure," Diane said. "And it's possible that you're right. But if there's one thing I've learned in twenty-three years of legal practice, it's that people are capable of all kinds of things that people who care about them think they could never have done in a million years. Every judge in the county has learned the same thing. And if the mother has displayed suicidal tendencies—"

"Mandy is *not* suicidal," Hope said. "She was depressed when she first came to prison, but who wouldn't be? When you're twenty-one years old, a five-year sentence might as well be life without parole. Plus, she was still under the influence of drugs. She's been clean for more than four years. She goes to meetings every week."

"Well, it's good that she's still been clean for so long. Maybe she could volunteer to undergo random drug testing for a specified period of time. But when it comes to the fight, who started it, and who had possession of the weapon, a judge can't just take your word on it. You're going to need proof.

"Do you have any? And if not, can you get any?"

Hope looked a question at Kate.

"I don't think *we* can," Kate said. "Hope is persona non grata at the prison right now. It might be possible for me to go and ask a few questions, but I doubt it would turn up much. But maybe . . ." Kate looked at Hope, her expression brightening. "Maybe I could get in touch with somebody who could ask questions? Somebody who knows everybody's business?"

"Deedee?" Hope asked.

"It's worth a try," Kate said.

"Good," Diane said. "Now we're getting somewhere. But even if you can prove that Mandy didn't instigate the fight or provide the weapon, there's still no guarantee that a judge won't terminate her parental rights. She's been convicted of a felony.

"Plus, the child has been in the custody of the grandparents for the last five years. If I was the attorney for the other side, I'd argue that being separated from the grandparents who, at this point, are the only parents she really remembers, and being placed into the care of a woman she barely knows, would cause the child to suffer irreparable psychological and emotional damage."

"But Talia does know her mother," Hope said. "She's crazy about her. Talia and Mandy have been participating in a program designed to maintain the mother-child bond so that family reunification will be easier once the parent is released. Until Mandy's father got the court involved, they saw each other every two weeks. And Mandy has taken a ton of parenting classes, every course the prison offers. Besides, I thought that courts were supposed to lean toward family reunification whenever possible."

"They are," Diane said. "But 'whenever possible' is open to interpretation. Judges can also take the best interests of the child into consideration. And they should."

Diane leaned forward, resting both elbows on her desk, looking Hope squarely in the eye.

"I do think Mandy is being treated unfairly; that's why I've agreed to represent her on a pro bono basis. But the least powerful person in this situation is Talia. When families start to battle, children often get used as pawns. So, before we go any further down this road, are you sure Mandy will be a fit parent?"

"I'm sure she will," Hope said. "I'm not saying she'll be a perfect parent, because there's no such thing. But I know she'll devote every ounce of energy and effort she has to being the best possible mother for Talia. The reason I know that is because she's already spent the last five years doing exactly that."

"I agree with Hope," Kate said. "Everything Mandy does she does with Talia in mind. She's been a model prisoner. I don't know if there's such a thing as a model mother, but if there is, I'd bet my last dollar that Mandy would be it."

Diane shifted her weight back in her chair.

"All right, then. If the two of you are sure, then so am I. I'll do everything I can to help Mandy regain custody of her daughter. Even so, I can't guarantee the outcome. There are so many things that can go wrong. The best thing would be if this case never got in front of a judge at all. Any chance you can talk the family into changing their minds about bringing the suit?"

"From what I hear," Hope said, "Mandy's father is adamant. He threw Mandy out of the house when she was sixteen, something about her using the car without permission and staying out after curfew. I'm sure there was more to it than that, but that's when Mandy started getting into serious trouble. She didn't have anywhere to go, ended up living with a boyfriend, who was older and a drug dealer. She got pregnant with Talia at age eighteen, was arrested at twenty and incarcerated at twenty-one.

"I guess I could try to talk to Mandy's dad, but he doesn't know me at all. And he doesn't sound like the sort of person who listens to reason."

Diane glanced at her watch and got to her feet. "You never know. As a teacher, you might carry some kind of influence with him. And if not? Well, maybe you can find someone who does."

Chapter 40

Rick and Hope parked just down the street from a small but tidy ranch-style home with blue siding, a gray front door, and a well-tended lawn. The bushes were neatly trimmed and the flower beds newly mulched, with green shoots of soon-to-bloom daffodils.

"Maybe I should go in with you," Rick said as he set the parking brake.

"I don't think it's a good idea," Hope said. "Mandy's mother seems kind of shy. I think she'll be much more likely to open up in a one-on-one conversation, and to another woman."

"You're sure the dad isn't in there? I don't like the idea of you being around that guy."

"He should be at work by now," Hope said. "And Talia will be at school. Anyway, from what Mandy told me, he's not violent. He never hit her, or her mother."

"Yeah, well. Some guys can hit without throwing a punch," Rick groused. "Mandy's dad sounds like one of them. I hate a bully. What kind of father tosses his daughter out into the woods and then blames her for getting eaten by wolves? I kind of wish he was home. I'd like about five minutes alone with him."

"Be right back." Hope leaned across the seat, kissed him on the lips, and then hopped out of the truck. Before closing the door, she turned back toward him and said, "By the way, I am very, very happy that I picked you to be the father of my children."

"Well, okay. Me too," Rick said, and gave Hope a lopsided sort of grin. "Good luck. If you need anything, I'll be right here."

"I know you will."

Hope passed a couple of lawns and climbed the front steps of the blue rancher. A few moments after she rang the bell Lola, Mandy's mother, opened the door.

"Mrs. Lopez? My name is Hope Carpenter." Lola frowned but said nothing. "I was Mandy's teacher."

"Is my Mandy in trouble? I haven't seen her for weeks."

"None that you don't already know about," Hope said. "That's what I wanted to talk to you about. Do you have a few minutes?"

Lola looked left and right, as if she was checking to see who might be watching, then opened the screen door that separated them.

"Okay," she said. "I have to go pick Talia up for a dentist appointment in about half an hour. But please. Come inside."

Rick sat in his truck, his eyes glued to the gray door his wife had disappeared through, waiting.

Doing nothing had never been his strong suit. He had always been a man of action, a doer. Even though Mandy's father wasn't home, he didn't like the idea of Hope being in a stranger's house alone. But worse than that was the idea that he had no role to play here, no way to help his wife deal with a problem that she very much wanted resolved. It was a situation he found himself in a lot of late, or at least far more often than he would have liked, which would have been never.

This thing with Mandy really mattered to Hope. It mattered to Rick too, but for different reasons. He never could stand by and do nothing when somebody was being bullied. As a kid, he'd spent a lot of time in the principal's office, but only for defending the rights of other kids who were getting picked on by

those who were stronger, or bigger, or just plain meaner. But Rick
didn't have a dog in this hunt, not the way Hope did. As much as
he felt bad for Mandy, he'd never met her. The wronged party
Rick most wanted to avenge in this situation was his wife, but
there was little, perhaps nothing, he could do to help her.

Rick stared at the door, waiting for it to open. After about
twenty minutes, he turned on the radio, found an eighties rock
station, and slumped against the seat with his arms crossed over
his chest, feeling useless and guilty.

He wished he'd been more supportive about Hope taking the
job at the prison. More supportive? He sniffed and shifted in his
seat. He hadn't even been tolerant. In fact, he'd gone out of his
way to make her life miserable. Yes, it was at least partly because his own life had been so miserable at the time, but that
was no excuse. The truth was, he'd bullied her. Or tried to.

Luckily for those women at the prison, and for him, Hope
wasn't the kind of woman who could be pushed around. Certainly not by the likes of him. He'd always loved that about
Hope, the feisty core of her. Not everybody got to see that side
of her, but Rick did. That was what made it so special. He knew
that she felt safe enough with him so she could always be herself. More than anything in the world, Rick wanted Hope to feel
safe. To be safe.

That was the other part of why he hadn't wanted her to work
in the prison, or to go into that house without him.

Hope said that Mandy's father wasn't home, said she'd be
fine on her own. Probably she would. But with her in there and
him sitting out here, being useless, there was no way to know
for sure. The prison was even worse because the danger there
was real and more prevalent.

Yes, there were safety procedures and precautions, lots of
them. Hope told him about all that. And when David was at the
house for Christmas, Rick had cornered him when Hope wasn't
looking, quizzed him about the safety systems and incidences of
violence between inmates and staff. According to David, it almost never happened. Violent altercations were almost always
between inmates. Also, they were at an all-time low since he'd

become superintendent. That was reassuring. But, still, if something did happen, Hope would be on the other side of that wall, alone.

That was what had really bothered him, the walls. The physical walls, of course, but also the emotional walls that had come between Hope and himself. Until he lost his job, he hadn't even known they were there. He'd always thought that he and Hope were on the same side, teammates. Getting fired had forced him to face the truth.

With the distraction of his work removed and his sense of power and purpose defeated, Rick had begun to see how he and Hope had built parallel but separate lives for themselves, each running along their own personal track, rarely conflicting but also rarely intersecting. He blamed himself, for so many things.

He'd been such an ass.

Miserable as it had been for both of them, a part of him was grateful. Sometimes you have to lose everything you think is important before you realize that none of it was. But Hope was important to him; so were his kids, his community, the opportunity to get up in the morning, work hard, and come home tired but satisfied because you knew what you'd accomplished that day and that it would make life at least a little bit better for somebody.

He'd always been so proud of his engineering work, of putting his stamp on the city skyline. He still was. But he understood now that there are all kinds of ways to have an impact. The imprint we leave on the lives of others can be deeper, more meaningful, and more lasting than any edifice. Buildings can be torn down but not what you do for other people, especially the people you love.

He was glad he'd learned that lesson, grateful that Hope had stood by while he did, regretful that he'd made them both so miserable in the process. He wished he could make it up to her. She said there was nothing to make up for, but still . . . He was a doer. That piece of him never had and never would change. Neither would the need to protect his wife and champion her cause, especially when she was in the right.

The work she'd done in the prison lit her up in a way that he'd never seen before. It was difficult, and frustrating, and pioneering, and risky, and she was passionate about it. She had pushed through every obstacle, including him, to make it happen, building something from nothing, something that mattered. He was no more enthusiastic about her working at the prison than he'd ever been, but he knew that what she was doing was important and necessary.

Rick had always loved Hope. Now he was impressed with her.

At long last, the gray door opened.

Hope stepped through. She wasn't smiling. A woman with gray hair and a slight build followed her. They stood on the walkway talking for a moment; then the woman climbed into a blue sedan that had been parked in the driveway and drove off. Hope retraced her path past the neighboring yards toward the truck.

"Well?" he asked after she climbed inside and closed the door. "How'd it go?"

"Honestly? I don't know. . . ." Hope paused, gazing sightlessly up the street toward the corner where the blue sedan had turned right and disappeared. "She was cautious about opening up to me, especially at first. She's got perfectly reasonable concerns about how this will impact Talia; she was so little when Mandy was sentenced that she doesn't remember another home. And, of course, Lola loves Talia. It must be hard to think about letting her go.

"Still, though she didn't come right out and say so, I think she's worried about what will happen when Talia gets older. Apparently, everything was fine between Mandy and her dad until Mandy hit puberty, but then . . . I don't know. Something changed. It sounds like he suddenly didn't trust her; everything she said or did made him suspicious. Maybe he thought he was protecting her?"

Rick sputtered, "Maybe he was being a jealous jerk. I'm telling you, babe. The guy's a bully."

"Yeah, maybe. I do think he's the one driving this, not Lola.

She knows that Mandy has changed and would move heaven and earth to make a good home for Talia. But I think she's afraid to stand up to her husband. He sounds like the kind of man who doesn't budge once he's turned against someone. He's certainly proven that with his daughter. I think Lola's afraid the same rule applies to wives."

Rick reached across the seat, grabbed Hope's hand, and then pulled it to his lips, placing a smacking kiss on the ridge of her knuckles.

"You're an amazing woman, do you know that?"

Hope let out an unconvinced little laugh. "Thanks. But if I was really amazing I'd have walked out of that house knowing that Lola was going to stand up to her husband."

"How about formidable then? Or at least determined? You never know; things still might work out."

"They might," Hope said, though her tone made her doubts clear. "I appealed to her as a woman and a mother. That's really all I can do. The rest is up to her."

"Well. Maybe," Rick said. "I've been sitting here thinking and I'm not so sure about that."

Hope tilted her head to one side, frowning. "What are you talking about?"

"When it comes to helping Mandy regain custody, I do think you've done everything you can. But the other inmates still need you. You didn't do anything wrong and neither did they. I think you should try to get your job back."

"Hang on," Hope said, shaking her head hard, as if she were trying to clear water out of her ears. "Did you just say you wanted me to go back to work at the prison? I thought you hated me working there."

"I did," he admitted. "And the truth is, I still do in a way. But that was before I saw how much it meant to you and what a difference you're making by being there. Besides, even if you lose, sometimes you've got to stand up for what's right."

"But how? David wouldn't budge. He said he didn't have a choice. The truth is: I'm not sure he did. Policy."

"So go over his head."

"How? It's not like I can complain to the supervisor; he *is* the supervisor. Of everything."

"Go *way* over his head. David enforces policy. Appeal to the person who actually makes it."

"Okay," Hope said slowly. "Sounds good to me, but once again, I ask the obvious question—how? Do you have a plan?"

Rick sniffed and turned the key in the ignition. The old truck sputtered and complained for a moment, then roared to life.

"Not a plan exactly. More of an idea."

"An idea. Uh-huh. Are explosives and pickaxes involved? Spies? Superhero capes? Because that's what I think it would take."

Rick looked over his shoulder to check for traffic and then gave the gearshift a shove. The old truck groaned in protest, then slipped into first.

"I was thinking more along the lines of you, Kate, and a quilt," he said, pressing his foot onto the gas pedal. "But capes would be a nice touch."

Chapter 41

The steady drizzle did nothing to dampen the enthusiasm of the crowd that was standing shoulder to shoulder in Seattle's Waterfront Park, waiting for the rally to begin.

"Four more years! Four more years!" they chanted, and clapped their hands and sang along to the recording of "We Take Care of Our Own" that played over the loudspeakers. When three older women carrying blue and green pompoms began shaking them and started shouting, "We love Norma! Yes, we do! We love Norma! How 'bout you?" the crowd took up the answering cheer, shouting that yes, they, too, loved Norma.

While all this was going on, Hope and Kate, who had been delayed by traffic on the drive from Olympia to Seattle and then had to park eight blocks away because several streets had been blocked off for the rally, tried to push and squeeze and sweet-talk their way to the front of the crowd. It was very slow going.

"Now I know how salmon feel," Kate said, calling over her shoulder to Hope as they inched forward. "It's like trying to swim upstream to the spawning grounds."

"Just keep moving!" Hope replied, shouting to make herself heard over the cheering and music and chaos. "We'll get there. Good thing they started late."

When her progress forward was blocked by a man with a huge, almost mountainous body, Kate tapped him on the shoulder and said, "Excuse me, sir. Can my friend and I get by? We're trying to get up front to see the governor."

The man turned around, scowling. His beard hung almost to his belt. He wore a plaid shirt and a gray and red WSU Cougars baseball cap. When he looked down at petite little Kate, water dripped from the brim of his hat and onto Kate's nose. She swiped it away with the back of her hand.

"Lady, we're all trying to see the governor. I've been standing out here for two solid hours waiting to see the governor. You should have shown up earlier."

"Yes," Kate said, smiling, "but there was terrible traffic. We drove all the way up from Olympia because we want to deliver a quilt to the governor."

"A quilt?" The mountainous man scowled again and looked at Hope, who was holding the quilt, wrapped in a clear plastic bag to keep it from getting wet. "Why would you come up here to give the governor a quilt? You were already in Olympia. Why not just drop it off at the capitol? Or mail it?"

"We want to deliver it to Governor Russman personally, along with a letter. We're hoping that she'll intervene to help some friends of ours." Seeing no softening in Mountainous Man's expression, Hope looked up at his hat and smiled. "Oh, are you a Cougar? My husband went to WSU. Wonderful school."

"Sure is. I grew up near Pullman."

"Really? What a small world. My aunt Marilyn was from Pullman."

After a couple of minutes of small talk about small worlds, Mountainous Man let them pass and Hope and Kate progressed a few more yards, until their path was blocked by someone else, only to be cleared by the finding of common ground a few minutes later. It went on like that for a good forty minutes, which was just about the time that Governor Norma Russman arrived on the scene.

She was a good speaker. The crowd of enthusiastic support-
ers interrupted her with cheers and chants throughout her address. Hope and Kate were more focused on trying to work
their way over toward the right side of the stage, where the governor had entered and where they assumed she would make her
exit, than on the speech itself. Even so, after the governor out-
lined a quite detailed plan to improve high school graduation
rates and offer more advanced technological training at the
community colleges, preparing students for high-paying jobs
without incurring big educational debts, Kate said, "You know,
I was thinking of voting for the other guy, but after listening to
her I've changed my mind."

"She seems pretty smart," Hope said. "I like that she was a
teacher before she went into politics. And that she's a mother.
That's got to be good for us, don't you think? A mother of four
is bound to be compassionate."

"I hope so," Kate replied. "But she's also a politician. So who
knows?"

"I guess we'll find out—if we can get close enough to talk to
her. Oh, wait! It sounds like she's wrapping up. Come on!"

As the governor thanked the crowd and waved an arm over
her head, bidding them farewell, Hope and Kate pressed forward toward a line of metal stanchions, meant to separate the
candidate from the crowd. Hundreds of other people did the
same, thrusting their hands out, hoping Governor Russman
would shake them. Grinning from ear to ear, leaning out to
touch as many hands as she could, stopping now and then to exchange a few words with people, the governor slowly worked
her way down the line of admirers.

Hope had never liked crowds and she was worried about
Kate. The old woman was feisty enough to take care of herself
in almost any situation. But the people kept pressing forward.
Kate was so petite that Hope worried about her getting tram-
pled. The fervor of the crowd was starting to feel frightening to
Hope, like a pot about to boil over.

Apparently, Hope wasn't the only one who felt that way.

When the governor was only a few feet away from them, nearly close enough to touch, and Hope was getting ready to hold the purple and gray quilt across the stanchions and re-hearsing, yet again, what she was going to say, four men in dark suits moved closer to the governor.

One of them leaned close to the governor's ear, saying something that made her smile disappear for a moment. She nodded, then smiled once again and waved her arm high and wide over her head, as if she were signaling to one of the boats bobbing in the water behind her.

The men in the suits formed a tight, impenetrable wall of protection around the governor and began to guide her to the left side of the stage, in the opposite direction from where Hope and Kate were standing.

"Governor!" Hope cried, leaning across the metal railing as far as she could, the quilt in her arms. "Governor, please! I have something I want to give you!"

Hope shouted as loud as she could, but it was impossible to make herself heard over the crowd. The men in the suits closed ranks and whisked the governor to a waiting SUV.

And then she was gone.

Fifteen minutes into what had been a largely silent journey back to Olympia, Kate said, "Oh, I forgot to tell you; I went to the prison on Tuesday and was able to talk to Deedee."

"And?"

"According to her, the rumor is that Mandy did steal the blade. They say that Nita was the one who started the fight but that Mandy had taken it because she was depressed, thinking of cutting herself, but then used it on Nita when she attacked."

"That's not possible," Hope declared. "She wouldn't do that. They did a count of the supplies afterward and none of the blades was missing. Everything was accounted for."

"I know. But some people are saying the count was off to start with."

"It wasn't," Hope said. "I counted them myself. There were four blades total. I know I'm no math whiz, but even I can count to four."

"Well, maybe Deedee will come up with something. I told her to start asking around, even gave her some money to buy a few bags of Fritos. Maybe a few incentives will convince people to start talking." Hope nodded but said nothing, her eyes glued to the back of the pokey motor home they'd been following since merging onto the freeway.

"At least we tried," Kate said after a long moment. "That's got to count for something, doesn't it?"

"I suppose."

"Oh, come on now. Don't be so gloomy. Another two minutes and we'd have been able to talk with the governor. Next time, we will. There'll be other rallies."

"Don't think so. Not for a long time anyway. I read a couple of articles that explained the strategy. She doesn't have a primary opponent and the election is months away yet. This event was just supposed to rally her base and send a message to the other side, demonstrate her popularity and scare off any serious opposition, convince them to sit this one out."

"Well," Kate said after a moment's rumination, "then we'll approach her at some other event, preferably one that's slightly less insane."

"Maybe. But she doesn't have any public events on her schedule for the next ten days or so. Apparently, she's getting ready for a big trip to Japan, promoting trade. After that, she's going to a conference of western governors; then she's speaking to some group in Pennsylvania about economic development."

Kate scowled. "Doesn't the woman ever stay home?" she harrumphed. "I'm thinking about switching back my vote. Well, don't worry. We struck out this time, but we've got ten days to think of something else."

"True," Hope said, sitting up taller in her seat, then taking advantage of a hole in the traffic to change lanes and pass the motor home. "All kinds of things can happen in that time. We just need to come up with a new plan."

"Right," Kate said. "Any ideas?"

Hope paused for a moment, glancing into the rearview mirror as she pulled back into the right lane.

"Not really. Except that a miracle would come in very handy about now. Who do I see about arranging one of those?"

Chapter 42

Four days later, the much hoped and prayed for miracle had not appeared. Nor was Hope getting anywhere with her job search. After calling the Boys & Girls Club the day before to check on the status of her application, she was told that the position had been filled.

She hadn't even gotten an interview.

"Why don't you come with me," Rick suggested as he was lacing up his running shoes after they finished breakfast. "It'd get your mind off things. Running's great for stress."

"I wouldn't run unless zombies were chasing me." Hope sighed heavily and poured herself another cup of coffee. "I was thinking of painting an accent wall in the living room—six-inch stripes of red—carmine and cardinal. What do you think?"

"Uh-huh. Sounds great."

"You don't think it'll be too bright?"

"You're asking me for decorating advice? If you think it'll look good, then I'm sure it will. And if it makes you happy, then I'm all for it." Rick took a final slurp of coffee and hopped to his feet.

Hope propped her elbow on the table and rested her chin in her hand. "I don't know if it'll make me happy. But at least that way I'll have accomplished *something* today."

Rick looked at her.

"Are you planning to spend the whole day feeling sorry for yourself?"

"Nancy called. They hired a new arts and crafts teacher at the prison."

Rick winced. "Ow. I'm sorry. Well, maybe you do get to spend the whole day feeling sorry for yourself."

Hope shook her head and lifted her coffee cup to her lips. "I already told you: I'm going to paint an accent wall in the living room this morning. I'll spend the *rest* of the day feeling sorry for myself."

Rick smiled and bent down to give her a kiss.

"See you in an hour," he said.

In thirty-nine minutes, before Hope had even finished taping off the wall, Rick was back. He was huffing and puffing so hard that he could barely speak. His face was as red as the splotch of cardinal paint Hope had put up as a test color.

"Honey! Are you okay? Do you need to sit down? Should I get you some water?"

Rick shook his head, then bent forward, resting his hands on his thighs, sucking air.

"It's okay," he gasped after a moment. "Just. Need to. Catch my breath. Ran all the way up the stairs."

Hope's eyes went wide. "All five flights? Why didn't you just take the elevator?"

"Somebody's using it," he said, his breathing slower but still ragged. "Delivering some furniture. Had to tell you right away. I saw her."

"Saw who?" Hope said, shaking her head in confusion.

Rick stood up straight, grinning, and took one more big breath.

"The governor and two of her bodyguards. Down at Marathon Park. She's a runner, Hope. Runs almost every day."

Hope's forehead was dripping with sweat. Her lungs felt like they were about to explode, and a pinch of pain on her left foot hinted that a blister was ready to rise on her heel. But she'd made up her mind.

She was going to run an entire quarter mile without stopping even if it killed her. At the moment, this seemed like a possibility. But the footbridge was only a few yards ahead of her. Once she crossed it, she'd have reached her goal. At least she'd have something to show for the last five days of misery and aching muscles.

Just before stepping onto the footbridge, she shifted her burden to her other arm. Even though Hope had rolled it tightly into a tube shape before wrapping it in plastic, Mandy's quilt made an awkward baton, especially when Hope's hands were sweating. Her feet thumped heavily over the wooden slats of the bridge, a slow and steady drumbeat.

Excruciatingly slow, Hope thought to herself, willing her leaden legs to keep moving. Excruciating in every sense. But she was almost there. Another twenty yards. Fifteen. Ten.

Hope felt the whoosh of disturbed air before she actually saw Rick pass her. Again. He sped past her with long, loping, gazelle-like strides, then ran to the end of the bridge and a few yards farther before turning around and slowing his pace to a jog, meeting Hope at the end of the footbridge.

"Great job, babe! You did it!"

Chest heaving, Hope let the quilt-baton drop to the ground and took the water bottle Rick held out to her, sucking down half of it before speaking.

"That was absolutely miserable."

"But you did it," Rick said. "And without zombies. Good job!"

"Slow as I run, it's a good thing there weren't any zombies involved. Otherwise, I'd already be among the undead. How many times did you go around?"

"Twice. That's all I have time for. I've got to get over to the jobsite. The building inspector is due this morning. You ready to go?"

Hope looked to the left and right, scanning the horizon, looking for a redheaded woman about her age who, according to Rick, would be running between two fit men in their early thirties. She saw only individual runners and none of them had red hair. She looked at Rick.

"No sign of her on the other side of the lake?"

"You think I'd have kept it from you if I had? Honey, you tried. That's all anybody can do."

"I guess. It was always kind of a crazy plan," she said, sounding more resigned than she felt. "She's leaving for Japan tomorrow. Maybe I should have just mailed it."

"You still can. Just because you don't hand it to her personally doesn't mean she won't actually see it or read the letter."

"True. But chances would be a lot better if I did. Plus, I feel like if I could just talk to her for even a few minutes, I could explain what happened and why the quilting program should be reinstated. At this point, I don't even care if I get my old job back. But the program should be saved.

"I know this is small potatoes compared to trade with Japan, but this program can make a difference in the lives of women who deserve a second chance. Giving these women a skill they can feel proud of, a chance to give something of value to someone else, sometimes for the first time in their—"

"Babe?" Rick looked at his watch.

"Sorry, sorry. I've rehearsed my speech so many times in my head that it just kind of popped out."

"You ready?"

Hope shook her head. "You go on without me. I want to finish the loop; then I'll walk home."

"It's a pretty long walk."

"I know," Hope said, bending down and picking up the plastic-wrapped quilt. "I want to stay a little longer. Just in case. And if I don't see her . . ." Hope shrugged. "Well, then I'll put it in the mail. You're right. All I can do is try."

Rick gave her a quick kiss. "See you tonight," he said before jogging off toward the truck.

"See you tonight."

Carrying the quilt under her arm, Hope finished walking the upper loop of Capitol Lake. She considered going around again, but that would be another three miles, not counting the walk back to the condo. Besides, it was almost ten o'clock. Either the governor wasn't running today or they'd missed her. Much as she hated giving up, it was time to admit defeat and head home.

It was a nice day. Since she didn't have anywhere special to be—that was one benefit of being jobless—Hope took her time. Strolling along the avenue, she peeked into shop windows and took note of a few restaurants she and Rick might want to try in the future. If the two of them could ever manage to be employed at the same time, maybe they'd be able to eat out more often.

She went inside the bookstore, petted the shop cat, checked out the children's section, smiling to herself as she flipped through some of the picture books, imagining future field trips with her future granddaughter, then placed an order for a new baking book that was coming out just before Rick's birthday.

She was glad Rick had cut back on his baking, it was better for both their waistlines, but she hoped he'd take the hint that perhaps he'd cut back a little too much. Hope hadn't had a decent cookie since McKenzie had come over that day. And she couldn't remember the last time she'd had a good loaf of homemade bread. At this point, she'd even have gotten excited about rosemary olive loaf.

On second thought, she decided, maybe not.

However, Hope was in luck. As she stepped through the bookstore's door and onto the street, her nose was greeted by a delicious aroma of coffee, baking butter, and sugar. Olympia Coffee Roasting Company was less than a block away.

Remembering that she'd stowed some money in the pocket of her jacket a few days before, Hope went inside, ordered a small latte and a chocolate croissant, then sat down at one of the tables to enjoy a well-deserved treat. Surely a four-mile walk would negate the calories in a chocolate croissant. And if not, she really didn't care.

After taking a moment to appreciate the pretty leaf design that the clever and creative barista had drawn into the latte foam, Hope took a sip. The coffee was deliciously strong but perfectly mellowed by the creamy flavor of the hot milk. Biting through the flaky crisp layers of croissant to the rich chocolate in the center, Hope decided she would be returning to this coffee shop as frequently as possible. Did McKenzie know about this place?

Looking around the mostly young and entirely hip clientele, Hope decided she probably did. There wasn't another over-fifty face in the room. At least at that moment. As Hope took another sip, the door opened. A middle-aged woman with red hair, wearing black running capris and a T-shirt, flanked by two fit young men in their early thirties, walked up to the counter and ordered three iced coffees.

Hope almost choked on her coffee.

It wasn't possible. After all this time, all the miles she'd clocked, carting Mandy's quilt around the lake, hoping beyond hope that she might almost literally run into the governor of the state, she stumbled upon her in a coffee shop entirely by accident?

Maybe it didn't qualify as a genuine miracle, but it was pretty close.

Hope swiped her hand across her lips to banish any traces of foam and retrieved the rolled-up quilt from the chair next to her. The governor was still at the counter, joking with the cashier. Hope approached slowly, not wanting to interrupt. When there was a lapse in the conversation, Hope cleared her throat.

"Excuse me? Governor Russman? Do you have a moment? There's something I wanted to give you."

Still smiling, the governor turned around to face Hope. But the instant Hope pulled the plastic-wrapped, tube-shaped quilt from under her arm, the governor's smile fled. Almost as instantly, the two fit young men stepped in front of her, glowering at Hope, putting a wall of muscle and menace between Hope and the governor.

"Step back, ma'am! Put the package on the floor and your hands up. Do it now!"

"The package?"

Seeing the look in those young men's eyes, feeling the crackling tension in the air, realizing it was fear and that she was the cause of it, Hope did as she was told.

"It's not a package. I mean, it is, but there's nothing danger-ous inside. It's a quilt. I just want to give the governor a quilt."

A red head popped up over the shoulders of the two fit young men.

"A quilt? Somebody made me a quilt? Can I see it?"

She muscled her way between the two men, who looked none too happy about the situation. Hope glanced at the taller of the two, her eyes silently asking permission to move. The man frowned and gave a short nod.

Hope knelt down, ripped away the plastic cover, and then got to her feet again, unfurling Mandy's quilt with a purple and periwinkle flourish. The governor gasped.

"Oh, it's gorgeous! What's the pattern? My grandmother was an avid quilter, but I don't recognize this block. And you made it for me?"

"It's called Dove in the Window, an old block and a beautiful one. A friend and I stitched a few of the blocks and finished the quilting and binding, but most of the piecing was done by a young woman named Mandy. She's an inmate at the women's prison and I'm her teacher, or was, until a couple of weeks ago when the program was ended."

"There's a letter pinned to the back of the quilt," Hope said, placing the quilt in Governor Russman's arms, "but if you have a few minutes, I'd like to tell you about it."

"Governor?" One of the tall and fit young men took a step forward. "Ma'am, you've got your final Japan briefing in forty-five minutes."

"And I need to shower and get changed beforehand," the governor said, then turned toward Hope. "What's your name?"

"Hope Carpenter."

"Nice to meet you, Hope. I'm Norma Russman." The gover-nor extended her hand. Hope shook it. "And I've got exactly five minutes."

Chapter 43

"Mr. Hernandez? Are you still there?"

"Yes."

"Please hold for the governor."

Though there was no one but himself in his office and Governor Russman wouldn't be able to see him through the phone, David suddenly felt the need to sit up in his chair, straighten his tie, and square his shoulders.

When Steve Vincent, the aide to the governor who served as the liaison for the commission on prison reform, called a couple of weeks before, David hadn't been surprised. They'd already chatted once or twice about David's forthcoming report on programming for the female prison population, a report David anticipated putting a lot of time into only to see it gather dust on some shelf at the capitol.

The surprising part was when Steve started asking specific questions about the quilting pilot program. David hadn't discussed it with him or really with anyone outside the prison. But somehow, Steve knew about it. Apparently, the governor did too and wanted to know more.

When David explained that the program, while initially promising, had been suspended because of safety concerns, Steve said that the governor wanted a report anyway, along with any information about the other programs they'd been working on—the arts and crafts classes, the family preservation project, and the practical living initiative.

"Well, the arts and crafts classes had to be suspended along with the quilting pilot. But the new teacher came on board last week, so that's back on track. The practical living initiative is still in the idea phase," David explained. "We'd target inmates who have less than a year left on their sentence and offer classes in basic life skills—budgeting, financial education, job interview techniques, even basic meal planning, nutrition, and grocery-shopping skills, real rubber-meets-the-road stuff, the kinds of skills that are assumed but which a lot of our population missed along the way."

"So? Kind of like Home Ec? Sounds interesting. Got somebody in mind who can teach all that?"

David paused, sighing inwardly. He'd sprouted a lot of gray hair in the last six months. He probably couldn't blame all of that on Hope—he *was* in his mid-forties—but it was hard not to believe she hadn't sped the process. The woman was very good at her job but *such* a pain. But, he had to admit, less so toward the end than she'd been in the beginning. If inmates could be reformed, maybe Hope could as well? Still . . .

"Uh, no," David said. "Not right now."

"Well, sounds like something worth exploring. Anyway, I'd like for you to write all this up—especially the quilting thing. The governor wants to dig into this."

"Okay," David replied. "Say, any idea how she heard about it?"

"Not a clue. All I know is she wants to put it on the front burner, so if you could write it up and send it over by ten o'clock tomorrow morning—"

"Tomorrow morning? What's the rush?"

"She's flying to Japan tomorrow and wants to read the report on the plane. Hey, David, gotta go. I'm late for a meeting. You on this?"

"Sure," David said. "Not a problem. You'll have it by ten tomorrow."

David had stayed up half the night writing the report and

e-mailed it to Steve at 9:51 a.m. the next day. Exactly six minutes later, Steve e-mailed back: *Thanks, buddy. Appreciate it.*

And then . . . nothing.

It was disappointing but not unexpected. This was far from
the first time that David had pushed to finish something somebody said they absolutely had to have as soon as humanly possible, only to send the work and never hear from them again. It
was part of the job.

But now the governor was calling.

Once they got through pleasantries and her apology for taking so long to get back to him, it was clear that Governor Russman had not only read his report but also spent a lot of time
thinking about it. Her questions were insightful and her commitment to prison reform and willingness to roll up her sleeves
and make it happen was genuine, the furthest thing from election year grandstanding. Next time, David told himself, he was
definitely voting for Russman.

"Well, I think the practical living program is definitely worth
pursuing," the governor said, about fifteen minutes into the
conversation. "I've already got people working on the funding. It looks like we've only got room in the budget to fund a
part-time position, but you might want to start thinking about
staffing."

"Yes, ma'am. I—I do have someone in mind."

"Good. Now let's talk about the quilting pilot program. As I
understand it, the cancellation was specifically based on safety
concerns. Otherwise, it had been very successful, is that right?"

David detailed the circumstances and thinking behind his decision.

"Uh-huh," the governor said. "I think that was a reasonable
response. But it also sounds like you limited participation to inmates with good behavior records and had very strict safety
procedures in place that, up until the incident, had been effective. And when it was looked into later, nothing was missing
from the cabinet?"

"That's right, ma'am. All four blades were still in the cabinet."

"So, the weapon in question might not have come from the classroom at all, isn't that true? I mean, if you were dealing with fifty blades, or even twenty, it's easier to believe there could have been a miscount. But four? You don't need to be an accountant to tally up four blades. So, it's possible the one used in the incident could have been smuggled in by some other means."

Before running for office, the governor had worked in the public defender's office. Her interrogation skills had not diminished. David wiped a sweating palm on his pants leg and coughed.

"We're very careful about screening and searches, but yes. That is a possibility. However, since we couldn't prove it one way or another, I thought it best to err on the side of safety."

"Agree completely," Governor Russman replied. "Safety has to take highest priority. And I wouldn't presume to tell you how to run your institution; your record speaks for itself. But if you *could* prove that the blade was smuggled in by some other means, then I assume you would have no qualms about reinstituting the program? Or even expanding it?"

"No, ma'am. None at all. As a matter of fact, there have been some rumors floating around among the inmates recently that suggest the blade might have come from the outside. Nothing I've been able to substantiate so far, but—"

"Is that so? Well, Mr. Superintendent, if you can get to the bottom of it and find out if the rumors are more than rumors, I'd definitely like to know about that."

"Certainly, Governor. I'll get on it right away."

"Good. Thank you for your time, David. And keep up the good work."

Ten minutes later, David was striding down a corridor that led to the cafeteria with even more than his usual energy and focus. When he saw Nancy exiting the cafeteria, talking with a red-eyed Ronda Bitters, a fairly recent arrival, he interrupted their conversation.

"Deedee?" Nancy said. "Oh yes. I saw her a few minutes ago. But she'd finished eating and was getting ready to leave.

Probably went out to the courtyard for a cigarette. I think Nita is out there too. I was surprised to see her back already. That flew by, didn't it? And so peacefully."

"Thank you," David said without commenting, then continued on his way, taking a left at the end of the hall instead of a right and exiting a pair of double doors into the courtyard, which appeared to be empty.

However, the sound of voices coming from the northwest corner, behind a bed of soon-to-bloom roses, caught his attention and he began walking in that direction. When the volume and intensity of the voices increased and was followed by a shout of surprise and pain, he started running.

Though the faces and bodies were obscured by the rosebushes, he saw two female forms circling each other like prizefighters before a bout, their movements tense and erratic, searching for an opening, a weakness to exploit, a hole through which to escape.

David ran as fast as he could, arms and legs pumping, adrenaline flooding his body, breath coming in bursts. When he was just a few yards away, the larger figure lunged and the smaller shrieked in anguish. David shouted as loud as he could, roaring warnings and demands. The figures froze for an instant, startled by the sound, then turned toward him.

He saw the silver glint of steel and the sickening red of gushing blood. He heard another cry of pain, this time his own, as the larger figure lunged again and he flung himself forward, putting himself between the smaller woman and the blade.

Chapter 44

In the middle of May, after weeks of dithering between dreary weather and fine, spring finally seemed to make up her mind about staying. This delay and indecision was annual and irritating, but once it had passed, Hope, like every other resident of the Pacific Northwest, quickly forgave and forgot, making the most of the sunny season.

Knowing it would be busy on a Saturday morning, she arrived at the coffee roasters early, hoping to snag a table by the sun-drenched front window. After ordering a large iced latte and half a dozen crispy, buttery French *palmiers* cookies, she leaned casually against the counter and sipped coffee through a straw, trying not to look like she was stalking people, even though she absolutely was.

The moment two young mothers with four preschoolers between them shifted their chairs back and started swiping up a small mountain of cookie crumbs, crumpled napkins, and broken crayons, Hope swooped in. "Oh, are you leaving? Do you mind? Don't worry about the crumbs. Let me take care of cleaning up. It looks like you've got your hands full." Since two of the four preschoolers had started to howl piteously, the young mothers gratefully accepted her offer.

McKenzie, looking like a balloon in danger of bursting, wearing a voluminous maternity dress and her only shoes that fit, a pair of blue Crocs, waddled through the door just as Hope finished wiping down the table. "Oh, good! You got us a seat by the window. It's such a pretty day."

Mandy arrived a couple of minutes later, looking around the café with an anxious expression until Hope caught her eye and waved her over. After introducing the two younger women, Hope hopped up from the table to place another order.

"Kenz, I know you'll want a chai. Iced or hot?"

"Iced, please. Large. And can you get some more cookies?"

"Sure. Mandy? What do you want?"

Mandy pressed her lips together. The anxious look returned to her eyes.

"I don't know. Just coffee? I've never been to one of these places before."

"Plain coffee?" McKenzie shook her head. "Uh-uh. Take a walk on the wild side. Get a chai. Or a mocha latte. You like chocolate?"

Mandy smiled. "Who doesn't?"

"Got it," Hope said. "One large iced chai. One large iced mocha. And six more *palmiers*. Is that all?"

"Some muffins?" McKenzie asked, making a pitiful "please, Mommy" face. "Your grandchild is starving."

"As usual." Hope chuckled. Mandy reached toward her purse, but Hope waved her off. "No, no. I've got it. This is your Coming Out party. You and McKenzie stay here and get to know each other. I'll get the food."

A line had formed at the counter, so Hope had to wait a few minutes before placing her order, but that was fine; she was in no hurry. By the time she returned, Mandy looked far more at ease. The two young women were gabbing like girlfriends and seemed to have hit it off, just as Hope had thought they would.

"Oh, I *know*," Mandy said, shaking her head in sympathy. "The last month before I had Talia the only thing I could fit into was flip-flops. And it was February. My feet were so cold they looked like two big, fat, blue slugs. It was awful." Mandy laughed. "When are you due?"

"Three more weeks," McKenzie sighed. "I wish I could have her right now. Today. I've been thinking about swallowing an eviction notice so she'll get the hint."

"Not today," Hope said, passing out the beverages after taking her seat. "I need to get back over to your place and finish wallpapering the nursery."

"She means re-wallpapering," McKenzie said. "I tried to do it on my own and made a total mess of it. It was totally crooked and the edges came up."

"It wasn't that bad," Hope said. "You didn't have the right tools, that's all."

"She's being kind," McKenzie said in a conspiratorial tone, leaning closer to Mandy. "It was a complete disaster. You see, Mandy, though I come from a long line of domestic divas, the crafty gene seemed to skip me. Well . . . except for crocheting. As it turns out, I am pretty good at that."

"Much better than me," Hope said.

"Not true," McKenzie said. "At least not yet. But I'm getting better. I finished the sweater last night. Do you want to see?"

Responding to Hope's and Mandy's eager assurances in the affirmative, McKenzie reached into her purse and pulled out a tiny pink cardigan with raglan sleeves. Seeing it, Mandy clutched her hand to her chest.

"Awww. It's so teeny and cute!" she exclaimed.

"Don't look too close. I messed up in a couple of places," McKenzie said. "But I don't think it's too terrible. Not for my first sleeves. It was a lot harder than the hat."

"I think you did a great job," Hope said.

"Me too," Mandy added. "I could never make something like that."

"But you can sew," McKenzie said. "Mom showed me your quilt before she gave it to the governor. It was just gorgeous."

"Thanks. I had a pretty good teacher," Mandy said, looking toward Hope. "Any word on how that went?"

"With the governor?" Hope asked, shaking her head when Mandy nodded. "She promised she'd look into it when she got back from her travels, but—nothing. At least not yet. But you never know," Hope said with more conviction than she felt. "The governor really loved your quilt. Purple is her favorite color too. Something still might come of it."

"I hope so," Mandy said, her eyes downcast as she picked up one of the *palmiers* and broke it in half. "I feel bad that the quilting program was canceled because of me."

"That wasn't your fault," Hope said firmly. "It wasn't."

"Yeah, well . . ." Mandy mumbled, crumbing the edge of the cookie.

McKenzie shifted her gaze to her mother and then, rightly reading Hope's silent permission to change the subject, she said, "So how are things going for you? Does it feel good to be out? Or weird?"

Mandy smiled a little. "Both, I guess. It's not like how I thought it would be. The halfway house is okay. The food is way better than it was at the prison. But I can't sleep at night. Too quiet." She puffed out a little laugh. "Who would ever have thought that I'd miss all that racket, huh? I guess I just got used to it.

"I miss my friends, too. Funny thing is, I didn't really start thinking of them as my friends until right before I got out. But you get close to people after a while, know? I spend a lot of my free time writing letters to the girls. Deedee wrote back, but it was mostly pictures. I don't really know anybody on the outside.

"Well, I do," Mandy said. "But my old friends are part of the reason I ended up getting into trouble, so I'm steering clear of them. And, you know, my parents and I aren't exactly on speaking terms."

"What about Talia?" Hope asked. "Have you been able to see her?"

"Not yet. Diane is petitioning to get me some supervised visits. Thanks for getting her to take my case," Mandy said, looking up. "I wouldn't have a chance without her."

"She's a good lawyer," Hope said. "I'm sure she'll be able to make it happen."

"I hope so," Mandy said. "I'm trying not to think about it too much right now. Diane says that the best thing I can do to convince the court that I'm ready to take care of Talia is to find a job. So, I'm just trying to focus on that."

"How's it going?"

"No luck so far. I've filled out a bunch of applications, fast-food places mostly. But they all have that question on the bottom: 'Have you ever been convicted of a felony?' Of course I check off 'yes.' I have to. But then, when I hand it back in and the manager sees that, even if he was real friendly before, he stops smiling and says he'll call if they're interested. No calls yet," Mandy said. "Big jerks.

"My counselor at the halfway house is going to set up an interview for me next week, though," she said, sounding more optimistic, "with a landscaping company. They've been able to place a few people there. It'd only be for the summer, pulling weeds and mowing lawns and stuff. But I wouldn't mind that. I like working outside."

Mandy lifted her head and gazed out the window onto the sunlit Saturday sidewalk, smiling as she took in the sight of trees, and people walking their dogs, or talking on their phones, or talking to each other.

"That's the good part," she mused. "Being able to walk out the door, go anyplace I want to go, and do anything I want to do. Well, as long as it's legal and I'm back by eight. The halfway house is pretty strict about curfew.

"What about you?" she asked Hope. "Any luck with the job hunt?"

Hope shook her head. "Not yet. Life on the outside is tough."

"It sure is," Mandy said.

The three women finished their coffee and pastries and got up to leave, yielding their prime table to another group. Hope offered to drive Mandy back to the halfway house but she demurred, saying she was going to walk around the area to see if anyone was hiring, then take the bus. Smiles and hugs were exchanged and Hope reminded Mandy that she'd be happy to serve as a reference if she needed one.

Just before they parted, McKenzie reached into her bag, pulled out a business card, and gave it to Mandy.

"So, listen, a couple of my friends and I have decided to start getting together on Wednesdays after work, here at the coffee shop, to talk and crochet. Well, one of them is actually a knitter, but . . . Anyway, if you'd like to come, give me a call."

Mandy held the card gingerly in her hand, as if she were cupping a baby bird in her palm, something fragile and precious and utterly unexpected. She looked up at McKenzie.

"Really?"

McKenzie nodded. "I'll probably only be able to come for a couple more weeks, you know, until the baby comes. But I think it'll be fun."

"Wow. Yeah. I'd like that. But . . ." Mandy's eager expression faded. "I don't have any needles or yarn or anything. And until I get a job—"

"Oh, don't worry about that," McKenzie said, flapping her hand. "Do what I do: shop in Mom's stash. She's got enough yarn to open a store."

"She's right," Hope said. "More than I could use in three lifetimes. Honestly, Mandy, you'd be doing me a favor by taking some of it off my hands."

"You sure?"

"Absolutely," McKenzie said. "I was planning to follow Mom home and find something for my next project. I can pick out something for you too, if you want. How about purple? You could make Talia a scarf."

"Okay," Mandy said, grinning. "That'd be great."

"Good," McKenzie replied. "See you on Wednesday."

When they got back to the condo, McKenzie parked and then rode upstairs with her mother.

"That was nice of you," Hope said as the elevator door opened.

"What was?"

"Inviting Mandy to your crocheting group."

"Oh, well," McKenzie said. "She seemed lonely. And, anyway, I like her."

"Well, it was still nice of you. It meant a lot to her. You're a nice person, you know that?"

"You think so?" McKenzie replied. "Well, don't let it get around. I'm aiming for another promotion after I get back from maternity leave. But I'll never make it in management if they think I'm too soft."

Hope laughed and opened the front door, then stopped dead in her tracks, sniffing the air.

"Oh no," Hope murmured.

"Dad's baking again?" McKenzie sniffed too. "What's wrong? Smells good."

Hope dropped her purse on the floor.

"Rosemary," she said, and strode straight to the kitchen.

Chapter 45

When Hope entered the kitchen, Rick was standing at the kitchen counter, slicing bread. Nancy was sitting at the kitchen table, eating it. Both of them looked up when Hope entered the room.

"Nancy! Oh, thank heaven," Hope said, shoulders slumping with relief. "I thought something bad had happened."

"Hope has a thing about rosemary," Rick explained to Nancy before putting his bread knife down on the cutting board. "I've got some work to do in the bedroom. So, I think I'll leave you two to talk."

He looked at McKenzie, who had entered the room shortly after her mother, with raised brows. McKenzie frowned for a moment, then said, "Right. Well, I'm going to go look for some yarn. Still in the guest room, Mom?"

"The blue plastic bin in the closet. Second shelf from the top on the right-hand side," Hope said automatically, keeping her eyes on Nancy's solemn face as she took a seat at the table while Rick and McKenzie left the room.

"I was going to say I was happy to see you, but something tells me I shouldn't be. Not today."

Nancy tipped her head to one side, her somber expression

softening into one of compassion. "Not today," she echoed. "It's not all bad news. But something happened at the prison."

Hope propped her elbow onto the table and covered her mouth with her hand, steeling herself for what was to come. Nancy took a deep breath, then began to speak.

"Deedee has been asking a lot of questions lately, trying to see if she can get any information about the fight between Nita and Mandy and where that rotary blade could have come from if not the sewing supplies. It seems that she was making progress.

"One of the new girls, Ronda, said she overheard one of the other prisoners saying that she'd heard that Nita had gotten close to one of the cafeteria workers and exchanged—shall we say favors—to get him to smuggle some blades in for her.

"According to Ronda, this prisoner said Nita wanted to get back at Mandy. She had to know she'd get sent back to medium for a while, but apparently, she thought it would be worth it because she knew Mandy had more to lose. Since Mandy was one of the only prisoners with access to the sewing cabinet and since rotary blades are so unusual, she reckoned she'd be able to pin everything on Mandy. And with Mandy being so depressed about possibly losing custody of Talia, and having been on suicide watch in the past—"

"*Years* ago," Hope said. "Right after she arrived."

"Nita thought people would believe it," Nancy continued, talking over Hope's interruption.

"Which is *exactly* what I said must have happened," Hope said, smacking the table with her hand. "So Deedee found out the truth?"

"Maybe," Nancy said, holding her hands up as if to warn Hope about getting ahead of herself. "It was all hearsay and speculation. And Ronda, while I wouldn't call her a pathological liar, seems to have a pretty flexible relationship with the truth.

"You know how things are inside. Rumors are rampant. Put a thousand women behind walls with too much time on their hands and they're going to spread all kinds of rumors and tell all kinds of tales, some true, some not.

"So even if Ronda overheard this conversation as she claims, that doesn't mean the people she was eavesdropping on were telling the truth. Plus, Deedee was offering rewards in exchange for information—"

Hope's face fell. "Kate. And the Fritos."

"Exactly," Nancy said. "If some of them were willing to make you cry and quit your job in exchange for a few bags of crisps, it's not a stretch to think that they'd make up a story about Nita smuggling blades for the same sort of prize."

"So you don't think the blade belonged to Nita?" Hope asked.

"I'm getting to that part," Nancy said, lifting her hand. "Apparently, Nita heard about the story that was going around and that Deedee was the one who'd been asking questions. On Friday, she found Deedee alone in a corner of the courtyard and attacked her."

"No!" Hope gasped. "Is she all right?"

"She will be. The doctors put twenty-two stitches in her forearms—she was trying to defend herself—but apart from the scars, they say she'll be fine. Nita pulled a blade on her," Nancy said. "A round one."

Hope's mouth dropped open. For a moment, it felt like she'd forgotten to breathe or that her heart had skipped a beat. But then it started pounding, double time, and her eyes brimmed.

"So, it wasn't Mandy. She didn't steal the blade from the cabinet."

Nancy shook her head. "She didn't."

"This is *amazing* news," Hope said, tears spilling over even as she began to laugh. She shoved her chair back from the table. "Amazing!

"I've got to call Diane. No, wait. First I should call Mandy; then I'll call Diane. And David! The only reason he canceled the quilting program was because of the blades. Does he know about this?"

Hope put her hands against the table to push herself up from her chair. Nancy grabbed her around the wrist.

"Hang on, Hope. You didn't let me finish."

There it was again, the feeling that she'd forgotten to breathe. But this time, instead of the thrill of good news, the sensation was caused by the dread that gripped her when she looked into Nancy's eyes.

"David was in the courtyard when the fight broke out. He was the first staff member on the scene. When he put himself between Nita and Deedee, Nita started going for him instead. The other staff got there as quickly as they could, but . . ." Nancy paused for a moment, swallowed, and blinked back tears. "He was hurt pretty badly."

Hope sank back down into her chair. "How badly? Is he going to be all right?" she whispered.

"I don't know. I was with him when the ambulance arrived. He lost a lot of blood. And his face . . ." Two tears rolled down Nancy's cheeks. "Oh, Hope. His face."

"Oh, my God." Hope shut her eyes. "Oh, my God. Please."

Nancy closed her eyes as well and grabbed Hope's hand. "Oh yes. Please. Please, God."

Hope sat there, clutching Nancy's hand, pleading with raw and honest ineloquence for the life of a man who, until that moment, Hope had not realized was her friend.

Even later, Hope could never say how long they sat there. But, after a time, her pleas were interrupted by the clunking sound of footsteps on the floor as McKenzie came up behind them, clomping into the kitchen in her Crocs.

"Mom? Are you okay?"

Hope wiped her eyes with the back of her hand. "I'm fine," she said, her voice stark and static. She rose to her feet. "Where's my purse?"

"Still in the foyer," McKenzie said. "You dropped it there when you smelled Dad's bread, remember?"

"That's right," Hope said, sniffling as she turned around and started to walk toward the door, where McKenzie was standing. "Okay. Good."

"Mom?" McKenzie said again, her face a mask of confusion. "Are you going somewhere?"

"Yes," she said, pushing past her daughter. "To the hospital."

"Oh. Can I come with you? I think my water just broke."

"Well, McKenzie, you're fully effaced and three centimeters dilated," the doctor said cheerfully, pulling the sheet down over McKenzie's knees. "Looks like we're going to have a baby today."

McKenzie's eyes went wide. "Today? Are you sure? I'm not due for three weeks." She clutched at Hope's hand. "It's too soon."

"No it's not," Hope said calmly. "You were early too, remember? And you weighed seven pounds and were healthy as a horse."

"The baby is fine," the doctor assured her. "I'm not at all concerned about her being early or underweight. She's ready."

"See?" Hope said when the doctor left to go check on some other patients. "Already a chip off the old block. She wants to make an entrance, just like you did."

McKenzie let out a short groan of pain and surprise, holding her breath for a moment and then letting it out in a whoosh.

"She might be ready," McKenzie said, looking at her mother, "but I don't know if I am."

"Yes, you are. One hundred percent. You've got this, Kenz. You are going to be a wonderful mother. This is one lucky little baby." Hope squeezed McKenzie's hand and blinked back tears, feeling like she was the lucky one.

"I love you, Mom."

"I love you too, baby."

Rick entered the room. "I called Zach. He's on his way."

"Good," Hope said. "What about Ted and Wanda? They wanted to be here for the birth."

Rick shook his head. "They're on vacation in Florida, but Zach said they'll be flying home the day after tomorrow. I don't think there's any need for them to change their plans, do you?" he asked, looking at McKenzie. "I don't think they'd get here in time anyway."

"And three birth coaches are more than enough," McKenzie said. "Mom, why don't you go and see how David is?"

Hope bit her lower lip, torn between the desire to stay by McKenzie's side and concern for her friend.

"It's okay," McKenzie said, rightly reading her mother's expression. "Nothing is going to happen for hours anyway. And even if it did, Dad's here."

"That's right," Rick said, smiling at his daughter and putting his arm over Hope's shoulders. "When it comes to birthing babies, I'm an old hand. Remember?"

Hope opened the door quietly. The form under the blanket, tethered to the bed by tubes, and wires, and monitors that blinked yellow and green, stirred as she crept into the dimly lit room.

"What now?" asked a weakened but still familiar voice. "Can't you people just let me sleep?"

"It's me, David."

Hope stepped nearer and David turned his head toward her. A pool of light from the wall sconce revealed a ravaged, almost unrecognizable face, swollen and purpled with bruises, his left eye covered with a thick white bandage, another on his throat, his cheeks, jaw, and formerly fine nose cragged by long, angry gashes that had been closed with black thread and uneven stitches, the patchwork visage of a mistreated scarecrow.

Pressing her lips tight together, Hope swallowed back a gasp of horror, then moved to the edge of the bed. To her surprise, he lifted his hand toward her. She took it in hers, blinking back tears.

"What are you doing here?"

"Seeing you. But my daughter is also here and in labor. I'm her birth coach, but her ex-husband is with her right now. It's going to be a few hours before the baby comes."

David blinked a couple of times. "Early, isn't it? The baby?"

"About three weeks. But the doctor says everything should be all right."

"Good," he rasped. "I'm glad. A girl, right?"

"Yes," Hope said, her eyes tearing anew. "Maybe I can bring her by and introduce the two of you later."

"Oh, I don't know. One look at me could scar her for life. Scarred for life," he repeated, chuckling as if he'd just picked up on the irony of his statement.

"No, it wouldn't. You don't look that bad. "

David rolled his head slowly to the left, fixing her gaze with his one good eye.

"Don't take up a life of crime, Hope. You're a terrible liar."

She smiled.

"But I'll be all right. I'm not planning to die, if that's what you're wondering." He released her hand and moved his own slowly to the bandage at his throat. "Nita tried her best; lucky for me, her aim was off."

"Lucky for all of us," Hope said.

David attempted a smile. "Wish you'd been in the operating room. Stitches would have been a lot smaller. Stitches . . ." he murmured, his words trailing off and his right eye becoming heavy.

Hope patted his arm. "I'm going to get out of here and let you get some sleep. I'll be back later, after the baby comes, to see how you're doing."

"Okay," he mumbled. "Sorry. I'm just so tired."

"It's all right."

"Hope?" His eyelids fluttered. "One thing. Did you take another job yet?"

"No, David. Not yet."

"Good," he mumbled. "Don't."

Chapter 46

Hope popped open the trunk of her car, took out a large, cube-shaped bakery box, and carried it to the gate. Wayne, looking uncharacteristically cheerful, was there to greet her.

"Mornin', Hope. Big day, eh? You didn't bake any files into that cake, did you?"

"Not a one," Hope said. "You want to see?"

When Wayne said that he did, she put her purse on the ground and lifted the lid of the box a few inches. Wayne peered over the edge.

"Well, that is just about the prettiest cake I ever saw. Too pretty to eat, really. You baked that?"

"It was a collaborative effort," Hope said. "My husband did the baking—lemon and vanilla layer cake with raspberry filling—and I did the decorating."

"Will you look at that? You got quilt blocks on the top *and* the sides. How'd you get 'em so even and keep the frosting from smearing?"

"I didn't. The frosting is only on the base. I made the blocks from colored marzipan. See?" she said, pointing to the pastel-colored decorations that circled the edge of the cake. "These are Sawtooth Stars. The blocks on the top are Carolina Lily, one of my favorites."

"Pretty. But sounds like a lot of work," Wayne said as Hope closed the box.

"It was. But as hard as the girls have worked over the last few months, I wanted to do something special for graduation. I'm really going to miss them."

"Well, it's not like most of them are going anywhere anytime soon," Wayne said. "Well, except Tonya. I hear she's getting out in a couple of months. And you've got a whole new class coming in next week, don't you?"

"*Two* classes. And a waiting list," Hope said, bending down carefully to retrieve her purse. "Is she here yet?"

Wayne shook his head. "They said to expect her around ten fifteen. The wife pressed my uniform extra special. Put so much starch on the collar I can hardly turn my head." He grinned.

"Well, you look good," Hope said, and began walking toward the door. "I'll save you a piece of the cake."

The governor actually didn't arrive until ten thirty, but she got there in time to help hand out the graduation certificates, present an award to Kate, who was so surprised that she was crying in all the pictures, and then give a short speech.

"The creativity and determination that you women have displayed is something you can be very proud of. But as all of you are aware, without the creativity and determination of some very remarkable people this program could easily have ended before it began.

"Facing enormous obstacles, your teachers refused to give up. When Mrs. Carpenter tracked me down to try and convince me that this program should be reinstated, it was her obvious passion and commitment to all of you that convinced me to investigate further. Another woman, a lesser and less determined woman, would have given up. But as all of you know, your teacher is not a lesser woman—"

"That's right!" Deedee shouted, pumping her fist in the air, a pinkish scar visible across her knuckles. "Amen to that!"

"Yeah, Mrs. C.!" whooped one of the other women, while another added, "You're the best!"

Grinning, Governor Russman went off script briefly to say, "She is indeed," nodding her agreement and allowing the inmates to have their say before continuing her remarks.

"And when I had the opportunity to read a previously unpublished report written by Superintendent Hernandez, the insights he offered and value he attributed to this program convinced me it should be saved, if possible. When I urged him to take steps to get to the bottom of the safety concerns that caused the program to be suspended, he did so with characteristic commitment and professionalism. A lesser man, a man not as committed to the job and to you, might not have approved this program to begin with, might not have placed his responsibility for his charges above his personal safety."

"Yes, ma'am!" Deedee cried, shouting again, as the other inmates clapped and cheered.

"And a less determined man," the governor said, looking toward the front row, where David sat, "might not have endured the hard work of rehabilitation so he could be present to celebrate your accomplishments today. I trust that determination will carry him through the remainder of his recovery so he may return and continue his good work here very soon."

More clapping and whooping greeted this pronouncement. Hope, who was seated next to David, clapped loudest of all.

"Now, I know you're all anxious to get to that delicious-looking cake I see on the back table," the governor said. "But before you do so, I want to remind you of something important.

"Though life isn't always fair—in fact, frequently isn't fair—the kind of determination that you have shown in completing this program, the same kind your teachers and superintendent displayed in keeping it going, is the thing that can tip the scales in your favor. You won't always have control over the circumstances of life, but you are in control of how you respond to those circumstances.

"If you didn't know it before, all of you now know that you have something meaningful to offer. The quilts that you have made, the hard work and creativity that you have put into them, have blessed the lives of others. I hope you will take that knowledge with you today and that you will continue to be a blessing to others, both within these walls and, someday, without.

"Congratulations, ladies. We are all very proud of you."

Applause broke out once again. Hope rose to her feet.

"Excuse me, everyone. But before we have our cake and punch, we have one last presentation. Deedee?" she said, beckoning her forward.

"Actually," Deedee said when she came to the front, bringing along a paper grocery sack, "we have *two* presentations."

Two?

Hope looked a question at Kate. The older woman spread out her hands, as if to say it was as much a mystery to her as anyone, but the twinkle in her eyes told Hope that might not be true.

Deedee moved forward, standing directly in front of David.

"Mr. Hernandez, when I started this program, the thing I was most excited about was making a quilt for me. I thought it'd be really nice to have my own quilt on the end of my bunk. But if it wasn't for you, I wouldn't even be here today. So I want to give you my quilt. Thank you for saving me. And I hope you get done with all your surgeries and come back real soon."

Hope never had seen, never would see, David Hernandez cry. But she could see his Adam's apple bob in his throat, moving under the scar where his life's blood had once poured out. And she saw the expression in his right eye, the damaged left covered by a black patch, and knew that he was deeply moved.

Deedee pulled the quilt from the bag, a pattern of scrappy red and white bow-tie blocks on a creamy background, and laid it over his knees. Hope saw his Adam's apple bob again as he swallowed.

"Well. This is . . . This is amazing. I don't know what to say."

Deedee propped a hand on her hip. "Well, when somebody gives you a present, you're supposed to say thank you."

There was a murmur of laughter. David joined in it, then smiled.

"Thank you, Deedee."

"You're welcome," she said. "Now, just one more present. Then we can eat. Miss Kate?"

Kate stood up and came forward.

"Several weeks ago," she said, addressing the audience, "a group of students came to me and said they wanted to do something for Mrs. Carpenter, to thank her for all she's done. All twelve of the original students, including one who has already been released, contributed two blocks to a baby quilt for Mrs. Carpenter's new granddaughter, Leesha."

Kate reached beneath the podium, pulled out a folded quilt, then unfurled it so that everyone could see it, a simple but cheerful pattern of brightly colored snowball blocks on a crisp white background, with white sashing and colorful cornerstone patches at the corners.

"Oh, it's beautiful!" Hope exclaimed. "But how did you ever manage to sew the blocks without me knowing what you were up to?"

"It was *not* easy," Deedee said in a dramatic tone. "We thought for sure you were going to find out. Miss Kate took the blocks home and finished the quilt for us. We hope the baby likes it."

"Well, if she doesn't then Grammy might just have to steal it from her," Hope said, laughing and clutching the quilt to her chest.

Hope turned forward to face the audience, but though the chairs were filled with many people—David, Kate, Nancy, Cindy, other guards and staff, the governor and her aides, and the photographers and reporters who had come to cover the event—in that moment, she only had eyes for her students.

Hope's gaze moved slowly down the row, pausing briefly to focus on every pair of eyes and every smiling face.

"For a teacher," she said, "the measure of a student is how much she learns from them. That's why I mean it when I say that you're the best class I've ever had."

"This is good cake," David said.

"Glad you're enjoying it," Hope replied.

"No, I mean it. This is seriously good cake. Like biblically good." He bobbed his head as he chewed, the look on his face somewhere between wonder and shock. He swallowed and pointed his plastic spork at the paper plate. "You made this?"

"Rick did. Oh, wait. That reminds me." Hope turned toward the table, where Kate was tidying up, picking up discarded paper napkins and crumb-strewn plates. "Kate? Could you wrap up a piece of cake and put it aside? I promised Wayne."

"I would, but there isn't any left."

"Seriously? It should have served fifty."

"I sent some home with the governor."

"Oh no," Hope groaned, then raised a finger to David and said, "Don't move. I'll be right back."

Hope carried her partially eaten slice of cake to the table, trimmed a ragged edge in hopes that Wayne wouldn't know the difference, asked Kate if she could carry it to the guard, and then went back to pick up the conversation.

"Sorry about that. Wayne isn't the kind of person who forgives easily."

"Oh, believe me, I know."

David lifted his spork toward Hope, silently offering her a bite of cake. She shook her head.

"You go ahead. I can always get more biblically good cake at home. Now that Rick has settled into his new job, he's started baking again. If he keeps this up, I may have to start running for real."

"So, Rick's liking his new job?"

"Loves it."

"And what about you?" he asked. "Liking your new-old job?"

"More than ever. The part-time schedule really is better for me. Rick and I get to spend our days off together and we're available to help McKenzie with the baby if and when she needs a backup or a break. They say you can't have it all but, for the moment at least, it feels like I do. And the work itself?" Hope spread her hands to indicate that the answer should be obvious. "Apart from seeing my kids turn out so well, this is the most satisfying thing I've ever done in my life."

"In some ways, it's kind of the same thing, isn't it?" David said, glancing around the room at the inmates who were still milling about, enjoying cake and one another's company. "We don't have as many success stories as I wish we did, but when they can leave here and make a new life for themselves on the outside? Well. There's something pretty great about that, isn't there?"

"Speaking of success stories," Hope said, "I saw Mandy a couple of weeks ago. She had a summer job with a landscaping company and they decided to keep her on over the winter. She's doing office work, mostly bookkeeping."

David grinned. "Really? Good for her. Guess those math classes paid off."

"Best of all is that she and her parents called a truce. Well, it was her mother, really. Apparently, Lola told her husband that if he kept up with his plan to rescind Mandy's parental rights she'd leave him. He didn't believe her—not until the moving truck pulled into the driveway."

"So the daughter is living with Mandy now?"

"Not quite. They're working out a gradual transition of custody. Right now, Mandy just has Talia on weekends. That was Mandy's idea; she thought it would be better for Talia. And they're all going to family therapy. That hasn't exactly been a picnic, but it sounds like they're working out some issues."

"Huh. Well, that is really good to hear. I always thought Mandy had a lot of potential, if she could just get herself straightened out. Sounds like she has."

"On the road to it anyway," Hope said. "But how are you doing? You look great."

David took another bite of cake.

"Still the world's worst liar," he said, his mouth half-full. "I don't look great. I didn't look great even before Nita tried to slice my face up like a Christmas ham. But I definitely look *better*. After this next surgery, I'm hoping I'll look kind of . . . rugged. Maybe pass myself off as a retired Navy SEAL. Or a reformed pirate." Hope laughed and David grinned. "Of course, if this corneal transplant works like the doctors hope it will, I probably won't be able to pull off the pirate thing. Who ever heard of a pirate without an eye patch?"

"Or a parrot?" Hope added.

"Good point. And," he said slowly, drawing out the word, "as far as when I'll come back, the answer is—I might not."

"What?" Hope gasped. "Why? David, I can only imagine how traumatic this has been for you. But you were a *great* super- intendent. Did you hear all that stuff the governor was saying about you? Before she left, she told me the report you wrote about the quilting program and ways to better serve the female prison population is being shared with correctional superinten- dents all over the country. She personally passed copies on to other governors at the last regional conference. And you were just saying, not ten seconds ago, how satisfying this is."

"I know, I know," David said, lifting his hands. "And it *is* satisfying. Or was. But even before this happened, I was starting to think I needed a break. A lot has happened to me in the last few years, Hope. I got cancer; my wife left me. I never really dealt with that. And now this?" He spread his hands.

"It's starting to feel like God is trying to tell me something. And since He seems to be trying pretty hard to get my attention . . ." David grinned. "Well, I don't really want to dig in my heels and see what comes next. Plagues of locusts, maybe."

"Well. Okay," Hope said grudgingly. "But I'll really miss you if you don't come back."

"I have a feeling we'll be running into each other."

"I hope so. So, what are you going to do? I mean, I know you've got some recovering to do yet, but after that? Will you look for another job? Go work for another prison?"

"Actually," he said, "I was thinking of going back to school, getting my master's degree."

"Criminal justice?"

David shook his head as he scraped the last smear of icing off the plate. "Secondary school education."

Hope's eyes went wide. "You want to be a teacher?"

"Thinking about it," David said, eating the last bite of icing. "I'm going to start classes down at Portland State in January, try a semester, and see how I feel about it."

"Well—Wow." Hope blinked twice. "That's great, David. Unexpected but great. So you're moving to Portland. Need the name of a good Realtor?"

"No, thanks. Already got one."

The twinkle in his eye was so mischievous and self-satisfied that, had David not had a patch over his other eye, Hope would have sworn she saw him wink.

"In fact," he said, his smile fading and lips flattening into something approaching uncertainty, "I was just talking to Hazel the other day. We'd been texting a lot, you know, before this happened. . . ."

"Yes, she told me."

"Right. Well, after I got hurt, I kind of cut it off."

"She told me that too," Hope said.

"Yeah." David sniffed and ducked his head. "That was pretty stupid of me. But I had a lot going on and I thought, if she saw me like this . . . Well. You know."

"I think Hazel really likes you, David. More than likes you."

David lifted his head to look at Hope.

"And I more than like her."

Hope nodded.

"So anyway," he said, then cleared his throat, "after I get this corneal transplant, I'm going to have to recover for a while and figured that I might as well do it someplace warm, with a beach. I've rented a condo for a couple of weeks down in La Jolla. I asked Hazel to come with me and she said okay. Did she tell you that?"

Hope shook her head. "No. She didn't."

"Ah." David pressed his lips together. "Well. That okay with you?"

"David," she said, her lips drawn into a bow, "not only is that okay with me; it's the best news I've heard in a long time."

Chapter 47

Knowing Hazel and David needed to drive back to Portland that night after Christmas dinner, Hope had moved the meal a few hours ahead this year. So even though it was still early evening when she walked them to the door to say goodbye, the candles were beginning to sputter.

The remaining revelers—just the family at this point, Kate, Nancy and John, and the other guests having already departed—were lolling on couches and chairs in the living room, digesting, apparently so bloated that they were unable to summon the energy to get up and say goodbye when Hazel said it was time they get going. The only exception was Pamela, who politely rose from the sofa and gave Hazel and David a farewell hug. The rest of the nephews and nieces held their ground, lifting arms to wave goodbye from their various places of collapse.

"See you, Hazel!"

"Bye, David!"

"Drive safe!"

"Thanks for the sweater!"

Hazel gave Hope another hug and kiss. "Thanks, Sis. Another amazing Christmas. I honestly don't know how you do it, but I'm really glad you do. It was wonderful, as always."

"I'm so glad you could come," Hope said, squeezing her sister one last time. "Are you sure you're not too tired to drive back? You could sleep here, get up early, and go back in the morning, you know. Reed and Pamela are staying over at McKenzie's place, so we've got room for you."

"No, but thanks. I've got a sales presentation tomorrow," Hazel said.

"And I have a huge pile of reading I need to get to," David added, shifting the armload of gifts he was carrying to one side and then kissing Hope on the cheek.

"The semester doesn't start for another two weeks," Hope protested. "And who schedules a sales presentation for the day after Christmas?" She clucked her tongue and shook her head. "You two, I guess. That's okay. Every family needs at least *one* overachiever. Or two," she said, smiling at David.

"Hey!" Reed shouted from his spot on the sofa. "Who are you calling an underachiever? I'm a tenure-track professor."

"Yeah, and I'm a doctor," Rory added.

"And I'm a single mother and head of my department," McKenzie said, leaning forward to kiss baby Leesha on the nose.

"And I'm . . ." Liam raised a fist over his head and then let it flop to his side. "Oh, wait. A total loser. Almost forgot."

"Oh, you are not," McKenzie said impatiently, rolling her eyes. "It was a small production company and it ran out of money. Big deal. You'll find another job. In the meantime, if you're looking to make yourself useful, here. Be a good uncle and play with your niece."

She handed the baby to Liam, who started making goofy faces at his niece and talking in a voice reminiscent of Kermit the Frog. He was instantly rewarded with a drooling, beaming, toothless infant grin.

After giving Hazel and David a final wave and reminding them that she and Rick were still coming to Portland for New Year's Eve, Hope closed the door, went back into the living room, and started picking up the abandoned and empty glasses. A moment later, Rick, still wearing his baker's apron, walked in and clapped his hands together.

"So. Who's ready for more pie?" he asked, and received a chorus of groans and protests in response.

"Maybe later," McKenzie said, seeing the disappointment on her father's face. "The pie was great, Dad. But right now, I couldn't eat another bite."

"So, what do you guys want to do?" asked Rory, scanning the faces of his siblings.

"If you're bored you can always help me clean up this mess," Hope suggested.

"I'll help." Pamela got to her feet and started picking up some of the discarded wrapping paper, only to be greeted with boos and heckling.

"Brownnoser!"

"Suck-up!"

"Knock it off," McKenzie said to her brothers before taking the baby back into her lap. "She's just trying to get on the in-laws' good side. I did the same thing with Zach's parents. She'll get over it after the wedding, trust me," she teased.

"Hey, I know what we can do," Liam said, sitting up straight and looking far more energetic than he had a moment before. "Let's go find a brew pub, order a pitcher, and toast Reed and Pamela's engagement."

"It's Christmas. Do you really think they'll be open?" Hope asked. "Besides, everyone said they were too full to eat anything else."

"Beer's different. Fits in the cracks." Liam stood up. "Come on, guys. Who wants to go out for a beer? Reed's buying."

"I am not buying. At least not for you," Reed said, looking fondly at Pamela, who looked fondly back, then came to stand next to him when he got to his feet, placing her left hand, with its bright and brand-new diamond ring, lightly on his arm. "But a beer sounds good."

"I'm in," Rory said. "Kenz?"

McKenzie thought about it for a moment, then said, "I probably shouldn't. I have to get up early and drive to Bellingham. We're meeting Zach at his parents' and doing Christmas all over again. Besides, it's almost Leesha's bedtime."

"Oh, come on," Liam moaned. "One beer."

"You go on," Hope urged her. "Dad and I can babysit."

"Sure you don't mind?" McKenzie said, sounding hopeful.

"Mind?" Hope put a glass back down on the coffee table and crossed the room, grinning widely and holding her arms wide. "As if I could ever mind spending time with the cutest, smartest, most advanced, and most beautiful baby on the face of the earth. Come here to Grammy, you sweet little girl."

After the kids left to drink beer, bond, and toast the expansion of the family fold, Hope propped baby Leesha on her hip and carried her around the condo, showing her the sparkling lights of the Christmas tree and explaining the history and origins of the various ornaments as if they were artifacts in the family museum and Hope was the curator of the collection, which, in a sense, was true.

"And that silver one there? The very old-looking one with the snow scene and sleigh? Your great-grandma painted that one by hand, way back when I was about your age.

"And those pinecones with the gold glitter? Rory and Reed made those when they were eight years old. Your uncle Liam painted that stained-glass cross when he was six. Isn't it pretty? Look at all the bright colors. And see the cross-stitched ornaments that say 'Baby's First Christmas' and the year? Grammy did those herself, when your mommy and uncles were born. Yes, she did.

"And see that funny reindeer with the red nose? Your mommy crocheted that one just for you! That's right. To celebrate Leesha's first Christmas! You come from a very talented family; did you know that?

"And someday, when you're just a little bit older, Grammy is going to teach you all kinds of things so you'll be able to add *your* ornaments to the tree. What do you think about that?"

Leesha, who had been listening solemnly to her grandmother's monologue, blinked twice and then yawned. Hope laughed and squeezed her.

"You are just too, too precious. Do you know *that*?"

Leesha offered no opinion. Hope carried her back into the living room, where Rick was lying prone on the sofa.

"This one is getting tired," Hope said. "Can you take her for a minute? I'm going to get her pajamas."

"Absolutely. I was beginning to wonder if you were ever going to share," Rick said, holding out his arms. "Come here, baby girl. Come and talk to your grandpa."

Leaving the baby with Rick, Hope went in search of the diaper bag. Somehow, it had ended up under a pile of coats in the guest room. When she returned to the living room a few minutes later, she found Rick still on the sofa with the baby on his chest, both sound asleep.

Hope stood there for a long moment, watching the rise and fall of Rick's breathing, and the look on her granddaughter's face as she went along for the ride: an expression of contentment and utter peace that matched Rick's own.

She considered waking them, but only briefly. Hope had lived long enough to know that such moments, though few and far between, must be treasured.

Instead, Hope lowered herself into a chair to keep watch, cherishing her life, and family, and home. And the knowledge it was exactly as it was meant to be.

All of it.

Dear Reader,

I hope you have enjoyed reading *Hope on the Inside*. This book is a labor of love that took many years in the making.

It began seven years ago, when I saw an exhibit of quilts made by inmates. Though the skill displayed by those incarcerated quilters varied from novice to expert, the quilts they produced were so honest, raw, and emotionally evocative that they truly rose to the level of art.

I was fascinated and immediately knew that I wanted to write a book set in a correctional setting. However, though I made a few attempts over the years, the story simply wouldn't come; the lives of the characters were just too far removed from my own experience. After several false starts, I shelved the idea.

Not long after I moved to Oregon, I stumbled across an article about the Coffee Creek Quilters, an entirely volunteer-run and -funded quilting program that has been operating inside the Coffee Creek Correctional Facility in Wilsonville, Oregon, since 2002.

Though my story is entirely fictional, my research about and visit to the Coffee Creek Quilters profoundly influenced *Hope on the Inside*. My conversations with the volunteers helped me to see that a tale about a woman at a crossroads of life, encountering this world for the first time, *was* a story I could tell. It's not too much to say that this book might never have been written if not for my encounters with the Coffee Creek Quilters. It is a remarkable program.

Unfortunately, it is, to my knowledge, the only such program for incarcerated women in the country. As I was writing this book, my fervent prayer has been that someone who reads this book becomes inspired to start a similar program in their area.

If you think that person might be you, visit www.coffeecreek quilters.org. There, under the "Get Involved" tab, you will find a detailed guide, written by the Coffee Creek Quilters, with detailed information on how you can begin a similar program at a correctional facility near you.

I hope you will read and consider it. And I really, *really* hope you will act on it.

Also, if you enjoyed reading *Hope on the Inside,* I would so appreciate it if you'd help spread the word. Tell your friends and family! Write an online review! Propose it to your book club! Word of mouth from passionate readers is the very best form of advertising and the greatest compliment that any author can receive. Thank you in advance for your support. It means so much.

I do love hearing from readers. I read every note personally and do my best to make sure each note receives a response. If you have a moment, drop me an e-mail at marie@mariebostwick.com or by regular mail. My mailing address is:

Marie Bostwick
18160 Cottonwood Road
PMB 118
Bend, Oregon 97707

Social media is the easiest, fastest way for me to stay in touch with readers.

You can find me on Facebook at facebook.com/mariebostwick/ and on Twitter, Pinterest, and Instagram by searching @marie bostwick. You can also connect with me at my new blog, www.fiercebeyond50.com, a lifestyle blog to help women age fifty and beyond celebrate this amazing season of life.

And, of course, I hope you'll take some time to visit my website, www.mariebostwick.com.

While you're there you can sign up for my monthly newsletter, check my calendar to see if I'll be making an appearance in your area, enter the monthly reader giveaway, and download free recipes and quilt patterns created exclusively for my readers. To find them, go to the "Quilt Central" tab on my website and choose "Quilt Patterns" from the pull-down menu. Recipes are found under the "Author" tab. (Please note, these patterns and recipes are for your personal use only and may not be copied to share with others or published by any means, either print or electronic.)

My dear friend the talented Deb Tucker and I began collaborating on the companion quilt for *Hope on the Inside* very early on. You are absolutely going to love the Dove in the Window quilt, inspired by the quilt Mandy made, which was designed to go with this book. It's gorgeous!

Part of what makes it so special is that we used a new collection of actual Island Batik fabrics, with the same colors and patterns I describe in the book, to create the quilt. That fabric collection, *Steam Engine* by Island Batik, will be available in the spring of 2019. Ask for it at your local quilt shop or visit www.Island Batik.com for information and inspiration.

Deb has also created many companion patterns for purchase to go with my books. To check them out, visit www.studio 180design.net, click the "Shop" tab on the menu, and look for the Cobbled Court section under "Specialty Collections." There are some beautiful patterns there!

In addition to the new quilt pattern, I'm sure that *Hope on the Inside* will inspire a few new additions to my collection of online recipes. Given Rick's love of baking, I'm sure that bread and pastry will be involved.

On the day I finished writing the draft for *Hope on the Inside,* I went for a long walk in the woods. As I strolled by a river and under the shade of evergreens, it suddenly hit me that I had just finished my fifteenth full-length novel.

That's a lot of books!

But it also hit me that I couldn't have reached this milestone without you, my readers. Time is the most precious commodity we have. I am sincerely grateful that you have chosen to spend some of yours with me and with my characters. It is a tremendous honor. Without you, my readers, I would not have been able to become a writer.

Thank you for making it all possible.

Blessings,

Marie Bostwick

HOPE ON THE INSIDE

Marie Bostwick

ABOUT THIS GUIDE

The following questions are intended to
enhance your group's reading of
Hope on the Inside.

DISCUSSION QUESTIONS

1. Ms. Bostwick's novels, including *Hope on the Inside*, emphasize the importance of creative pursuits in everyday life. Hope has her crafting and quilting; Rick has his baking. In what ways do the individual characters' creative activities inform their relationships and sense of self-worth? In what ways do you think your own creative pursuits enrich your life?

2. Career and vocational change during different stages of life play an important role in the story. When the book opens, Rick views himself as the family breadwinner, viewing his identity in terms of his work. Hope, though she has recently returned to teaching, views herself primarily as a homemaker. How was their view of themselves and each other influenced or altered by their career changes? Do you think these were changes for the better or the worse? Have you experienced similar types of career changes in your life? How have those changes impacted your sense of self and your relationships?

3. David's relationship with Hope changes radically from the start of the novel to the end. In the beginning, he seems antagonistic toward Hope and her plans for the inmates, but later he appears more supportive and even reveals a shared desire to teach. What do you think accounts for the change in the way David treats Hope? Was he always on her side or did his attitude toward the program change over time?

4. Based on the depiction of the prison system in the novel, in what ways do you think the system could be improved? What negative and positive effects does such an environment have on the inmates as well as the people who work there (the guards, teachers, and administrators)?

5. The relationship between Hope and her daughter, McKenzie, evolves considerably throughout the story. Why do you think their relationship is so tense in the beginning of the story? What part did both mother and daughter play in contributing to that tension? What factors or events helped ease the tension and helped Hope and McKenzie develop the "close, cozy" mother-daughter relationship that Hope had always longed for? What about your relationship with your parents? Did it change over time? How and why?

6. Hope and Rick fall into the "empty nesters" category. Hope struggles to find new purpose after many years of being a full-time wife and mother. Do you think our current culture is better preparing parents of adult children to anticipate and handle similar situations? Are there certain expectations for personal reinvention and career choices that come with this stage of life? How does Hope and Rick's financial situation inform their later lifestyle choices?

7. Nancy and others emphasize the role that men played in the female inmates' incarceration. Do you think this is a fair assessment? Do you believe the inmates' relationships with men are at least partly responsible for the women's situations?

8. Do you think McKenzie's reaction toward her father's suspected infidelity is normal given the situation, or was she overly influenced by her own marital problems? Was she justified in confronting Rick at Kate's home, or was she only looking to channel her anger at her own husband?

9. Hope downplays the symptoms of her hyperthyroidism until it becomes a medical crisis. How does this connect or conflict with Hope's other personality traits, such as her tendency to put others before herself?

10. The title of the book, *Hope on the Inside,* is a play on words, a hint about the content of the book and the fact that Hope teaches inside a correctional facility. In what other ways does the title shed light on the story line and the lives of the characters?

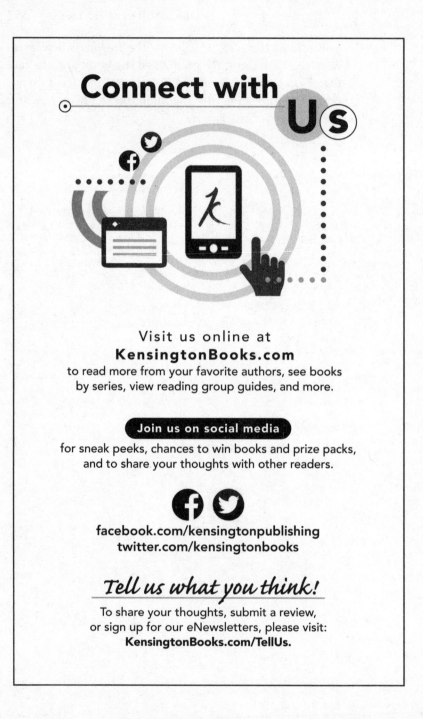

Connect with Us

Visit us online at
KensingtonBooks.com
to read more from your favorite authors, see books
by series, view reading group guides, and more.

Join us on social media

for sneak peeks, chances to win books and prize packs,
and to share your thoughts with other readers.

facebook.com/kensingtonpublishing
twitter.com/kensingtonbooks

Tell us what you think!

To share your thoughts, submit a review,
or sign up for our eNewsletters, please visit:
KensingtonBooks.com/TellUs.